KOGAIONON

CAVE OF ZALMOXIS

UNCHARTED WILDLANDS

SOLOMANTHA BELL TOWER

THE CROSS ROADS

THE ALPINE SEA

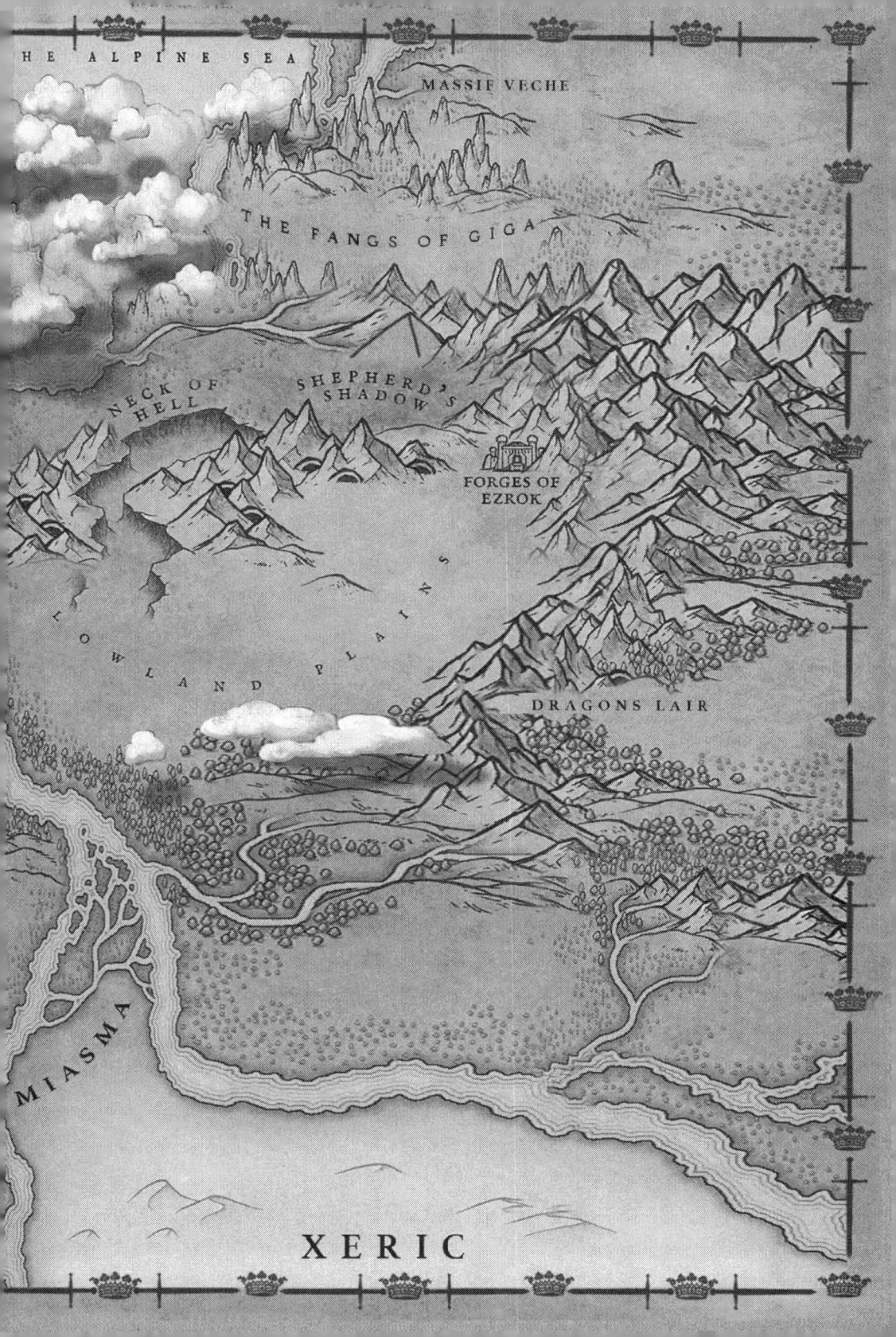

MASSIF VECHE

THE FANGS OF GIGA

NECK OF HELL

SHEPHERD'S SHADOW

FORGES OF EZROK

LOWLAND PLAINS

DRAGONS LAIR

MIASMA

XERIC

Stefan
and the
Celestial Sword

To Scott,
Celebrate Stefan!
Ecc 3:17
Frank Amoroso

F.L. Amoroso

simply francis publishing company

Wrightsville Beach, North Carolina

Copyright 2022 Frank Amoroso. All rights reserved.

This book is a work of fiction. Any references to historical events, real people, or real places are used fictitiously. Other names, characters, places, and events are products of the author's imagination, and any resemblance to actual events or places or persons, living or dead, is entirely coincidental.

Library of Congress Control Number: 2022900013
ISBN: 978-1-63062-034-9 paperback
ISBN: 978-1-63062-035-6 ebook
Printed in the United States of America
Cover and Interior Design: Christy King Meares

No part of this publication may be reproduced, stored in a retrieval system or transmitted, in any form or by any means-electronic, mechanical, photocopying, recording, or by any information storage device - without the prior written permission from the publisher, except for the inclusions of brief quotations in a review.

For information about this title or to order books and/or electronic media, contact the publisher:

simply francis publishing company
P.O. Box 329, Wrightsville Beach, NC 28480
www.simplyfrancispublishing.com
simplyfrancispublishing@gmail.com

OTHER BOOKS BY THE AUTHOR

Behind Every Great Fortune®
"... boldly imaginative historical novel that is sumptuously detailed and filled with intrigue, betrayal and plot twists that surprise and entertain the reader."

Dread the Fed
"... a gripping story of a crime so bold, so ingenious and so perfect, that a century later, the plunder continues and the People venerate the banksters who commit it."

**Behind Every Great Recipe:
From Latkes to Vodkas & Beets to Meats**
"... a charming and unique companion book containing delicious period recipes and vignettes featuring the characters from the historical novel *Behind Every Great Fortune®*."

**Wopper - How Babe Ruth Lost His Father and Won The 1918 World Series Against The Cubs
Volume 1 Pigtown**
"... a fantastical Ruthian novel based on the life of Babe Ruth!"

**Wopper - How Babe Ruth Lost His Father and WonThe 1918 World Series Against The Cubs
Volume 1 Pigtown YOUNG ADULT VERSION**

**Wopper - How Babe Ruth Lost His Father and Won The 1918 World Series Against The Cubs
Volume 2 The Show**
"... follow Babe's exhilarating journey from the sandlots of Baltimore to superstardom in Fenway Park."

**Wopper - How Babe Ruth Lost His Father and Won The 1918 World Series Against The Cubs
Volume 3 The Series**
"... the explosive culmination of the trilogy as Babe learns of the death of his father and battles not only the Cubs but anti-German zealots, anarchists, and pure evil."

German-Americans and Our National Pastime
"... study of the enduring greatness of German-Americans in baseball."

Korea: Forgotten Sacrifice
"... forgotten sacrifice is the shame of a nation."

DEDICATION

To my son Louis Paul who served in Romania in the Peace Corps and always inspired me with his love of life and his spirit of adventure. Sadly, he succumbed to pancreatic cancer earlier this year.

F.L. Amoroso
Wilmington, N.C.
October, 2021

Foreword

Several years ago, my wife and I visited Moldova with our dear friends Donna and Jerry Flake. The trip was in furtherance of the North Carolina-Moldova Bilateral Partnership which had been established after the Soviet Union collapsed. We had the good fortune to meet Dr. Ion Ababii who was the head of the Moldovan Medical University system. During a press conference to acknowledge the purpose of our visit which was to provide educational support to Moldovan medical libraries, Dr. Ababii introduced me as a writer and suggested that I might write a book about Moldova. I accepted the challenge and this novel was born.

While in Moldova I was fascinated by the national hero of the country, *Stefan cel Mare,* or Stefan the Great. He ruled Moldova from 1457 to 1504 and was a great leader. I admit that writing about a national hero from another culture might be considered presumptuous and perhaps insulting. The encouragement I received from every Moldovan I discussed this project with led me to conclude that it was welcome. To any who might feel otherwise or take offense, I assure you that no offense was intended and that I have the greatest respect for Stefan and his legacy.

I would also note that I have tried to incorporate Romanian words to give this work verisimilitude. These words and phrases are denoted by italics. However, in deference to English-speaking readers I have refrained from using diacritical marks which often appear in Romanian words to indicate accent or pronunciation.

An intriguing sidenote about Stefan is that his cousin was Vlad Tepes, known in western popular lore as Count Dracula. For his efforts in holding off the advance of the Ottoman Turks into Europe, Stefan was declared the Champion of Christ by the Pope and was ultimately canonized by the Orthodox Church. His likeness appears on Moldovan currency, postage, and in innumerable statues throughout the land.

I became so enamored with the distinctive crown which Stefan wore that I decided to write a fantasy quest novel about Stefan and the genesis of the crown. This germ of an idea led me to create a world inhabited by fairies, angels, dragons, and other assorted magical creatures. Unique among these creations is Telly, a telepathic land octopus with extraordinary capabilities and an exasperating, yet endearing, personality. I set out to write a novel using magical realism and came to learn that I had written an historical fantasy.

I invite you to escape to medieval Moldova where there are murders, monsters, and mortals clashing in a ferocious battle between good and evil.

F. L. Amoroso

Prologue

"Tell me the story of Aparator, Papa."

"What? Again? You've heard that tale more times than there are fairies in the enchanted forest," said the father with a puckish grin.

"So? It's fun, please, please tell it again."

"I've told you that legend so many times while we travel in this wagon that I bet old Sophie here could tell it," said the father, gesturing toward the mare pulling the wagon up the hill.

"Don't you ever get tired of it?"

The youngster shook his head so rapidly from side-to-side that his lips fluttered like Sophie's did when she had finished drinking from the trough.

"*Da*," said the father breaking into a broad smile that transformed his weathered face into the cheery aspect of a traveling minstrel. "If you don't stop that blubbering, your face will freeze like that forever."

The chides of his own parent echoed in his memory. Funny how that works, he thought.

"It was in the time right after the dawn of man. The earth was newly formed. Volcanoes erupted, sending boulders and molten lava into the land. Majestic geysers gushed steam and boiling water hundreds of feet into the air. These were difficult times for man to survive. They had none of the modern conveniences that we have now. They did not have wagons and wheels; they had to carry everything on their backs. Daily life was hard; it left them stooped and withered like a frostbitten apple.

"To eat, they had to follow the great herds of auroch and hunt the warty boars. Killing these creatures was dangerous because these people did not have bows and arrows or swords. They used rocks or wooden branches sharpened to a point by scraping against a boulder. Life was especially harsh if you were weak or sick. They had no knowledge of the herbs and incantations that we have today to heal. As if that was not enough, they faced mortal danger from Hyaenodon gigas, man-eating hyenas as big as a pony. Or, they had to fight nimraveks, large ferocious animals with pairs of long sharp teeth, slanted forwards to bite and tear flesh."

The boy shivered at the thought of such a creature tearing and ripping at Sophie while he tried to poke it with a stick. The man clicked for Sophie to quicken the pace so they could be home for supper.

"Oh, yes, life was harsh. The greatest threat to the people came from a race of brutes known as the Uriasi. They were giants of unbelievable size and strength whose favorite meal was human stew. They made it by boiling men they captured in a massive cauldron. Of course, they spiced it up with roots, leaves, and berries. The Uriasi were so destructive of man that there were very few humans left on this earth."

"Didn't the men know how to fight the Uriasi?"

"They tried, but their weapons were primitive and the Uriasi were too strong. The sticks and rocks of men were unable to penetrate the thick scales which covered the skin of the Uriasi. They laughed at the weak men as they scooped them up in their huge hands and dropped them into the stew pot."

"Papa, what if there are some Uriasi still roaming the wilderness?"

"Not to worry, my son."

"It was a terrible time for men. They lived in fear until an answer appeared from the heavens. They did not understand the weather the way we do today. They had no idea of seasons the way we do. I have to admit that they were pretty dumb.

"There came a season of storms. The sun disappeared and it grew dark except for bolts of lightning which crackled across the sky. Great claps of thunder shook the ground. It was as if there was a war rocking the heavens. This lasted for many days, weeks, so long that people forgot when the sky had been calm. Then, a shower of fiery meteors raced across the sky as if chased by the guardians of heaven. They fled over the horizon."

The man paused to gulp some water. He offered the canteen to his son who shook his head, not wanting to delay the story.

"A short time later, the sky settled and an orange glow appeared in the east. With it followed the sun and daylight returned. One man awoke and crept from the cave where the men huddled in fear. A glorious sunrise greeted him. Since he was thirsty, he walked toward a nearby stream. He looked from here to there, wary that the Uriasi might have seen the sun and were out hunting. As he bent toward the water to drink, he saw something glittering near the opposite shore. A light breeze rippled the water and the sunlight bounced off the surface. He blinked not sure he had seen anything at all.

"Suddenly, he heard crunching in the brush behind him. It was a band of Uriasi, sniffing the air for prey. The man's heart began to beat in his chest faster than the knocking of a woodpecker on a tree filled with bugs. He thought that his heart was making as much noise. His only escape was to slip into the water and glide to the opposite shore. Submerged, he propelled himself along by grabbing rocks and tugging himself forward. In a short time, his lungs burned and arms ached from the effort. When he could no longer stand it, he surfaced to breathe. Gasping for air, he looked for the Uriasi. One of the beasts saw him and summoned his comrades with the cruel screech that passed for language with their kind.

"The man retreated back under the water. A shiny object near a ledge by the shore drew his eyes to it. The water was now vibrating with the thrashing of the Uriasi who were racing toward him howling as if they smelled blood. A reality which was only moments away. Fearing that his life was about to end, the man reached for the object. He felt a handle. He yanked. It was a sword!

"As he grasped the hilt with both hands, energy surged through his body. The man hurtled himself out of the water. With water diamonds dripping from his body, he swung the sword in a deadly arc. The blade sparkled before it sliced off the arm of the nearest Uriasi. An instant of silence followed, before he bellowed in pain. It was the first time a man had pierced the hide of a Uriasi. Vile blood the color of pus spurted from the wounded beast.

"Surprised and encouraged by his success, the man whipped the sword in a fury that made a tornado appear like a puff of air. He hacked and stabbed and thrust his sword into every giant he could reach. A few of the Uriasi were so shocked at the murderous rage directed at them that they ran. No problem. Our hero raced after them, reaching them as they entered their camp. The man attacked the giants with such force and skill that the blade glowed and hummed with power.

Dead Uriasi bodies piled high as he fought and slayed his enemies.

"Finally, when all but one of the Uriasi remained, the man came face-to-face with the largest, meanest, and ugliest giant in the colony. He wielded a granite club larger than an oak tree. The giant roared in disdain at the man.

"'You are puny and weak,' screeched the Urias while thumping his chest. 'I am **Kogaionon**, leader of the Uriasi. I will smite you and drop you in my stew. Then I will devour you and excrete you from my rear in the morning!'

"The giant roared and saw a flicker of doubt enter the man's eyes. The man vowed to slay this monster even if it cost his life. He crouched low and moved to the side careful to stay out of reach of the massive club which would mash him into pulp if it hit him. He knew that he might only get one chance to kill Kogaionon so he had to plan his attack wisely. The most vulnerable spot on the beast was the front of his neck which was devoid of scales. The man feinted, ducked, and dodged the giant's blows until he saw an opening.

"Screaming a battle cry, the man exploded from his crouch, jumping so high that he was even with **Kogaionon's** throat. He swung the sword with lightning speed and caught the giant under his chin. The man felt the blade slice through skin, muscle, and bone. He propelled the blade in a radius that continued through to the opposite side. The sword did not stop until it struck the club. There was a loud crash as the man felt the sword hit the stone. The force of the blow sent shock waves back through the man's arms.

"When he returned to the ground, he held only the hilt and half the blade. Looking up he saw the other half of the blade stuck in the granite club. Kogaionon's face was a picture of shocked bewilderment as he looked toward the man. The club fell from his hand with a thud which caused the earth to tremble. His mouth opened as if preparing to hurl insults, but there was no sound save the gurgling of purulent blood. He dropped to his knees and his huge head thumped onto the club.

"The man's eyes turned skyward in gratitude. Then, he watched, astonished, as a beam of light crossed the land, turning the bodies of the Uriasi into stone. In moments, a mountain range stood where the Uriasi had fallen."

The father smiled down on his boy who stared up expectantly. Knowing that his son was waiting for the finale, the man continued.

"As the wave of stone conversion swept toward Kogaionon, the man drove the sword into his lifeless mouth. The man went back to his cave and told his people about the sword delivered from heaven and his destruction of the Uriasi. He named the sword Aparator, the Defender. There is a legend told by the people who live in those mountains that whoever finds the pieces of the sword and connects them with a pure heart will become a brave and powerful prince."

"Papa, has anyone found this celestial sword?"

"Son, as far back as memory goes, people have searched these mountains. No one has found the sword. Maybe, someday..." he replied, turning to his son with a wistful smile, thinking of the time he spent as a youth searching the hills and valleys of the Carpathian Mountains for the elusive sword.

BOOK ONE

CHAPTER 1

"Hey, Bogdan, look who's here," shouted Bako the blacksmith, a squat, powerfully-built man with straight black hair who could have descended from Genghis Khan.

"Ah, my little wolf cub, *Lupusor*, where have you been? Come join us. We have much to celebrate!" said Bogdan Musatin.

As the old Romanian word *musat,* or handsome, implies, Bogdan had a handsome face framed by shoulder-length chestnut hair. There was a scar over his left eye, a reminder to duck faster when encountering a Turkish scimitar. Although he had been a warrior renowned for his prodigious strength,

Chapter 1

age and a comfortable life had softened his physique. He bore the telltale paunch of middle age.

Stefan glanced toward his mother who smiled and nodded encouragement. Eyes down, Stefan shuffled over to his father.

"Behold the future *voivode!*" shouted the group, amidst laughter. Beer and wine spilled from uplifted mugs. With an unsettled look, Stefan put his arms around his father.

"My son, today is a great day. It is the day that I have been selected *voivode* of our country."

Turning to his wife, Bogdan shouted, "Can't you see that flagons are empty? Bring out several barrels of our finest ale for these *gentlemen*. And I use that term because if I call them what they really are, the women and children would be scandalized."

Raucous laughter and catcalls followed. Shouts of "*Noroc!* Long live Bogdan!" reverberated through the crowd.

As the men crowded around the entrance to the brew shed, Bogdan knelt next to his son.

"Some of these men are our friends and some are supporters."

"Aren't they the same thing?"

"No," scoffed Bogdan. "Real friends are loyal and will fight with you to the death. Supporters are fickle and will abandon you if it suits their selfish interests."

"How do you tell the difference?"

"By actions, not words. See Bako over there? He's my best friend. When we were soldiers together in the Holy Land, he rushed in front of me to intercept an arrow aimed my way. He was wounded and I carried him to safety."

Stefan's eyes widened.

"We have similar scars on our backs; a reminder of our time as prisoners of war. Experiences like that tell you who is a friend. Today, Bako is the leader of the *Calusari*, a secret fraternal order of horsemen. We can count on them to the death."

With plenty of ale to go around, Bako incited the revelers to chant.

"We want Bogdan. We want Bogdan!"

Bogdan waded into the crowd, accepting congratulations and beverages from well-wishers. At that moment, his mother tugged Stefan aside. She cast a worried glance toward her husband.

"Stefan, I need help. We have to feed these people before they get sick from drinking on empty stomachs. Fetch hams, sausages, and *brinza*, cheese, from the larder."

Before Stefan could protest, she disappeared into the kitchen. He heard her exhorting the women to slice the bread, cut the cucumbers and tomatoes, and plate the *placinte*. At the mention of the savory pastries, Stefan's mouth watered. His hunger would have to wait until after he had finished helping his mother.

While the celebrants gorged themselves, a mounted rider handed a message to Bogdan. As he perused the missive, Stefan saw a change flit across his father's face with the dark suddenness of a late summer thunderstorm. Bogdan beckoned to his closest friends and huddled with them in subdued conversation. Between outward smiles and raised flagons to shouts of congratulations, grave expressions guarded their faces. As Stefan helped clear the tables, he caught snatches of what was said, but could only discern a few words, 'Petru Aron,' 'danger,' and 'ruthless.'

A chorus of "Speech, speech, speech!" erupted from the increasingly inebriated crowd.

Chapter 1

Feigning reluctance, Bogdan shrugged to his wife and mounted one of the tables. As he surveyed those gathered, he rubbed his clean-shaven chin as if lost in thought.

"Friends, I am humbled by your presence to help us celebrate my selection as *voivode*. Thank you. We are blessed to live as freemen in a wondrous country. I promise to give you my best to make it even better. On this occasion, I think it is appropriate to recount the birth of Moldova."

The crowd cheered in anticipation of their cherished story.

"Every autumn, our countrymen prepared for winter by hunting the wild herds of auroch for meat to eat and hides for warmth. One day in the year of the blight, the auroch disappeared from the grasslands. A mighty bull-bison led them away. Knowing that the survival of their people depended on the success of the hunt, a brave warrior named Dragos tracked the herd over the mountains. Out of respect for the nobility of the mighty bull-bison, Dragos named him Urias, after the legendary giants of the creation myth.

"The hero of this story is not who you would expect. Sure, Dragos was brave and handsome, however, another proved even braver. When all was said and done, Dragos owed his life to Molda, a Molossian dog. She had a short, wide muzzle framed by bone-crunching jaw muscles. Molda traced her lineage to the war dogs of Alexander the Great."

As if on cue, Bogdan's rambunctious Molossian puppy leaped onto the table and slobbered on his master with his pink tongue. He was named Panda on account of the unique black and white markings around his eyes and face. Bogdan lowered his flagon to the dog. As Panda drank the ale without coming up for air, the crowd cheered and counted until he finished. When the ensuing hilarity and toasts to Panda subsided, Bogdan resumed the story of how Molda was killed by the bull-bison while saving her master's life. In gratitude, Dragos settled the land and named it Moldova.

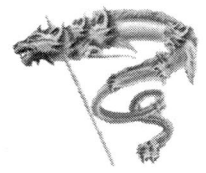

Months later after many seasons passed, other men held a secret parley in a remote place to prevent prying eyes and ears from learning about their plans. There was nothing new or original about the plot. The merger of greed and jealousy to eliminate a common obstacle was as old as the folklore describing the creation of the mountain range where the meeting was held. Nor was the perfidy involved particularly unique. What made this alliance noteworthy was the events it would trigger.

"How is my greedy, round friend?" shouted the man with the neatly trimmed beard as he dismounted his charger. One of his lackeys carried a banner on a pole into the center of the camp and planted it into a pile of rocks as if staking a territorial claim. The blood red flag bore the image of many silver vipers, bodies interlaced and heads with mouths displaying fangs, facing outward to form a circle. One could almost hear the snakes hissing malevolently as the heads seemed to strike and lunge as the wind rippled the banner.

The horsemen accompanying the leader fanned out to form a loose perimeter around the encampment. Hoofbeats and the noises of buckles, leather and steel created an unsettling dissonance at the bucolic campground. They appeared gaunt and wary, eyes scanning the forest for signs of any hostile presence. By their dress and arms, it was clear that they were mercenaries, who had no use for civilized discourse. They

Chapter 1

preferred to take whatever they wanted, whenever it suited them.

The merchant watched the soldiers maneuver into position with admiration for their discipline. At the same time, he felt corrosive doubt over what he had gotten himself into. It lasted only an instant, erased by visions of sparkling gems piled high in his treasury. The portly man smiled as the leader strode up to him and embraced him. The older man winced from the pressure of the hilts of several daggers against his corpulence.

The taut, leather-clad man pushed his face next to the ear of the kaftan-wearing boyar and said, "As a favor to you my friend, a squad of my stoutest men escorts your lovely daughter to the harvest festival. Trust that she is as safe as our plans are solid."

The boyar told himself that it was the chill autumn air that caused him to shiver. He forced a smile. With a twinge of covetousness, the soldier eyed the gaudy gold rings on the plump hand holding the canvas flap of the tent. They retired to the cozy interior where the aroma of lamb roasting on a brazier enveloped them.

"While we wait for dinner, would you care for a beverage?"

The soldier nodded. His ruddy beard bristled against the strap of his headgear as he removed it. He wore his leather clothes like a protective crust. Lean, tending toward boniness, he exuded a hungry look. With thin reptilian lips which were utterly mirthless, it was hard to imagine him with a genuine smile. He had a high forehead that sloped down to hooded brows that seemed to cantilever over his eye-sockets. His eyes were gray like tarnished metal and the pupils were surrounded by a dull, tint of yellow which gave him an alien look. The bridge of his nose was sunken, in a way which brought to mind a sinkhole. Some claimed that it was from the impact of the hilt of a Saracen sword; while others whispered that it was the result of growing up in a brothel. Either way, none dare ask him about it.

"Make yourself comfortable," said the boyar. With muddy boots, the soldier stepped onto the thick Bijar rug which covered the floor of the sumptuously decorated tent. He sat on a tufted divan and rested his leonine head on a silken pillow artfully embroidered with an elaborate dragon. Sweat and grime marred the surface. The boyar grimaced.

"I acquired that treasure from a Chinese baron who assured me that it came from the house of Zheng He, the legendary explorer," said the merchant who gave a sign to one of his attendants to rescue the valuable pillow. Before the attendant could snare the object under the guise of fluffing it, the warrior rubbed his head into the pillow and released a sigh of contentment. The boyar rolled his eyes.

"Tell me your plan to deliver that swine to me so I can remove his crown and see his head on a silver platter," said the brute in a coarse nasal voice. "I will have what is rightfully mine!"

The merchant closed his eyes and reminded himself that Bogdan had rejected his plan to take control of the silver mines near Rodna. Consorting with this savage was the price for assurance that he would gain control of the lucrative mines once the deed was done. Still, he cringed at the thought of associating with a man who went by the name the Bloody Scourge. A title he apparently acquired for his penchant for bloody solutions to problems. The boyar hoped that the Bloody Scourge never considered him a problem.

"The plan has been set in motion," said the portly merchant. "You will be most happy with my arrangements."

Chapter 1

The soldier grunted impatiently and spat out enough invective to poison a small city.

"You understand that I have spent my life fighting for scraps while my father bestowed every privilege on that pampered worm? And the irony is that I am the first-born," said the soldier, slamming his fist on an adjacent table.

The boyar squirmed uncomfortably during this diatribe. As the last piece of information hung in the air, he sputtered in his cup.

With spittle of wine dripping from his chin, he asked, "How is that possible?"

"How is it possible, you ask? I'll tell you how it's possible. When the Lady Mariana was unwilling to service the *lord of the manor,* she cast a spell on her sister and maneuvered her into the marital bed. The lord bedded her sister who became pregnant with me. After I was born, my *sainted* father resumed relations with that witch he called his wife. She spawned my younger half-brother one year after I was born."

"But that *voivode* was known as *the Good.*"

"Ha! *The Good,* my ass. He was complicit in his wife's sorcery and reveled in impregnating her sister. He was a lecherous beast whose appetites knew no bounds.... Ah, I see you doubt me. Just take a look at this royal symbol," he said, lowering his trousers to expose his butt.

The merchant stared at a puckered white scar depicting a winged dragon. He grimaced at the thought of how painful the branding of that crude scar must have been.

"*Da,* it hurt like the devil himself scorched my skin."

The soldier emitted a shriek so piercing and loathsome that the skin on boyar's arms prickled. The sound reverberated in the silence which followed. Unsure of how to react, the boyar fussed with the utensils on the table. When he was reasonably sure the other had vented fully, the boyar spoke.

"We know that the *voivode's* wife stayed behind to nurse one of her youngsters who mysteriously fell ill on the eve of the *petrecere*. The daughter of my head servant is the babe's nursemaid, so there will be no sudden recovery," he said through a smug smirk. "The unaccompanied *voivode* will succumb to the feminine wiles of my most alluring courtesan whose name, get this, is Salome just like the tart who demanded the head of John the Baptizer. She will deliver him in a, shall we say distracted state, to your *sicarii*."

"How can you be sure he will lie with your Salome?"

"With this," said the boyar. From deep in his robes, he produced a vial of scarlet liquid. "A magic aphrodisiac from the far east will ensure his attention," said the man trying to suppress a sinister leer.

"When?"

"This will be done before dawn on the night after the wedding ceremony. I don't want to disrupt my daughter's wedding."

Quicker than a snake strike, the soldier was behind the boyar, blade at his throat. He shushed the quivering man and deftly lifted the red vial from his pudgy hand.

"That's better," said the soldier, his voice oozing contempt. "I will determine *when* Bogdan will be distracted."

"But . . ."

A venomous glare from the mercenary silenced the boyar. As if he were weighing the advisability of finishing off the other man right there, the soldier regarded him over the rim of his cup. The boyar released an involuntary whimper. The soldier exhaled as if to say that he grew weary of this game.

"What about his vile offspring?"

Chapter 1

"Alas, when the boy goes to his bedroll, he will find something which will inflict a painful demise," responded the merchant trying to regain his poise.

A servant entered the tent with a platter of delicacies. The fat man turned his greedy gaze to the timely distraction. Before the boyar could reach the food, the soldier grabbed a couple of spicy lamb meatballs, popped them into his mouth, and cackled,

"Soon, his balls and his crown will be mine!"

CHAPTER 2

After a modest coronation ceremony, Bogdan embraced the challenges of leadership by traveling throughout the realm. Stefan often traveled with him. While on the road, Bogdan taught his son more than the history of his country, he taught him about the soul of his country.

As they traveled, Stefan's thoughts drifted to one especially memorable trip. Stefan was sitting against a barn listening to Bogdan explain the secrets to success that his father had passed on to him. According to Alexandru the Good, there were three secrets to a long, successful reign. First, cultivate as many friends and allies as possible. Second, wield the levers of power with fairness and justice. Third, pray for a healthy supply of luck.

Chapter 2

"But never rely too much on luck because she is a fickle mistress who will turn on you before you can say *placinte*. And you know how much I love our cabbage pastry."

The *voivode* smiled to himself. Stefan furrowed his brows as he absorbed what his father told him. The autumn sun warmed his cheeks. The warble of a songbird was replaced by the jangle of spurs. The shadow of a man covered Stefan. Bogdan sprang to his feet with a shout that was surprise mingled with joy.

"Commander, what an unexpected pleasure. What brings you to these parts?"

"I'm hunting scoundrels. Have you seen any?"

"As a matter of fact, I have. There is a youngster who they call *Lupusor*, the wolf cub, who has been raiding the sweet biscuit jar," said Bogdan tousling his son's hair.

"Stefan, I want you to meet an important man and great friend of our family – my patron, Commander Janos Hunyadi. With God's grace and the support of this noble gentleman, the council chose me as prince of Moldova."

A man with dark, expressive eyes stood before them. His thick, black moustache curved across his face like the cropped bristles on a Roman war helmet. His swarthy complexion contrasted sharply with his white tunic, his trademark attire befitting the title the White Knight of Wallachia he had earned during the Ottoman wars. His unmistakable martial posture coupled with a deep, authoritative voice completed the image of a formidable warrior. To Stefan, Hunyadi was an ideal to aspire to, a Christian knight.

Hunyadi smiled down at the boy and knelt next to him. In a voice intended only for Stefan, the knight said, "As I pledge my fealty to your father, I promise to support you when you become *voivode*."

Stefan blushed, speechless for a moment, until he found his voice and whispered a thank you.

"Look sharp, Lupusor, we are nearing a village and we must be amiable."

Seeing that his son was dozing, Bogdan jostled his shoulder. Stefan shook the cobwebs from his head and smiled at the field hands. They waved back their faces lit with the joy of nurturing the earth after the darkness of winter.

"According to custom, our family will host the fall harvest festival. This autumn the *petrecere* will be held in our region in the city of Reuseni."

"Papa, I hate all those strangers. They are so loud and smelly."

"Ah, you were young the last time our region hosted. You will see. It's a good thing. The mingling of the farmers, tradesmen, mechanics, and gentry reinforces our common history and our national identity. Without the *petrecere* we are random, disconnected, unable to repel attackers."

Stefan slouched and pouted.

"Besides, this is the year you train with the warriors."

Energized, Stefan sat up straight.

"I've been so busy that I had completely forgotten. This *petrecere* is going to be the best ever."

After months of planning, the *petrecere* was here. Over the previous year, Stefan had experienced a growth spurt that propelled him into manhood. With reddish-brown hair, fair skin, and a strong Musatin nose, he was the perfect combination of his mother's refinement and his father's

Chapter 2

masculinity. In an effort to emulate his warrior father, Stefan effected a pronounced strut complete with jutting chin. When he was agitated, the golden flecks of his brown eyes sparkled like meteors streaking across a moonless sky. When he was tired or bored, his eyes projected the fuzzy brown skin of an unpeeled chestnut.

While his father was preoccupied with solidifying his alliances, Stefan amused himself by wandering around the hollow where the tradesmen, cooks, and entertainers were setting up their tents. There, he encountered a kaleidoscope of people from many nations, colors, and creeds. Stefan was engaged in a knife-throwing contest into a circular target with several dark-skinned boys dressed in colorful striped apparel, when a young man came up behind him.

As Stefan was about to release his knife, a deep voice said, "Make sure that your spin technique is tight. Otherwise ..."

The knife thudded into the post below the target. Stefan whirled toward the source of the distraction. His expression changed from anger to elation when he recognized his cousin. Stefan stepped forward and the young men clasped forearms in an affectionate salute.

"How are you, Stefan?" said Vlad, whose face was split in an uncharacteristically broad grin.

"I'm so glad to see you, Vlad. I can't wait to go exploring the cliffs with you. Papa won't let me go alone. He told me to wait until you get here. You will be my protector."

"Ha, I'm two years older than you and already I'm your protector," said an amused Vlad. "I guess I've been through enough to qualify."

Vlad was the son of Vlad Dracul, who prior to his untimely death, had been the *voivode* of the nearby principality of Wallachia. Under his prominent nose, the young man wore a dashing moustache. It snaked across his upper lip and onto his cheeks in a way that menaced like a sinister asp when he spoke. Shielded by thick, scowling eyebrows, his obsidian eyes gave Vlad a dark countenance. His hair was the color of the pitch Stefan had seen applied to his father's ships. Vlad fashioned his locks in long, corkscrew plaits, similar to the mythical nocturnal bogey man feared by the superstitious peasants. He was frequently described as morose and melancholy. It was as if he had cultivated an aura of dread after the murder of his father.

"Don't be idling about cliffs, you won't have the strength to leave your tent each night after the rigorous training ahead."

"If you were able to do it, how can it be that demanding, Vlad?"

Before Vlad could respond, Stefan snatched his cap and darted into an alleyway. Vlad stomped after him, threatening his cousin with dire consequences if anything happened to his new, velvet cap. Stefan ran backwards, waving the hat aloft to taunt his pursuer. When Vlad was out of breath, he stopped and bent at the waist clutching his side.

"Who is going to be too exhausted each night after training?" mocked Stefan.

"You'll find out soon enough, *Lupusor*. There's a lot more to combat training than racing about. Wait 'til the Cossacks have you carrying barrels on your back while you hurl weighted spears."

The jibe pierced its target and Stefan's playful grin withered like the fading light at dusk. The acid of doubt flashed in his eyes.

"Hey, Stefan, not to worry. You'll be fine; you're of Musatin stock."

Chapter 2

The training for the young men alternated between classroom sessions taught by intellectuals and physical training inflicted by Cossacks. Stefan's favorite subject was war strategy and battle tactics. His least favorite, the endurance trials which were so physically demanding that he fell into his cot exhausted from the sustained intensity and stress of the Cossack drills. On most nights, not even the healing balms applied by Vlad could rouse him enough to take supper. On the rare nights he made it to the mess tent, he fell asleep with his face in his plate.

When the final segment of training began, the sun had not risen. Emitting vapor clouds with each breath, Stefan stood in the courtyard of a nondescript building on the outskirts of the city. About two dozen boys loitered, waiting for the taskmaster to arrive. Stefan tried to disguise his nervousness by slouching against a wall. He chatted with his friend Viorico and Vlad.

In contrast to his two privileged companions, Viorico Baltraz had an enigmatic lineage. No one knew where he was born. He came with the people who arrived every spring when the rivers flowed high from the thaw after the long cold winter. It may have been a coincidence, but then again, probably not, since they came at the same time as the great herds of auroch. Although he was a young lad there was a special aura about him. It was as if a shimmering glow emanated from him. His friends called him Rico.

He was tall for his age and, although he was the same age as Stefan, he was often mistaken for someone much older. It was natural for him to run with a surge of a terrestrial predator. His stride combined catlike lightness, caprine agility and the power of a Hyaenodon giga. In contrast to his sinewy legs, his core was muscular, even brawny. He had a neck that was short and thick to support a large high-domed head crowned with a mane of shaggy, brown hair.

His true distinction came from his eyes which were alert and piercing. By a strange quirk, his left eye was hazel almost tawny and his right eye was cerulean blue. When he was alarmed, his eyes blazed clear and bright like the fires of Sumedru.

"Vlad, congratulations on winning the archery competition. What is your secret?" asked Stefan.

"I don't let anything distract me from my aim. Using my father's bow, the only thing I think about is the face of the bastard who killed my father."

As he spoke, Vlad adopted an archer's stance and pantomimed aiming and firing a phantom arrow. Stefan admired the thick, muscular forearms of his cousin. In contrast to Stefan's litheness of youth, Vlad was big boned with the sturdy frame of a mature man. He was flat-footed and lumbering, almost bearlike. And, like a bear, he was ferocious when angered.

"Excuse me Vlad," said Rico, "I'm new here. What happened to your father?"

Vlad swiveled his head to ensure that no one was listening. Then, in a low voice he said, "My father was a faithful ally of Sigismund von Luxembourg, the King of Hungary who later became Holy Roman Emperor. He made my father a member of the Order of the Dragon. I wear the dragon-badge under my tunic," said Vlad with a catch in his throat.

Vlad slid his shirt to the side to expose a red cross medallion encircled by a dragon with its tail coiled around its neck.

"After he fought in the Crusade of Varna, my father was *voivode* of Wallachia. I was still young, but I remember him as

Chapter 2

a large man with a big belly. He had long black mustaches that tickled my cheek when he hugged me. Four years ago, he angered Janos Hunyadi over a disagreement about paying tribute to the Ottomans. The bastards took my father from our home and killed him in the marshes by the river. Now, Hunyadi and his henchmen rule Wallachia," said Vlad, as a single tear slid down his cheek.

"I'm sorry, Vlad," said Rico, as a metal gate clanged against the wall of the courtyard. Vlad gasped.

"Line up, you runts," shouted a giant of a man who wore chain mail which was so highly polished that its reflection was painful to the eyes.

Although he was above average in size, he moved with the grace and agility of a circus gymnast. Scars or tattoos covered every bit of his exposed skin. He was the bastard son of the leader of a clan that inhabited the Wild Fields north of the Black Sea. At twelve, he ran away to join a troop of knights heading south to fight the Moslems. He became squire to Janos Hunyadi and made his fortune in service to the Hungarian commander. His reputation for inflicting pain was so renown that he had spent the last few years employed by a villain of equal cruelty. His *nom de guerre* was the 'Butcher of Greben.'

"There are two kinds of swordsmen – the quick and the dead. For the next few days, you will learn swordsmanship; the art of close quarter combat using a blade made of Damascus steel, sharpened to a razor's edge," he said, throwing a feather into the air.

The boys watched as it fluttered earthward in a lazy spiral. With a sweep that was barely visible, he sliced the feather in two with his sword. The sword cut the shaft of the feather so cleanly that not a single barb was displaced.

"I am Dryger of Greben. You will call me 'Sir' or 'Knight' when I give you permission to speak. Otherwise, you will remain silent."

Throughout the morning of vigorous exercise wielding the heavy metal swords according to maneuvers choreographed by Dryger, Stefan sensed that Vlad was disturbed. He swung his sword so violently at times that Stefan feared that Vlad might impale someone by accident.

Later, at the midday meal when they could talk, Stefan asked, "What's bothering you, Vlad? You almost chopped my ear off during that parrying drill."

Vlad shook his head and looked down to hide the welling up in his eyes. Rico nudged Stefan and signaled him to give Vlad privacy. They went to the food line for a bowl of cornmeal porridge, *mamaliga* and a glob of sour cream. The young men ate while sitting against a walnut tree. Shortly, Vlad joined them.

"It's hard for me, here. I am considered the spawn of a dead *voivode*. Many would rather see me dead," said Vlad, sweeping the courtyard with his dark eyes.

"I'm sorry, Vlad, but I don't see it," said Stefan.

"Are you blind? Look at that bastard Dryger. He would laugh if I were to be the *victim* of a training accident."

"Keep your voice down, or we'll be cleaning stables for a week," said Rico.

"I think you are letting your imagination get the best of you," said Stefan.

"Really? Would you say that if you knew that that bastard was with Hunyadi when they came for my father? Would you say the same if you followed them as they dragged your father into the swamp? Would you say the same if you saw Dryger pin your father's arms behind him as that rat Hunyadi slit his

Chapter 2

throat? Bah, you have a charmed life. Your path to the throne is guaranteed."

Blank stares and open mouths replaced the expressions on the faces of Stefan and Rico. Vlad threw his bowl. It splattered the mushy contents against a nearby tree creating a mess. It reminded the boys of the brain matter from yesterday's demonstration of the effect of a war hammer on a calf. As Vlad hurried away, Stefan heard him mutter, "I *will* get that bastard."

Stefan's expression slackened and a shiver like an ice bolt ran down his spine. He wondered whether Vlad knew that Hunyadi was the reason Bogdan was *voivode* of Moldova. Recalling his positive experience with Hunyadi, Stefan felt a pang of guilt.

Later that week, after the conclusion of swordsmanship training, Stefan headed toward the outskirts of the camp. The muscles in his legs rebelled as Stefan ascended the rise to the children's theater. The burning in his quads reminded him to climb the incline gingerly. From atop the hill, he heard someone tittering. All he saw was the flash of white cloth disappearing behind the trunk of an oak. Stefan crouched low advancing along a row of scrub pines. He grimaced as his legs barked at the effort.

Again, the sound of light laughter enticed his ears. He cocked his head expectantly. With a sly smile, he dropped to all fours and ascended toward his prey. As he caught a glimpse of a forehead at the edge of the trunk, a feminine form slipped deeper into the woods. A siren's laughter wafted in his direction.

Intrigued, Stefan realized that she would continue to elude him unless he devised another tactic. He slipped from the path into a slight ravine which concealed his location. He backtracked down the rise to where he located another branch of the ravine. Stefan scrambled hand-over-hand up the second ravine until he ascended the hill about ten yards from the oak tree. Straight ahead he could see a figure dressed in a white shawl peering around the tree toward where he had been. On tip-toe, he crept up on the figure. Closer and closer, he drew.

A slight breeze loosened a cluster of acorns which fell between them. Startled, the white figure turned toward Stefan. For an instant, their eyes met. A hush enveloped them, as if some force silenced all the forest noises. An indescribable radiance passed between them. A strange serenity melted Stefan's anxiety. Then, he blinked and she was gone.

With the grace and alacrity of a frightened doe, she ran into the brush. Her shawl flapped like the wings of an angel. Stefan grinned as he watched the mystery lady's head bobbing away until she disappeared in the thicket. Stefan decided not to pursue her; he did not want to be late in picking up his younger relative because he had arranged to meet his friends for some fun before the banquet that night.

Stefan headed toward the amphitheater which nestled in a natural hollow which was surrounded by tiered seating built into the gentle slope of a hill. Built by the Romans over a millennium ago, it was a marvel of engineering and acoustics.

Scanning the crowd for his charge, he spied him near the front row. Content that he would reach him when the show ended, his eyes were drawn to the woman on stage. She gesticulated wildly as she portrayed multiple characters in an elaborate fairy tale. She was Ruxandra the gypsy queen – a master storyteller.

Chapter 2

Perspiration glistened on the folds of the olive skin of her forehead. The knotted tail of her colorful head scarf ran down her neck. As she pranced across the stage, intensely-hued scarves of her costume fluttered hypnotically in her wake. Her movements were as bold and grand as her voice. The audience alternately gasped, laughed, and shrieked as the gypsy wove a tale of treachery, danger, and heroism.

Watching Ruxandra cavort with feline grace, Stefan smiled as he found a seat in the back. In mid-whirl, she spied him. Her eyes flashed in acknowledgement. He nodded imperceptibly. Despite numerous liver spots on her face and hands, Stefan thought that time had been kind to her. She was nimble and her dark eyes were captivating. Stefan recalled her enthralling performances in years past when he was a youngster. As she danced, she sang of a witch who danced with the devil creating a whirlwind that snatched an unwary soul in its grasp and pulled him into the underworld. The children giggled nervously.

Gesticulating languorously, Ruxandra moved toward a circle of stones at the edge of the stage. A black cast-iron kettle hung by an arc-shaped hanger over an open flame. In a low voice, she chanted. As if in a trance, her eyes glazed over. She shuffled toward the cauldron. In a flurry of motion and sound, Ruxandra screeched and jerked her right hand skyward. As the audience followed her misdirection, she slipped a tablet into the cauldron. A scrim of smoke blossomed into a swirling grey plume above the pot. All eyes watched as Ruxandra exclaimed an unrecognizable name. First one, then another, then a dozen snakes slithered out of the cauldron onto the stage.

Shrieks, wails, and shouts filled the air. While the audience was transfixed in horror, Ruxandra waved dramatically and the snakes disappeared into a hidden channel in the floor. Before the crowd could recover from the shock, Ruxandra swept in front of the cauldron and raised the folds of her costume above her until she was encased in a cocoon of bright silk. From somewhere behind the stage, a thunderclap exploded. Startled, the crowd jumped. When the audience returned their attention to the stage, Ruxandra was gone, leaving behind a pile of silken robes. There was stunned silence. Then the crowd erupted into loud cheering, whistling, and stamping of feet.

After a few minutes of raucous noise, Ruxandra returned stage left and trotted to the center where she bowed. With his pinkies at the edge of his lips, Stefan whistled loudly. He and others tossed coins onto the stage. Ruxandra beamed proudly and scooped up the tribute.

Moments later, as the crowd cleared, Stefan felt a slight tug on his jacket. Fearing a pickpocket, he grabbed a hand. Turning toward the perpetrator, Stefan prepared to strike. Much to his surprise, Ruxandra stood beside him. She placed a note in his pocket and mouthed the words, "When you are alone..."

Stefan patted his pocket and nodded. Something about the solemn look in the gypsy's eyes raised goosebumps on his arms. Up ahead he glimpsed a figure covered with a white shawl. She was too far ahead in the crowd. He hoped that he might see her at the evening banquet.

Much to the relief of the trio of friends, the training week was over. The fun part of the *petrecere* was here. With the arrival of the families from every region, the atmosphere in the encampment transformed from one of spartan existence into one gigantic party. Gone were the military weapons, austere drillmasters, and cowering trainees. In their place, musicians, clowns, and minstrels roamed spreading a special joy. The most dramatic change was the delicious aroma of pastries emanating from conical brick ovens which had been hastily-constructed for the *petrecere*.

Fresh from a cleansing in a nearby stream to remove the stench of a week's training, Stefan, Rico, and Vlad ventured into the camp. The young men wore achievement badges - Stefan for battle tactics and swordsmanship, Rico for horsemanship, and Vlad for archery.

"My nose tells me that the pastry booths are open," said Vlad, smacking his lips in exaggeration.

"I can taste the *alivanca* now," said Stefan, rubbing his stomach.

With a quizzical look, Rico asked "What's an alive cow?"

Stefan and Vlad giggled at their clueless friend.

"Silly, it's not a live cow. *Alivanca* is a delicious custard tart," said Stefan.

"My *bunica*, granny, makes the best *alivenci* in Wallachia," boasted Vlad.

"I'll bet you that the peasant woman over there makes a better *alivanca*," said Stefan.

"How can you know that?" said Rico.

"Because, her *alivenci* are the only ones we can eat now," laughed Stefan.

As they made their way toward the pastry tent, a group of young girls passed. They were whispering and pointing surreptitiously at the trio. Feeling a surge of pride at his new status, Stefan puffed out his chest **like a bantam rooster** to show off his badges. He wished he could grow a moustache as dashing as his cousin's. Stefan cursed the wispy caricature of a moustache which sat on his upper lip. He lifted his chin to such a ridiculous level that he failed to see a small dog by his feet and tripped over it. With arms flailing, he fell into the back of a soldier clad in black leather just as he was about to bite into a pastry.

When the man turned toward them, custard cream splotched his face. A titter of laughter rose from the crowd. The man's companion tried to wipe the cream away, but only made matters worse as the cream smeared giving him the visage of a demented clown.

"Stop it, you fool," said the man as he slapped the other's hands away.

"You!" shouted the irate man, pointing at Stefan. "You will pay for this insult."

His right hand flashed out and struck Stefan in the face. The sound of the open-handed slap reverberated throughout the area. Stefan staggered as much from shock as from the blow. As his left cheek turned bright crimson, Stefan clenched his fists and propelled himself at his assailant. Like a matador avoiding a charging bull, the soldier eluded Stefan with a deft slide-step. As Stefan passed, the soldier gave him a swift kick in the butt which sent Stefan sprawling into a pile of baskets.

"Time to leave," said the soldier as he wiped his face with an apron hanging on a tent pole. A reluctant glob of cream filled the dent in the bridge of his nose.

"These worthless whelps have no respect for their betters."

With gall roiling in the back of his throat, Stefan called for worms, cancer, and maggots to penetrate his tormentor's head and cause him an undignified death. The soldier grabbed the hilt of his sword and turned with an expression of malevolence so vile that the crowd recoiled.

"What did you say, you sniveling rodent?" shouted the soldier in a voice so loud that it eclipsed the sound of the unsheathing of his sword.

CHAPTER 3

Bogdan sat at the high banquet table at the front of the great tent. As host it was his duty to oversee and direct the festivities. His face betrayed no emotion as he listened to Tramo, one of his best friends and captain of Bogdan's retinue. Tramo was a big, strapping man who came from a long line of miners. His thick chest and cannonball biceps made him a formidable presence.

"The good news is that I arrived in time to avert an ugly incident. I persuaded him to return his sword to its proper place. He deferred to our superior numbers, but his eyes blazed with hatred. Your son was shaken but unharmed. One of my best men is shadowing the bastard so we will know what he is plotting."

"Nothing good, Tramo. I can assure you of that."

With a nod of grateful recognition, Bogdan stood and waited for the crowd to quiet and focus its attention on him. Given that the wine and ale had been flowing for some time, it took a few minutes for the noise to abate. A shrill whistle and impatient glare by Tramo brought silence.

"I raise my glass to welcome our honored guests. According to tradition, we hold this year's *petrecere* under the Hunter's Moon. We are honored to have no fewer than five *voivodes* join us. Unfortunately, our great friend and military leader, Janos Hunyadi sends his regrets – he has been called to duty on the frontier. I am pleased to announce that we have agreement on measures to ensure that our regions will have great success in the coming year. We raise our glasses in friendship to our fellow *voivodes*. May they live a hundred years! *Noroc!*" roared *Voivode* Bogdan as he hoisted his flagon.

"Congratulations to all who contributed to the most prosperous and safest season of our realm. I thank God for His blessings and am pleased to announce that when you return to your homesteads each family will receive six hens, two dairy cows, and a horse."

He punctuated his last statement by drinking deeply and belching loudly. The leader's boorishness resonated with the rustics and provoked a mimetic retort, much to the dismay of the ladies present.

The atmosphere at the party skyrocketed from cheerful to jubilant.

When the jubilation subsided, Bogdan voiced a perfunctory introduction of Theoctist, the resident Metropolitan of the Church. As the cleric rose to join Bogdan, the *voivode* admonished him in a stage whisper to be brief so as not to delay the feast.

Chapter 3

He barely uttered the words, "Bless this food" when Bogdan shouted, "And now, we feast! Enjoy the celebratory *masa* dinner!"

As the *voivode* raised his flagon, his beverage splashed onto Theoctist. As the monk wiped the stinging liquid from his eyes, he shot an anguished glance at Stefan in the wings.

Shouts of "Here, here. Hooray for Bogdan! Long live the *voivode*!" erupted from the crowd which cheered and jumped in unison.

At one end of the hall, *jongleurs* wearing colorful native costumes sang songs about the joys and beauty of their country. Across the span, *lautari*, oral poets, warbled tributes to the great leaders to the accompaniment of stringed instruments. Men and women danced and sang as the alcohol flowed. The temperament of the people tended to be melancholy except when they were dancing. Then, they seemed radiant and happy.

"Sir, it is *entrée* time. We have followed your instructions to prepare everything that has four legs which is not a table," said the head chef.

As he spoke, he followed the *voivode's* gaze to the sensuous vixen prancing before them. Her movements were so enticing that the chef momentarily forgot why he had come to Bogdan.

Without interrupting his stare, Bogdan said, "What can I do for you, Giacomo?"

A long second passed before the chef came to his senses. "The food, sir, we must serve the food."

"*Da, da.*"

A parade of servers carrying trays piled high with Russian-style trout, chicken smothered in garlic sauce, orange-glazed duck, and mushroom encrusted bison fanned out through the crowded tent. Giacomo glanced at Bogdan who nodded in approval.

Stefan had no appetite and avoided his father because he did not want to explain the bright red welt on his face. As he sat toying with his food, he felt that he was being watched. Out of the corner of his eye he saw a feminine figure dart behind one of the tent's supporting poles. Stefan sidled over to the pole only to find no one there. He saw a figure in white across the room.

When he attempted to follow her, he bumped into a waiter carrying a tray overflowing with slabs of roasted beef. For a brief second, it appeared that the platter would topple onto one of the guests. Stefan stiffened as the tray tilted precariously toward his nemesis. As the waiter struggled for control, the mercenary glared at Stefan, his steely eyes conveying murderous thoughts. The back-and-forth swaying of the tray captured the attention of those in the nearby tables. More than one soul rooted for the tray to crash onto the mean bastard. With Herculean effort, the server steadied the tray and an ugly incident was averted.

At the end of the feast, Bogdan rose to address the crowd.

"My dear friends, I trust that your bellies have been sated. Now, it is my pleasure to present the Fires of Sumedru, our celebration of life, freedom, and fertility."

This last word elicited a lascivious roar from the drunken men who grabbed and pinched any woman within reach. The older women cringed while the nubile ones blushed. With a subtle signal, he ordered the ignition of the Fires of Sumedru.

The crowd gasped in awe as the bonfire burst into flames. It crackled and sprayed a geyser of fiery embers into the night sky. When the huge pyre was roaring, the fire-tender strutted toward it. Shouting incantations, he cast a powder into the

Chapter 3

flames. The fire changed into a satanic red that acknowledged the evil spirits. Many voices wailed in pain and screamed for protection.

He reached into his bag and threw another powder into the conflagration. Instantly, the flames turned purple, symbolizing winter and death of evil. He allowed the flames to temper. Several women sang a dirge. Like a gypsy violinist hovering over a mournful note as the mood darkened to sadness, but before despair, the fire-tender chanted a rejoicing incantation. To a crescendo of drums that blared from the edge of the crowd, he cast another powder into the fire. It erupted into a magnificent green. Rebirth and spring.

It was time for the Dance of the Colts. As Bogdan took his place, he nodded toward Bako Fotino, a swarthy man with a flowing mane of onyx hair and eyes the color of kalamata olives. As a result of his years as a blacksmith and wrangler on the Eurasian steppes, he was built like a human anvil. Bako was responsible for the Dance of the Colts, a ritualistic performance glorifying equine majesty and fairy magic.

Bako raised his hands like a maestro and signaled the commencement of the Dance of the Colts. From the outskirts of the crowd, a percussive thumping filled the air. At first, it was a single drum creating a rhythmic beat. The drummer walked out from the darkness, circled the fire and mounted a makeshift stage. His white costume shone in the bright firelight. His bare arms glistened as he beat the taut drumskin with rounded knobs on the end of a sticks which resembled the femurs of a deer. The crowd joined in, clapping to the beat. The lone drummer smiled and varied the beats leading the crowd in evermore complex rhythms. Soon, everyone was clapping and dancing.

The crowd cheered when a second drummer dressed in white entered the light, drumming in counterpoint. He was followed by another, then another until there were seven drummers beating an ancient composition. They formed a semi-circle on the platform facing the bonfire, the blaze reflecting orange on their faces. The audience was so engrossed with the music that a gasp of surprise and excitement rang out when a group of dancers sprang onto the stage. They were the tambourine nymphs, young girls dressed in flowing white gowns with flowered garlands in their hair. Colorful ribbons twitched and fluttered around their instruments as they shook and rapped their tambourines.

Moments later, a group of male dancers pranced onto the stage. They wore white costumes girded around the waist by wide belts decorated with vivid native patterns. These men wore tiny bells on their ankles which tradition had it were meant to ward off evil spirits. As the dancers jumped, rolled, and whirled with the skill of trained acrobats, the metallic tinkling of the bells and tambourines were perfect complements to the drumming.

From the wings, a dancer entered wearing a garish, diamond-patterned costume fringed with tassels and ruffs. He wore a black-and-red mask with grotesque features. The jester pranced and pantomimed the flips and cartwheels of the dancers. As he mimicked the virtuosity of the dancers with a clumsy bounce or pratfall, the gathering laughed and pointed at his silly antics. He mugged and fawned to the crowd before exiting to raucous cheering.

With the atmosphere charged with energy, it was time for the finale. Six young men stood off to the side looking out at the joyful gathering. They were the oldest sons of the *voivodes* present at the *petrecere*. Since Bogdan was the host, Stefan

Chapter 3

stood at the rear of the line. One by one they entered the stage and joined the dancing. Once they were all on the stage, the tempo changed and the drummers beat a rising crescendo. As the musical tension built, the first son sprinted across the stage toward the bonfire and leapt. Many gasped as he silhouetted against the night sky. There was an audible sigh of relief when he landed safely.

Stefan stared in awe as each of the jumpers, added twists and somersaults to his leap in an effort to outdo the previous jump. He shuffled forward, his heart thumping faster with the uproar following each jump. Stefan smiled at the youngster ahead of him in line. He smiled back, then sprinted toward the edge of the platform and sailed high into the air. After he passed the bonfire, Stefan lost track of him. The roar of the crowd turned to a cry of dismay. The background drumming ceased. After what seemed like as long as Stefan took to grow enough hair on his lip for a scraggily moustache, someone shouted, "He's all right. Just fell awkwardly and broke his ankle. He'll be fine by spring."

As the drumming resumed, Stefan closed his eyes. Memories from a childhood accident revived the pain of his own ankle twisted and bleeding after a fall off a horse. He bit his lower lip and began to doubt the advice of Vlad. It seemed so simple when Vlad proposed it, but now, with hundreds of eyes following him Stefan was tempted to slink away into the darkness.

Of course, that was not possible. His stomach fluttered and he thought he might vomit. Somehow above the din, a gentle female voice reached his ears and whispered, "Don't be afraid. You can do it."

Trying to locate the speaker, Stefan spun around, but only the fire loomed in his sight, a bright, flaming mass. Then, a creature with a black-and-red face, distorted by carbuncles and deformities into a grotesque mask, filled his vision. Stefan started. The crowd laughed at the absurdity of the jester leading the hesitant young man onto the forefront of the stage.

He heard more words of encouragement. Emboldened, Stefan ran and cartwheeled himself off the stage into the void between the stage and the bonfire. He disappeared from view. Shouts of fright and dismay punctured the night.

A long second later, Stefan catapulted into sight as if expelled from a volcano. He flew so high in the air that he performed four somersaults before he sped earthward. Some covered their eyes, others inhaled in apprehension, but most watched in awe as the slender figure accelerated head first toward the ground. At the moment of impact, Stefan tucked his shoulder and rolled several times before springing to his feet. Stefan lifted his arms in triumph and bowed so low that his hair touched the ground. His smile did not betray the astonishment he felt at being in one piece.

"And that concludes our 'Dance of the Colts.' There are tents serving wine and ale over there," exclaimed the jester.

Stefan was exuberant as he bounded to Vlad who was stationed behind the stage. The young men embraced while laughing so hard they could hardly breathe.

"That was beyond amazing, cuz," said Vlad. Then, in a conspiratorial voice, he whispered, "The crowd was so focused on you that I retrieved the jumping frame and hid it before anyone noticed."

From his vantage point, Bogdan watched his son and Vlad walk toward the drink tents with their arms draped over the other's shoulders. The *voivode* smiled as he tried to keep his heart from swelling too much.

Chapter 3

That night, Stefan was exhilarated, validated, and mystified. It was as if his miraculous jump over the bonfire were a lamp and all the beautiful young girls were attracted like moths. Beauties who did not know he existed during the banquet showered him with so much attention that he began to feel irresistible. Those vying for his attention assumed that the bruise on his face was from his landing and made sympathetic offers of cooling salves to ease his pain. He had to admit that the jump was quite remarkable, even though he felt a little uneasy about using a jumping frame. Vlad persuaded him that his spring-loaded jump was perfectly acceptable. Who was he to argue, thought Stefan?

The voice he heard at his moment of doubt was mystifying. The silken voice imploring him to disregard his fear. The beautiful message of encouragement. It was not the first time he heard it. Whose voice was it? Was it the girl in the white cloak with the radiant face? If so, why was she so elusive? He scoured the crowd at the drink tents, but he had not seen her. Stefan could not tell Vlad about the voice because he would say that Stefan was crazy or weak.

Inside the libation tent, at a table reserved for dignitaries, Stefan saw Bogdan gesticulating wildly with an imaginary sword and laughing with Tramo and Bako. It must have been a grand joke because the three comrades roared with hilarity. Bogdan saw his son.

"*Lupusor*, come here for a second. I was just telling my friends that you won the award for swordsmanship and how you used to wave your wooden sword when you were a pup."

"Vlad, there's Papa with Bako and Tramo. You go ahead and find Rico. I'll catch up."

As Stefan came to them, he heard Tramo say with a touch of envy in his voice, "Bogdan, you are a lucky dog. Your son is turning into a fine young man right before our eyes, eh. Oltea certainly provided you with a worthy male successor. My Sorina is good at pushing out only girls."

"Stop complaining, my friend. Your daughters are so beautiful that they will have suitors crossing far oceans banging on your door. Maybe, one of them will snag the heart of my son," said Bogdan, clamping his hand roughly on Stefan's shoulder.

"Papa, Vlad and I are exploring the cliffs tomorrow. Don't worry, we'll be back for dinner."

Bogdan gave him a nod which was the equivalent of swatting away a fly.

"Come, son, sit here."

He squeezed to make room on the bench, making sure that his son was on his left.

"Is everything alright?"

No response.

"Are you having fun?"

Again, with eyes downcast, Stefan was quiet. He slouched, wishing he could disappear. Bogdan exhaled as he thought of his own father when neither wanted to press an important conversation.

"I want you to understand that being the son of the *voivode* brings with it many benefits . . . and many responsibilities. When you are in public, you must carry yourself with dignity and restraint."

Stefan wrinkled his nose as if he was about to say something, but he ended up just nodding.

"*Lupusor*, now that you have become a warrior, there is something I want to give you."

He twisted off a gold signet from his hand and gestured for Stefan to put it on his finger.

"This ring has been in our family for generations. The face of the auroch covers the signet. When troubles come, which they surely will, look to the auroch," said Bogdan, with a catch in his throat. "I want you to have it."

"No, Papa, I cannot take this. I don't deserve it."

"Don't be silly, *Lupusor*, of course you do. When your grandfather gave it to me, I felt the same way as you do. But he saw me for the man I would become; just as I see greatness in you. It's a family blessing, take it."

"Papa, I can't tell you how much this means. I have always admired it. I promise to bring honor to our family."

"Anyway, this design might look familiar because it was imprinted on your rump when you were born."

Bogdan's eyes shifted from Stefan to something or someone behind his son. The merriment which filled his face a moment earlier, drained as quickly as a ship sucked into a maelstrom.

"What is it?" said Tramo, searching in the direction of Bogdan's gaze.

"Petru Aron, he's standing with Dryger," said Bako in a hushed whisper, looking at the figure wearing black leather. Hidden from their view was the receding figure of a sensuous vixen.

"What is that brazen bastard doing here? No one invited him to the banquet," said Bogdan through clenched teeth.

"Did you know that since he has returned from the frontier wars, he wants to be called the Bloody Scourge?"

"Forget about that mongrel. This is your celebration and nothing he can do will ruin it. I'll make sure of that," said Tramo.

Stefan turned to where they were looking and saw the man with the bent nose from the pastry tent. The young man inhaled sharply as he grasped the identity of his nemesis.

"*Da*," said Bako. "Your *petrecere* has been the best ever. We must celebrate."

"You are right, my friends. We have the whole night to enjoy the fruits of our labor," said Bogdan. "*Lupusor*, enjoy the revelry with your friends. This is our time."

"So, it's good to go to the cliffs, Papa?" said Stefan as he headed for his friends.

"*Da, da*, don't get hurt. Enjoy the caves," said Bogdan.

"Did you just say caves, Papa? You know I can't stand being confined in caves!"

"Sorry, *Lupusor*, the wine got in the way of my tongue. Enjoy the cliffs."

"Hey, Stefan, you are falling behind. Here, have a drink," said Vlad, as he lifted a flagon from the tray of a passing waiter.

"No, I'm not in the mood."

"What's the matter?" asked Rico.

"That ruffian from the pastry tent is Petru Aron, my father's bastard step-brother."

"He gives me the creeps," said Rico.

"Forget about him. There are too many young virgins here who need our services," said Vlad, rotating his hips for emphasis.

"Is that all you care about?" said Stefan.

"Did you ever find your mystery lady in white?" asked Rico, looking to diffuse the situation.

"No," said Stefan curtly, folding his arms to his chest.

"Look, the night is young and filled with possibilities. Let's drink to something joyful," said Rico.

Chapter 3

"To deflowering virgins!" said Vlad, in a voice that was a little too loud.

Each scanned the room over the rim of his mug– Vlad for the fiery gypsy girl he had trysted with the previous night, Rico for one of the stable girls he had befriended while he was grooming the horses, and Stefan for the mysterious woman in white.

Stefan was so engrossed in searching for his mystery lady that when he scanned past the dignitary table, he failed to notice a sensual young dancer gyrating toward his father. She snaked her way onto his lap and ran her fingers through his hair. When Bogdan turned to Tramo, the beauty removed a vial from her bodice and poured the contents into Bogdan's glass. A drop of red liquid fell onto Bogdan's sleeve, leaving a crimson stain that looked like blood. No one noticed it.

As he sipped his drink, Stefan remembered the note from Ruxandra. He unfolded it.

"Snake strike, Hunter's Moon,
Musatin Mortal Danger, Run!"

His skin chilled as if father frost had enveloped him in a block of ice. He looked to where his father had been. His chair was empty. *Bogdan would not leave the party. Something is seriously wrong.*

Stefan raced to his tent for weapons. He entered the tent hoping that no one had seen him. He forced himself to breathe taking quick, shallow breaths. Something was moving in his tent. He reached for the lantern. Gripping it so tightly that his fingernails pierced his palms, he lit it.

In the second that it took for his eyes to adjust to the light, he saw his bedroll undulating and writhing in an odd fashion as if something inside was trying to get out. Stefan touched the bedroll with the toe of his boot. There was an agitation under the blanket. He heard hissing.

As his brain registered 'snakes,' a black viper escaped and struck at him. The fangs caught the heel of his boot. Stefan kicked at the snake as it prepared to renew its attack. In a panic, Stefan flung the lantern at it. The lantern landed on the blanket and shattered. Flaming oil engulfed the bedroll. Stefan heard the sizzling of flesh as dozens of vipers caught fire. In a flash, fire consumed the tent. Stefan grabbed his dagger and ran. His only thought was to get to his father.

Willing himself into invisibility, he crept toward his father's tent. An icicle of dread stabbed his spine when he saw the bodies of several bodyguards lying prone on the ground with their throats slashed. The blood was morbid black and still liquid in the pallid moonlight. Stefan recognized the large form of Tramo lying inert near the entrance to the tent. The eerie moonlight reflected off a knife protruding from his back.

Stefan's eyes bulged as he saw a figure whom he recognized as Petru Aron come out of Bogdan's tent. Silhouetted against the fire, he was holding something. As Stefan struggled to see through the smoke, Petru Aron raised an object so incomprehensible that Stefan blinked in disbelief. Stefan's stomach lurched at the realization that the bastard was holding his father's severed head by the hair. As it twisted, Stefan saw Bogdan's dead eyes and pained expression.

Saying a silent prayer, the young prince clutched the handle of his weapon and fixated on Petru Aron's throat where he planned to plunge his dagger. Exhaling, **Stefan coiled his legs, ready to pounce and wreak revenge.**

CHAPTER 4

Before Stefan could rise in fury, a rough hand clamped over his mouth and a figure pushed him down into the foliage. As Stefan turned, he grasped the hilt of his dagger. A second before he plunged it into the ribs of his assailant, Stefan recognized the voice of his cousin Vlad.

"Stay still. They murdered your father and are searching for you. We must leave here as quietly as possible. Understand?"

He kept his hand over Stefan's mouth until his cousin nodded. His breathing quickened as he swallowed his sobs. Slithering on their bellies, Vlad led Stefan along a path which was illuminated by the Hunter's Moon. When they spotted a band of men carrying torches, the lads halted, quivering in place like trained falcons waiting for removal of their hoods. After a few minutes, they heard the baying of hounds. Without communicating, both bolted up and sprinted away up a rocky incline.

"Wait, Vlad, look," said Stefan, stopping and pointing to mounted silhouettes ahead.

"Friends," he shouted without breaking stride. Vlad was already mounted when Stefan reached the top. Vlad spurred his horse and held the reins of a horse for Stefan. With a burst of speed that he didn't know he had left, Stefan caught up to the running horse, grabbed the pommel, stepped into the stirrup, and launched himself into the saddle. He barely dodged a low branch before righting himself. There was nothing left to do but follow the racing horses in front of him. With the moon behind them, they headed northwest toward the mountains.

He counted three riders ahead of him. Vlad, of course; but Stefan was in the dark about the identity of the others. They rode like banshees, hunched forward with their whip-hands exhorting their steeds to fly. They wore hooded cloaks against the early winter cold. Recalling his mother's admonition that rushing wind on his face would cause illness, Stefan made sure that his muffler covered his face and mouth as a precaution to protect him.

As time passed and their plight seemed less perilous, Stefan felt overwhelmed by the gruesome death of his father. Bogdan had been a rock – a pillar of strength to his family and country. Tears streamed down his face and vanished into the rushing night. Who would bring the killers to justice? What would happen to his family? How would his country survive? Should he go back to help his family? Did he even know how to find them? As the uncertainties multiplied, he clenched his jaw conjuring up every curse he could imagine.

Chapter 4

Hours later, when they reached a junction in their path the party stopped for a brief rest. Stefan dismounted and knelt to check the front hoof of his horse. At a noise in the underbrush, he jerked his head up in time to see a black and white blur pounce toward him. He was knocked onto his back by a large creature which lunged for his face. Stefan grunted from the impact.

Vlad sprang to his aid, dagger drawn. He grabbed the creature's lower jaw and lifted. Stefan lay on his back with an amused look on his face. Vlad was about to slit the creature's throat when he heard a shout.

"Stop, Vlad! It's Panda, our Molossian," said Stefan, as he reached to scratch his pet's neck. Vlad released his grip and looked toward the woman, nodding.

Vlad pointed toward one trail and said, "That trail heads west. They will expect us to head in that direction – toward civilization. The other heads north toward the wilderness. That's the path you will take."

"No, Vlad," said Stefan. "I must return to Borszeti to save my family."

"That's not wise, Stefan. It's exactly what Petru Aron will expect you to do. You will be walking into his trap alone," said the woman.

As Stefan regarded her, he struggled with the thought of abandoning his family. He petted Panda who flopped onto his back for a belly-scratch. The sight of his dog, exposed, vulnerable, brought to mind the teaching of Tramo that it is folly for a skillful warrior to attack a superior enemy when weak. His face adopted a veil of agony as he punched the ground.

"We must ride to safety, Stefan," she said.

"Godspeed," said Vlad.

"What? You are not coming?" said Stefan, in a voice harsh with agitation.

"No, cousin."

"What do you mean? What will you do?"

"I'm going to climb that tree with my bow. I have a blood score to settle."

"What? Are you crazy?" said Stefan, raising his voice in disbelief.

"Doubtless, that pig Dryger is with the group that is chasing us. I will avenge the murder of my father," said Vlad, in a voice so filled with venom that Stefan hardly recognized it as his cousin's.

Stefan moved closer to Vlad. "My cousin, I now know the depth of your loss, but this is madness. We will be greatly outnumbered. They will slaughter us."

"You cannot stay, Stefan. We will help you escape," said Rico.

"Cousin, I mean to stay alone," said Vlad.

"Vlad, it's certain death," pleaded Stefan. "Don't!"

"Don't worry, I have a plan," said the older cousin. Stefan cast him a dubious look.

"I will hide in that tree," said Vlad. "Rico and I have already dragged the ground to make a scent for hounds to follow. When they arrive at this junction, they will stop to determine which way to go. Once they stop, I will have the perfect shot at Dryger. After I put an arrow through his heart, I will jump onto my horse and outrace them to the river."

"They will catch you," said Stefan in a plaintive tone.

"No. I know a perfect spot to ford and they do not. Further, they will be slowed by the surprise attack and confused over whether to attend to the blackguard or chase me."

"Vlad, please come with us," pleaded Stefan.

Chapter 4

"No, I will kill him and save you all from their pursuit. That is final!" said Vlad as he climbed the tree.

While the young men were arguing, the woman in white walked over to Panda, petting the enthusiastic canine. With no one watching, she reached up her sleeve and withdrew a soft, pliable substance which she rolled into a ball. She fed it to the hungry dog. Seconds after he gobbled it down, he collapsed at the base of the tree.

The woman dashed to her horse and mounted.

"Let's go," she shouted.

When they reached the trail north, Stefan glanced back for Panda. His heart dropped as he saw his dog lying by the tree.

"Wait, we have to get Panda," shouted Stefan. His voice was drowned out by the sound of hounds baying. The villains were close.

"No time," shouted Rico.

The woman grabbed the bridle of Stefan's horse and yanked hard, as she spurred her horse into a gallop. The three riders were out of sight and sound when the pursuers entered the clearing.

Vlad adjusted his position straddling a tree limb, his bow at the ready. Beads of perspiration formed on his forehead as he waited. Long moments passed before the pursuers appeared. The hounds came first and surrounded Panda, whimpering and nuzzling the inert form. Then, with a harried flourish, the contingent of riders came into the opening. Sweat-flecked horses chomped at their bits as they stomped restlessly.

"What's lying by that tree?" shouted the lead horseman, pointing toward a black furry creature. Vlad stretched the bowstring taut as his eyes narrowed on Dryger.

CHAPTER 5

They rode in silence as they ascended into the evergreen forest. Thick branches bristling with pine needles concealed their presence from any observers who might be below them. In the early going, the path was clearly defined. While the stony ground made the journey more difficult for the horses, it served to reduce evidence of their passage. Stefan watched the puffs of breath vapor gush from his horse's nostrils. He felt the powerful haunches propel the animal up the steepening slope. As his mount labored, Stefan felt heat enter his own muscles and dispel the chill of the crisp autumn morning.

Stefan rode behind the woman with Rico bringing up the rear. Daylight and the fragrance of pine were invigorating. When he wasn't obsessing about the hollow groaning in his belly, he

Chapter 5

pondered the loss of those close to him. He squeezed his eyes shut in an effort to eradicate the tableau of Petru Aron swinging Bogdan's head. Tramo was dead at his feet. The scene was backlit against the blazing tents. The barbarity of the images was so overwhelming that Stefan's tears blurred his vision.

They rode and rode until well after the sun had dwindled in the western sky. Always in the lead, the woman periodically checked her compass making sure that they stayed on a northern trajectory. When they had reached the limit of their ability to continue, she halted, listening for sounds of pursuit. Hearing none, she dismounted and led her horse to a stream. Following Rico's lead, Stefan unsaddled his horse and removed the bridle before taking them for water. While the horses drank, the young men also slaked their thirst and filled their water sacks.

When they returned from the stream, the woman had set up camp against a large boulder, facing the trail in case they had unwanted visitors. They understood that a fire was out of the question and ate whatever dried food they found in the saddlebags.

Each was lost in thought over the carnage they had seen and the tension of their flight. Stefan looked from one companion to the other. In Rico, he saw his training partner and his comrade in arms. In the woman, he saw a mystery.

"Who are you?" blurted Stefan in an exasperated tone.

"I'm Isabella, your guardian."

"My what?"

"Your guardian. My job is to keep track of you; which I might add is pretty boring."

Rico let out a great guffaw.

"You mean to say that all the while I thought I was following you, you were actually following me?" asked Stefan with a bemused look.

"Precisely."

"Where are we going?"

"We head north to your destiny, Stefan."

Over the days and weeks ahead, these words often sustained and troubled Stefan as he rode ever northward into the unknown.

As time passed, the urgency of their flight changed from frantic terror into a determined routine of pressing forward. The constant scanning the land behind them for sounds or signs of pursuit faded to an occasional glance rearward. Stefan reviewed their last conversation with Vlad. He worried about his cousin. Did his plan work? Where was he?

Once they passed above the tree line, the wild beauty of the forest landscape gave way to a barren windswept mountain scape. No longer were they shielded from the piercing wind. The change impacted the animals most; the horses could no longer find water or forage in the underbrush. As the days passed their mounts became emaciated; their tongues lolled and their ribs and hip bones etched against sagging skin.

"If we don't dismount, these horses will surely die," said Rico after watching Stefan's horse stumble several times on the rocky terrain.

"I agree," said Stefan, patting his horse on the neck as he swung his leg over the saddle. They were on a ridge and as far as the eye could see there was an endless vista of craggy mountains. The weary travelers gave no thought to the majestic undulation of stony promontories which lay before them like a graveyard of petrified giants. Their only concern was survival.

"We have to push ahead. The horses are doomed. To save ourselves, we must ride them until they drop," said Isabella in a dry, logical tone. Her scarf wrapped her face so that only her eyes were visible. For a brief moment, Stefan was entranced by the blue

Chapter 5

of her pupils which shone like brilliant sapphires in the mountain sunlight.

"We have no right to sacrifice these creatures for our selfish reasons," answered Rico.

It was clear that Stefan was the deciding vote. He knew that Isabella was correct, yet, he did not want to disregard Rico's empathy for the horses. While his companions looked to him, a cloud covered the sun and a Siberian gale raged around them. The horses whinnied and skittered, their metal shoes screeching on the rocks. Isabella pumped her arms to stay warm and Rico shivered without expression.

"We must keep riding," said Stefan in a determined voice. "It is our best chance. Unless we ride, we will all perish."

And so, they rode.

"I don't think my sorrel can take another step," said Stefan, as his horse faltered on the high ridge trail. Three weeks after their escape, their party was withering. Stefan dismounted and patted the horse's neck.

"It's alright, boy. You've given everything you have."

Understanding Stefan's words as a release from further effort, the horse sank to his knees, then rolled onto his side. Stefan unhooked the cinch on the saddle trying to comfort the dying animal. Rico was tight-lipped as he walked up to the horse. Withdrawing his dagger, he leaned forward and whispered words of endearment into the horse's ear. With a forceful thrust, he stabbed the horse in the neck, perpendicular to the skull. The sickening sound of the blade crunching bones, severing the spinal cord, and entering the brain was followed by death spasms. Within minutes, the sorrel was gone.

Over the next few days, this process was repeated twice. The party staggered forward northbound to where they were not sure.

On the verge of total exhaustion, each of the travelers knew that their journey was nearing its end.

The three were perched on a ledge overlooking the mountain range. They sat in front of a rock wall that reached into the wispy clouds above. The wall shielded them from the wind. Stefan could hear the incessant gales hitting the windward side of the mountain face. It sounded like the moaning of spirits of a long extinct race. Stefan's eyes unfocused as he tried to decipher the wind noise. Was it some sort of call?

He shivered and blinked back to the present. They huddled together, trying to conserve as much body warmth as possible. As he embraced his friends, Stefan observed them. What he could see of Isabella's face was bluish-white, the color of a fish belly. Rico had grayish-yellow skin and his ears looked hard and brittle as if they were about to crack and break off. Looking into Isabella's eyes, he saw sadness and an emotion which caused him to well up. Stefan wished that he and Isabella soon would find normalcy to explore that emotion.

The sun had risen revealing a sublime scarlet panorama. The morning sun provided only light and no warmth. What was that old sailor's rhyme he wondered? A voice interrupted his thoughts.

"I no longer believe that I have toes," said Rico through cracked and chapped lips. "I stopped feeling them when we crossed the last ridge."

In a scratchy voice, Stefan replied, "Nothing has entered my stomach for so long that it has ceased tormenting me. I guess it finally concluded that it is futile."

Isabella stood and stretched. Sunbeams outlined her. Stefan thought that with her arms outstretched, she looked like an angel preparing for flight. When the snapping noises of her joints and her grunting reached his ears, he knew that he was losing his grip on reality.

Chapter 5

"*Tovaras,* guys, we must press forward, I can feel it in my bones that the weather is changing. Make sure you fill your crocks with snow so that you will have water later. Come now," she urged.

Checking her compass, Isabella tapped it to release the needle. Satisfied of their orientation north, she took the lead. Stefan winced at the necessity of putting the snow-filled container under his clothing so that it would melt. He trembled as the crock touched his shirt under his cloak. It felt like the frigid icicle of death jabbing his ribs as he followed his companions.

With Isabella leading the way, they followed the ledge. To contend with the monotony of trudging behind, Stefan transported himself elsewhere. The grief over his father's murder was gradually replaced by darker thoughts. He was slow to form ideas and his mind wandered before an idea crystallized. Horror seized him like icy fingers clutching his heart when it dawned on him that Petru Aron would not have assassinated his father without a plan to murder his mother and the rest of his family. This thought weighed heavily on him and was transmitted to his feet which felt like he was lifting anvils with each step.

Sensing that the energy of her party was waning, Isabella halted.

"We'll take a break here," she said, after finding a shallow depression in the rock. She scurried back to Stefan. Grabbing his hands, she looked into his eyes and saw despair advancing like a gathering storm.

"Be of strong heart, Stefan. Your destiny lies ahead."

Despite the dullness which had suffused his consciousness, he nodded. Isabella pressed her lips to the brim of his cap.

"Viorico, are you with us?" said Isabella as she turned toward him. She shook him gently. "Stay awake. You must stay awake."

With a determination which would have made Moses proud, Isabella forged ahead. They had cleared the leeward face and marched up on the windward side. They gasped and shuddered when the wind hit them. Stefan stumbled, almost losing his footing. Rico grumbled something about wishing he was a chamois.

"What's that?" asked Stefan.

"A chamois is a goat-antelope creature which lives in these mountains. They are sure-footed."

"Can we eat them?"

"I would rather ride them, Stefan."

"We have to keep moving," pleaded Isabella, as she scanned the sky. The temperature rose slightly and the wind battered them with snow pellets which stung when they hit skin. As they plodded along, the ledge narrowed. It would soon be obliterated. One slip could mean death. Isabella halted to tie a rope around her waist and gestured for the others to do the same. By the time they had accomplished this, the storm was in full fury.

The blizzard roared around them, making progress halting and treacherous. Isabella slogged through snow that drifted above her knees. Although she was less than six feet ahead, Stefan could no longer see her. It was as if she had been swallowed by an opaque snow creature. His mind wandered and he stumbled into Rico who paused in front of him. Stefan brushed away icicles from his eyebrows and cleared the accumulated ice from under his nostrils. He was so sleepy. *Let me stay here for a while*, he thought.

The rope connecting them grew taut. Isabella appeared in his line-of-sight. She corralled her companions until they were on their knees facing each other in a tight circle. Stefan sank back on his haunches, his face stained with lines of exhaustion.

Though his eyelids were almost stuck together, Stefan watched Isabella as she unfastened her pack and removed a container of some sort. She lifted the lid and removed three pieces of something that resembled teardrop-shaped confections. They were glacial blue and shimmered in the wane light. Stefan thought that he must be dreaming.

"Here, eat one of these. It will help sustain you," said Isabella, slipping each a diamond-shaped lozenge.

"What is this?" asked Rico, casting a wary eye on the object.

"I saved it for an emergency. It is a form of paximadion, a type of military ration."

"Umm, it tastes good once it softens, sweet like honey," said Stefan.

"What are the solid flecks I'm feeling?" asked Rico.

"Dried auroch meat," said Isabella gripping their hands.

"Now is the time to pray. Dear God, hallowed be thy name. We know that your plan may be as unknowable and dense as this blizzard. Your humble servants beseech you to deliver us from this trial."

At that moment, Stefan looked at Isabella, her face as shining as the sun, and her cloak was as white as the light. Their heads bowed together for support, touching like the sides of triangular pyramid. The last thought Stefan had, before drifting away was that in the spring some goatherd would find them frozen together.

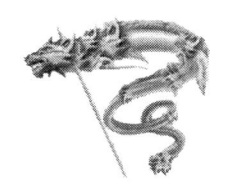

BOOK TWO

CHAPTER 6

The falling snow rapidly covered the three travelers who were huddled in a tight triangle. Although they were resigned to their fate of freezing to death, the snow had an opposite effect. It shielded them from the biting wind, trapped their body heat, and created a cocoon of warmth. Isabella opened her eyes and saw Viorico with his eyes clamped shut, his lips barely moving in what sounded like a mantra. She glanced at the snowflakes nestled on Stefan's eyelashes and watched as he nithered, trembling from the cold. Her heart fell like a stone tossed into a pond at the thought that she had failed to guard him from this calamity.

At the point of conceding failure, she heard it. A trickle. Isabella's gaze widened as she cocked her head to focus her hearing. Yes, she heard it more distinctly now. Where was it? She released her grip on the hands of the others and wriggled her fingers into the snow next to her right knee. The tips of her fingers were so cold that she could not be sure that she felt water. She pushed her hand through the crust of snow and felt water flowing under the surface. If the snow was melting there must be a heat source. Finding it might save their lives.

Chapter 6

Isabella crawled up the path, her knees pushing the accumulated snow aside. A slight smile formed on her face as she felt the water becoming increasingly warmer. Ahead she saw a cloud of moisture. She had read about thermal fissures in high-altitude mountains, but they were rare. Could this be the source of the warmth she felt, or, was she hallucinating?

Eating another paximadion for energy, she forced herself to cross the last few yards on her knees. When she arrived at the fissure, the relief she felt was indescribable. As the warm air flowed over her, she absorbed its life-saving heat the way a sponge absorbs water. While her body thawed, something gnawed at her brain. Stefan and Viorico! Isabella panicked, remembering her companions. How long had she luxuriated in the warmth?

Isabella rushed to her companions who had fallen onto their sides, appearing as buried lumps in the snow. She removed her pack and dragged Viorico to the fissure, his legs barely pushing in the right direction. By the time she returned for Stefan, she feared the worst. Stefan was unconscious, oblivious to her entreaties to assist as she dragged him toward the heat. After an interminable slog, Isabella thrust Stefan against the fissure. Her breath was rapid and ragged, her heart raced as she rubbed his arms and legs.

"Wake up! Darn you. Wake up!"

Viorico stirred and blinked toward Isabella as she flailed in desperation to revive Stefan. Agitated puffs of white frost burst from her nose and mouth. Rico crept to them and added his efforts.

Stefan was far away, floating through space atop a magnificent charger. He wore a radiant battle helm adorned with dazzling gemstones. His mouth was shouting a battle cry as he raised his great sword. At the end of the handle, he saw the words "*I, voivod Stefan.*" He searched the battlefield for the murderer of his father. From a distance, he heard voices calling him and felt hands rubbing and kneading his extremities....

Long minutes passed before Stefan opened his eyes. He coughed and nodded, signaling that he was back.

"I can feel warmth. Where is it coming from? Are we still alive?"

"Yes," said Isabella. "Praise the Lord. He has delivered this life-saving stream of warmth."

Satisfied that her companions were stable, Isabella crawled along the ledge looking for an opening in the rock where they might find shelter.

Stefan and Rico sat at the fissure, as feeling returned to their fingers and toes.

"Rico, where's Isabella?"

"She went to look for shelter."

"How long has she been gone?" Stefan frowned and grimaced as his raw skin grated against his muffler.

"Too long."

"We better go find her. She might be in danger."

Both crawled in the direction Isabella had gone. Due to swirling winds, there was no trace of her. Stefan was despondent at the prospect of losing her. The feeling was similar to the emotion he experienced on the night of Bogdan's assassination. It drove him to manic action. He pawed at the snow, but made little progress.

"Isabella! Answer. Where are you?" he shouted with a hoarse, raspy voice.

Rico echoed Stefan's calls until his voice gave out.

What little light existed was waning along with their hopes.

Chapter 6

Between gusts of wind, Stefan heard a faint sound. His heart rallied and propelled him to redouble his efforts. He stopped and held up a hand to Rico for silence.

"Stefan, Viorico, help."

A feeble call led them to an opening.

"Isabella? Where are you?" rasped Stefan.

After an anxious moment, she responded. "Thank God, you found me. I fell through an ice wall onto a ledge about ten feet down. Get my pack and drop it to me."

Once she got her pack, she retrieved a silver tube from a pocket and she placed it to her lips, blowing across an opening.

"Well, that's something," scoffed Stefan. "I didn't hear a blasted thing."

"You're not supposed to, unless . . . ," said Isabella who inclined her head to one side.

"Unless wha_?" asked Stefan, who stopped in mid-word. Turning toward the driving snow, his mouth gaped open as he saw a glowing swarm flowing toward them. Rico covered his head with his arms in a gesture of protection. A look of bemusement spread across Isabella's face.

"No need to worry. Say hello to the *zine*. They are friends," said Isabella, as a shining mass hovered near her face, flittering and sparkling. As if struck dumb, the young men stared at Isabella and her friends. Once the cloud of *zine* was stationary, Stefan saw that the swarm was actually a collection of radiant individuals.

Isabella nodded, hummed, and clicked her tongue apparently conversing with the *zine*.

"They extend warm greetings and agree to help us navigate the caves," said Isabella. She opted to withhold the admonition of the *zine* that no one leaves the caves in the same condition as they enter. While that was ambiguous, she thought, there was no need to create any more dread than there already was.

Stefan and Viorico wriggled into the cave and dropped to the lip alongside Isabella. They experienced a remarkable change in temperature, much like entering the hot thermal springs of the Herculean Baths that the Romans built in the Cerna Valley. From the light emitted by the *zine* they could see the floor of a long tunnel leading into the mountain.

"In case you have not heard of *zine* before, you should know that there are good and bad fairies, and some who are just pranksters. My . . . our friends here are the most beneficent fairies. As you can see, they are as beautiful as the daylight. The light comes from their luminescent skin and is magnified by their robes of sparkling diamonds," said Isabella to a buzz of affirmation and pulsing glow from the mass.

"Allow me to introduce Clopotica who is the decoder for this coterie," said Isabella, as a singular *zina* flashed a slow pulse.

"Where do they live?" asked Stefan.

"This coterie lives in these mountains, in hives made of flower petals. Although they never sleep, they have resting chambers filled with cushions encrusted with diamonds and emeralds," said Isabella. "Any mortal who disturbs the home of a *zina* will be stricken blind."

"They will help us find our way in the caves," said Isabella, her face aglow. "But they insist that you shut your gaping mouths lest you swallow one of them in a backdraft. That would be quite messy."

The companions exchanged looks of bewilderment and both clamped their jaws tight. Isabella laughed and the *zine* buzzed in accord. Stefan had the distinct feeling that the tone of the *zine* was mocking.

Chapter 6

As soon as they found a flat, dry area to rest, they unburdened themselves and settled into comfortable positions. Isabella explained that the source of the constant flow of warm air upward toward the entrance came from intrusions of molten rock from volcanic areas.

"Do you know where we are?" asked Stefan.

Viorico shrugged while Isabella turned to Clopotica. A floral white glow suffused Isabella's face.

"According to our friends, throughout all antiquity this mountain has had many names. The most common recognizable name is Kogaionon."

Stefan was in the middle of a yawn when Isabella spoke the name Kogaionon. He stifled his yawn and his eyes widened.

"Do you mean to say that this is the mountain where the man who slayed the evil giants according to Dacian origin myth?"

"Where they turned into rock?" interjected Rico.

After conferring with Clopoţica, Isabella answered, "Yes, this is the mountain named after the leader of the Uriasi."

"My father would be thrilled knowing that we found Kogaionon," said Stefan as he gazed absently at the cave. He wiped something from his eye.

"Are you alright, Stefan?"

"I guess. We've been running for so long that it just hit me that my father is dead."

"I'm so sorry, Stefan," said Rico.

"I know, thanks. It's just that I always thought he was impregnable, you know, like the rock of Gibraltor. How could he be dead?" said Stefan, his voice trailing off.

"Stefan, he would want you to finish the work he started . . . and his father before him . . . you are of noble stock. Things will improve," said Isabella.

Stefan sat cross-legged with his chin resting on a fist, eyes down. After a few minutes, he looked up. His eyes beamed with renewed vigor.

"Can the *zine* lead us to the celestial sword?" said Stefan, holding his breath as he remembered the times when Bogdan told him the story of man's victory over the race of giants.

Again, Isabella conferred.

"Although that knowledge is hidden from them, they will not stop you from looking. Now it's time to rest."

With that, the *zine* turned off their illumination. In the pitch blackness, Stefan closed his eyes and thought that it was as dark as the heart of Kogaionon. Exhausted and, at last warm, they slept the sleep of the just.

When they awoke, they walked into the tunnel led by the *zine*. Even though the *zine* provided adequate illumination to the front, the travelers soon felt oppressed by the darkness surrounding them. As before, they tied a rope to each other. Isabella led, followed by Stefan with Viorico bringing up the rear. They traveled for countless miles through natural and manmade underground passages. At times the passage narrowed and the ceilings were low. To avoid missteps, they crouched, taking small, shuffling steps. Aside from the faint buzzing of the *zine,* the silence was interrupted only by the occasional dripping of water, or the sounds of stones careening down a cliff into oblivion.

The deeper into the mountain they went, the warmer it became. At first, they exulted in the heat. Soon, the thermal currents became oppressive. From the exertion of traversing the up-and-down surfaces in the heat, a film of gritty sweat covered their bodies. Stefan mused that only a day before they wished with all their might for warmth. Now that they had it, they forgot the cold and complained about the heat. What strange, ungrateful creatures.

Fearing that he might lose contact with Isabella if he freed his grip to wipe his eyes, Stefan shook his head and squeezed droplets of sweat from his eyes. His throat and eyes burned. Shadows flitted among the irregular surfaces.

"I fear that I am beginning to hallucinate," said Stefan.

"*Da*," said Isabella, "the combination of darkness and strange noises is enough to unsettle a bat."

After more than a few knocks on the head from low ceilings and more than a few close calls where he almost plunged off a cliff, Stefan saw something ahead that would be emblazoned on his memory for the rest of his life. He blinked and pinched himself to make sure that he wasn't dreaming.

Stefan gasped when he turned the last corner and saw the phosphorescent blue-green glow of a placid lake. It was set in a cavern that reminded him of a grand cathedral. He craned his neck to see the high walls that rose scores of *stanjeni*, hundreds of feet, before arching into a dome ceiling. The grey stone walls were speckled with black splotches like the eggshells of the chickens which patrolled his family barnyard. Gazing up at the crags and cavities pockmarking the walls, he wondered whether any living creatures inhabited in the vaulted roosts.

So vast and magnificent was the space that he felt pitiful and insignificant. He thought that this is what it must be like to come before the throne of God. Stefan closed his eyes and listened to the hum from the wings of the *zine* as the sound reverberated throughout the vast chamber. It was as if choirs of angels were serenading them.

"What's that?" he heard Isabella ask Clopotica, gesturing toward the ethereal vista before them.

"According to antiquity, it is Lake Zalmoxis. The *zine* call it Mirror Lake due to its stillness. This is where we will stop and rest."

They walked to the shore and stood in awe. Stefan felt as if he were in a trance, his movements and perceptions were slow and almost childlike in wonder. The lake was so still that to Stefan it was like glimmer glass. The only animation came from the celadon light which seemed to swirl magically below the unmoving surface.

"Look at this. The sand is made of fine grains of emeralds," said Rico, as he filtered a handful of sand through his fingers. The facets of the particles glittered and sparkled in the ambient light.

"How is this possible?" uttered Stefan to himself. He toed the sand and sparks of light flew around his foot. A feeling of elation coursed through him. Although he wanted to think that this was the end of their wandering, he sensed that it was more like the beginning of their adventure.

While the *zine* retired on the nearest wall for a well-deserved respite, Isabella walked to the water with Clopotica on her shoulder. Kneeling, Isabella swished the water with her hand.

"Can we drink it?" she clicked.

"I'll have one of my fairies test it," said Clopotica, in a buzz devoid of emotion. She signaled to one of her group and a point of light flitted to her.

Isabella raised her hand in protest.

"No, what if it is poison? I won't let her risk her life for us," said the guardian.

Chapter 6

"Don't worry, the *zine* are different from humans. We are a collective being. As the leader, I am separate, but all the others are one," said Clopotica.

"Still, I . . . we cannot allow her to make this sacrifice."

Before Isabella could finish her sentence, Clopotica swooped down and grabbed a droplet of lake water and thrust the *zina* in it. Isabella's hands went to her mouth in shock as she watched the tiny *zina* flutter her wings languorously from within her bubble. The droplet floated, suspended in air, as the light coming from it turned chartreuse as the *zina* melded with the green water. Isabella focused on the *zina* whose mouth was moving as if she were consuming the droplet which was shrinking.

Suddenly, the light in the droplet went dark. The droplet was no longer suspended, but was falling rapidly toward the ground like an errant raindrop. Isabella shrieked and lurched forward to catch it. On contacting Isabella's skin, the droplet flexed and bounced before rolling to a halt. After a few anxious seconds, the *zina* appeared, shook herself in the manner of a dog coming in from the rain, and flew to Clopotica. An animated buzzing ensued.

"She has reported that the water is safe for humans," said Clopotica with a hint of annoyance.

"Is something wrong?" asked Isabella.

"Oh, nothing."

"What was all that buzzing about?"

"If you must know, I berated the *zina* for being a drama queen," said Clopotica.

"I'm not familiar with that term. What does it mean?" asked Isabella.

"It's *Zinese* for someone who shamelessly exaggerates a reaction simply to attract attention," said Clopotica, stifling a chuckle. "Although I must admit, her act was quite entertaining."

Both laughed, as much a release of the strain accumulated during the journey, as for the *zina's* performance. The sound of splashing broke the moment. Isabella turned to see the young men releasing tension by enjoying a swim. Uplit by the phosphorescent light rising from the lake, they looked like mythic heroes glowing translucent pale green.

Aware of her own need to bathe, Isabella removed her outer-garments and plunged into the smoothing water. When she surfaced, Stefan was staring at her with a strange look on his face. As Stefan waded toward her, Rico announced that he was going to gather some wila.

"What's that?" asked Isabella.

"It's edible lichen. I thought I saw some on the wall over there," said Rico, pointing.

As Stefan closed the distance between them, Isabella felt flush.

"I have not properly thanked you for saving me," he said in a husky voice.

"It's what I was made to do, Stefan."

His breath warmed her cheek. He reached to embrace her.

"Please, Stefan, not now, not here. I can't."

A look of befuddlement came over his features, almost as if she had slapped him. An emotion which he was not used to surged in him, only to be squelched by her distress. He thought that she shared his feelings – the look in her eyes when she regarded him, the concern in her voice when she revived him, the many signs of love communicated during the journey. Could he be so mistaken? His mind drift was broken by a stentorian shout.

Chapter 6

"Hey, you are not going to believe this," shouted Rico. He was high on the wall above the lake.

"Come now, hurry!"

Awkwardly at first, Stefan and Isabella untangled and paddled ashore. They avoided eye contact, dressing quickly. As he put on his shirt, Stefan felt his signet ring spin loosely on his finger. *We must eat or we will starve to death.*

By the time Stefan and Isabella clambered up the rocks to where Rico had been, he was gone into a narrow slit in the rockface. The *zine* preceded them into the aperture, providing illumination. Rico stood in front of a wall covered in runic symbols.

"Look at this. What do you think it could be?" he said, bursting with excitement. They stared at the faded pigments depicting symbols and figures with a mixture of awe and curiosity.

"It looks Dacian. I recall something like this in Bogdan's books," said Stefan.

"Definitely Dacian," she opined, perusing the symbols.

"Oh, my goodness," she exclaimed. "It can't be. No, that's not possible," she exclaimed.

"What?" asked Stefan and Rico at the same time.

"I think we found the cave of Zalmoxis," replied Isabella in a voice that tapered off in her own disbelief. It was one of those moments when the grasp of what you are seeing contradicts your understanding of reality. She blinked again and again, trying to absorb the enormity of their discovery.

"Remind me, who was this Zalmoltis guy?" said Rico.

"Zal – **mox** - is," said Stefan, as though repeating the name for a dull child.

"He was a major religious figure for the Dacians. According to Dacian belief, he was born wrapped in a bear's skin and named after the word for bear, *zalmus*. At a young age he was enslaved in Egypt where he learned from Pythagoras. Zalmoxis was so favored that he was freed and moved to Dacia where he became a learned teacher and prophet.

"At the height of his popularity, he disappeared. Most thought he had died, but what he really did was to retreat to a cave on the sacred mountain. He lived there for three years. When he returned, many proclaimed that he was a deity who had conquered death. Zalmoxis denied being a deity, rather, he preached that there was one eternal God who promises us a life in paradise enjoying eternal life and everlasting pleasure after we have finished our life on earth."

"These wall writings tell the story of Zalmoxis as far as I can tell," said Isabella.

An excited buzz from the *zine*, broke the spell.

"What do they want?" asked Isabella.

"They saw the wila that Viorico gathered and they are hungry," said Clopotica with a shrug of her tiny shoulders that mirrored a parent acknowledging the imperative for food communicated by children. It was an unstoppable force of nature.

"Let's eat and rest and tackle this mystery tomorrow," suggested Isabella.

"Yeah, *da*," said Stefan. "It's not going anywhere in the next few hours."

In short order, with the enthusiastic help of the *zine*, Rico was cooking wila soup in a kettle scavenged from the cave of Zalmoxis. As the aroma permeated their makeshift campsite, Stefan considered their meager rations since they had fled Reuseni and he salivated. Hunger, which had been suppressed during their arduous journey now returned with the virulence of a whirlwind.

CHAPTER 7

Many leagues away, Vlad listened to his friends ride away from the crossroads. When he could no longer hear them, he smiled. It was time to settle a personal score with the usurper's second in command. Straddling the tree limb overlooking the crossroads seemed like a good idea when he climbed the tree searching for an advantageous shooting position. It was the early morning hours after the assassination of Bogdan II and no matter how frequently Vlad shifted, his legs kept falling asleep. The tingling sensation served a positive purpose of keeping him uncomfortable enough to stay alert. Not that staying alert was an issue for the young man who was poised to kill the man instrumental in his father's murder.

It was fitting that he was waiting in ambush under a Hunter's Moon. Also called the Blood Moon, it was the time of year when hunters stalked summer-fattened prey over fields laid bare in autumn. Years before, Dryger had lured Vlad's father into a trap and held his arms while Janos Hunyadi slit his father's throat. Now, Dryger was the prey.

In the bright lunar light, Vlad studied the end of his broadhead arrow. The three-razor tip shone like a malevolent avenger. He vowed to the memory of his father that his arrow would cause Dryger's blood to spill as much as Vlad Dracul's had. His most perfect arrow was nocked ready to fire. All Vlad had to do was draw the bowstring when Dryger entered the clearing and let it fly.

The hunting dogs arrived first. Sensing that they were closing in on their prey, they bayed for all they were worth. On reaching the clearing, they were distracted by the body of Bogdan's favorite Molossian which lay at the base of the tree where Vlad perched.

"It's Panda," said the houndsman, as he waded through the pack to see what had caught their attention.

"Dead?" asked Dryger who reined in his horse.

"Appears so."

"Pity, he was a good tracker."

Dryger dismounted. He was standing almost directly below Vlad who was struggling to get a clear shot. He cursed to himself for not firing as soon as Dryger entered the clearing.

Several of the men dismounted to examine the tracks at the crossroads.

"What are you doing? We don't have time for that," snapped Dryger. "Get the dogs back on the scent. We are so close I can feel it."

The pack continued to roil around the tree. A few rose on their hind legs with their front paws scratching at the trunk. Dryger lifted his head. At the instant he saw a figure hiding, Vlad released the bow string. His aim was true. The arrow sped toward its mark when the horse suddenly reared jostling Dryger. The big man twisted.

The arrow struck a glancing blow above his cheekbone. The cutting edge sliced through the globe of his eye. The tip broke through the orbital bone and continued its flight. Dryger

Chapter 7

screamed in pain and clutched his face. The arrow struck one of the dogs in the hind quarter. As Dryger staggered, there was blood and chaos everywhere.

"My eye . . . the tree . . . my eye."

Vlad leaped from the tree and sprinted toward his horse. A few of the hounds pursued him. One reached him as he rammed his foot into the stirrup and vaulted into his saddle. The dog bit his leg and held on as Vlad whipped the horse into action. The other dogs nipped at the horse's hamstrings attempting to bring down the fleeing animal. The horse was battle-trained and lashed out with its hooves. One dog took a hoof in the face and fell whining in pain. Vlad was last seen heading toward the river with a determined canine dangling from his leg.

Back at the crossroads, three men ministered to Dryger who cursed and thrashed. The rest of the patrol reacted to the attack by pursuing the archer. They followed the sounds of the hounds and heard one yelping in pain. The riders overtook the injured dog and saw Vlad not far ahead.

Each time Vlad bounced on the galloping horse, he experienced searing pain in his calf where the powerful dog had clamped its jaws. As he entered the river, Vlad veered toward a large rock and moved his leg enough to cause the hound to smash into it. He heard bones crunch. The canine's jaws went limp. Freed from the weight of the animal, Vlad urged his horse forward. He knew that once the riders found the shallow ford, he could not outrace them, especially in the dark. His pursuers shouted in hot pursuit. Vlad turned back to see where they were. He failed to see a low hanging branch and was knocked off his mount. The horse was so agitated by the chase and dogs that it continued racing full speed away from danger.

When the pursuers reached the river, they found the hound severely injured, lying near a boulder which bore traces of blood where the unfortunate dog collided with it. The patrol followed the sound of splashing heading upstream. It did not take them long before they caught up with the fleeing horse. It was rider-less.

The men separated and searched the riverbed. With the sight of Dryger bleeding like a stuck pig all too vivid in their minds, they moved slowly keeping a wary eye out for a sniper.

Dazed, Vlad crawled toward the riverbank. His bow and quiver of arrows were still strapped across his back as he tried to regain his wits. He was formulating a plan to climb a tree and pick off his pursuers when a pair of hands grabbed him by the collar and dragged him into the woods. Vlad was able to get to his feet but he could not stop being tugged forward. He reached for his dagger but the sheath was empty. Vlad cursed at the misfortune of losing his weapon in the fall.

"Quiet," hissed a voice.

The next thing Vlad experienced was total darkness. Strong hands pushed him down on to a dirt floor. He bumped into a wall which was oddly slanted. The air was moist in an earthy way and smelled like mushrooms and dried herbs. He heard voices outside and felt around for something, anything to use as a weapon. The person with him, urged him to be silent. In time, the voices faded into the distance.

"Are you hurt?" asked a muted voice.

Vlad shook his head.

"I asked if you were injured," said the person, with a tone of insistence.

"No."

"Good. My name is Seraphim. I will stand guard against these mercenaries. You rest."

Chapter 7

Vlad thought to ask how his guardian knew that he was being hunted by mercenaries but decided to disclose as little as possible until he knew for certain who this stranger was. In the darkness, Vlad felt his calf swelling from the bite of the war-dog. He folded his cloak into a headrest and fell into a fitful sleep.

Many hours later he roused only to be in complete darkness. It must be morning he thought, but remembered that he was in some sort of wooden structure. He returned to sleep until he heard the sound of a horse snorting and rooting nearby.

"Seraphim?"

There was no reply.

"Hello there. What do we have here? It sounds like a horse. Nice, boy."

"Seraphim, is that you?" said Vlad in a stronger voice.

"Ah, our sleeping beauty awakens."

Vlad stood and cracked his head on the low ceiling.

"I'll be right there."

When Seraphim yanked open a heavy wooden door, a blaze of sunlight blinded Vlad. His hands rushed to shield his eyes and he stumbled forward like a blind man.

"Is that any way to treat a guest?" he said in a voice whose harshness he regretted instantly. As he adjusted to the light, Vlad saw an elderly man in tattered robes standing before him. The man stared vacantly ahead out of opaque eyes the color of robin's eggs.

"Seraphim . . . you're blind."

"I can tell that you are a master of the obvious. Does this animal look familiar?"

"*Da*, that's my horse."

"It helps if the rider stays on the creature's back, no?"

"I got knocked from the saddle by . . ." said Vlad, slow to grasp that Seraphim was mocking him. The old man rested his staff on a log and sat down. He motioned for Vlad to join him.

"When there was no sign of you along the riverbank, your pursuers gave up the search. Their party returned to the city to get medical aid for their leader."

Vlad breathed a sigh of relief. He had a brief time before they will be after him again.

"Tell me why those thugs were chasing you."

Vlad detailed the assassination of the *voivode* and the chase to kill his son. Vlad omitted his vendetta against Dryger.

"I was afraid that treachery was afoot."

"How?"

"For some time, there have been rumors of violence targeting Bogdan and his family. Is Stefan out of harm's way?"

"Honestly, I have no idea. I parted with him and two others late last night and stayed behind to divert the hunters."

"That was a selfless act . . . what did you say your name was?"

"Vlad Tepes."

"Where are you headed?"

"To Solomanta. Do you know of it?"

"*Da*, my son. It is a place of immense energy. Those who enter with a pure heart will have their wishes granted."

While Vlad considered this, the Blind Monk turned to him with a grave look.

"Woe to those who enter with darkness in their hearts."

"How does one know?"

"This earth is like a disc. On one side live the gentle folk who are grateful. On the other side live the avaricious who are never satisfied. When you go to Solomanta, your true nature will be revealed."

Chapter 7

As Vlad prepared to leave, the Monk's words traveled through his head like a bird trying to escape a cage. Trepidation flooded Vlad's thoughts. *What was his true nature? What if his true nature was despicable? Was change possible?* An urgency to get to Solomanta possessed him.

"I can tell that you are upset. Here have some mead. It cures all," said the Monk, handing Vlad an earthen jug. Vlad gagged when his lips touched a layer of strange purple-green ooze around the opening.

"What the . . ."

"This is an elixir the peasants use to dispel fear. Drink up."

"Smells like *marcat,* rancid milk. It's so vile I cannot make it pass my lips."

"Stop being a baby. . . . Vlad?"

Vlad placed the jug on the Monk's lap and mounted his horse.

"Farewell, my friend. I hope our paths cross again."

With a vacant stare, the Blind Monk waved haphazardly at his departing guest. Standing framed in the doorway of the tree abode, the low, autumn sun shone on his bearded face giving him an otherworldly look. Twisting his shoulder back toward the Monk, Vlad half-expected to see him rise majestically and disappear into the heavens.

CHAPTER 8

*H*e settled in his lair for the long winter's nap. His metabolism, heart, and respiratory rates slowed. Yawning, his tongue flicked over his whiskers. He exhaled and placed his head on his paws so wide that they functioned like snowshoes. As he slipped into sleep, he saw himself chasing a wild ibex through the snowy boulders of his homeland. The frightened creature bleated frantically, its hooves clicking on the rocks. Pumping his powerful rear legs, his traction was perfect. He closed in for the kill.

The sound of a stone bouncing down a drop interrupted his reverie. His pointy ears snapped forward. Hearing nothing further, his eyes fluttered, and he returned to slumber. His long, bushy tail wrapped around his body like the stole worn by a baroness to a jubilee.

Several hundred feet below, a motley party entered the cavern. A cloud of glowing light preceded them. Due to the vastness of the cavern and the routine sounds of the mountain with its contractions, shifts and ice falling, he was too deep in his rest to awaken. Noise would not trigger him. It would take something more primal.

Chapter 8

"Stefan, help me carry this pot down to the shore," said Rico. "Isabella, you can help get a fire started. There is some kindling and fuel behind the stalagmite."

Using rocks scattered around the cave's entrance, Stefan built a firepit. Before long, wila soup was simmering. A delightful aroma wafted upward. Rico returned to the cave to scavenge pottery cups for their dinner. Stefan tended the fire.

High above, the smell of the soup reached the snow leopard's nose. His whiskers twitched. As the aroma traveling to his lair intensified, his stupor eroded. The smell of food activated his salivary glands and stomach juices which signaled his brain to wake up. He opened his eyes and perked up his ears. Time to investigate. Known for his stealth, mountain people gave him the sobriquet the Ghost of the Mountains.

Rico came out of the cave carrying an armful of cups and bowls.

"Hey, Stefan, look what I found."

Stefan was glad to see the broad grin which creased his friend's face. There had been few opportunities to smile during their journey. This was a pleasant break from the danger.

"Did you find any growlers of ale while you were rummaging through Zalmoxis' larder?" said Stefan, in a tone that was jocular, with a tinge of wistfulness.

Isabella smiled at the banter. Stefan was about to ask whether Rico had conjured up a loaf of crusty bread to soak up the soup, when movement behind Rico caught his eye. Stefan stared at the cavern wall, but could not discern anything. The distinctive dark rosettes of the leopard's grey coat blended perfectly with the black specks in the grey rock of the cavern. About thirty feet above Rico, a blur launched itself from the wall toward him.

"Look out! Look out!" shouted Stefan. An instant before the leopard landed, Rico twisted and ducked. The pottery smashed onto the path, shattering on impact. The leopard's claws struck a glancing blow. Rico fell, banging his head on a stone. He lay there unconscious.

With fangs bared, the leopard bounded toward Stefan. He reached for his dagger and braced himself.

"Clopotica! Help!" shrieked Isabella who withdrew her flute and sounded an urgent alarm.

The leader buzzed and the *zine* mobilized into an angry cloud.

A tiny voice in Stefan's head reminded him of the mantra of his martial arts teacher. 'Use your opponent's force against him.'

When the leopard reached him, Stefan dipped his shoulder and flipped the leopard with his forearm. Sharp claws grabbed vainly for purchase as the beast elevated over Stefan. With astounding agility, the big cat landed on his feet and skidded to a stop. Emerald dust sparked under his powerful legs. Tensing his haunches for a fatal leap, the leopard snarled at Stefan.

In the instant that the snow leopard paused, the *zine* struck. They swarmed around the leopard's head. They flashed on and off so rapidly that it appeared like an intense meteor shower was attacking him. The brilliant, pulsing bursts of light disoriented the snow leopard. He swiped at the *zine* with fierce desperation. His paws flailed at the air as the *zine* darted back and forth so fast that he lost his balance. Stefan seized the opportunity to plunge his dagger deep into the leopard's side right behind his shoulder.

The snow leopard bucked and spasmed in pain as Stefan stabbed and stabbed until the creature lay lifeless before him.

Chapter 8

When Stefan mastered his heavy breathing, he rose and teetered to where Isabella was ministering to Viorico. She was sitting with Viorico's head and torso propped on her lap. Her face radiated beneficence as she applied a damp compress to a nasty bump on his temple. For an instant, Stefan's mind flashed to the painted icons of Mary mourning her dead son at the foot of the cross.

"Where am I? What happened?" murmured Viorico, trying to rise.

"Viorico, stay still. You banged your head when a snow leopard knocked you down."

"What? Owww. That hurts."

He relaxed back into Isabella. Worry lines etched onto Stefan's face. Blood streamed from his friend's side.

"Don't move, I need to look at this wound," ordered Stefan in a voice that barely concealed his concern. He tore aside the fabric of Viorico's shirt revealing four gashes in the pasty-white skin.

Stefan went to the lake to soak a cloth. The water felt cool as it sluiced through his fingers. He tried to recall the lessons on treating different wounds during training. Try as he might, his mind was blank when it came to treating claw injuries. Spears, yes, arrows, yes, knife wounds, yes, but no animal claws. Figuring that knife wounds were the closest, Stefan dabbed and stroked until he removed all foreign material and the wounds bled freely. Soon the blood coagulated except for the deepest cut which continued to seep.

"That one is going to need stitching," said Isabella who was monitoring Stefan's ministrations. She smiled at him. Handing him her compress, she said, "Please rinse this out and get my pack."

"Don't worry buddy. You'll be as good as new."

As he rinsed the compress, his eyes were drawn to the snow leopard. *What a magnificent creature. We must honor it by eating his flesh and using his coat to save ourselves. Thank you, God.*

"Stefan, what's taking you so long?" Isabella called.

He flipped her the kit. She found the needle and thread and began sewing Viorico's wound. Concentrating on her task, she lost track of Stefan. When she was almost finished, Isabella looked up from her patient and saw Stefan cooking leopard steaks on the fire. The smell of grilling flesh filled the area. Her stomach growled in anticipation.

Viorico moaned and started convulsing. His limbs spasmed and flailed like tree branches in a gale storm. His body twisted and bucked in sudden violent movements as if he were a wild horse trying to shed a rider. Isabella pushed Viorico onto his side and called for Stefan to help.

"Shouldn't we hold him down?" asked Stefan.

"No, he is shaking because of the blow to his head. It will pass. We have to make sure he doesn't swallow his tongue."

As he knelt over Viorico, Stefan cursed Petru Aron. They wouldn't be in this fix if it weren't for that bastard.

"Don't let your heart turn as black as obsidian with hatred, Stefan," said Isabella.

"How do you know what is going on in my heart?"

She touched his arm.

"As I told you, I am your guardian. It's my job to help and protect you. You have a great destiny to fulfill and I cannot watch you succumb to the poison of hatred. You are better than that."

"I don't know," he replied in a low voice.

"I do."

Chapter 8

With those two simple words, Stefan felt a great hardness in his heart soften. With eyes closed, he leaned his head toward Isabella until their foreheads touched. They remained like this for a while, breathing quietly. When they opened their eyes, they saw their injured friend at peace, lying still.

The smell of burnt leopard drifted to them.

"Oh, well," remarked Stefan. "That meat was probably too tough to eat."

Isabella allowed herself a slight smile.

"Here," said Isabella, extending her hand to him.

"What is it?"

"Dessert."

Isabella opened her hand over his and dropped a blue paximadion into his hand.

"Thanks," he said, smiling.

Later, when Viorico was comfortable and they all had consumed the soup, Stefan went off with some of the *zine* to explore the cave of Zalmoxis. He hoped to find something useful there. Fearing the possibility of more snow leopards, Clopotica decided that the remaining *zine* would keep watch. No one objected.

Although Stefan had to bend to enter, the interior of the cave was high enough for him to walk around upright. At first glance, Stefan noticed that there were three compartments. In the compartment to his right there were indentations that served as shelves. This is where Viorico must have found the pottery vessels he was carrying when the snow leopard attacked. Opposite the entrance, there was an area that looked like it was for sleeping. It was not very high and had indentations about two feet above the floor which must have been shelves to hold objects for someone lying down. To the left of the entrance was a shallow area which might have been for storage. Faded paintings of strange symbols and images covered the walls throughout the cave. He could only imagine what they meant.

A sudden weariness overcame Stefan.

"Alright, *zine,* I'm going to lie down and rest."

He crawled into the sleep chamber and fell fast asleep. The *zine* dimmed and joined him. Stefan was deep in sleep when he dreamed that he was sitting on the bed looking out at the glowing lake. He was not alone. Sitting by the entrance was a man who stared at him with eyes that were a color he had never seen before – they shimmered like a fabled auroral display. He was wearing a garment which covered one shoulder and flowed kilt-like midway down his muscular thighs. Stefan smiled when he appreciated that the garment was made from the same greyish-white fur of the snow leopard he had skinned. The man's body was trim and athletic like a young warrior. Yet, his face was weathered and lined like an older sage. His forehead was high and what hair he had started well back on his head. A full beard covered his mouth and jaw.

Stefan's attention was drawn to a scepter or shaft which the sage held crooked in his right elbow. Atop the scepter was the living head of a wolf. This was no ordinary wolf; it was connected to the body of a dragon which was curled around the shaft of the scepter. The sharp, yellow fangs of the wolf glistened with saliva and menace. Stefan glanced from the creature to a faded image painted on the wall and recognized it as the embodiment of the Dacian symbol of war.

"Who are you?" whispered Stefan.

"I am Zalmoxis. Who are you?"

"I am Stefan, son of Bogdan of the Musatin family."

Chapter 8

"Stefan, what are you doing here?" asked Zalmoxis. His gaze was at once imperious befitting a monarch, but also warm and comforting like that of a close friend.

"I am merely a traveler seeking his destiny."

"*Da*, it's been a long time. You are finally here. Know this, you are in the right place."

The man rose and faded.

"Wait! What am I supposed to do? What is my destiny?"

A faint voice from far-away said, "Look . . ."

In his sleep, Stefan experienced intense agitation. He wanted to yell, 'Wait! Stop! Help!' but it was too late. The vision had gone. Stefan settled into a restless and shallow sleep.

He awoke hours later, not knowing where he was. When his senses returned, he remembered he was in the cave of Zalmoxis. A panic seized him when he recalled the injuries to his friend. He was so intent on seeing Viorico that he rose quickly and banged his head on the ceiling of the cramped sleeping chamber. Dust fell into his eyes. Rubbing his eyes, Stefan carefully rolled and stood. From his perch above the camp, he saw Isabella kneeling next to Viorico holding a cup of water to his lips.

"How is he?" asked Stefan.

"Better, but still not out of the woods. The swelling has gone down. He gets dizzy when he sits up, so, he must remain immobile for another few days."

"Thank, God."

Stefan busied himself with preparing more wila for the soup. He replayed the dream encounter with Zalmoxis in his head. Why did Zalmoxis disappear so suddenly? Where was he supposed to look? Stefan yanked on the wila to release his frustration. He concluded that he would sleep in the chamber again and maybe Zalmoxis would reappear.

For the next few nights, Stefan returned to the sleep chamber. He tossed and turned all night, unable to sleep. He was fiddling with the signet and staring at the auroch head on the face of the ring. In the dim light coming off the lake, he noticed something he had never seen before. Numbers ... the numerals 317 were engraved there, incorporated into the design. He blinked and refocused. Like with a puzzle, once you've seen the solution, that's all you can see. Until you see it, you are left to wonder: *what did it mean?*

When he returned to the camp, Isabella was waiting for him.

"Stefan, the *zine* have told me that you are tossing and mumbling in your sleep. What's going on? Can I help you?"

"No, I'm fine. I guess I would rather be moving than waiting here."

"You know that Viorico cannot travel yet."

"He looks fine to me," said Stefan. Isabella flinched at his abruptness.

"A few more days..."

"*Da*, a few more days . . . You don't understand. Confinement in this cave is killing me. I hate being locked up. I must see the sky bespeckled with puffy white clouds in the day and sparkling with stars in the dark velvet night."

"Patience is a virtue," said Isabella in voice intended to soothe him.

"Patience, you say? Patience is for women!"

His voice echoed through the cavern. Feeling heat rising in his neck and ears, Stefan lowered his gaze. With a foolish grin, he swallowed deeply, then, as if nothing had transpired, he said, "In the meantime, I'm going to explore these tunnels."

Chapter 8

"Make sure the *zine* are with you. I don't need you getting hurt."

"Of course, chief lady."

"You don't have to be sarcastic," said Isabella to his back.

Before he entered the tunnels, he pantomimed to the *zine* his desire that they divide into three squads – one near his feet, another near his head, and the third behind him. This arrangement prevented painful bashes to his head and helped avoid tripping. It also gave him a sense of perspective to be surrounded by light. If Stefan had been able to understand *Zinese*, he would have understood that the highly social *zine* were angry at being separated from their customary companions. It inhibited their greatest joy, the delicious pastime of gossip. Moreover, they resented being bossed around by an inferior being. Stefan was oblivious to this festering mutiny.

His sense of time left him as he walked through the labyrinth of tunnels which radiated out from the lake. After many hours of exploration, he had little to show for his efforts. He found a handful of arrow and spear heads, flint blades and a few oddly-chiseled pieces of obsidian. Nothing useful. At times his mind wandered to thoughts of home with his family. Sadness engulfed him. His chin quivered from the effort to hold back the flood of tears which he knew would be difficult to stanch. Something sparkling up ahead diverted his attention. Maybe it was something they could use.

When he reached the object, it turned out to be a rock striated with mica. He lashed out with his boot and kicked the rock, only to feel his leg buckle from the impact. Stifling a cry of pain, he limped forward. As the throbbing of his big toe subsided, he muttered to himself, decrying the futility of his search.

Accompanied by the buzzing of the *zine* and his own dark thoughts, Stefan wandered until he saw a narrow opening which appeared to be sculpted by human hands. Stefan bent to examine the edges of opening. He observed scrape marks like those made by the pickaxe used by miners. Stefan fingered the splintered tailings at the base of the opening. They crumbled under finger pressure.

The *zine* buzzed impatiently. They were not used to obeying humans for hours and hours. They were tired and hungry. As Stefan crawled through the entrance, sweat dripped into his eyes. Pointed stones on the ground savaged his hands and knees. The low ceiling was so confining that Stefan imagined it was shrinking and would trap him. The air was dank and dusty. He was unsure whether he should back out or continue forward.

Suddenly, the *zine* lighting his way disappeared. Where did they go? Were they playing a trick on him? Thrust into darkness, he squeezed his eyes shut. He tried to turn around and bumped his shoulder against the ceiling. A gush of rocks, stone, and gravel fell on him. His head and arms were free of the rubble. He was stuck in an awkward position in the tunnel with his shoulders buried.

Stefan coughed as a grimy film covered him attaching to the sweat on his face. He sputtered in disgust at his careless stupidity. When he tried to twist himself around, he failed. He wiggled the foot on one leg and felt no resistance. His other leg was flexed in a vain attempt to crawl. His knee was wedged against the tunnel wall.

His eyes welled up and tears etched streaks in the dust on his cheeks. Placing his head on his forearm, Stefan weighed

Chapter 8

his options. No one knew where he was and that he was immobile. How long would it take for Isabella to figure out that he was missing? What could she do to get him out? Stefan pounded the rubble until the fleshy edge of his hand bled. This only resulted in more loose material falling on his head.

Clopotica sat on Isabella's shoulder as she tended to Viorico's wounds. Since the attack by the Ghost of the Mountains, he had slept almost continuously. Viorico would waken every six hours or so to drink some water or broth. Isabella confided in Clopotica that her initial concern that he had a fractured skull had lessened over time. His periods of wakefulness were increasing and his eyes were more focused. Although he still had not spoken, she could see improvement.

An excited group of *zine* interrupted their discussion.

"What do you mean you quit?" asked Clopotica in *Zinese*. From the agitated conversation, Isabella sensed a problem. Although she could not translate all the words, a cold fear crept into her. The *zine* and Clopotica jabbered on about their gripes and hunger.

Sensing no end to the bickering, Isabella's impatience rose like steam in a boiling tea kettle.

"Where's Stefan!?"

The buzzing and clacking stopped in embarrassed silence.

Clopotica's wings flapped faster than a hummingbird being chased by a redtail hawk. The flashing of the *zine* went from zero to rapid in seconds.

Clopotica advised Isabella that the *zine* had last seen Stefan in one of the caves. After they quit, they raced to the camp to eat. Worry lines formed on Isabella's face as she comprehended what had happened. The *zine* had left Stefan behind figuring that he would find his way back.

"Tell them to take us to him, immediately!"

The *zine* needed no translation. They zoomed in the direction of Zalmoxis' cave with Clopotica and Isabella close behind.

The *zine* led them to the rear of a series of tunnels where there was a scant opening. Isabella peered in and saw what appeared to be a boot.

"Stefan, Stefan, are you alright? Are you injured?" shouted Isabella with her voice edging on panic. How would she explain her failure to guard Stefan? How could she handle two injured companions? When there was no response, her heart sank.

CHAPTER 9

Isabella's eyes were blank as she squatted inside the cave opening. She had led them away from their pursuers and navigated the treacherous mountains until she stumbled upon the fissure emitting life-saving heat. They had found refuge at Lake Zalmoxis. Now, Viorico was recovering from the snow leopard attack and Stefan was buried in a narrow cave. Isabella clenched her fists and pounded her legs groping for an answer.

"Isabella, where is Stefan?"

Startled, she bumped her head on the ceiling of the cave.

"Isabella, where is Stefan?" asked a weak voice, again.

Her eyes widened when she comprehended that Viorico had joined her.

"Viorico, it's you. Thank, God. How? What?"

"Isabella, where is Stefan?"

"He's back in the tunnels, stuck."

"Oh, no! He has a morbid fear of being confined in a small space. We must rescue him."

Viorico shuffled alongside Isabella through the tunnels until he found the *zine* who were hovering outside the collapsed tunnel. He peered in.

"Is that his foot?"

"Yes . . . at least I think it is," said Isabella.

"Have you pulled on it?"

"No, I can't reach it. Maybe you can."

Viorico reached in and winced when his temple grazed the top of the hole.

"Careful."

The young man grunted and stretched until he grasped the heel of the boot.

"I got it," he said, tugging on the boot. "Oww."

"What happened?"

"He kicked me," said Viorico, withdrawing his hand and sucking on his fingers.

Isabella and Viorico heard a muffled voice. It was Stefan. Although the words were indistinguishable, his voice reeked with despair.

Moments later, they heard scaping in the hole and movement of the boot. Gradually, the boot and, more important, the leg appeared. When his first leg released, Stefan's hips shifted, pulling his knee away from the wall. He stretched his other leg toward the opening.

When the second leg appeared, Isabella and Viorico each grabbed a leg and pulled. The trapped man struggled, grunted, and twisted as if he were a crab trying to back out of a trap. As he slid toward his rescuers, loose dirt fell on him. Rico scraped away the rubble giving his friend more room to wriggle. His shirt slid up; his bare skin scraped along the rocky bottom. He cautioned his friends to pull slowly lest the roof collapse on him. After inching his way back, he was sufficiently free of the debris that they succeeded in pulling him out. Sweaty and weepy, the three hugged.

Chapter 9

"I thought I was going to explode. Being stuck in that wretched hole, all I could think of was a coffin," said Stefan, breathing in and out deeply.

Isabella led Stefan to the sleeping niche while Viorico went for water. As Stefan lay covered with dust and rubble, a cloud of *zine* hovered over him in a gesture that was almost caressing. Although he could not speak *Zinese*, Stefan understood that they were apologizing. He smiled a weary smile and closed his eyes.

Isabella removed her jacket and folded it into a pillow for him. Stefan was asleep before Rico returned. It didn't take long before Stefan was snoring, sounding like an approaching thunderstorm. Isabella touched her lips, and brought her fingers to Stefan's lips. She gestured for all to leave the cave and let him sleep.

For Stefan, sleep was a satisfying release from his ordeal. His eyelids fluttered from the rapid movement of his eyes. Stefan envisioned himself in an open field in bright daylight. He breathed deeply imagining the fresh air of a spring day in the meadow near his home. His features relaxed and a slight smile graced his lips. In his dream, he watched Panda frolic in the grass while chasing a pair of butterflies. Suddenly, Panda cocked his head toward a copse of trees. His ears perked, listening.

The first thing Stefan saw was the shaft of a scepter, followed by the sandal, then a figure. He had a noble bearing and easily wielded the scepter bearing the wolf head-dragon body. Stefan greeted Zalmoxis whose face split into a welcoming smile.

"How are you, my son?"

"Zalmoxis, sir, I am sore and baffled."

"Baffled? Why?"

"You told me to 'Look,' but, I don't know where? Help me," mumbled Stefan.

"Simple. Look up!" said Zalmoxis who smiled and waved as he disappeared into the woods.

Several hours later, Stefan awoke. He stretched his arms upward. With a yawn, he touched the ceiling of the niche. A puff of dust floated onto his face. As he blinked away the fine powder, he thought, the ceiling of the bedchamber was not supposed to move. It was solid rock. Or, was it?

Stefan bolted upright and pressed against the ceiling – there was play in the slab above him. He wiggled it and caulking around the edges fell aside. Excited, he stood to gain leverage. Ever-so-slowly, the slab slid open. Stefan placed his hands inside the crack. With a loud grunt, he yanked with all his strength until the slab slid to reveal a hollow area.

He was tempted to climb through the opening, but the maw of darkness convinced him that he needed light. Stefan sprinted out of the dwelling, almost smashing his head on the entrance.

"Isabella, Rico, come quickly! Bring the *zine*!"

His companions looked to him with surprise etched on their faces. *Was Stefan delirious? Why was he screaming? What was wrong?*

"Zalmoxis came to me in a dream. Come look!" said Stefan, rushing toward them with arms waving wildly. Breathless, he reached them and grabbed their hands. He tugged them toward the bed niche. Isabella hopped on one foot as she tried to wriggle into one of her boots.

"Wait, Stefan. Slow down. We're coming."

Stefan was like a man possessed. Rico dug his feet into the emerald sand and slowed Stefan enough for Isabella to get her

Chapter 9

other boot on. By this time, the *zine* were aroused. Clopotica pressed to the front and alighted on Isabella's shoulder.

"Stefan found something. We need light."

Once inside the dwelling, the *zine* flew directly into the opening above the sleeping niche. Stefan hesitated, breathed deeply, then followed, shimmying up into the now-illuminated area.

"Wow, this is amazing!" said Stefan to no one in particular.

Isabella and Rico stood on tiptoes, eager to see what Stefan saw. The sound of his voice echoed and diminished as he crawled further into the recesses of the passage. Isabella whispered a prayer that Stefan be safe from another collapse. Minutes passed before Stefan returned. When his face appeared in the opening, he was beaming. His eyes shone as brilliant as the midsummer sun.

"Here, Rico, take this."

They heard a grating sound as if Stefan was dragging a heavy object along the passage to the opening. The bottom of a terracotta urn appeared in the opening. Stefan slid the urn until it balanced on the edge.

"Got it?"

"*Da*," said Rico, as he grasped the piece and levered it into his arms. Isabella steadied his legs and helped him slide the pottery onto the surface of the bed. Stefan followed, bringing a shower of dust and pebbles onto his friends.

"What do we have here?" said Stefan, chest expanded and sporting a self-satisfied grin. He rapped on the surface and heard a hollow sound. The urn stood about three feet high. A cap with a pyramidal handle sealed the vessel.

"Let me try to pry it open," said Rico.

With his knife, Rico stabbed and twisted at the seal without success. Rico scraped at the seal and wedged the tip of the dagger in as far as he could which wasn't much. Shouting "Hyaahh" as they had been taught in fencing class when delivering a lethal blow, he forced the knife handle downward violently. The tip of the knife snapped off, sending a piece of jagged metal toward Isabella. With a deft step to the side, she dodged it.

"I guess Zalmoxis knew how to make a glue that would last," remarked Rico in a tone of defeat. "You would think that after more than a millennium, the sealant would be dried out."

"Or, he made it secure to keep air out and preserve whatever is inside," offered Isabella.

Stefan lifted the urn and shook it.

"There is definitely something inside. I can feel something shift when I shake it," said Stefan who put the object down on the floor.

Isabella was about to unsheathe her dagger to work on the resinous seal when Stefan exclaimed, "Enough!"

He lifted the urn over his head. With a sound that released all of his frustration, he hurled the urn against the wall. It splintered. Pottery shards and rags littered the chamber.

When the dust settled, the three travelers stared in disbelief at a white linen sack coated with a shiny material that lay before them. Protruding from the top was a leather tube. It was dark brown and preserved as if it had been placed in the urn a day earlier.

Isabella picked it up. Something inside rattled.

"Maybe it contains some of the lost scrolls of Zalmoxis," said Stefan with rising excitement. "Bogdan used to tell me about the myths of the mysterious writings of Zalmoxis. He

Chapter 9

appeared to me for a reason. Let's go to the camp where we can work on this with more room."

Isabella and Viorico followed Clopotica and the *zine* out of the confined space. Stefan was about to leave when he noticed something in the rags. In the retreating light of the *zine*, he saw a flicker of light, a reflection, perhaps. He toed the edge of rags back and gasped. *Was it the hilt of a sword?* Stefan dropped to his knees and fumbled in the rubble. His heart was pounding. Shaking his head in disbelief, a wave of giddiness overcame him.

"Wait!" he said, in a voice that was more of a croak than a shout. The others stopped and stared.

Stefan stood at the cave entrance holding two parts of a majestic sword in his upraised hands.

"It's true! We found the heavenly sword that killed Kogaionon!"

He dropped to his knees and wept for joy. Stefan felt as if he were floating in a globe separated from all the travails which brought them to this moment.

When the elation of the discovery waned, Rico looked at the two pieces of the sword and said, "This is a great find, Stefan, but you do know it is useless. Who can use a broken sword?"

Stefan stared at Rico as if he had shattered the protective globe that Stefan felt shielded him from the pain of recent events. Stefan grabbed both pieces of the sword and pressed them together, hoping that some cosmic magnetic force would unite them. He tried rubbing them on his woolen cloak, he tried wet emerald sand from the shore of the lake. Nothing worked to connect the two pieces.

"You are right. It is useless. I thought for one instant that it was the key to our survival. You are right."

With slumped shoulders and drooping head, Stefan shuffled away leaving the broken sword in pieces on the ground.

Rico started to say, 'I'm sorry' but a glance from Isabella silenced him.

CHAPTER 10

Isabella sighed from a weariness which she felt deep into the marrow of her bones. Watching Stefan's dejection when he realized that a broken sword is useless was a major blow to their morale. She did not know how much more they could take.

"I'm going to harvest some more wila so that we can replenish our soup," said Viorico. Even though he seemed better, Isabella noticed that he wobbled every so often when climbing. She hoped that his balance would return before the group embarked from here. An unspoken reality which they avoided discussing was the need to leave.

Stefan sat on a rock on the shore with the pieces of the sword at his feet. Placed end-to-end, the sword measured almost three feet long. Beveled grooves, or blood gutters, ran the length of the pointed double-edged blade. Stefan leaned forward and grasped the hilt. His hands fit comfortably between the pommel and the cross-guard.

He stood and waved it as if he was battling a fire-breathing dragon. His heart pumped with the energy which accompanies wielding an exquisite weapon. Stefan rotated the sword and brought the pommel to eye level. The rod of the handle joined the circular pommel at the end of the sword. The large, round pommel was designed to keep hands from slipping off during battle. His eyes widened as he peered into the hole in the center of the pommel ring. He imagined the jewel which must have filled this space. In his mind's eye he saw a faceted jewel which glowed with an otherworldly luminescence. It was unlike any gemstone that he had ever seen. When the sword was in motion, the jewel would flash all the colors of the rainbow thought Stefan. He beamed with excitement at the uses he would make of this weapon – that is, if they could discover how to fix the blade and replace the pommel gemstone.

Isabella thrummed her fingers on her thighs as she decided what to do. She spied the leather tube which was angled against her backpack. Isabella reached for it and placed it on her legs as she sat cross-legged. The tube was constructed of sturdy hide which she assumed came from an auroch. The cap was hinged to the top of the tube and secured by a slim strap. The craftsman who made this container had used a heated metal tool to burn intricate designs along its length. Although the designs had faded over time, Isabella thought that she recognized the word 'Zalmoxis.' The remainder of the surface bore curlicues, runes, and hieroglyphs revealing no pattern which could be considered language.

Taking her dagger Isabella placed the blade under the strap and slit it. The leather band separated in a puff of dust. Her eyebrows arched at the ease of this procedure. She twisted the cap in the hope that she would be able to unfasten by aligning the notches she felt so that they fell into place like the tumblers of a lock. No matter how much she jiggered and twisted it, the cap refused to open.

Chapter 10

"Stefan, I need your help," she said raising the tube and beckoning him.

Slouching slightly, he took his time walking to her. She sighed, thinking that maybe there was still a residue of the sullen teenager in him.

"Here," she said, handing him the tube. "We need to remove the cap."

Stefan held the tube to his chest and tried to wrench the cap loose. He took a deep breath and tugged at the top until his face reddened. His features contorted into a mask resembling a gargoyle. With an exasperated howl which would have made a wolf proud, he released the tube. His face bore a look of frustrated disgust.

"What now?" asked Isabella.

Stefan shrugged.

"I wish I had the blacksmith tools from our barn back home."

All of a sudden, he jumped up and carried the tube to the fire.

"Maybe we can melt the sealant."

Stefan dangled the end of the tube over the fire. Isabella reached over and raised the tube above the flames.

"We don't want the tube to catch fire," she said in a gentle voice.

With the seam directly above the hottest part of the fire, they saw a dark, gooey substance trickle into the fire. It sizzled sending a pungent wisp of smoke upward. Stefan coughed and his eyes watered. The tube smoldered and was on the verge of igniting when he pulled it away.

"That was close to a disaster," Isabella said.

Stefan nodded. He would never forgive himself if the tube and its contents had caught fire. Stefan rotated the tube with care until the entire seam had melted.

Rico carried an armful of wila to the camp. When he surmised what they were doing he watched with a curious look on his face. Stefan grasped the cap and yelped in pain. Shaking his hand, he passed the tube to Isabella. She blew on the end until it stopped smoking. With the triumphant look of a magician awing the crowd with a brilliant trick, Isabella yanked the cap from the tube. Rico and Stefan cheered in mock admiration.

Cupping the opening, Isabella upended the tube. Several scrolls made of vellum slid into her hands. Viorico gathered stones to hold the corners and they knelt around the scroll.

"Legend has it that before Zalmoxis came to Dacia, he was a slave in Greece. With some luck, maybe these scrolls are written in Greek," said Isabella.

She unrolled the largest first, treating it as a gossamer butterfly wing. The document gave off a stale, musty smell. Aside some singeing on one edge, the document was intact.

Often, expectations lead to misperception. Isabella's eyes brightened as she focused on the characters on the vellum. She shook her head in disbelief. Dejection settled in her eyes. She sagged backwards onto her haunches.

"It's not Greek," she said in a low voice. Isabella set her jaw and studied the document. "It's either lambskin or goatskin covered with ancient writing, probably Dacian."

Clopotica and the *zine* joined them, buzzing in an animated fashion.

"What's it say?" asked Viorico.

"It's not that simple," said Isabella. "This language has been extinct for centuries."

Chapter 10

"Maybe we can figure out what it says by analyzing the symbols as pictures?" said Stefan.

"Let's hope so. Many ancient languages were based on picture symbols used as what we know as words," said Isabella as her eyes scanned the scroll for clues.

The three of them stared at the scroll for a long time. When Rico's stomach growled, he suggested, "Maybe it's time we take a break. My gut is cancelling my brain."

Isabella glared at him.

"Do you have any idea how long this mystery has been hidden? No food until we figure this out," she snapped.

"We're getting nowhere with this one, let's examine the other scroll," said Stefan.

"Good idea," said Rico who shifted over to unroll the second scroll.

"Careful," said Isabella. "It's fragile."

The three of them moved to the smaller scroll. Stefan whistled a happy note.

"It's a map!" said Rico.

"Let's see if we can decipher it," replied Isabella with an undertone of caution.

"See these squiggly lines? Don't they look like mountains?" asked Stefan.

"*Da,* and the puffy figures above them look like clouds," said Rico.

"Hhmmm," said Isabella. "There's a notation near that. It looks like Greek . . . . The Way of the Sky over the Alpine Sea. I wonder what that means?"

"Look," said Stefan. "These are spikes rising from the ground."

"Are they some kind of rock formation?" asked Rico.

"*Da,* they look familiar, don't they?"

"Hold on, there are words under it," said Isabella.

"What's it say?" asked Viorico, impatiently.

"Hold on, hold, . . . the teeth, no, the Fangs of Giga," offered Isabella. "I wonder what that means?"

"I remember on one of my trips with my father hearing a story about a dark spirit which lives between two rocky peaks who prevents anyone from passing. Maybe that's it," said Stefan.

"Could be," added Rico, barely able to contain his rising excitement.

While they were studying the map, Isabella lifted her head and rubbed her neck to relieve the tightness from bending over the scrolls for so long. Twisting her neck from side-to-side, she noticed a glowing swarm over the larger scroll. Clopotica lifted above the swarm and blinked rapidly to her before re-entering the swarm. Isabella knotted her eyebrows and shrugged her shoulders. Before she could interpret Clopotica's movement, Isabella felt Stefan tug her sleeve.

"Check this," he said, pointing to a figure on the map.

"That's a pyramid," said Viorico. "What's it say?"

"It says Shepherd's Shadow," said Isabella.

"Huh?" uttered Rico and Stefan together.

All three laughed.

"Can we eat now?"

Isabella chuckled, "*Da*, we've earned it."

As Rico stirred the soup, Stefan noticed how Rico's clothes were hanging off him like a wet cloak on a door hook. His movements were so slow and deliberate that he appeared to be swimming through molasses. Most disturbing was the dullness which was replacing the brightness of his eyes.

Chapter 10

Stefan examined his own sagging garments and could only imagine how much he had deteriorated. His index finger traced the outlines of his ribcage. The usual cushion was lacking. A profound sadness seeped into Stefan's core.

Oddly, Isabella retained her vitality. Given his ignorance of the gentler sex, Stefan concluded that it was because women are different.

While they supped, Rico advised them that the supply of wila was almost all gone. They knew that their stay by Lake Zalmoxis would have to end soon. But how?

Each plunged into their own private thoughts.

Stefan longed for the feel of the bright sun on his face and the brisk autumn wind flowing through his hair as he galloped on his steed through the forest. He missed the flavorful aromas of pies baking in the kitchen. He craved the sharp crunch of a carrot or a freshly picked cucumber. As much as he had grown to love Rico and Isabella, he missed the hustle and bustle of the communal market, the camaraderie of his mates and the warmth of the hearth with his family gathered around while his father told stories of their ancestors.

Helplessness encircled his heart with the inexorability of vines reclaiming an untended orchard. Each thought of long-gone pleasures was another tendril entwining and strangling him. Soon, there would be nothing but vines. He struggled to breathe.

"What good is a map if we don't know where the starting point is, and what's at the end? Pwaa, we're wasting our time. We're stuck here until . . . ."

Stefan flipped his bowl onto the ground in disgust.

Later, after he had recovered his composure, Stefan noticed that Isabella and Viorico were with Clopotica who hovered over the larger scroll. Timidly, he joined them.

The *zina* buzzed rapidly. She flitted up and down, left to right, then bottom to top and right to left.

"Nothing," said Isabella. Stefan and Rico sank back, their arms like props supporting them. Another hope dashed.

Rico took a flat stone and twirled it on the tip of his index finger. With a vacant stare, Isabella watched him. Each time the stone turned, it caught the light of the fire and a reflection crossed Isabella's face. She seemed entranced by the flashing light. Bored with his twirling, Rico threw the stone into the lake.

"That's it," shrieked Isabella who grabbed Clopotica and whispered into her ear.

The *zina* bolted to the center of the scroll and flew concentric circles over the scroll. She flew so fast that the scroll appeared to be on fire. In the force of her wake, the stones shifted from the edges and the scroll began to spin. Stefan's jaw dropped at the sight.

When Clopotica finally stopped, she staggered like a *clurichaun,* her Irish fairy kin, known for their legendary binge drinking. Then, she collapsed onto the scroll.

Isabella held her ear over the fallen *zina*. She heard nothing. With a look of horror, Isabella rasped, "She's not breathing."

A talc-white cloud of *zine* rushed to Clopotica. They buzzed and pulsed in evident concern. Time seemed to stop. Stefan read the anguish on Isabella's face and he fell to his knees. Viorico's mouth formed a question that never came as the light from the *zine* flickered, growing dimmer.

"Can't you do something?" Stefan whispered to Isabella.

"I don't know. Fairies are not like humans."

"We have to do something. We can't let her lie there," said Stefan.

Chapter 10

Rico bent over and lifted Clopotica in his hands and held her to his chest. He remained as motionless as a cliff, except for his lips which quivered imperceptibly. His companions heard a low hum. The *zine* stopped flitting and the usual buzzing noise also stopped. Rico's eyes were closed in concentration. Stefan reached for Isabella's hand.

She entwined her fingers in his.

Rico's humming stopped. He felt movement by his heart and he opened his eyes to see Clopotica smiling up at him.

"What . . . what did you do?" stuttered Stefan. Isabella rushed to Clopotica mouthing, "How are you?"

"She says that the flying in circles made her so dizzy that she lost control and shut down. Viorico's humming restored her equilibrium and now she's fine."

Clopotica flew to him and, in an uncharacteristic display of gratitude, pecked him on the cheek. He blushed.

"How did you know what to do?" asked Stefan.

"I learned that charm from the fairies of the steppes. I wasn't sure if it would work on a mountain fairy, but I'm glad it did."

At the sight of their beloved Clopotica, the *zine* rushed to her, glowing and clacking as if it were the summer solstice. After a lengthy celebration, Clopotica separated from the swarm and went to Isabella.

"Clopotica says that she has unlocked the secrets of the scrolls."

Over the next hour, Clopotica explained that they were indeed from antiquity as they had surmised. The larger scroll was written by several prophets, the last being the successor to Zalmoxis. However, it was not a document; rather it was some sort of recording. What looked like symbols were really minute indentations in the surface that reverberated with a narrative when she flew over it in an ever-widening spiral.

In the beginning, earth was occupied by men who lived harsh lives. The biggest danger they faced were giants called Uriasi who hunted men and ate them. There came a time when the sun disappeared and thunder and lightning filled the sky. It was as if a heavenly battle was raging. One man ventured out from his cave. While he was drinking from a stream, fiery meteors crossed the sky. The man hid underwater when Uriasi came to the stream. One of the Uriasi saw him and summoned others.

The man was doomed, but then he spied something gleaming in the water. He grasped it – it was a sword. He wielded the sword with such savagery that he slew all the Uriasi but the leader. His name was Kogaionon and he was the biggest, cruelest, nastiest giant. After a ferocious battle, the man chopped off Kogaionon's head. The final blow was so powerful that it severed the monster's spinal cord and shattered from the impact with Kogaionon's club.

The man watched in awe as a ray of light came down from the heavens and turned the dead Uriasi into mountains. As the beam reached the spot where the man had slain Kogaionon, he shoved the pieces of the heavenly sword into the skull of Kogaionon where it stayed for many centuries.

"That's the story of Aparator. Every child knows this story. We're right back where we started," said Stefan who threw up his hands in a disconsolate gesture.

"Patience."

"Patience is for women," said Stefan.

The way Isabella raised her eyebrows in admonishment reminded him of how his mother chided his father when he was too stubborn to listen. Isabella touched Stefan's hand gently. It was as if she infused a calmness in him. Tenseness left his shoulders and the muscles on his face loosened from annoyance into an attentive expression.

"Patience," said Isabella. "There's more."

More than a millennium ago, a wise man sought refuge from the excesses of his society. He went to the mountain which the Dacians believed was as sacred as Mount Olympus was to the Greeks. He found solace in a cave. His name was Zalmoxis, and he learned that his cave was none other than the skull of Kogaionon.

While purifying himself on a diet of mushrooms and honey, he found an auxiliary tunnel not far from the lake. Deep inside this tunnel, he discovered an area where the cave opened into a chamber where sound and light bounced off the stone walls in a sublime way.

This was where he found shapes, lines, and zigzags inscribed on the walls. At first, he dismissed these figures as primitive paintings without meaning. Something drew him back to this area again and again. Over time, he discerned a pattern to these markings and understood that they represented a code. What he learned when he deciphered it led him to find an ancient artifact.

"Aparator," said Stefan.

"Correct."

After Zalmoxis found the sword, a celestial being visited him in a dream. The being told him that during the battle in which Michael the Archangel drove Lucifer from heaven, the sword fell to earth. Zalmoxis asked whether the sword could be repaired. The being said that only Faur, the cosmic blacksmith, could fix it.

"Isn't Faur just a bedtime story?" said Stefan. "My father always told me that if I did not behave, I would be sent to Faur."

"My people told a similar tale of the powerful blacksmith who had a magical forge."

"That's right, the Forges of Ezrok," said Isabella in a cheerful voice.

"How do we get to the Forges of Ezrok?" asked Stefan.

"The map?" asked Rico.

"Maybe, but, we don't even know where the starting point is, or, whether it leads to the Forges of Ezrok. All we have is the pyramid called Shepherd's Shadow, whatever that means?" said Stefan. He ran his hands through his unkempt hair.

"The answer is here somewhere. We have to figure it out," answered Isabella in a placid tone which irritated him.

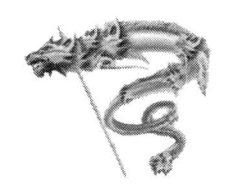

CHAPTER 11

In a manner which reminded Viorico of a mother goose nudging her goslings into the water, Isabella shepherded her charges into Lake Zalmoxis.

"Listen, with all the bumps you two have taken, you need to soak. It'll do you good."

"But," protested Rico. "I'm too busy. I have things to do."

A cynical stare from Isabella quelled that line of avoidance.

Stefan was reclining against his pack, feigning sleep. Isabella nudged his foot to get him moving.

"Come on, Stefan, you can't fool me. Get into the lake. You need to heal up before our journey."

Without opening his eyes, Stefan considered what Isabella had said. He had to admit that the warm waters of the lake did help heal injuries and soothe aches. He recalled with fondness trips with his father to the healing mineral springs along the Slanic River in the Nemira Mountains. Bogdan would sigh and smile as he slipped into the hot water.

"Thermal baths are God's reward for diligent service. We must not disappoint our Lord by failing to indulge in this divine gift," he would say.

Although Stefan knew Isabella was right about the healing properties of the water, his teenage mind resisted admitting it.

"If the lake is so great, Isabella, why don't you jump in?"

Isabella was too smart to engage in that debate.

"You're right. I'm going for a swim whether you join us or not," she said as she stripped off her outer garments and dove into the soothing water.

"Ahh, that is just what the healer ordered," cooed Isabella.

Recognizing that he had been out-maneuvered, Stefan followed suit.

He immersed himself in the waters of Lake Zalmoxis and tried to clear his mind; but that was not possible. The preceding days had been too eventful. They had found Aparator which he would use to vanquish Petru Aron and bring glory to God and his country. Of equal importance, they had decoded the scrolls of Zalmoxis which explained the ancient myths in a dynamic way.

The revelations of the scrolls of Zalmoxis resonated deeply within Stefan's soul. He felt like a layer of gauze which blurred his vision had been lifted. For once in his life, he recognized his destiny. With youthful optimism, he vowed to destroy any obstacle that might impede him. An older, more mature Stefan might have appreciated that there is never a straight path to one's destiny and that there were always perils in the way.

When their fingertips started resembling the grooved wrinkles on prunes, they left the healing waters. The waters worked their magic and the three companions left the lake reinvigorated. It was not the relaxing sort of reinvigoration which follows a restful sleep. Rather, it renewed their resolve to crack the puzzle. Unspoken was the fear that failure to find the answer would result in slow death by starvation in this sunless cavern.

Chapter 11

Stefan, Isabella, and Viorico, sat cross-legged around the campfire. Seeing the conference, Clopotica joined them.

"Let's review our information. We must be missing something," said Isabella. "We have the large scroll which Clopotica interpreted for us. That provides the history and significance of the artifacts. Stefan?"

Stefan who was toying with the hilt of the sword, looked up.

"We have two pieces of the sword man used to destroy the oppressor giants. We know that only Faur can repair it. We have a map to the Forges of Ezrok but we don't know the starting point and what the notations mean. That leaves us with no idea how to find Faur, or if he even exists."

"Viorico, are you listening?"

He was holding the leather tube in front of him. It reminded him of the instruments used by the shepherds of the steppes on moonless nights to stave off loneliness. He blew across the open top. A deep, mournful sound emanated from the cylinder. Rico tapped a percussive rhythm on the tube.

The sound was hypnotic. The three were as if transported to another time, a time when giants ruled and men huddled in fear inside caves. Shivers ran down their spines as they heard the hunting call of the Uriasi. Thrashing in the nearby forest signaled that the hunters were close. Primal fear gripped them.

Seeing his companions cowering, Stefan knew he had to act. He seized the instrument from Rico and shouted, "Halt!"

It was as if the sun broke through the clouds and sunlight shone on their faces. Stefan thought that Isabella had an angelic glow, like she had when he first saw her face outside the amphitheater. The light had a different effect on Rico. Due to the abundance of hair on his head and beard, the otherworldly light was absorbed. Rico appeared simian, hunched over.

At that moment, Stefan heard an animated buzzing. It was the *zine*, flitting from one companion to the next out of concern that their human friends seemed locked in place.

The spell broke.

Stefan blinked, as did the others.

"What was that?"

"What?" said Rico, dazed.

Still holding the tube, Stefan stared at it. His focus shifted to the markings on the tube. Maybe these inscriptions were the answer to the enigma.

"Isabella, we need Clopotica here. Now!"

Isabella translated for Stefan who explained that he wanted her to read the symbols which decorated the tube. To avoid a repeat of her dizziness, he rotated it slowly as the fairy hovered before it.

When Clopotica finished, she alighted on Isabella's shoulder and clacked and clucked intensely. Isabella nodded and smiled while Stefan and Viorico leaned forward, barely breathing. When the *Zinese* conversation stopped, Isabella closed her eyes to order her thoughts. She turned to her companions. For the first time since the beginning of their ordeal, her eyes beamed with hope. The lines around her mouth formed a smile.

"Gentlemen, Clopotica told me that the markings are runes and hieroglyphs of ancient origin. Her translation is detailed and wondrous. Here's what she found on the cylinder:

This attestation is addressed to the uncrowned prince who will bring glory to God and humanity as the defender of the people against evil malefactors.

ATTESTATION of ZALMOXIS of SARMIZEGETUSA

Chapter 11

I, ZALMOXIS, doth attest on my honor that the contents of this sealed cylinder are true and authentic. It contains four objects: a scroll, the hilt and blade sections of the heavenly sword, and a map.

The scroll chronicles the history of events relating to the sword and man.

The hilt and the blade are the genuine sections of the sword used by man to slay the race of giants, thus saving humanity.

The map depicts the route to the FORGES of EZROK where FAUR maintains his foundry. The journey to the FORGES of EZROK commences at KOGAIONON. It proceeds across the ALPINE SEA, down through the FANGS of GIGA and continues to the SHEPHERD'S SHADOW. The entrance is designated by the pyramid which appears on the day of the winter solstice.

UPON PRESENTATION of this cylinder and the broken sword to FAUR, the cosmic blacksmith, he shall forthwith restore the sword to its original condition with full functionality.

Signed and dated, Zalmoxis of Sarmizegetusa

"Wahoo!"

"Excellent!"

"When do we leave?"

"Wait, there is more," said Isabella.

WHOMEVER FINDS THIS BUNDLE SHALL TRIGGER THE PROPHECY

After purification in the crucible,
the dragon-stones crest the defender.
In the wilderness, the cub razes the enemy and
banishes the usurper at the neck of hell,

liberating the land of the war dog.

The three travelers exchanged quizzical glances. Viorico scratched his head as if he were calculating one of Tramo's tactical problems, like if one soldier eats one pound of grain per day, how many wagons of grain does it take to feed a cohort for a month-long campaign? Isabella adopted a faraway look as she mouthed the words to herself. Stefan watched her pause at certain words, trying to decipher the prophecy by building on certain known words. The look of frustration which clouded her face told him that she was not making much progress.

Stefan sat with his chin resting on his fist. Although they were trying to interpret an ancient language, they had clearly recognized several words. Something about one of the words in the attestation nagged at his mind. It was at the edge of his conscious thought. It was important. What was it?

He broke the silence.

"What day is it?"

"Who cares?" said Rico, his eyebrows scrunched together in concentration.

"I do. Everything depends on it."

"Huh?"

"Solstice!" blurted Stefan. "That's it. Based on the message from Zalmoxis, we have to be at the pyramid by the winter solstice. If we are not there in time, we won't find the entrance to the Forges of Ezrok."

"Stefan's right. If we are late, we will have to wait another twelve months," said Isabella.

"By my calculation, we have less than three weeks to get there," said Stefan.

"We'd better get moving."

Chapter 11

They shouldered their packs and bundled up for the cold. Stefan rigged a strap to the leather tube and slung it across his back. Trying to burn the image of the spectacular glowing lake into his memory, he stared at Lake Zalmoxis. He would never forget the lake which had healed, sustained, and saved them; but it was time to seek his destiny.

The pure white swarm of *zine* led them through the caverns back to the mountain ledge. During the hike, Stefan kept repeating the prophecy in his head to unravel it's meaning. Whenever he was on the verge of understanding one of the phrases, the thought dissipated like a swamp gas bubble puncturing. There was nothing concrete to grasp.

When they arrived at the fissure, a tearful Clopotica advised that it was time for the *zine* to return home. Although the travelers knew that this parting was inevitable, it came as a surprise. None of them anticipated how difficult it would be to say goodbye to the *zine*. 'No, not yet' their eyes pleaded. In the end, after all manner of goodbyes had been expressed, they stood, the humans on one side and the glowing swarm facing them, with nothing more to say. In her fairy way, Clopotica rallied her coterie to her and the cloud of *zine* flew away.

"Clopotica told me that we will find the Alpine Sea at the summit. My goal is to get to the top during daylight."

It did not take long for the bitter cold to embrace them in its clutches. Viorico followed Isabella and the chattering of his teeth helped to guide Stefan who brought up the rear. He followed Rico's footsteps in robotic fashion. Around midday they took their first break in a sheltered nook.

As they huddled together Isabella gave each a piece of paximadion. Stefan savored the bitter sweetness as it dissolved in his mouth. A slight smile formed under his scarf as Stefan watched Rico swallow his in a quick gulp. His friend disliked the strong flavor of Isabella's concoction.

The summit loomed over them. To Rico it seemed to be as far away as when they started. Stefan looked at Isabella and saw only her eyes. They were red from bearing the brunt of the wind-driven ice and snow whipping off the surface of the path. He offered to take the lead, but she refused, pulling her scarf high to protect her face.

Before they set off again, she tied a rope from her waist to Viorico, and then Stefan's waist. No words were needed.

They trudged on for hours. Each was silent, figuring out how to distract themselves from the bone-chilling cold. The elements numbed their fingers and toes and chapped their faces and lips. Most serious, their cores were losing heat. At last Isabella found a narrow crevice out of the wind. As they huddled together Isabella spoke.

"We are near the summit. We have to climb this rockface ahead. It is steep, so we will have to go hand over hand. Go slow and make sure of your footing before you step."

She broke a paximadion in half and offered a triangular-shaped piece to each.

"Last one," she said, a look of resignation.

Viorico refused. He sat there holding his head. Stefan and Isabella exchanged a glance. Their eyes conveyed concern over their companion, and whether the bump on his head from the snow leopard was bothering him. There was not much they could do about it now, except to watch him. Stefan sucked on the lozenge and Isabella did the same.

Before they returned to their climb, she lengthened the rope between them, giving more play in the event one of them lost their footing. Their eyes were beacons of grim determination. To steel himself for the ordeal, Stefan told

Chapter 11

himself that there was a spa at the top complete with hot springs. Though his head was throbbing, Rico imagined that he was a mountain goat which would handle the cliff like it had evolved to do. He wondered whether mountain goats got headaches, especially when the alpha males butted heads during mating season. Isabella crossed herself and forged ahead.

They were about ten yards from the top when it happened.

The light was behind them as they made their final push for the summit. What little warmth that the sun had provided disappeared. Whether it was the diminishing light or packing of the snow on the footholds, it was solid ice when Stefan shifted his weight onto his left leg. His foot slipped and he fell. After about five feet, the rope around his waist caught. Rico heard Stefan fall before he felt the sharp tug. He braced himself as best he could. He used all of his strength to break the momentum of Stefan's fall.

When Stefan fell, he swung out and banged into the rockface hard. After that, he jerked awkwardly, sagging helplessly like a broken marionette. He came to an abrupt stop as Rico grunted, holding the rope with both hands.

As Stefan swayed, the leather cylinder slipped free from his shoulder and fell. He caught it with the toe of his boot. As it dangled over the abyss below them, a million thoughts raced through his mind. He refused to believe that his destiny would be so cruelly taken from him.

CHAPTER 12

At the sight of the lifeline dangling over the precipice with Viorico straining to save Stefan, Isabella reversed her climb and found an indentation to brace herself on and help Viorico. His face was a mask of desperate urgency.

"Did he bang his head when he fell? Is he still conscious?" yelled Isabella, over the whistling wind.

"I don't know. He feels like dead weight . . . ," said Viorico, regretting his poor choice of words.

"We must pull in unison if we hope to get him up here."

"Pull . . . pull . . . pull," he shouted. Large frosty clouds billowed from their mouths, obscuring their vision. All they could see was the rope trailing into the bottomless gray beneath them. Their yells for Stefan to keep heart went unanswered. Each tug brought Stefan closer to safety. As their strength waned, the pulls became intermittent. Isabella and Viorico exchanged glances. A flicker of doubt passed between them.

At the end of the rope, Stefan struggled to recover his senses after a forceful collision with the mountain face. After a few shakes of the head, a calmness infused him. One thing at a time, he told himself. He disregarded the shouts of his

Chapter 12

companions and focused only on the cylinder. Crooking his ankle, Stefan willed the strap to slide across the top of his foot and come to rest. Good, now the leg. Careful to keep his ankle bent, Stefan lifted his leg toward his waist. As he did so he released his left hand and grabbed the strap. In one swift motion, he flipped the strap over his head and brought his hand back to his lifeline. He exhaled a frosty cloud of air.

Although Rico was not that far from him, his voice sounded like it was coming from the other side of the mountain. Stefan squeezed his eyes shut to concentrate. He felt an updraft bringing with it a swirl of granular ice particles which surrounded them like a mist off a lake when the weather changes. The ice was sharp and biting and stung his exposed skin. Through the hazy cloud, he saw someone coming his way. He blinked rapidly.

It was Zalmoxis holding his wolf-dragon scepter aloft walking toward him. With a voice as soothing as a lullaby, the prophet told him not to be afraid, that he needed to step out in faith. Stefan squinted so that he could barely see out. What he saw made him inhale sharply and squeeze his eyelids so tight that bright points of light appeared. He released the tension on his eyelids and looked into the eyes of the wolf-dragon.

The annals of Dacia were replete with images of the wolf-dragon. When the Dacian army fought the Romans, its battle flag was a wolf's head mounted on a dragon's body.

The wolf-dragon in front of Stefan was not some fabric war banner. It was an actual wolf-dragon. As Stefan dangled, the wolf-dragon alighted from the scepter and positioned the ridges on his back next to him.

"This is Zeuta-Draco, my wolf-dragon. Use his back like a staircase to reach your friends," said Zalmoxis.

Sliding his foot forward, Stefan took a tentative step and felt an unexpected sensation. Zeuta's back was spongy. Stefan's feet adhered to Zeuta in a most reassuring way. Stefan climbed these unusual stairs until he reached the perch where Viorico and Isabella wrestled him to safety.

Zeuta-Draco remounted the scepter of Zalmoxis. As the pair faded into space, the sage whispered to Stefan, "Remember Zeuta for wolves and Draco for dragons."

Stefan nodded as if he understood. The moment his saviors disappeared his presumed understanding evaporated like a vapor in the wind.

"Thank goodness you are safe. It's a miracle that you were able to climb back up," said Isabella as she embraced Stefan like a miser clutching her last coin.

"Lucky, I guess."

Viorico shot him a look of unbelief. Although he had no idea how Stefan had managed to elevate himself to them, he doubted it was luck. Stefan shrugged.

"We are close to the summit. I think there is a place not far ahead for us to rest for the night," said Viorico, pointing to a shadow above their position.

When they arrived at the ledge, they engaged in a communal hug. They stayed as if glued together until the winter sun disappeared. From the snow on the ledge, the weary travelers scooped out enough space to lie down. They huddled like spoons tucked together by size in a silverware chest – Isabella, Stefan, then Viorico.

By morning, a blanket of snow covered them with the beneficial effect of retaining their warmth. Isabella woke first and took inventory. She reminded herself to keep an eye on Viorico to see if there were any lingering effects from the blow to his head. She was encouraged by the return of brightness to

Chapter 12

his eyes. They weren't as bright as when she first met him, but the cold mountain air worked as a tonic which she hoped would continue.

Her concern for Stefan was greater. She rolled over and faced him. With her hands on his back, she probed for sore spots. Stefan winced and opened his eyes. Surprised to see her face, he hugged her close. They lay like this for several minutes until the spell was broken by a stretching, groaning Viorico. Fearful that he might roll off the cliff, she rose and reached for him.

"You have to see this," she said to her companions. They followed her gaze to see a splendid panorama. The sun shone on a billowy, white covering which stretched to the horizon like a carpet of luscious marshmallow.

"There's the Alpine Sea," said Viorico.

"It's there, as Clopotica told us it would be."

"But how do we cross it?" asked Viorico with a note of deflation.

"Let me see the map," asked Stefan.

Unrolling the scroll, Stefan tapped his finger on a notation and said, "That's it. That's the key. We have to find the Way of the Sky."

"I wish that we were celestial beings who could skip lightly across the surface," said Viorico.

"One thing is certain, we are not beings like Jesus who walked on water," remarked Stefan.

Isabella knelt and whisked her hand through the fluffy cloud. As wisps of moisture followed her fingers, Stefan thought of the gypsy dance performed by Ruxandra before she disappeared into the smoke. He was convinced that there had to be a solution. Stefan pursed his lips and tried to force his brain to disgorge something, something that he saw in the caves, something in the wall writings.

When a gust of wind caused him to reach for his pack, his hand produced a puff of snow which dissipated into nothingness. This triggered Stefan's memory. He recalled a saying scrawled in faded ochre paint, 'The Way of the Sky is covered . . . no, paved with sand.' What did that mean?

"Stefan, are you alright? You look pained," said Isabella.

"I'm fine," he stammered. "I've remembered one of the wall writings in the caves."

"What?"

"The Way of the Sky is paved with sand."

"I can see why you are holding your head. It seems like gibberish," she quipped.

Viorico sat, his eyes narrow in concentration. His eyes brightened as though he had received a revelation. He snapped his fingers.

"That's it. That's got to be it."

He opened his pack and removed a pouch. He walked to the edge and sprinkled a green powder on the cloud. Stefan recognized the powder as the emerald sand from the shore of Lake Zalmoxis.

The emerald sand remained on the surface, bubbling until two dark bands materialized on either side of a strong and strange light. Rico thought that a rainbow was the closest phenomenon he could use to describe the strong central band of light bordered by dark bands of light.

Viorico placed his spare water sack on the patch. It steadied as if he had set it on a groaning board. The companions smiled with joy and relief, until Stefan said, "That's not strong enough to hold our weight."

Chapter 12

He placed his toe on the sand patch. It resisted for a bit, then, disintegrated into the cloud. A sense of defeat surrounded them like an evil miasma.

Isabella reached into her backpack and removed her dagger. Stefan gasped, thinking that she intended to end her misery.

"Not to worry," she said, lifting her face to reveal a smile. She removed the pelt of the snow leopard and started to slice it.

"What?" asked Rico and Stefan at the same time.

Isabella said, "I remembered thinking when you were skinning the snow leopard, Stefan, that the creature had huge paws."

"So?"

"The paws are wide to spread the weight so that it can run fast on top of the snow."

"Like snow shoes," said Viorico.

"Brilliant," said Stefan. Then, half to himself, he muttered, "I hope it works."

When she finished cutting, she had six pieces. They each tied them to their boots.

"Wait, where are we going to get enough emerald sand to cross this expanse?" asked Stefan.

"Not a problem," replied Viorico.

Stefan and Isabella looked at him incredulously.

"Check your packs. You each have a pouch of emerald sand."

"What? How?" It was Stefan and Isabella's turn to speak at the same time.

Rico chuckled.

"Before we left, I thought that we might need something we could use as money in case we had to pay for anything on our journey. I figured that we might be able to use emerald dust to purchase a meal. I never dreamed that it would help us cross the Alpine Sea."

The three companions shared the uneasy laugh of explorers with nothing left to lose.

The sun was high in the sky when they embarked from the summit. Isabella checked the map against her compass to make sure they were on the right heading. They were quite a sight, bundled up to their noses and wearing ragged, leopard skin swatches on their feet. When Stefan dubbed them sky-shoes, Rico signaled thumbs up.

Isabella went first, taking tiny tentative steps. Holding to a lifeline in case the path did not hold. Then, something most remarkable occurred. With each handful of dust she threw in front of her, a crystalline web radiated from the strange central light until it formed a path edged by the parallel dark bands. It was almost as if the emerald sand had the magical power to form a path.

She thought of the Apostle Peter stepping over the gunnel onto the water to walk to Jesus. As she walked, she repeated mantra-like, "Do not lose faith. This is our destiny."

Viorico and Stefan followed her, initially walking like they were on egg shells. As they gained confidence, they quickened their pace so that they did not fall too far behind Isabella. For the first time in weeks, they were free. Unlimited openness and the purest air they had ever experienced surrounded them. It felt as if they shed the film of cave gloom which had covered them for weeks in the same way a snake molts its extra skin.

Overcome by bonhomie, they picked up Isabella's refrain.

"Do not lose faith. This is our destiny."

By the time they reached the halfway point, they were singing full-throated in three-part harmony.

Chapter 12

The view matched their elation. They were in a world of billowy, pure white vapors. Instead of the biting cold of the mountain, the temperature during the trip across the clouds was comfortable, owing to the insulating nature of the clouds which trapped the sun's warmth and enfolded the cloud walkers. Rico tapped Stefan on the shoulder and pointed toward the west. He saw a cluster of dark gray clouds which were illuminated with flashes of brilliant light, no doubt a thunderstorm.

Later, Stefan scanned toward the east. He saw a mountain peak which looked alien in the white cloudscape. Suddenly, two large birds flew into view. Their plumage was dark brown turning to golden around their necks.

"Those are golden eagles. They mate for life," said Rico who had followed his gaze. "They are fierce predators. My uncle calls them flying killing machines. They hunt in pairs – one stalks the prey and drives it to the other who takes it down."

"I'm sorry to interrupt your lesson, Rico, but I think we have their attention. Here they come."

"Don't make any quick movements. They are probably curious."

"Probably?" said Stefan to himself.

As the lead bird swooped in, Stefan became as still as a statue. The second eagle glided above and to the side of its partner, ready to attack if necessary.

Stefan could hear the rippling of its flight feathers as the first bird modulated its speed and direction. The sound reminded him of the *petrecere* where the heraldic banners behind the dais were flapping in the wind. The eagle was so close that Stefan could clearly see its large round eyes which were brilliant orange-gold punctuated in the center by black pupils. Was he imagining it or did the eagle wink at him? As the bird passed over Stefan and cawed, the young man flinched.

Rico laughed.

"Not to worry. It's telling its mate that you are not prey. Wow, look at that!" Rico said as he pointed to the male eagle which was performing intricate dives and loops.

"It's called sky dancing. It's a mating ritual. We are privileged to see this aerial display from this perspective," said Rico, his voice brimming with admiration.

Stefan saluted the pair as they soared toward the mountain top. His heart beat fast. He wondered how the great bird knew that he would not make a decent meal. Maybe it was the grungy smell of the clothes that he had worn for months. Good thing.

Isabella turned to her companions and smiled. After all the danger they had experienced, this was a welcome interlude.

As they progressed, the light path kept pace with them and disappeared behind them. There will be no turning back. She thought about bringing it to their attention, but decided that it was better to maintain the current equanimity. Isabella felt like one of the acrobats in the circus who refuses to look down because she doesn't want to consider how high she is. Better to enjoy the journey and trust whatever power was enabling them to cross the Alpine Sea.

"Do not lose faith. This is our destiny."

While crossing the Alpine Sea, Isabella checked her compass against the map often. Each step brought them closer to a mountain peak which was depicted on the map as Massif Veche. As the day wore on, their eyelids narrowed to avoid the bright sunlight. It reminded Rico of winter on the steppes where the blinding light paralyzed herds of Saiga antelope,

Chapter 12

rendering them vulnerable to predators, human and otherwise. He brought his hat down close to his scarf so that his eyes looked through a narrow slit. It helped to reduce the incessant ache in his head.

Unsure of the durability of their pathway, Isabella urged them to keep moving. By midday, their steps slowed until their trek resembled a ponderous slog. Keeping his eyes forward, Stefan adjusted the shoulder strap attached to the storage tube. The sword shifted and his mind raced ahead to the time when he would wield a repaired sword. He saw himself swinging the great sword on a trajectory toward Petru Aron's neck. The villain would suffer beheading just as Stefan's father had.

The refrain of Isabella and Viorico singing interrupted his reverie.

"Do not lose faith. This is our destiny."

He joined in.

Isabella had stared at their destination for so many hours that she starting seeing it double. She blinked herself back into alertness and focused on Massif Veche. It was so close she could almost touch it. But what would they find there, she wondered?

When they reached the massif, the Alpine Sea thinned in the way that the sea gets shallower when it reaches the shore. They were walking on a cloud that was turning translucent and they could see the tops of trees as if they were on the ocean floor. Birds flew among the trees like fish darting through underwater forests of kelp. While Stefan and Isabella enjoyed the aerial perspective of the mountainside, Viorico experienced vertigo. When he focused on one pine tree at a time, the unsteadiness left.

Nearing the end of their journey, the travelers were stunned by what they saw. Rising through the mist was, a wooden structure built to receive arriving voyagers.

They alighted the dock with the ease of sailors reaching port. It led to a path which brought them into a thick forest. Now that they were out of the insulating warmth of the sun, a late winter afternoon chill settled on them. Isabella led them to a fallen tree trunk where they sat. Glad to be off their feet, they removed their backpacks.

"We made it," said a weary Isabella, with as much enthusiasm as she could muster. She rubbed her hands together and looked to her companions.

Rico straddled the log. He leaned forward and said, "It's going to get cold on top of this mountain. We need to find shelter soon."

"That goes without saying," said Stefan. "There's a bigger question here. What do we do when the sun rises?"

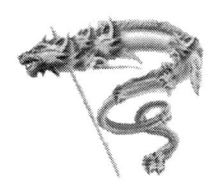

CHAPTER 13

"First things, first, gentlemen."

Reaching into her pack Isabella withdrew her silver instrument. She blew into it and waited for a cloud of *zine* to come to their assistance. After a while, she tried again. The temperature dropped as the sunlight lessened. A sense of futility that manifested as 'what now?' hovered over them.

Stefan stood and lifted his pack and the cylinder onto his back.

"We need to head down that path while we have some light remaining."

Viorico joined him. Isabella looked up with a gesture of 'a little while longer.' Stefan rested one foot on a log. His friend sat.

Her patience was rewarded a few minutes later, when a buzzing green cloud arrived. A singular figure separated from the mass and went up to Isabella. While the two clacked and clicked back and forth, Isabella's eyes drifted between her friends, communicating optimism.

"The lead *zina* is named Lulica. Her dialect is different from Clopotica's. I . . . think she is going to lead us to food and shelter. She says it's not far."

"Good," said Rico. "I'm cabbage, *varza*."

"You are not the only one who is tired, my friend," said Stefan.

With a renewed feeling of purpose, the three followed the *zine* into the forest. They walked through a hilly landscape. The scent of pine needles carried by a light breeze was an appreciated improvement from the still air of the cavern.

Lulica buzzed incessantly to Isabella as if she were a tour guide noting the scenic highlights. Stefan noticed a massive sparkling boulder near one of the streams they crossed. When he saw that boulder a second, and then a third time, he knew that the *zine* were playing a cruel joke on them. He stopped at the boulder.

"Isabella, we are taking a spike here, *a luat teapa*. We are being deluded," he shouted.

She turned to see her companions nearly collapsed on the rock. She was bone-weary herself. Clopotica had told her that there were some *zine* who were mischievous, and others who were downright malicious. Stefan had never seen Isabella lose her temper before this. She beckoned Lulica and began ranting about how deceitful, and hurtful the *zine* were. Lulica blinked a few times and her cohorts seemed to be clucking in a mocking tone at Isabella.

Stefan slipped off the boulder and quietly got behind Lulica. He grabbed her forcefully and shouted,

"You better apologize and take us to shelter, or I will clip your wings with my dagger," said Stefan, his knife gleaming in the pulsing light of the *zine*. Before he could move, his face

Chapter 13

disappeared under a swarm of animated *zine* who flashed, battered, and pecked at him.

"Owww," he screamed. "She bit me."

With that Lulica and her band of miscreant *zine* flew off into the woods. As Rico assessed Stefan's wounds in the dim moonlight, Isabella got a cloth from her pack and dipped it in the stream. She dabbed where the little demons, as she called them, had broken the surface.

"What were you thinking?" asked Isabella.

"I hated that they made fools of us."

"You showed them, alright," said Rico, stifling a laugh.

When she finished, Stefan's face was covered with red splotches as if he had chickenpox.

"I know, I know," said Stefan. "It must have been a funny sight watching those tiny witches, use my face like a dartboard."

"Actually, it was," said Rico who burst into a full-out laughing fit.

Isabella brought her hand to her mouth to hide her laughter. Tears filled her eyes as she tried to contain it. When it forced its way out, the sound from her throat was like a laugh bomb. The sight of his companions doubled-over in laughter was so ludicrous that Stefan burst into raucous laughter himself. This contagion lasted several minutes, because whenever one of them stopped, the others laughed and pointed until the laughing fit re-ignited with the one not laughing.

When their composure had returned, Isabella asked, "Are you sure you are alright?"

"Look at his mug," sputtered Viorico. That brought about another fit of laughter.

"I think my pride is wounded more than my face."

"Good. I'm exhausted," said Isabella.

"I guess it's another night under the stars," said Rico as he rested his head on his backpack and closed his eyes.

"We've done worse," said Stefan.

"Good night."

A shaft of light sliced through the evergreen branches and traveled toward Isabella. When the sunbeam crossed her eyelids, her sleeping brain responded by nudging her into consciousness. It had been a while since the sun had woken her. While at the Lake Zalmoxis cavern, her circadian rhythms were disrupted by the absence of sunrises. When the sunlight glowed red on the insides of her eyelids, she needed an extra second to orient herself. Right, they had crossed the Alpine Sea and were sleeping in the forest after the wicked *zine* misled and abandoned them. Let's not forgot how the tiny demons attacked Stefan, she thought.

She sat up and looked for him. Against a log next to Viorico, Stefan was sleeping with his forearm covering his face. His jaw was exposed but his beard obscured any marks left by the *zine* attack. Isabella shook her head, recalling the bizarre scene of Stefan swatting at a green swarm surrounding his head. Except for its malevolence, she was reminded of the crown of light that shone from the face of Moses when he descended from Mount Sinai after speaking with God. Exhaling a sigh of relief, her lips formed the smile which follows a narrow escape from a potentially ugly situation.

After reviewing the map for the hundredth time, she rose to reconnoiter the immediate area while her fellow travelers indulged in some much-needed sleep. She hoped rest would bring mental clarity because they were going to need it.

Chapter 13

There was not much underbrush in this section of the forest, so Isabella walked in ever-widening circles while maintaining visual contact with their location. A short walk led her to the stream which she followed up-mountain to its source. Dipping her hand in the frigid water reminded her of how fortunate they were to be in a pocket of temperate weather.

Sounds of distress alarmed Isabella. Hoping that the bad *zine* had not returned to torment them further, she hurried back to the camp. Not far from where the young men slept, there was rustling in a nest located in the crotch between the trunk and a branch of an old beech tree. A black woodpecker screeched a loud, plaintive "keeaaa" as it bolted skyward. The plumage of the large bird was pitch dark, except for crimson feathers gracing its crown. He launched from the tree as if a snow leopard were chasing it.

Awakened by the racket, Stefan said, "I wonder what spooked him?"

"I hope it wasn't a flock of *zine,*" cracked Rico.

Stefan zipped a pine cone towards Rico's noggin. The missile grazed his shoulder as he vaulted behind the log.

"Duck and cover like our ground warfare instructor taught," taunted Rico. A return volley sent Stefan scurrying for the safety of a tree trunk.

Isabella entered the kill zone between the combatants and was pelted with several pine cones before they realized that an innocent civilian was in the line of fire.

"Enough horsing around, lads. We are on a mission, remember?" she said, with her hands planted on both hips like an overbearing school teacher.

"*Da, da*, sorry," both said emerging from their shelters, heads down, embarrassed that Isabella had caught them playing like children.

"Not far through the woods over there," she said pointing, "There is a rough wagon path. Maybe it will lead us to a settlement where we can get some food."

"Sounds good to me," replied Rico.

"Hold on," said Stefan whose voice was shrill, bordering on panic. "Where's the Zalmoxis tube? It was here, leaning on this log."

He bent over and felt the strap but he could not see it. The tube was gone from sight. As he pulled on the strap, two appendages grabbed his wrist and tried to pull the strap from his hand.

"Help! Something is pulling the cylinder."

Isabella reached for an area near Stefan's hand and grabbed the strap. Two appendages ripped her hands away from the strap. Rico rushed over and yanked on the invisible strap. The un-seeable cylinder flew toward him and slapped against his shins halting his momentum. Two appendages gripped his forearms.

The band of three struggled against an invisible being.

A voice entered Stefan's mind urging him to relax and let go of the strap. At the same time a voice told Isabella not to worry. Another voice told Rico that excessive force would sunder the strap. Unbeknownst to the companions, someone or something was simultaneously sending a different message to each of them. To an outside observer the three appeared like befuddled Maypole dancers circling against an unseen force.

Stefan saw a mixture of bewilderment and fear in the faces of his friends. Isabella's eyebrows were pinched inward and her mouth formed an empty circle. The muscles on the side of

Chapter 13

Rico's face were clenched as if in anticipation of a blow. Stefan imagined the angry, panicked look on his own face.

"What is happening?" said Isabella.

"Whatever happens, we can NOT let go of the strap. The sword is everything!" Stefan fumbled for his dagger, thinking that he might slash the enemy. He puzzled over how to do this without cutting his companions.

"I will hold onto this until my enemy pries it out of my cold, dead hands," said Rico through gritted teeth.

"Let's start over," said an inaudible voice to all three at once.

"I can hear you, but I cannot see you. Where are you? What are you?" said Stefan.

"*Escusi.* Excuse me, I forgot that I am in camouflage mode," said the creature.

"Let go of the cylinder and then we'll talk," said Stefan.

An instant later, the tension on the Zalmoxis tube released. It reappeared. Looks of astonishment replaced their bewilderment and fear. As their minds grappled with the freakish battle over their most valuable possession, something even more startling occurred. A formless creature appeared on the log. Lidless, watery eyes beheld them.

"You mentioned camouflage, what is that?" asked Stefan.

"I can adapt my body to any color or shape that I am in contact with. See?" said the creature as he blended into the log, becoming mottled-brown and gnarly. Like a blind man, Stefan ran his hands along the log trying to find him. A moment later, the thing left the log.

"Over here," he said, appearing on a rock behind Stefan.

Stefan wheeled around and saw the creature curled on a rock.

"Watch carefully."

The three companions watched as the octopus blended into the rock with such detail, texture, and composition that they were unable to discern where the creature ended and the rock began. Stefan shook his head as if it would clear his mind to understand the trick. He blinked repeatedly to refocus on the enigmatic animal.

"What are you?" asked Stefan.

The response in his mind was, "I am an octopus. Isn't that obvious?"

"What did you say your name was?" asked Stefan, stalling for time while his brain processed what he was seeing. He thought to himself, *"Have I gone mad . . . talking to an octopus?"*

"I didn't say but now that you ask. In your tongue, I am called Vivaldi, which means 'power, strength in combat.' My full name is Tellaro Antonio Vivaldi."

"I like it," replied Stefan, playing along.

"*Da*, I can hear you, but I hear no sound. How is that possible?" said Rico.

"Simple, I communicate by creating thoughts which I transfer to your brain by using my beak to transmit waves to you."

"Where are you from?" asked Isabella.

"I was born in Italia. I come from a long line of octopuses. My first name is Tellaro, named after my great grandfather who saved the town of Tellaro, Italia from marauding pirates. On seeing danger of the impending attack, he went to the cathedral and rang the warning bells. My great grandfather's quick thinking saved the town from murder, rape, and plunder. In honor of his heroism, the town erected a huge octopus statue in the piazza. It is so large that it serves as a band shell for musicians to entertain the people. Every July

28th, Tellaro sponsors a concert to commemorate the day and affirm the bond between the town and the Vivaldi octopuses."

"That's an impressive story," said Stefan, who thought of his own noble lineage which was now in mortal danger. He let his own troubles recede in the face of this intriguing situation.

"What do your friends call you?"

"You can call me Telly..., but don't ever call me Telly Tony. That's what some of the cuttlefish in my neighborhood called me when they wanted to bust my tentacles. I hate it!"

"*Da, da*, we get it. Don't worry, we will only call you Telly. I'm Stefan, this is Viorico, and this is Isabella."

His eyebrows knit over wary eyes. He scanned the faces of his companions. Isabella exhibited wide-eyed wonder. Rico scowled, while clinching his fists.

"Telly, I'm confused. I thought that octopuses were sea creatures. Obviously, you are able to survive out of the water. How is that possible?"

Puffing himself to his full expanse, Telly replied, "Over the millennium, we have evolved so that we are able to breathe through our skin, which you can see is quite plentiful. That is not to say that we do not need water. I must be submerged in water occasionally, or I will shrivel and die. Usually when I am on land, the overnight dew and rain suffice to replenish my moisture; otherwise, I must find a lake, stream, or even a well."

Stefan crossed himself and murmured, "*Gloria in excelsis Deo*, Glory to God in the highest."

He again wondered whether this encounter was happening.

"So, tell me, how is it that you are here in this forest with us?"

"At a young age, I decided to travel, you know, to see the world. I travel by boat or drift with the tides or flow with a river. . . wherever, fate may take me. I always seek adventure. When I saw the situation of you and your friends, I thought, 'There's a young man on a quest.' Maybe I can help him.'"

"Would you excuse us for a second?" said Stefan motioning for his friends to join him. When they were shielded by a large tree, Stefan said, "Do you believe this? What should we do?"

"It's an abomination. I say we grab stones and bash it to pieces," said Rico.

"Keep your voice down," urged Stefan. "I'm not sure that we could overpower it, even if we wanted to. It would be like fighting eight enemies. Who knows what other powers it possesses?"

"What's it going to do, spray us with ink?" said Rico, his voice dripping with sarcasm.

"I hadn't thought of that. What if the ink is acid? Or poison? Then what?"

The dejection evident in his voice, showed on his face.

"We could run away."

"Rico, it will follow us."

"Let's consider the positives," said Isabella.

"Like what? That he's good at stealing," said Rico.

"Listen, we are not sure that we can subdue it and we can't run from it. Maybe we should embrace him. Maybe this is an opportunity," said Isabella.

"Oh, now it's a 'he'" Rico hurumphed, turning his back and bending around the tree to stare at the creature.

"We know it can disappear. We know it is strong," said Stefan as he rubbed the suction marks on his wrist. "We know it can send thoughts to our heads . . . . With those talents it would be a great sentry. It could guard us while we sleep."

Chapter 13

"I'm not sleeping with that thing slinking around. What if it sends thoughts to our enemies? We wouldn't even know it," hissed Rico, his face reddening in frustration.

"He is intelligent, strong, has unique abilities to communicate and disappear. I say he can help us," said Isabella.

"He comes from a noble background and he wants to help," added Stefan.

"You believe that *minciuni*, malarkey?" huffed Rico.

"Yes," said Stefan, giving his friend a steely look.

"I agree with Isabella that we take him with us and keep a close eye on him at all times. We tell him nothing of the scroll and our goal. Most important, one of us has to guard the Zalmoxis cylinder every second of the day or night. Agreed?"

"*Da*," Isabella. Rico nodded.

They put their heads together and clasped hands and joined in a brief invocation for the Lord's help.

Stefan stepped out from behind the tree first.

"We have decided that you may join us . . . Provided you swear an oath of allegiance to us and agree to follow orders."

He mused to himself how he had considered demanding that Telly kneel and kiss his ring, like his father had done with his sub-vassals. Trying hard to keep a dignified mien, Stefan swallowed a smile at the absurdity of that image. *How does an octopus kneel? Can an octopus kiss? What were they getting into with this alien creature, he wondered?*

"*Si, si, certo*, yes, yes, certainly" said Telly into their minds. "Now, may I tell you something?"

"*Da*, what?"

"There is a group of horsemen approaching on the wagon trail. I suggest we hide."

Puzzled, they looked to each other. Moments later, the sounds of hooves pounding, horse tack jangling, and men shouting reached to them. Isabella's hand went to her mouth in surprise. Viorico grabbed her hand and pulled her out of sight behind a large boulder. Stefan scrambled to recover the cylinder before dashing under a **juniper** bush.

CHAPTER 14

"Halt!" shouted one of the men. "I saw the glint of a stream over there. We will stop to fill our canteens and water the horses."

Something about that voice was familiar, thought Stefan as he shrunk further into the shrub. The riding party dismounted. The sounds from their spurs and weapons were amplified in the forest stillness. Horses slurped water and men knelt to drink.

Isabella saw it first. Their backpacks were out, leaning against the log. She squeezed her eyes shut and concentrated, trying to signal Telly. Movement caught Isabella's eye. With the stealth of a ghost, the octopus crawled to the packs and covered them with his malleable body. A second later a large man stepped through the trees and walked toward the boulder. Stefan's eyes widened as he recognized the man associated with the voice. It was Dryger. He was wearing an eye-patch. He was headed right to where his companions hid.

Stefan's hand reached for his dagger as he calculated the distance to Dryger if he had to attack. He trembled.

"I'm with you, chief," said another man who Stefan recognized from training camp. There were two men to handle if they found his friends. He listened to determine how many more were in the patrol. Six, or seven, maximum. His heart sank. As the two men moved toward the boulder, he reconciled himself to his fate. They stopped in front of the boulder. He held his breath.

He saw the boulder darken and heard splashing as the urine fell to the ground. He watched as they shook and turned back toward the stream. Stefan exhaled.

"Dryger, I wonder if the report we got was wrong."

"I'm telling you our spies are never wrong. If they are here, our spies will find them. We have to keep looking. Tell the men to mount up, we have a lot of ground to cover."

"Yes, chief."

Dryger hesitated as he passed a log which was oddly-shaped. He stared for a long second, then muttered, "This damn eyepatch has my eye playing tricks on me."

"You said something, chief?"

"Nah," he said, shaking his head like a desert sojourner trying to dismiss a mirage. "Let's ride."

Stefan thought that the receding sound of the horsemen riding up the mountain was among the sweetest sounds he had ever heard.

Isabella was pale when she and Viorico came out from their hiding place. Stefan went to the log and patted Telly, or he thought he patted Telly, he couldn't tell for sure where the octopus began and the log ended.

"Thanks, you saved us."

"*Da*, thanks," said Rico, who stood with arms crossed and his eyes trying to fathom what to make of their new ally.

"Thank Isabella. She alerted me that the packs were exposed," said Telly.

Isabella was pensive.

Chapter 14

"Dryger mentioned scouts. Do you think the *zine* betrayed us?"

"Who else could it be? What do you think, Stefan?"

Stefan did not respond; he was somewhere else. His face showed the turmoil and sadness of his thoughts. If Dryger was here, that means that Vlad failed to kill him. He pictured Vlad with his bow and how he vowed vengeance on the man who held his father when his throat was slit. Vlad must be dead. Stefan's eyes welled up. *Were there any loved ones, immune from the Bloody Scourge, he wondered?*

The arrival of Dryger and his band of assassins marred the beautiful early winter morning. Since the murders at the *petrecere*, the three travelers had eluded their pursuers. Over days and weeks without the ominous shadow of their enemies looming over their every move, they had developed a sense of security which now proved unfounded. They were in immediate, mortal danger. The appearance of an active, mounted patrol rattled the group.

"We must get as far away from Dryger's brutes as possible," said Isabella.

"How? They found us here," said Rico.

"The eagles," offered Telly.

"What? How?" thought the trio.

"I heard the leader think that the eagles are never wrong."

This comment drew a skeptical glance from Rico.

"This map is the best way to elude Petru Aron's patrols," said Isabella, withdrawing the map from her inner pocket. "We must stay under the forest canopy to avoid them."

As she bent to pick up stones to secure the corners of the map, Telly's voice told her not to bother; he would hold it down with his tentacles. He added that they would find him helpful in handling a wide variety of chores. She responded silently.

Isabella had decided to practice this skill with Telly since she foresaw instances where it could be crucial. Still, she had doubts. As if the process of communicating soundlessly with an octopus wasn't strange enough, she wondered whether it opened her mind for Telly to access thoughts which she wished to keep private. If this was the case, it was imperative that she determine whether she could block Telly's access. Although she was adept at reading people, the same might not be possible with an octopus.

If Telly could "read" her mind, was it a two-way street? Could she access his thoughts? Isabella knew that she would need considerable mental discipline to control this process. She shuddered at the idea that their lives may well depend on it.

Another issue surfaced almost immediately. During their short time together with the octopus, Telly had been extremely loquacious. She found that his constant chatter interrupted her own thoughts to the point where it was impeding her ability to think clearly. She had to figure out how to turn a deaf ear on Telly.

As Isabella struggled with the ramifications, she questioned whether her decision to open her mind to Telly was a mistake. Stefan and Viorico had adamantly refused.

"I don't want some octopus swimming around in my head. My hearing is as sharp as my retriever hunting quail. I don't need some critter with a lot of arms interfering."

Stefan was more diplomatic, but no less forceful in his rejection.

"No offense, Telly, but my father always told me to keep my own counsel."

Chapter 14

"Enough. Let's focus. We have crossed the Alpine Sea and are high up in the Carpathian Mountains. We do not have mounts and lack food and weapons. A few minutes ago, we almost came face-to-face with a patrol that wants to kill us. Needless to say, our situation has gotten much more perilous. We have at least one major advantage," Isabella said as she pointed to the fragile vellum map.

"We need to find the most direct route to the Fangs of Giga," said Stefan.

"... without using roads," added Rico.

"Why not use roads but travel at night?" said Telly using the only means at his disposal, his gift of telepathy.

"Traveling in the dark is not an option. We've already had a bad experience with the forest *zine*," said Isabella.

"Look here. We can follow the tree line along these ridges until we reach this river," said Stefan. He traced a route on the map which tacked toward the Fangs.

"What about that river? Will we be able to cross it?" asked Rico. "This other way seems more direct."

"More direct but right through a settlement where we could run into trouble with Petru Aron's men," said Isabella.

"*Da*," said Stefan. "We will cross that river when we get to it."

"We should get moving," said Isabella.

"Make sure you top off your canteens with water before we go. We might be hard pressed to find water near the tree line," said Stefan.

Telly followed them to the stream in his awkward way of ambulating, rising onto four tentacles and using the other four for balance. The octopus slipped into the stream and propelled to a small pool where an eddy of collected water swirled. As Telly gamboled in the water, twisting, diving, and accelerating with ease, Rico noted the transformation from an ungainly terrestrial creature into a graceful and powerful swimmer.

"Wait," said Rico. "Telly's manner of walking is slow and clumsy. How is he going to keep up with us?"

"I can carry him," offered Stefan.

"No need," was the answer. "I will tenaculate."

"Huh?"

"I use my tentacles to swing through the trees using limbs the way a trapeze artist swings from one swing to another. I must say that it's quite exhilarating."

With Isabella taking point, they settled into a steady rhythm and made good progress, despite checking constantly for any sign that Dryger's men might be near. The drudgery of the hike was relieved by the antics of Telly. He was a natural show-off who entertained them with a display of acrobatics that defied description. The spectacle of an eight-limbed creature navigating through the forest was made more memorable by Telly's telepathic commentary.

"Watch this quadruple somersault with a twisting flyaway. I can perform these feats because I have no bones to get in my way. I can bend, twist and contort in every direction. Multiple suction cups line my tentacles giving me superior gripping power."

"Don't you ever get tired?" asked Isabella, testing the range of his ability to hear her.

"I have no lungs. The skin over my entire body absorbs oxygen, so I never get winded. In addition, I have three hearts pumping blood which by the way is not red, but the color of lapis mixed with carbon. My blood is the same color as your ink. I have been truly blessed by God."

Isabella could have sworn that he winked at her when he made that last statement.

Chapter 14

Miles away, Dryger and his horsemen reached the top of the mountain. His face contorted with anger and his vacant eye socket throbbed. The report of sighting Stefan and his companions had led them on a fruitless errand. He grumbled to himself that he was tired of riding over mountains and valleys chasing apparitions. The only thing he knew for certain was that they could not return to Petru Aron empty-handed. Not if they wanted to keep their heads attached to their necks.

Along the wagon path, he spied a reflection of water. He signaled his men to stop. The large boulder not far from the stream attested to the fact that it was the same watering area they had used earlier in the day. Looking at the boulder, Dryger thought that it would make a good hiding place for an ambush. When he dismounted and walked around it, he changed his mind. The trees were too close to conceal enough men. Something caught his attention. He noticed that the grass around the boulder was trampled. Recalling that he and some of the men had relieved themselves against the boulder, he disregarded it.

"Hey, chief. You gotta see this."

He was on the far side of the stream, pointing to strange markings in the mud. Dryger waded across the stream and stared at the ground.

"How can this be?"

"That's exactly what I thought."

"These marks look like the suction cups of an octopus, the kind we used to hunt when we were stationed in the Holy Land. We would grab them by the tentacles and smash their heads against the rocks before we grilled them over hot coals," said Dryger who closed his good eye and imagined enjoying a feast of charred octopus with a squeeze of lemon.

"Hey, chief, I found some footprints. Look, there are three sets."

"These tracks head into the forest. It must be them," said Dryger, assuming, the bloodthirsty look of a hunter who has identified his prey. All that was left was stalking the victims before the slaughter.

"It'll be dark soon. They are on foot so they can't get far. We will go back to the village and enjoy a nice, hot meal while they shiver in the forest. Tomorrow, we will return here with the dogs and track the prince and his minions down like defenseless rabbits."

The day of forced march had taken its toll on their group. At times they had to ascend several hundred feet to reach the tree line. Once there, they left the soft, needle-clad forest for the rocky crust of the mountainside.

"These rocks are tearing up my boots," said Stefan when they stopped for a rest.

"You think you have problems? My blisters have blisters," said Viorico.

Isabella sat with the map on her thighs.

"We are about here," she pointed. "We should be able to find shelter over here, above the gorge. We'll rest there tonight."

"What about our friend?" said Stefan tilting his head toward Telly who lingered in the trees about forty yards from them. Stefan waved and received a half-hearted wave in return.

"The effort of tenaculating is wearing him down," said Viorico.

"*Da*, he stopped showboating about an hour ago," added Stefan.

Chapter 14

"When we get near the river later, he will be able to revive himself. For now, I think I've learned something we may find useful," she said.

"What?" asked Stefan.

"All morning I've been testing the range of his ability to talk to our minds. I calculate that, thirty yards is the extent of it. Beyond that he cannot enter our thoughts."

"Good to know. I'll make sure to stay far enough away so I do not have to listen to him singing Roman ballads about Trajan defeating my ancestors," said Stefan.

"Do I detect a note of bitterness?" teased his buddy.

"Time to push on," said Isabella.

Several hours later, they heard the sound of rushing water which got louder as they descended back into the trees. When they reached a flat ledge partially covered by another boulder, Isabella indicated that they would camp there. With an exhausted sigh, Stefan unslung his pack and the cylinder.

"Where's Telly?" asked Isabella.

"I hear splashing over there," said Stefan, cocking his head toward the noise.

Viorico was about to flop down beside him but changed his mind.

"I'm going to join him. These feet could sure use a soak."

He walked from the clearing to the water. He sat and gingerly removed his boots.

"Ahh, that feels sooo good."

Moments later, all three companions were sitting on the bank with their feet swishing in the cold, mountain water. The daylong tension seemed to drift away with the pains of their aching feet. The unexpected pleasure was so divine that they did not pay attention when Telly announced that he was going foraging in the woods.

When they returned to the camp, they were startled by what they saw . . . and smelled.

In a niche below the ledge, Telly had built a small fire. Stefan unhooked his water sack and prepared to extinguish the fire. Even a small amount of smoke could betray their position. He stood dumbfounded like a schoolboy trying to comprehend a magic trick when he saw that none of the escaping smoke was visible. Telly explained that above the flames there was a natural rock formation shaped like a reverse funnel riddled with channels rising to openings in the rock high above them. This "chimney" served to attenuate the smoke to such a degree that no trace of the fire was visible.

Telly was off to the side working like an octopus possessed. He was peeling root vegetables, kneading some sort of gummy dough, stirring a soup, washing dirt off radishes, slicing ramps, and removing pine nuts from pinecones.

"Sometimes, I have trouble walking and chewing mint. How in the world do you do that?" marveled Stefan.

"Do what?" asked Telly, his face wrinkled into a quizzical look. Isabella made a mental note, registering another facial expression of the octopus. So far, she had seen elation when he was tenaculating, pride when he was explaining camouflage, and now confusion when he did not comprehend Stefan's question. By focusing on the space around his eyes, the posture of his mantle, and detecting slight color variations, Isabella catalogued Telly's emotions. At least she hoped she was.

Stefan stammered.

"Oh, you mean, perform all these chores at the same time?"

"Yes," blustered Stefan. "How do you do it?"

"It's easy. You see, I am different from you."

"No kidding," retorted Stefan.

Chapter 14

"I have eight appendages and each one has a brain of its own. So, while tentacle one is washing, tentacle two is peeling, tentacle three is chopping. . ."

"*Da*, I get it," said Stefan, shaking his head in awe or shock, he wasn't sure which.

When he was through with his preparation, Telly insisted that his guests allow him to cook in privacy. Unaccustomed to being served, the three travelers spent their time studying the map.

"We are close to the second milestone," said Isabella. "By this time tomorrow we should be at the Fangs of Giga."

"Provided we don't run into Dryger and his gang," said Stefan through gritted teeth.

"Don't worry. I'll sense them long before they get near," said Telly.

Annoyance creased Isabella's face as she mouthed, "We need to move out of range."

The young men nodded. They moved to a cluster of pines near the flowing water.

"This tributary joins with other streams which flow into the river. The land drops off as the river widens and enters a valley," said Isabella, keeping her voice low so that it would barely rise above the gurgle of the water.

Leaning forward, Rico said, "Why don't we cross the water here where it is not wide?"

"There's one obstacle," said Stefan. "This way becomes a promontory which is high, relatively flat, and surrounded by cliffs. If we went that way, we would be trapped with nowhere to go."

"Stefan's correct. The only way to get to the Fangs is to follow the map to this point and cross the river before we descend toward the valley. This is where we will find the Fangs," said Isabella. Her index finger stopped at the depiction of the Fangs on the map, leaving unanswered the question of what then.

"One thing is for sure," said Viorico. "We will know if we miss the pyramid."

"How?"

"On the far side of the Shepard's Shadow is the Neck of Hell."

"So?"

"I've been to the Neck of Hell. It is an extremely forsaken place, as its name implies. It is a skinny path, about only one horse-width, with vertical rock walls on both sides. When you go through it, you feel as if you have fallen into the deepest well. It is so deep that you cannot see the sky. At the end it opens into a circular bowl known as Lucifer's dome.

"There is a legend that it was originally a solid mountain but a crack formed into the narrow opening when a trickster stole the staff of Ciobanul, the shepherd's guardian, and stabbed it into a tiny crack trying to access living water. The crevice opened and trickster fell to his death. Now, if the spirit of that place is disturbed, the walls will come together and crush anyone who happens to be there."

"That's a bunch of rubbish designed to scare children," said Stefan.

"I wouldn't be so dismissive, Stefan, there are many unexplained legends associated with these mountains," said Rico who turned to Isabella. "What do you think?"

Her face had a pensive look as if she were debating whether to disclose a profound secret. The answer never came because as quiet as a shadow, Telly joined their threesome. He startled

Chapter 14

Rico who jerked erect as though yanked by a puppet master. Stefan bolted into a fighting stance, reaching for his dagger.

"Telly," screamed Isabella, "for God's sake! You can't sneak up on us! It's dangerous."

This outburst brought a new expression to the octopus' face, if that was possible, thought Isabella. He looked chastised, sheepish.

"I'm sorry. I wanted to be part of the team. I did not want to interrupt. . ."

The annoyed glowers of the group were replaced by reluctant but forgiving expressions.

Telly brightened and announced with a flourish which involved too many tentacles, "Dinner is served."

If ever the old adage that hunger is the best seasoning applied, it was to that meal in the mountains.

"Telly, this pesto gnocchi is fantastic. If I close my eyes, I can imagine that I'm dining in the banquet hall of Charlemagne," said Stefan.

"How did you do this?" asked Isabella.

Rico loosened his belt a notch and scooped up another helping.

"I gathered as many acorns as I could find and boiled the toxins out. Then, I ground them with my suckers until I had a flour. I combined the flour with boiled root vegetables and formed fluffy gnocchi like my grandmother in Tellaro taught me. You must roll them off your small sucker."

"And the pesto?" asked Isabella.

"Ah, for that I had to be creative. Using the nuts from inside pinecones, in Italia we call them *pignoli*, I mashed them with ramps that I found near the stream. To finish the dish, I scraped some truffle which I was fortunate to find in the roots of that tree over there," said Telly, showing his proud expression.

"*Fantastico!*" said Stefan who joined the others in a round of applause.

CHAPTER 15

*I*n a settlement not far away, another team prepared to depart in the pre-dawn darkness. Their plan was to ride their horses to the stream on the wagon path where they had seen the footprints of their quarry and track them with hunting dogs. After months of futility in their search for the "wormy spawn of Bogdan" as Petru Aron called him, the riders were excited to hunt in earnest. As they rode, they bantered about the possibility of being home for Christmas.

After his culinary triumph, Telly basked in the glow that comes from a job well done and acceptance by his teammates as a contributor. He rewarded himself by sleeping in the stream to restore his moisture and the luxuriate in the flowing water. The unfortunate consequence of submersion was that his exceptional hearing was diminished by the insulation of the water. When he finally awoke, his sense of happy satisfaction was shattered by what he heard.

"Wake up, everyone!" he screamed into their minds. "The hunters are near."

Isabella was the first to respond, "Tell us what is happening. How much time do we have?"

"I hear Dryger's men and the baying of hounds closing in. They are minutes away!"

Stefan hoisted the Zalmoxis tube over his shoulder and raced to where Rico was stuffing their things into the packs.

"Leave everything. We have to run now!"

Rico shouldered his half-filled pack and dashed after his friends.

Isabella shouted, "Follow me. We must get to the bridge before they arrive and slaughter us."

The three travelers sprinted into the woods, heading toward what appeared on the map as a single line crossing the river. She hoped that her interpretation was correct and that whatever was on the map was still there. Their lives depended on it.

Telly tenaculated ahead, exhilarated at the prospect of playing scout in this unfolding drama. He forced himself to stay within sight of his friends while communicating the most effective route to Isabella. Not long after they ran into the woods, they heard barking and howling as the pack arrived at their camp site.

When Stefan looked back through the trees, he thought he saw Dryger's men entering the camp. Stefan pumped his legs harder. The sound of crashing and tumbling water, was at once soothing and terrifying. They had to get to the other side of the river. A chilling thought crept into his mind; *how do we stop Dryger from following us across the river?*

"I see it," cried Telly, with relief in his telepathic message, if that were possible. "It's a rope and board affair with a span of about thirty yards. Looks in decent shape."

Stefan's lungs burned and a stitch formed in his side. He could see glimpses of the bridge through the foliage. It was a rudimentary rope bridge with planks of wood tied together

Chapter 15

and waist-high ropes on either side serving as handrails. There were two posts on each end serving as anchors for the structure. About sixty feet below the crossing the river raged, white and foamy as it descended downward toward the distant valley. Stefan assessed the vertical cliffs on each side of the river and knew that the bridge was the only crossing option.

Stefan ushered Isabella on to the rickety boards, figuring that she was the best to test the sturdiness of the bridge. When she had crossed and signaled it was solid, Rico pushed Stefan on to the bridge.

"You go, you must survive," he shouted over the din of the rushing water. "I'll cut the supports so they cannot follow us."

As Stefan reached the midpoint, he turned to see the dogs clear the last rise which led to the bridge. Dryger and his men were right behind them. Dryger stood out by his size but also by the covering of his left eye. The patch was pitch black overlaid with a spectral skull which sent a chill through Stefan. He swore on the memory of his cousin Vlad that he would rid the earth of this evildoer in the same way that Odysseus had defeated the Cyclops.

The faces of their pursuers were filled with the same blood lust as the hounds. At the sight of their prey on the bridge, they screeched a war cry and bounded down the slope toward the bridge. At the sight of the frenzied warriors led by the voracious dogs, Stefan felt like the guest of honor at a fox hunt. He set his jaw and vowed that it would not end like this.

"Come on, Rico. They're right behind you!"

He wondered whether his friend heard him since he continued hacking at the rope support. It was clear that the killers would reach him before he would finish cutting the supports on both sides.

"Rico, you must go. I'll take over cutting the rope supports," said Telly.

A startled look from Rico changed into recognition before melting into resignation. He handed his knife to Telly who was already hacking away at the ropes on one post. The octopus quickly steadied himself on the bridge with four tentacles and used his other four to slash at both posts with the speed and intensity of a jagged streak of lightning.

The bridge swayed wildly from the force of Rico's frantic dash and Telly's manic efforts to sever the support ropes. Sensing that the bridge might collapse at any second, Stefan edged onto the bridge and stretched out his hand. Not knowing what else to do, Isabella withdrew her flute and played a silent, high-pitched distress signal. With long, loping strides Rico closed the gap and reached for Stefan. The bridge buckled and twisted as Telly succeeded in cutting another rope.

Rico was almost across the bridge when Dryger unslung his crossbow. His countenance was more like a clenched fist than a human face. Stefan would never forget the way his black eye patch seemed to exude malevolence. Dryger lowered his good eye to his crossbow, aimed, and fired. As the bolt flew toward its target, it seemed to Stefan that time slowed.

He watched in horror as the bolt spun on its axis, the feather vanes providing stability. Dryger's aim was true. Sweat poured into Stefan's eyes as he stretched toward his friend. The Zalmoxis tube slipped and Stefan hitched his shoulder to steady it. This movement shortened his reach. Their fingers were almost touching when the arrow hit Rico in the back. There was a sharp thud. Stefan watched in horror as Rico jerked, lost his balance, and grabbed the top rope only to find no support. With a pained look, Rico tumbled into space. He

Chapter 15

hurtled, end over end until he splashed into the river and disappeared.

Dryger reloaded and fired another shot, this time at Telly. The arrow pierced one of his tentacles at the instant he completed severing the supporting ropes on the near side. With Telly clinging to it, the bridge swung to the other side of the gorge where Stefan and Isabella watched, helpless. They heard Telly screaming as he flew in an arc across the chasm. He would explain later that his scream was one of delight at the sensation of flying. He insisted that he was elated, not terrified. Neither of his friends believed him.

The bridge struck the cliff and bounced several times before coming to rest. As Telly climbed the fallen bridge using it like a ladder, a flurry of arrows crossed the divide. Telly camouflaged himself, assuming the shape and color of the bridge. The archers fired like blind men and missed their unseen target.

As Telly came to them, Stefan and Isabella heard him proclaiming that there was nothing more exhilarating than being shot at without result. Dryger yelled the loudest and most profane curses to no avail. The shouts and curses of the frustrated killers served only to increase Stefan's vocabulary.

Isabella stared into the roiling river below. Those villains were the least of their concerns. Their friend had been shot and had fallen off the bridge. She turned toward Stefan and saw him trembling. Lines of pain and grief etched his face.

"Stefan, do you hear the splashing noise from the river? That has to be Rico. He's a strong swimmer. Remember how he swam across Lake Zalmoxis?"

"We cannot deny reality, Isabella. Dryger shot him squarely in the back. Plus, the fall itself would have taken him.

My . . . our trusted friend is gone," he sobbed. "How am I supposed to restore the sword and save my country? Not long ago, my biggest responsibility was to muck the stables. Now, I'm supposed to be some kind of hero who saves the world? I can't do it, especially without Rico and Bogdan and Vlad."

He gripped the strap of the Zalmoxis tube with such vehemence that his knuckles turned white.

With the gentleness of a butterfly landing on a flower petal, Isabella touched his hand. She looked deeply into his eyes

"Do not lose faith. With this celestial sword you will fulfill your destiny."

"It's because of this stupid sword that I wasn't able to reach Rico."

Angry shouts from across the chasm brought them back to their situation.

Isabella knelt to examine the arrow embedded in one of Telly's tentacles. Before Telly could protest, she took her knife and slit the skin on either side of the bolt. Telly grabbed the shaft with the tip of another tentacle and yanked the bolt free in one swift movement. A small geyser of midnight-blue blood squirted up several inches and fell over the gash. The suction cups at the end of the injured tentacle wrapped tightly over the wound.

"There, the suckers will seal the opening and my body will regenerate replacement skin over the injured tissue in no time."

He drew the arrow to his eyes. "Humans are so primitive. Why do you have to use barbs on the points of your projectiles when a simple paralyzing toxin accomplishes the same result?"

Chapter 15

"We have to keep moving. Those evil creatures will never stop chasing us. It will take them at least a day to find a place to ford the river. We must not squander our lead. Let's go."

CHAPTER 16

*I*sabella led them to a path parallel to the river which wound down into the valley. The Fangs of Giga were in the mountains on the other end of the valley. They hiked in silence; even Telly was uncharacteristically quiet. Stefan's stride was wooden as he followed Isabella's footfalls.

As the three traversed the valley, they stayed below the tree line to avoid detection. The sun was low and to their left. Although the sky was clear, little warmth came from the light. Stefan thought that the dim light matched his gloomy frame of mind. Not even the freakish sight of Telly walking with a limp due to his injured appendage could bring a smile to Stefan. He missed Rico's reassuring presence. To distract himself from the ache in his heart, he concentrated on calculating the days they had been running. Then, he slapped his forehead as if a flint had flashed in his head.

"The winter solstice is tomorrow."

The small party digested this information and increased their pace. When they climbed a ridge at the end of the valley, they hoped that the Fangs of Giga would appear.

Chapter 16

"I cannot believe it," said Stefan as he took in the panorama before them.

Stretching before them for miles was an undulating landscape punctuated by pairs of huge, pointed stones rising vertically toward the sky like fangs. At first glance, the granite formations seemed to sprout haphazardly from the earth. On closer examination there was a pattern, arrayed somewhat like the willow hoops on a croquet court. The meaning of the pattern eluded them.

"It's going to take us days to search for the Fangs we are looking for," groaned Stefan.

Isabella had her nose buried in the map. She exhaled, frustrated.

Telly sidled over to her and viewed the map.

"Stay here," said Telly. With a rush of movement, he bounded toward the strange rock formations.

As the sun crossed the sky, Stefan's anxiety increased. He sat on a boulder next to Isabella, his heel tapping an annoying, staccato beat.

"Please stop that. You're giving me a headache."

Stefan relented, only to resume his tapping a few minutes later.

Muttering to herself, Isabella rose and paced.

"You can wait for him here if you like. I'm going to keep moving. We have less than twenty-four hours to solve this riddle," said Stefan as he clutched the tube to his side and headed toward the nearest pair of towering rocks.

After he had disappeared beyond a rise, Isabella regretted not going with him. She gathered what little there was to carry and set off in the same direction. By now midday had passed and the sinking sun cast a lengthening shadow before her. At each rise, she scanned the horizon for either of her companions without success. Her shoulders slumped and her feet dragged through the low shrubbery. A growing wind pressed against her back. She recalled an old legend about a shepherd whose flute playing was answered by the whistling wind.

"Isabella, I found it. I found it." It was Telly.

"Over here," she yelled. Never in her life was she so glad to see an octopus.

He was so excited that his telepathic communication was virtually incoherent. Isabella was able to discern the words serrated and whistling. She told him to take her there. As they headed toward the Fangs, they called out to Stefan. They got no answer.

When he had calmed down, Telly explained how he found the correct formation.

"I concluded that the Giga must relate to the Hyaenodon gigas which were prehistoric carnivores, predecessors of current-day hyenas. One unique aspect of these creatures was that they had serrated teeth, better for ripping and tearing their prey. So, I decided to limit my search to rock formations which had serrated edges. That's when I found it – the only formation with inward-facing serrations. It's up ahead, over the next rise."

"I see it. I'll go there. You search for Stefan. It is imperative that we find him before the sun goes down."

When Isabella reached the stones, she imagined a giga buried under her with only these fangs showing above the surface. She felt a powerful energy below her. A gust of wind flew between the fangs producing a low, subtle whistle.

As the wind increased, a low, dirge-like whistle swelled. Its volume increased to the point where she felt it was resounding through the hills. The dirge was so sad that it would have

Chapter 16

driven most people to despair. The sound brought to her mind the belief that a higher purpose may be achieved through sacrifice. In the diminished light of the rising moon, she removed her flute and played a complementary melody. The music combined, intertwined and formed an ethereal song that spoke of eternal longing and struggle. It summoned the spirit of shepherds over the eons.

A figure approached as if walking out of a vapor plume. His form solidified as he got closer. She thought that the mist was incongruous because the night was clear and the wind was gusting.

He wore the traditional *sarica*, a shaggy sheepskin cloak which draped past his knees. A fine astrakhan wool hat covered his head. Although his face was weathered and his trim goatee was grey, his stride belied his age.

"Good evening, my daughter. It has been a long time since I have returned to this place. Your playing was so mournful and plaintive that it summoned me. May I join you?"

Isabella nodded in assent, not trusting her voice in the face of this apparition in rustic clothes.

"I am Ciobanul, the patron of shepherds," he said with the soothing tone of a confessor. "What so troubles you that I can hear your heart rending in your music?"

Her voice was tremulous at first, but gathered assurance as she looked into his clear, brown eyes. They were eyes that missed nothing. Perhaps, his guidance might help her bear the burden which she had assumed while leading the group through their perils.

"We are sojourners through this land in search of the blacksmith who operates the Forges of Ezrok. Our map is less detailed than we would want. We need to locate the pyramid at Shepherd's Shadow."

"I see," he said, stroking his chin. "You mention 'we' but I see just you. Where are your companions?"

"They are out among the rocks, . . . searching. I feel so alone."

"Do not worry, my child. Ciobanul is the protector of his flock. These hills are filled with others, lynxes, wolves, and bobcats, who prey on the vulnerable. Fear most the two-legged predators. You and your friends must be wary, for there are men with evil hearts lurking in these parts."

Isabella shivered and pulled her cloak around her.

"The pyramid you look for is rare. It is formed when the sunlight hits those two mountain peaks on the day of the solstice. It appears for only eighty minutes. Tomorrow is the winter solstice. You have no time to lose. If you want to be there when the pyramid appears, you must hike through the night. Then you will be in position to see it point to the entrance of the Forges."

Ciobanul rose and pointed his staff toward a looming mountain.

"There, you will find a path which will lead you to your destination." With a wink, he added, "Follow your heart, Stefan will bring you joy."

Isabella thanked him, bowing deeply. *What did he mean? Was she so obvious that he could tell? Was there a way out of this dilemma?* Thoughts flitted through her mind like squirrels in a cage.

"One more thing, child. Faur is a master blacksmith. True. But he always exacts a price for his work. Only you can decide whether the work is worth the price."

Ciobanul smiled and vanished into the mist.

Chapter 16

It wasn't until she had force-marched well into the night that Isabella grasped the depth of her desperation that she was chasing a shadow based on the assertions of a ghost.

CHAPTER 17

*A*fter Telly left Isabella to find Stefan, he found a stream. It had been a long day out on the hills, so he decided to enter the stream and remoisturize while he tenaculated on the bottom. The cold water energized him. He sent telepathic calls to Stefan in hopes of locating him. Based on what Telly knew of the direction Stefan headed that morning and his likely pace, Telly calculated where he might locate him. He followed the stream to the intersection point.

Quite a distance away, Stefan looked at the rising moon and recounted the pairs of vertical stone formations he had checked throughout the day. None were the Fangs of Giga. He was exhausted. He had trouble remembering exactly what he was searching for and how he would know when he found it. Demoralized, he sat.

The sound of water rippling over rocks caught Stefan's attention. As he walked toward it, he heard another, more ominous, sound. The snorting and heavy breathing of horses climbing a rise was unmistakable. Stefan dashed into a clump of bushes bordering the stream. Moments later, he saw a trio of horsemen dismount to water their horses a few yards from him.

Chapter 17

"The chief is obsessed with finding these fugitives," said one of the riders whose voice Stefan recognized from their close encounter near the wagon path.

"Splitting into teams of three was a good idea. We can cover a lot more territory," said another rider who cast stones across the stream. "Hey, did you see that one? It skipped four times."

"When I told the chief that this is my last shift, that I was leaving so I could be home by Christmas, I thought he was going to burst a blood vessel. He nearly turned purple with rage. He blames these curs for losing his eye. He won't stop until they are dead."

Stefan relaxed as they prepared to remount. Something squishy and wet touched his shoulder. Stefan jumped from fright and surprise. His foot slipped into the water, splashing noisily.

"What was that?" asked the leader, cocking his head to listen.

"It was probably a stone flipped by this dunce bouncing for the tenth time."

"I actually once threw one that skipped eleven times . . . ."

"*Da*, enough! If we leave now, we can be back to camp in time for supper."

Telly told Stefan not to worry, he had his back. In the darkening gloom, the young man glared at the octopus. They huddled in silence as the patrol rode away.

"Where did you come from?"

"I followed this stream to where I thought you might be."

"Where's Isabella?"

"She's at the Fangs, waiting for us. She sent me to find you."

"Take me to her. We are running out of time."

When they reached the Fangs, Isabella was gone.

"Where could she be?"

"Look here, I see footprints. Wait, there are two sets. Then only one set onto this path. They are smaller, like Isabella's. We have to find her!" said Stefan, his voice rising with concern.

Isabella trekked in the dwindling light until she found herself stumbling in the dark. She continued despite bruised shins and scratches from low branches. Once the moon rose, her progress improved. She snapped branches whenever she could in the hope that Stefan and Telly might follow her trail. On more than one occasion she thought she heard a large animal prowling nearby. The prospect of confronting a hungry lynx or pack of wolves kept her moving quickly. She thought of the attack of the snow leopard in the cave of Zalmoxis and how they had barely avoided disaster.

Weariness began to seep into her limbs. Isabella resisted the urge to rest, knowing that falling asleep would risk missing the pyramid. The fate of their mission depended on her perseverance. With Stefan and Telly somewhere behind her, it was imperative that she find the entrance to the Forges of Ezrok.

When the moon reached its apex, Isabella had enough light to adopt a steady pace. To help keep rhythm, she resurrected the mantra they had chanted while on the Alpine Sea.

"Do not lose faith. This is our destiny."

Repetition of this refrain got her through the night. She cleared a ridge on one of the mountains as the sky lightened. She made it!

Not knowing what to expect, Isabella checked the map and continued to descend to the valley floor. She concentrated her attention behind her for any sign of her companions. A wave of doubt flowed over her. Had she been rash in abandoning

Chapter 17

her post? Had she lost sight of her primary mission to protect Stefan? She bit her lower lip in self-recrimination.

"Do not lose faith. This is our destiny."

Isabella settled onto a log and waited. The sun gradually rose into a sparkling, clear sky. After a night of marching, a slight patina of perspiration covered her. She shivered in the breeze. Her mind was tuned for any communication from Telly. Silence prevailed.

The sun cleared the ridge opposite her position and, almost instantaneously, a three-dimensional pyramid materialized in the space between the two mountains. She gasped at its enormity. Her heart leapt in her chest and she thanked God for the privilege of experiencing this phenomenon. Her eyes widened as she scoured the area for an indication of where the entrance was. *All I need is a clue*, she thought. Then, she saw a weak blinking along the base of the pyramid. Maybe it was a facet on a piece of quartz reflecting through the rustling leaves. When it persisted, she walked toward it.

Darn, she chided herself, she forgot to mark the exact time the pyramid appeared. Ciobanul had been quite insistent that the pyramid would only be there for eighty minutes. She hastened her step while she questioned herself about how much time had elapsed. *Time is a relentless arrow speeding toward its target heedless of those in its path.*

Her pulse raced as she neared the blinking light. She found nothing. Dread spread over her like ink in a cup of water as she comprehended that all their efforts might be for naught if she didn't find the entrance.

Out of frustration, Isabella picked up a quartz rock. She was about to heave it as far as she could when a beam of sunlight struck it and bounced across the valley where it reflected off a stone and back to a rock wall behind her. The ricochet of the light beam was like a magical arrow flying through space locked onto its intended target.

The ground under her rumbled. Instinctively, she reached for something to brace herself. Like a stone rolling aside to open a tomb, the wall slid open. Isabella crossed herself and ran to the opening. Inside was a stairway down. *To where, she wondered?*

Isabella peered in and saw nothing but darkness. She considered using her flute to summon *zine* for illumination, but refrained. Her concern for her friends was paramount. *Where are you?*

The rising of the sun well above the ridge was a reminder of how tenuous their situation was. Her eyes scanned the elevations around her in every direction. There was no sign of them. She fell to her knees in despair. Tears brimmed on her eyelids and threatened to overflow into a torrent.

CHAPTER 18

After escaping from his failed attempt to kill Dryger, Vlad rode for days on end. Doubt seeped into his mind as he wandered, map-less. Staying in the shadows and streams, he searched for a sign. Late one afternoon, Vlad saw a rock formation shaped like a bell tower. *That must be it.*

A gale wind whistled between the tower and the adjacent mountain, a testament to the creation of a unique formation by centuries of abrasion. A glorious sunset between the tower and the mount reminded him that he needed a place to camp. He spied a cave in the mountain near the tower. After refreshing in a nearby stream, Vlad built a fire and set a pot of water to boil for his *mamaliga*.

He fashioned a makeshift torch and explored the cave. The floor was level as if chiseled by human hands. Well within the cave, he discovered a larger area configured as a meeting place. A dome-like ceiling was decorated with paintings of celestial figures. He recognized different constellations of the night sky. At the apex of the dome, he got a glimpse of the sky. This cave must be at the base of the rock formation which appeared like a bell tower. The sound of faint whistling indicated that it was safe to build a fire here.

By the time he returned to his campfire, his pot had boiled dry. He refilled the pot and resigned himself to a meal the flavor of burnt metal. This time he paid more attention to his cooking. He would explore the cave later when his belly was satisfied. Thoughts of his cousin Stefan flooded his mind.

Where had the mysterious woman in white taken him and Rico? Were they safe and warm, he wondered as he pulled his blanket over his shoulders to ward off the chill? What types of adventures were they having? What dangers were they facing? Vlad's imagination drew him into all sorts of wild scenarios which he dismissed saying to himself that life is never that exciting.

Although the moon was bright, clouds would soon obscure it. He moved inside. Once the fire was blazing and his bed roll set, he explored the room. The walls were covered with paintings of symbols and primitive icons. In a niche at the head of the room he found remnants of candles and what appeared to be burnt offerings. This must be an area of religious worship. He crossed himself and kissed the Order of the Dragon pendant hanging from his neck. A vision of his father floated into Vlad's mind. *Papa, next time I will succeed. For now, you have to be satisfied with an eye.*

As if the wind crossing the opening of the tower was a lullaby bringing rest, Vlad fell asleep. His subconscious drifted to recent events. The wind increased and it brought dreams of serenading the young gypsy girl in Reuseni and the pleasure they shared behind the wagons. Before long the wind turned into a gale and his reverie rose in intensity. Vlad was standing behind Stefan watching Petru Aron prance around the fiery camp brandishing Bogdan's head. Then, he and Stefan were mounted, racing away from danger. The wind increased, seemingly in sync with their pace. The tempest

Chapter 18

reverberated through the tower creating a mournful howl. The sound grew to a crescendo which awakened Vlad at the moment he released the bowstring.

Drenched in sweat, Vlad sat up. The fire was reduced to embers and in the dim light he took stock of where he was and returned his head to his bundled cloak. Trying to erase the image of Dryger from his mind, he stared at the wall paintings.

His gaze settled on one which was in front of a semi-circular bench. It depicted winged creatures, some with equine bodies with white tusks and others with human forms, their faces tattooed with alien symbols. The background was cobalt blue with slashes of bright yellow shaped like lightning. The tableau recorded a cosmic battle with cohorts of armed figures confronting each other.

When sleep returned, Vlad was seated in a lyceum of learning with others. The sun beat down on them as they waited for the teacher. A towering figure with a ginger beard glided into their space. The cowl of his white cape covered his head and eyes. Cinched around his waist was a leather belt bearing unrecognizable tools, no doubt with unique attributes.

"You would not be able to pronounce my formal name. You will address me as Molie."

A crack of thunder echoed through the cave. Vlad tossed and almost awoke. The storm moved rapidly and the noise subsided into a steady patter. Vlad settled back to sleep.

"You are the result of a fervent search for students of exceptional abilities. If you complete your studies at Solomanta successfully, you will be a member of the finest. If you fail, you will plunge into eternal servitude."

Molie told them that every night he would teach them magic secrets, the language of animals, and spells to vanquish their enemies. When a blue luminescence in the opening above them signaled the dawn, Molie wrapped himself in his cape and dissolved.

Vlad felt velvet lips nuzzle his cheek. As he edged toward consciousness, he envisioned the gypsy girl snuggling next to him. His dream and vision evaporated into reality. He was staring into the face of his horse who had entered the cave to avoid the storm. Vlad stroked the muzzle and whispered words of comfort to his only friend at the moment.

Vlad exited the warmth of the cave to find several inches of snow on the ground. The whiteness imparted a gentleness to the landscape that would have been pleasing if Vlad had not been fleeing from evildoers bent on his demise. He spent the day gathering plants and roots to make a stew or potion.

That evening back in the cave, he fell into a deep sleep. Once again, Vlad dreamed he was seated in a lyceum of learning. Molie glided into the space and pointed to various objects on his leather belt.

"These are the essential tools of our craft. Who can identify this?" he said withdrawing a slender wooden stick from a holster.

"It's a wand."

"*Da*, and every conjurer uses it for protection and as a weapon. And what is this?" he asked lifting a silver metal mesh device by its handle.

"It's a bug cage."

"A receptacle for coins?"

"Tea strainer."

"I'm afraid you are not even close. It's a soul catcher."

Without pausing, Molie produced another device. Tubular with a molded grip which came to a metal point, it had a clear glass reservoir of red liquid.

"It's a pen."

Chapter 18

"What type of pen?"
"For love letters?"
"To write curses?"
"How?"
"Dunno."
"It's called a blood stylus."
"What's it do?"

"It creates a blood tattoo under the skin of your subject which guarantees that they will always tell you the truth."

Molie surveyed the class as they processed this information. The pupils were leaning forward on the edge of the benches exchanging excited glances as they tried to curry favor with the teacher with their cleverness and alacrity. All except one who leaned back as if he were a spectator. The teacher nodded to Vlad. Challenge accepted.

When Vlad awoke the next morning, he again went foraging. He returned to the cave as the sun slipped behind the mountain range. After eating a modest meal, he fell into a deep sleep. He dreamed of benches in front of a vast mural painted in vivid colors. There were subtle changes to the painting as if a new layer of detail had been applied. This version contained all sorts of creatures from mythology – griffins, centaurs, dragons and an androgynous bald figure. Molie appeared out of thin air. His red beard bobbed like the head of a parrot as he explained the characteristics of the legendary beasts.

"Over the next days and weeks, you will learn how to summon and master these creatures. Most of you will be able to bend them to your will. Only the best will learn to call the dragon and ride it to your destiny. If you work hard and practice the lessons in your books, you can be that special student. Follow me."

Molie guided the students to cave opening. It led to a massive cavern which enclosed a lake as large as the top of a volcano. There was no discernible source of light except the luminescence rising from below the surface. Hot humid air stinking of decomposed eggs engulfed them. Steamy vapor clouds hovered over the surface of the water which was an iridescent swirl of vibrant colors. The instructor brought them to a perch over the lake and motioned for them to kneel toward the far end of the lake.

To maintain quiet, Molie used hand language. He explained that this was an ancient birthing chamber and they were about to witness the miracle of the birth of a brood of dragons. In some ancient codices this was called Lake Amnios. No sooner had he signed this, a large dragon with a swollen belly approached the far shore. It roared in distress as it waddled into the shallow water. When its belly was submerged, the great tail swung around and under its legs. The beast settled into a semi-reclining position supported by it wings.

Waves rippled toward them and lapped against their perch. Molie warned them to avoid contact with the water. Several students in the first row failed to protect themselves. Where water touched their skin, ghastly red pustules erupted. Molie assured the afflicted that, though painful, these sores would heal in a few days.

The dragon bellowed in what could only be described as anguish. Molie directed their attention to the water several yards from where the belly met the water. First one, then another a translucent bubble popped to the surface. With each howl another bubble appeared, until there were six in all.

Vlad leaned forward to gain a better view. Uplit by the volcanic light, he saw miniature dragons, each complete with wings and four legs. Molie explained that these bubbles contained dragon emuki in the late stage of formation. They would float in the birthing lake for several weeks receiving oxygen and nourishment. When they were fully developed, the bubbles would burst and the emuki would find their way to the lair.

Freed from the confines of the dragon belly, the emuki stretched and moved in their bubbles. Vlad noticed that one of the emuki was inanimate in its bubble. Recovered from its ordeal, the dragon was back on its feet. It was examining the bubbles when it saw the stillness in one of the bubbles. As quick as a spark from flint on steel, the dragon spewed flames at the bubble with such ferocity that the bubble sank. When the smoking lump bobbed to the surface, the dragon seized it and thrust it into its gaping mouth.

Molie signaled that with that dramatic end, the class on dragon birth was over.

CHAPTER 19

Back in the wilderness, the travelers continued to search for the Shepherd's Shadow and each other. For Stefan and Telly, the night had been one of frantic scrambling in the dark. It did not take long to detect an occasional broken twig on the path which Isabella had left as a sign. They could not be certain that every broken twig was made by Isabella. Instead of speeding their trek, it slowed them down as they examined each clue to discern whether it was a true marker, or happenstance. On more than one occasion, they veered off course due to an imagined clue.

"This is not good. It is costing us valuable time, Stefan."

"Do you have a better idea?"

"Yes, the next time we see a questionable clue, we split up and each follows a different path."

"We cannot split up, Telly. We never split up! That, will only guarantee that one of us will be wrong. Shhh, what was that?"

"You mean the rustling in the brush back there?"

Stefan nodded while withdrawing his dagger.

Chapter 19

"It's a pack of wolves which has been following us for a while."

"And when were you going to let me in on this secret?" Stefan hissed.

He heard several forms padding through the brush around them. Fiendish yellow eyes appeared on dark shadowy figures around them. Stefan searched for a tree to use as protection from attack from behind. He looked down for Telly. The octopus was gone, camouflaged.

"Telly, that is not helping me. Do something!"

"*Si, da*. I've never tried this before, but it might work."

The head of a large alpha male rose from the bushes. In the moonlight, Stefan could see his long, canine teeth dripping saliva in anticipation of a late-night meal.

"Telly, hurry," urged Stefan as several more wolves came into view. They were crouching slightly, preparing to attack. Telly's telepathic voice boomed.

"Attention, all wolves! We are not worth your trouble."

The leader stopped. He cocked his head as if trying to comprehend what had just happened in his head.

"Keep going, Telly. It's working."

"We are sure that you are hungry and want to eat us, but we are poisonous. You will get sick and die a painful death if you attack us."

The pack howled a baleful cry. They mimicked the leader who relaxed from his crouch into a stance that was more curious than menacing.

"Have you ever seen such strange creatures as us? No, we are messengers from the Great Alpha. Do not interfere with us or you risk the infernal wrath of the Zeuta, the wolf-dragon of Dacia and warrior companion of Zalmoxis."

Stefan inched closer to Telly, thinking 'I hope that these wolves do not consider Zeuta and Zalmoxis their enemies.'

At Telly's proclamation, the leader sat back on his haunches. A quizzical look took over his face as if he were trying to formulate a response. Then, in gruff, halting language, he communicated with Telly. Stefan watched in amazement.

"What is he saying?"

"He says that the Great Alpha has foretold of the coming of strange creatures that become invisible. The teachings of the pack say that it is to give safe passage to these strangers."

Behind the leader, the next largest wolf spoke in a menacing canine voice which was more of a growl than words.

Stefan shot a questioning look toward Telly.

"He is advising the leader that only one of us is invisible," came the telepathic answer.

Several members of the pack resumed a pre-attack posture. The leader growled to Telly for a response. Stefan contemplated rushing the leader and bringing his dagger to his throat. The wolf was as muscular as he was large. On his hind legs he would stand taller than Stefan. Even if Stefan could surprise the leader and was able to grab his throat, he would not be able to hold him still. Plus, Stefan would be exposed to attacks by the rest of the pack. They would tear him to pieces. As he visualized how such a scenario was likely to play out, Stefan recalled the admonition of Bogdan that when confronted with superior force, finesse and subtlety were better weapons than brute force.

A pronouncement by Telly interrupted his train of thought.

"Behold Stefan the Great who traces his lineage to Zalmoxis. He is a fierce warrior who rescued Zeuta-Draco

Chapter 19

from the evil clutches of the barbarians when they hunted the wolf packs of the steppes."

Sensing the wolves' reverence for Zeuta-Draco, Telly pressed on.

"Stefan nursed Zeuta back to health from grievous wounds. Zeuta was so grateful that he decreed that Stefan would forever be called *Lupusor,* Child of the Wolf."

The wolf pack relaxed the tension in their limbs. Some of the smaller members of the pack began vocalizing in what Stefan interpreted as a joyful refrain. Stefan stood before the pack with his hands at his sides and his eyes lowered in humility. Telly sidled over to him, telepathing for to him to stay still. Before he could assent, Stefan was plunged in an eerie half-light as Telly enveloped him. The sensation was unlike anything Stefan had ever experienced. It was as if he had returned to the womb. He detected light and blurry shapes through Telly's pliable, membranous skin.

In unison, each member of the wolf pack lowered his head in submission. The eyes of the leader darted anxiously, hoping that they had not offended the special visitors.

"We have no time to waste. The Great Alpha has foretold this moment. Oh, mighty leader, we want you to take us to the Shepherd's Shadow where the pyramid comes when the sun is low."

The leader seemed to evaluate this information. He nodded.

"What's going on, Telly?"

"He says that he knows of this place. It is sacred. He and his followers will take us there."

"What are we waiting for? Let's go!"

The head wolf sprinted ahead, followed by the travelers. The pack ran alongside like a regal escort. As the sky lightened,

Shepherd's Shadow loomed closer. Stefan had trouble keeping the pace. His legs grew heavy and he began to falter. He signaled to Telly to go on ahead, that he would catch up.

"Oh, no! You were the one who said 'We never split up!' I will ask the leader for help."

Moments later the strange convoy stopped. Sweat drenched Stefan. He doubled over, hands on his knees, wheezing to catch his breath.

"Stefan, the leader says his warriors will carry you, but you have to lie face down so that your weight will be evenly distributed on four of them."

At some silent command, four wolves lined up in front of Stefan, offering their backs. He lowered his torso onto the first pair and lifted his legs onto the second pair. Wrapping his arms around the necks and his legs around the ribs of his 'carriage,' Stefan secured the Zalmoxis tube across his back.

With nary an audible sound, the convoy moved out. It took Stefan a few minutes to adjust to the rhythm of the wolves. He felt the sharp bristles of their fur on his face and marveled at their effortless breathing as they covered great stretches of terrain. Freed from the agony of the run, Stefan's thoughts turned to Isabella and the pyramid. He looked at the brightening sky and prayed.

As they neared the mountain, Stefan saw the ephemeral pyramid rising tall against the backdrop of the other peaks. The ridge leading to the valley was ahead when Stefan noticed the eastern side of the pyramid flicker. Fearing that the window of the pyramid's appearance was closing, Stefan urged his carriers to quicken the pace. They responded to this command by lowering their heads and sprinting across the ridge as though propelled toward the finish line of a mythic race.

Chapter 19

With each second, the sun traveled its inexorable path to the west. To Stefan's horror, the pyramid seemed to fade with the passing sun. At last, they cleared the ridge and careened into the valley. Telly saw her first. Isabella was standing before a rock wall on the western edge of the pyramid. Tenaculating furiously, Telly shouted their arrival. Isabella looked toward them and waved frantically with both arms. Stefan watched as her face turned incredulous as they got closer.

"Hurry! Hurry!" she yelled. "The door is closing."

Sure enough, Stefan heard a low rumble and felt a vibration through the limbs of the wolves.

"Take us to that woman at the opening as quickly as you can!" Telly exhorted the alpha leader. The sprint turned into a manic dash.

Isabella pressed against the stone door in a futile effort to slow its progress. The passage through was shrinking rapidly. Telly made it first and vaulted into the opening. He thanked the lead wolf profusely while he watched Stefan's escort straining with every bit of energy.

As they neared the door, they skidded to a stop. Stefan went flying over them and sailed toward the opening. He hit the door and fell, stunned. The door inched further toward closing. Isabella grabbed Stefan under the armpits. She dragged Stefan toward the rumbling door. Telly watched in horror as the stone poised to crush Stefan's legs.

The octopus slithered next to Isabella. Stretching his tentacles to their fullest, he snatched Stefan's ankles into the cave as the door crashed against the jamb. They collapsed in a heap inside the cave. Stefan came to his senses in the dark. He rubbed the bump on his forehead where he had hit the stone door. He groaned.

In a rush of panic, he blurted, "The tube! Where's the tube?"

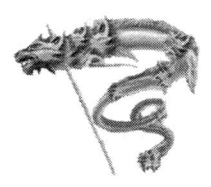

CHAPTER 20

The blackness within the cave was so complete that for a second, Stefan imagined that he had gone blind. Raising his hand to his forehead, he felt the stickiness of blood. The last thing he remembered was hurtling toward the stone door when the wolves screeched to a stop. How could that be? Where was he? From the hard rock he sat on, he knew he wasn't home. As his senses returned, his situation solidified.

Isabella shimmied toward him.

"Oh, Stefan, I'm so glad you are safe!"

She reached over and hugged him. Stefan leaned into her hug and closed his eyes, wishing he was back at home with her. He fought the urge to succumb to the reality that home as he knew it no longer existed. Full alertness returned and Stefan reached on the ground beside him.

"The tube! Where's the tube?"

"Not to worry," said Telly. "I saw it lying on the ground after we carried you in. I pulled it to safety as the door slammed shut. Having eight arms comes in handy."

Telly nudged the tube into Stefan's hands. He breathed a sigh of relief when he pulled it to his chest and kissed it.

"Now what?"

"I guess we have no choice but to summon the *zine*," said Isabella, reaching for her flute.

"Isabella, that did not work out so well when you tried it after crossing the Alpine Sea. Plus, I doubt that they can hear you from inside this sealed rock chamber."

"Wait," said Telly. "I think I can help."

Telly reared up on his four back tentacles and extended the front tentacles to their full width. He activated the bioluminescence in his suckers. Suddenly, the passageway was illuminated with a neon blue light.

Stefan was spellbound.

"Is there anything you cannot do?"

Telly issued the octopus version of a chuckle.

"Time to get back on task, we have a sword that needs fixing."

As they progressed downward, a low hum rose up toward them. At first, they thought that the sound was machinery. At some point they understood that the sound was human voices speaking in an indecipherable jumble. They were afraid that the voices meant enemies. As they closed the gap, the voices took on a cadence like parishioners marching in procession repeating a Gregorian chant.

Up ahead the tunnel widened into a cavernous opening, dimly lit with torches. Huddled against the wall, the three friends peeked around the corner to see a line of men dressed in rough fabric overalls, thick leather gloves and sturdy boots. The people shuffled mindlessly toward a tunnel in the cavern wall.

Stefan pointed to the opposite end of the cavern. Similarly-clad figures walked from another tunnel carrying baskets filled

Chapter 20

with large, cloudy crystals. They dumped the contents onto a wagon and followed the line back to the tunnel.

"They must be mining crystals," said Stefan.

"Why are their movements so stiff?" asked Telly.

"It looks like they are under a spell which imposes a collective group mind. Once that happens, they are controlled by an egregore. These poor creatures walk an endless loop into the mine, fill their baskets and dump the crystals into the wagons. We've got to free them," said Isabella, rising from their hiding place.

"Not now," whispered Stefan. "We have to avoid coming under the spell ourselves and get to Faur. We can free these drones after we complete our mission."

His companions nodded solemnly and followed Stefan as he made his way along the perimeter. Stefan and Telly knelt to drink some water from a stream which gurgled along the path. As they cupped water in their hands, they remarked about its appealing silvery quality.

Before Isabella knew what was happening, they were humming in cadence with the miners. Isabella dove toward them to swat their hands away from the stream. It was too late. Stefan and Telly had already gulped the accursed water. They stiffened erect and walked toward the miners, falling in line. Isabella watched with her eyes stretched wide as if she were watching a wagon drive off a cliff. As they followed the others into the mine, Isabella did the only thing she could think of, she slipped in behind them.

She mimicked their stiff movements and pretended to load chunks of crystals into a basket. They walked in a widening spiral through the mine in a slow, numbing rhythm. Deprived of natural light and unfettered by normal sounds, the mine took on a surreal quality – artificial and timeless. The stone and support work of the tunnel was so monotonous that she lost track of how far they had traveled. It was akin to the root system of some giant tree. As they proceeded, she observed auxiliary tunnels, snaking off to the left and right. The eerie sounds of wind whistling through the abandoned tunnels reminded her of banshees howling. There was a wounded hunger in the winds haunting the tunnels that made the hair on Isabella's arms prickle.

She had to pinch herself to avoid succumbing to the repetitive chanting. After several hours, she experienced a profound sense of loneliness. It was as if a lamprey had attached to her being, sapping her energy. Looking down was a mistake because it exposed her neck. Drops of frigid water struck her neck and slithered down her spine spreading a chill through her body.

Whenever they turned a corner, Isabella tried to push them or whisper to them. It was no use. Nothing roused them from the spell.

Her legs felt leaden from the shuffling pace, her eyes strained in the darkness, her throat was scratched raw from the dust. On the verge of despair, Isabella wracked her brain for something that might counteract the spell. In front of her, Stefan followed the cadence like a worker bee. Telly must have reverted to camouflage mode because Isabella lost track of him.

That's it, screamed Isabella to herself. I have to find the egregore, the source of this psychic power and stop it. Her step quickened as she spied a beam of light that surely led to an opening. Isabella left the line and stooped into a low tunnel. As she reached a large rock formation, a flutter of wings burst toward her. She hit the ground to avoid the creatures rushing over her.

Chapter 20

"Bats."

Isabella watched as a colony of bats passed over her. Despite covering her ears, Isabella was overwhelmed by the sounds of leathery wings flapping and the high-pitched shrieking of the bats as they navigated through the tunnel. Revulsion swept over her like an insatiable animal as she crawled over viscous bat guano. The musty acrid smell permeated her nostrils. It was all Isabella could do to avoid retching. She steeled herself against the smell and slime of the guano and crawled toward the light. When she finally reached the opening, a pair of burly guards were waiting for her. They seized her under her arms and dragged her kicking and screaming toward an ogre of a man.

"What do we have here?"

"We saw an unusual flurry of bats from one of the side tunnels and found this one crawling out, Sir," said the senior guard. The other guard held Isabella from behind, pinning her arms back in a painful grip.

"Take her to my vault."

The guards led her through the huge cavern past rows upon rows of cargo wagons. Before she was roughly thrust into a stone chamber, Isabella saw the egregore. A carved wooden image of an unidentifiable person stood in a glass-lined booth. Like a marionette operated by strings, the egregore pulsed in concert with the chants of the drone miners.

The vault was lit by torches which gave off grimy black smoke as they sputtered. The guards forced Isabella into a rough-hewn chair and tied her wrists to the armrests. She faced a massive table, littered with books, scrolls and drawings. When the guards left, she heard someone or something breathing. The sound came from a darkened corner of the room. Smarting from the acrid smoke, her eyes could not penetrate the darkness.

Minutes turned into hours of waiting. Isabella's mouth was parched and her wrists were chafed from the coarse rope that bound them. The constant chanting of the drones had a hypnotic effect on her. She stared forward, hardly blinking.

A flood of light startled her when the door opened. The master entered and sat behind the table. Two guards flanked the entrance. Isabella straightened and looked at her captor. He was a large, heavily-muscled brute of a man. A multitude of tattoos covered his arms and face. The deep blue ink depicted dragons, devils, and maidens burning at stakes. His narrow pig-eyes squinted at her.

"Who are you? And, what are you doing skulking around my mine?"

"I wasn't skulking. I . . ." said Isabella. The sound of a ham-like fist slamming onto the table interrupted her. It struck with such force that several scrolls rolled off and onto the floor. She flinched into silence.

"Who are you?"

"My name is Isabella. I am looking for Faur, the cosmic blacksmith."

"Why?"

"My purpose is for only him to know."

Another crash brutalized the desk.

"You will tell me!"

"I cannot . . . sir."

"If you cannot, maybe he can."

He nodded to the guards who marched to the dark corner and dragged a body into view. Isabella pressed her lips together and squeezed her eyes shut. A single tear from each eye rolled down her cheeks. It was Stefan. He was hog-tied,

Chapter 20

blindfolded and gagged. The guards unshackled him enough to thrust him onto a chair where he wobbled, almost falling.

Another nod directed the guards to remove the blindfold and gag. Stefan inhaled deeply. He blinked.

"Isabella!"

Before she could respond, the ogre-man thundered, "Why do you seek Faur?"

"Our destiny has brought us to Faur for help with a special project."

"What is this project?"

"I am not at liberty to say. Only to Faur, himself," said Stefan in a tone of defiant finality.

"You forfeited your liberty when you trespassed into my crystal mines. Now, tell me the nature of your business with Faur, or, I will resort to unpleasant measures to loosen your tongues."

Addressing the guards, Adnor said, "Rouse the torturer-in-chief and tell it to prepare the chamber." He added matter-of-factly, "I'm going to change into something more suitable for blood."

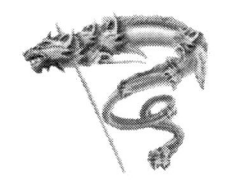

CHAPTER 21

A sense of dread enveloped Stefan. He and Isabella were held captive by a brutal slave-master who was intent on torturing them. He seemed well-acquainted with torture techniques, after all, who has a torturer-in-chief on staff unless it is a regular part of your operation. Stefan thought (hoped) that he could withstand torture, but he could not bear the thought of Isabella being tortured. *Where was that octopus when you needed him most?*

Before Adnor reached the door, there was a commotion in the cavern. With silent fanfare, a man dressed in a vibrant red uniform, different from the other guards, entered the room. He marched to the table and bowed. He was about one half the size of the man he addressed and his skin was buttercup yellow. With his cute little tricorn hat, he looked more like a garden ornament than a diplomat. His demeanor was that of a no-nonsense military officer who was used to being obeyed.

"M'lord Adnor, I have been sent here to request that you immediately release these prisoners into my custody."

"I'm afraid that is not possible. We have scheduled a torture session for them. You know how difficult it is to

Chapter 21

arrange for a competent torture crew, what with all the turmoil in the land above."

"As a show of good faith, my master has delivered ten barrels of wine and twelve sides of beef as collateral for their return in the event that the claim made by these prisoners is invalid."

Adnor grunted his assent, disappointed at the lost opportunity. He nodded to his guards who untied the prisoners. Rubbing their wrists, Isabella and Stefan followed the red uniform.

"Where's the tube?" whispered Isabella.

Stefan reached for the strap on his shoulder. A look of surprise and dismay crossed his face. With a pained expression, he shrugged.

"Right this way, please," said the emissary who opened a coach door for them. Stefan followed Isabella into the vehicle. Their deliverer smiled as he sat opposite them.

"My name is Calin, chamberlain to Lord Faur."

That was all he said as the coach rumbled through a tunnel traveling on a downward trajectory. An eerie darkness surrounded them as the coach bounced along. With the clip-clop of the horses' hooves echoing off the stone walls, Stefan wondered where the tube was. His last recollection before awakening in Adnor's chamber, was drinking from the silvery stream. Since they were underground again, he had no way to tell how much time had passed. Where was Telly? Where was the tube? Without it, all this sacrifice was meaningless. He glanced at Isabella who was biting her lower lip as her hands fingered an imaginary rosary.

As the coach descended along a winding path into the bowels of the earth, the temperature rose. Both of them perspired profusely while the diminutive emissary showed no signs of the heat. They lost all concept of time or place during the ride. When they finally arrived, Isabella exhaled a sigh of relief and sent a reassuring smile toward Stefan who returned a wan smile.

"Follow me, please," said Calin.

They stood before a stone structure which seemed oddly out of place. It was a proper cottage with a decidedly feminine air. It was enclosed by an elaborate wrought iron fence. Delicate metal creatures ranging from eagles, to foxes, and turtles adorned the fence. Inside the gates was a veritable Garden of Eden containing flowers of every description captured in exquisite detail, each with enameled petals of vibrant cloisonné. Among the most stunning were the roses, lilies, and tulips. As Stefan absorbed this beauty, he sensed that there was something missing, just what it was eluded him.

Calin brought them to a room and told them to make themselves comfortable. The furnishings were made of metal hammered into textures which belied their composition. Stefan and Isabella exchanged anxious glances. The stone floor vibrated. Stefan braced his legs in case he had to bolt upright. They watched the door knob twist. Calin entered and, mustering as much dignity as he could, announced, "All rise for Lord Faur, blacksmith to the gods."

At long last, they set eyes on Faur who walked past them toward Calin who had scurried to an object covered by a large sheet. With a flourish worthy of a stage magician, he whipped the covering away to reveal a bejeweled throne. When Faur was comfortably ensconced, Calin withdrew, bowing low.

Faur had a noble bearing and regarded them with a look that was a mixture of disdain and weary curiosity, as if there was a minimal possibility that they might offer something useful. He wore a sleeveless leather vest over his bare chest.

Chapter 21

Tapered slashes scarred his massive arms. Isabella surmised that these marks came from fragments of hot metal which sparked from his anvil. There was something about his ruddy face that evoked a sense of profound sadness. From the haunted look in his dark eyes, to his haggard cheeks, and the downward etching of the lines of his face, Faur was the picture of loss.

"What brings you to my domain?"

Stefan searched his memory for the appropriate protocol. He remembered his father once telling him about meeting the Pope and how he handled that honor. Stefan stepped forward, bowed, and reached to kiss the gigantic ring on Faur's hand. Faur waved him away.

"I asked you a question."

Isabella opened her mouth to speak, but, Faur silenced her by raising a thickly callused hand. He glowered at Stefan and braced his hands on the arms of his throne as if he was about to rise.

"We come to the mighty Faur because he is the only one capable of repairing the celestial sword."

Intrigued, Faur relaxed his grip on the armrests and leaned forward. He grunted for Stefan to continue.

"When Man slayed Kogiaonon, the sword broke in two after he cleaved the giant's head."

"Who told you this fairy tale?"

Stefan appeared stumped at the simplicity of the question. He started to say that it is a saga told by every parent over the generations. Something warned him that his inquisitor sought an answer beyond the obvious. Stefan stroked his upper lip in thought. During the ordeal of the last months, his moustache had thickened. It was now a luxurious, chestnut brown.

"Zalmoxis. We found the scrolls of Zalmoxis along with the broken sword. The prophet stated that only the mighty Faur could repair the sword and restore the kingdom."

"*Blathra.* Where is this mythical sword?"

Faur's eyes danced like those of a cat toying with a helpless mouse. Stefan cast his eyes down, praying for inspiration. With a pained expression, Stefan peeked toward Isabella, but her expression was as barren as her mind.

"Calin, these humans are wasting my time. Escort them away."

After all their trials and hardships, to come this close, only to fail was too much. Mustering his last vestige of dignity, Stefan took Isabella's elbow and turned to leave. Something near the blacksmith caught Stefan's eye. As they passed the fireplace, Stefan grabbed a poker and rushed toward Faur. He swung the poker down hard. It made a squishy sound when it struck something next to the blacksmith. Slowly, a dazed octopus shed his camouflage and appeared. Stefan used the poker to lift several tentacles to reveal the Zalmoxis tube.

Faur's expression went from alarm to stunned amusement when Stefan opened the tube and withdrew the sword pieces. Quaking like the eruption of Vesuvius, Faur's belly shook with laughter. He laughed so hard that he lost his breath. As he gasped for air, Faur's ruddy face turned as crimson as the burning coals of his forges.

"I was going to return you to Adnor's mines as slaves, but I must say that I have never seen a more spectacular turnaround. Please sit."

Isabella complied while Stefan and Telly bickered.

"What in God's name were you doing?"

"I was protecting the tube in case he was not the blacksmith we are looking for."

Chapter 21

"You are unbelievable!"

"Who do you think told Calin that you were prisoners of Adnor? It was me, Telly."

"Shhh," admonished Isabella.

"Calin, show our guests to the Lodge so they can freshen up before dinner. In the meantime, I will examine this sword."

As they exited, Stefan snuck a backwards glance at Faur whose expression had changed dramatically from gentility to something else. Was it avarice? Stefan signaled for Telly to stay behind undercover and keep watch over the sword lest their host take it for himself. Telly responded with a four-tentacle salute while he faded into camo-mode.

Stefan had to admit that despite his annoying tendencies, the octopus could be useful at times.

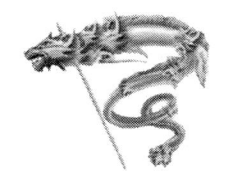

CHAPTER 22

Like any good chamberlain, Calin took his cue from his master. His initial contact with Stefan and Isabella had been business-like, sharing only needed information. Now that Faur had decided against banishing them, Calin adopted an air of friendliness. He spoke effusively about Faur's estate, giving them a tour of the metallic gardens that his liege had crafted over the centuries. His buttercup skin transformed to a bright saffron yellow when he described his master's floral creations. Stefan reflected on how the pigment of the chamberlain's skin varied with his moods. Interesting.

"Faur adores flowers. He travels above ground on occasion to draw inspiration from their delicate forms. He tries to re-create the intricacy of their structure in his artwork," said Calin as he gestured toward a bed of daffodils.

"How does he get the metal so thin that it appears so lifelike, so translucent?"

"Ah, Isabella, you have a sharp eye. Faur is a cosmic blacksmith with unsurpassed skill. He spends untold hours fabricating each petal until it is wafer thin. Then, he coats them with the thinnest layer of enamel which he formulates himself by crushing gems and crystals."

Chapter 22

"The colors are as vibrant as I would imagine the blossoms in the Garden of Eden," said Stefan.

"Yes, Faur has sought inspiration from there. And, I'd say he has succeeded. Although I must tell you his biggest frustration is the lack of fragrance. He works on that incessantly; yet, without success. Faur complains that the only smell he experiences is the acrid odor of the forge. He thinks it may come from the reaction of the metal with skin, but I don't know. That sounds improbable to me."

"Ah, we have arrived at the Lodge. This way, please."

They walked through a massive metal door which was decorated with detailed reliefs and embossings.

"These doors are magnificent," remarked Stefan.

"Faur invented the art of Toreutics. These are some of his masterworks."

"Toreutics?" asked Isabella.

"It is the art of creating surface ornamentation on metal. Using rare acids and distillates, Faur developed this process which decorates without weakening the metal."

"I have seen this before," said Stefan with a starry look. "Of course, this . . . toreutics are on the blade of the sword . . ."

"Yes, that is how Faur identified the sword you brought as genuine. Here are your rooms. Uh, where is your friend with all those arms?"

"Telly? Oh, he slipped into one of the fountain pools a while back. He needs to replenish," said Stefan, stepping into his room.

Calin shrugged at the abrupt end of the discussion. He figured that they must be tired or they were up to something. As Stefan closed the door, he noticed a slight yellow brilliance spark on Calin's face.

"I'll return for you at seven. Ring the bell near the bed if you need anything."

Faur experienced a feeling akin to the discovery of a long-lost set of keys when he examined the bisected sword. He admired the fine balance and handiwork of the pommel and pictured himself polishing the finished product eons ago. Carrying the hilt end of the sword, the smithy hummed to himself as he went to a bookshelf stuffed with tomes, scrolls, and detailed metallurgical recipes. Using a jeweler's loupe, he examined the ricasso where the blade intersected with the cross guard. Withdrawing of the most ancient books, Faur riffled through it until he reached the page he sought. His finger glided down searching a list of symbols and corresponding names.

"Ah, yes," he murmured in a confirmatory grunt. "That one was always careless."

To Faur, this was not just a sword, it was a piece of him. He poured himself into every project, especially those ordered for the heavenly host. To hold this precious object again made him momentarily forget his immense sadness. It sparked a determination to remedy the desecration of his masterpiece while at the same time solving his dilemma. A cursory evaluation revealed that multiple layers of the blade would have to be reconstructed. This was imperative to ensure a strong, transverse ridge that would withstand maximum force on impact. His mind worked furiously on calculations for implementing a series of interlocking layers of different composition which he would plait then pound to mend the break. The last thing he wanted was his reputation destroyed when the blade shattered when stressed in battle. No, this was a project that was more daunting than manufacturing a new sword. His excitement produced a slight upturn at the corners of his mouth.

Faur had a bounce in his step as he entered his workshop. Out of habit, he put on his long, leather apron and sat at his workbench. He withdrew a sketchpad and made notes and drawings of ideas to reconstruct a strong blade. Faur scribbled a list of the different metals, including high-carbon steel and several alloys. He would meld these using pattern welding to produce a blade of incomparable strength, flexibility, and sharpness. His concentration was so intense that he did not seem to notice a shadow made by a slinking figure as he passed in front of one of the torches lighting the shop. Telly conformed to a wooden beam with a vantage point over Faur's shoulder.

"You might as well reveal yourself and come down. I know you are there."

Telly stiffened. Never before had he been detected. How could Faur know he was watching? Telly wondered whether he should try to bluff his way through this when a strange thing happened. Faur turned toward him and spoke without moving his lips.

"Surprised, my friend? Do you think you are the only one who can communicate telepathically? I have been tending these forges for ages, long before your species was even created. I've learned a few tricks along the way."

"But how?"

"I knew you were in my reception chamber even though your friends were unaware."

"You were? Then, why did you almost drive Stefan to tears?"

"I wanted to test his mettle to see if he was worthy of the sword."

"And, you've known that I was here while you examined the sword?"

"Of course, I heard you tell Stefan that you would follow me to keep track of the sword. Now come here next to me and learn something."

Faur spent several hours schooling Telly on the finer points of metallurgy and various techniques of sword making. When Calin chimed the dinner bell, neither wanted to leave.

The chamberlain escorted the guests through Faur's expansive abode, all the while expostulating about the history of the Forges of Ezrok. Standing in the banquet hall, Stefan and Isabella could hardly contain their amazement at the sight of Faur and Telly entering arm-in-tentacle. They were engrossed in mental conversation.

After a bountiful dinner, the conversation turned to the business at hand.

"As I have demonstrated to our friend Telly, the repair of this sword is complex. It will require unique skill to reconstruct the blade to its former strength. The last thing a swordsman would want would be for his sword to snap in two during battle. That might prove fatal," said Faur, pausing for emphasis while casting an admonitory look at Stefan.

"We are confident that the great Faur, the cosmic blacksmith, is the only bladesmith able to make this repair. There are only two questions: one, how long will it take, and, two, what is your price for this service?"

"I will have the sword restored in time for your mission which coincidentally is the price for this work."

On the one hand, Stefan was relieved that Faur did not name a monetary figure because Stefan's belongings consisted of what he carried on his back. On the other hand, there was something ominous lurking within the term mission. Stefan

Chapter 22

nodded and opened his palm as if to say, lay out the mission. A look of profound sadness settled in the giant blacksmith's eyes.

"As you may have surmised, there is something missing in my abode."

He nodded toward an empty chair and place setting which Isabella had noticed but declined to draw attention to out of politeness.

"My wife, my dear Liubove, is a prisoner of *Ismeju*. He is a fiendish dragon who many believe is a fallen angel. His lair is across the valley to the south. This vile creature has teeth the size of a Viking seax. He has two rows of armored plates along his tail which he wields like the deadly war club of Bhima. His most formidable weapon is his ability to shoot fire from his nostrils. *Ismeju* delights in incinerating his foes."

The pupils of Stefan's eyes grew large. He tried to gulp without anyone noticing. Isabella touched his sleeve. Telly refrained from reassuring Stefan because he did not want Faur to eavesdrop on their conversations.

"Your mission has three parts. First, save my wife from this fiend. Second, kill him. And, third, bring me a vial filled with the saliva of *Ismeju*."

He let the scope of the mission sink in.

"During the time you are away on this mission I will fashion a battle helm and crown for you. You will leave once I have repaired Aparator. It is a sword of great power which was lost during the battle of the heavenly host. Under no circumstances is *Ismeju* to gain control over Aparator. He is one of the rebellious angels who was expelled from above. Were he or one of his minions to possess Aparator, I shudder to contemplate the evil he would create."

"You can keep the sword. I cannot do this. Find someone else."

"Stefan, there is no one else."

Those words hung in the air like a sword of Damocles suspended over his head held by a single horsehair. Stefan grew pensive, his eyes looking far off. Faur seized his chance to seal the deal.

"When you return, I will embed the battle helm with magic gemstones. Using the dragon saliva, I will create the stones to work with Aparator. The combination will generate power beyond any seen on this planet. A power so great that your enemies will quake in fear and submit to your demands."

Faur's words created a vision of Stefan wielding that power to vanquish the enemies of Moldova. His thoughts of the peril of a mere mortal confronting a fallen angel were replaced by images of eliminating the pestilence named Petru Aron from this earth.

"One warning, my friend, the saliva must be gathered from *Ismeju* while he is alive. Once the dragon perishes, the magical properties of his saliva die with him. Saliva from a live dragon is essential to the future of your country." He paused. "Any questions?"

Faur looked over his guests and saw blank expressions.

"Good. Calin will take you to your rooms while I prepare everything you will need for your journey. Sleep well. I will see you off bright and early in the morning three days hence."

As Stefan watched the blacksmith exit, the young man felt the enormity of the mission pressing down on him as if he were Atlas holding up the world. The words of assurance from Isabella and Telly were like dull echoes far off in the mountains. Their sentiments drifted into the ether without penetrating their target.

Chapter 22

"I need to work on these problems, so, I'm going to retire early."

"I'm going for a soak," said Telly, who tenaculated toward the fountain.

Stefan watched as Isabella and Calin went down the hall. Moments later they turned a corner toward Isabella's room and were out of sight. Stefan closed his door and sat down at a table to work on plans.

Over the next several days, the trio huddled in Stefan's chambers working on various scenarios which might arise. They took stock of their weapons, including Isabella's flute, Telly's ability to camouflage, and, of course, Aparator.

"Since we are only three, our best chance will be to have a single attack, with you covering my flanks."

"I wish Rico was with us so that he could bolster the center attack with you," said Isabella.

"He'd only get in Stefan's way. You know how clumsy he can be."

Isabella shot Telly a look.

"Enough, Telly. Don't be so petty. Rico's presence would improve our chances," said Stefan.

He wondered how Bogdan would conquer *Ismeju*? His father's military mind would have already devised a brilliant plan and he would be enjoying the companionship of his fellow warriors. Stefan was struggling for days to plan an attack with a woman and an octopus. It was hopeless.

As the days of plans, back-up plans, and contingency plans passed, Stefan's appetite waned and his time sleeping diminished. He experienced headaches and a nervous stomach. Whenever he tried to reach out to Faur, Calin thwarted him saying that Faur was busy repairing the sword and he could not spare a minute. The wait was excruciating.

Isabella watched and feared the toll that it was having on her charge.

At long last the three days passed and they were treated to a farewell dinner in the dining hall.

"My master sends his regrets that he cannot join you on the eve of your departure. He is conducting final stress tests on Aparator before giving one last sharpening. Faur will see you bright and early in the morning."

They ate in silence. Stefan barely touched his food despite the presence of his favorite *placinte.* As usual, Telly gorged himself on what he called free food. Isabella was so occupied studying Stefan that she ate with the stiff movements of a manikin. At the end of the meal, she looked at her empty plate with no memory of tasting any of the food.

Calin escorted them back to their rooms. Telly detoured to the fountains for one last soak. When Calin started to tell Stefan that he would provide a wake-up summons, Stefan interrupted him with an abrupt "No need" and disappeared into his room.

On the appointed day, the noise from the establishment awakening for the day had no effect on him. The halls were vacant as he made his way down to the kitchen for breakfast. Faur was enjoying a hearty breakfast when Stefan entered. Telly sat next to the blacksmith as they huddled over a map. Near the backdoor, Stefan saw the gear Faur had promised. His attention was drawn to a scabbard with the pommel of a sword sticking out. The cross was gilt-bronze. An interlaced design of shiny silver covered the scabbard. Stefan reached for the hilt. The sword seemed to spring from the scabbard. Stefan whipped it in a series of thrusts and parries. With each movement, a melodious humming emanated from the sword.

Chapter 22

"It sounds the way I imagine a celestial choir would – sweet, well-balanced, powerful."

Something strange happened. An inaudible statement entered his head.

"Yes, I think it is the perfect match for you."

Stefan stiffened. The voice in his head was not the one he had become accustomed to hearing. It was not Telly, it was Faur. Stefan dropped the sword. It clattered on the stone floor as Faur and Telly laughed at his surprise. Even their laughter was telepathic, thought Stefan. I must be going mad. His face reddened from a mixture of embarrassment and anger.

Looking over the breakfast spread on the table, Stefan shrugged; his appetite had vanished. He felt like an outsider as Telly and Faur engaged in a discussion of the tactical situation at the dragon's lair. Finally, he blurted out,

"Where's Isabella? We have to leave. Where's Isabella?"

The only sound audible was a kettle boiling gently on the stove. Stefan rose and raced toward the hallway.

"You won't find her, Stefan. Calin has taken her to a secret location. She is safe and will remain our guest until you return from your mission."

"You bastard! You mean she is your prisoner, your hostage!"

"That's a less kind way to say it. But, yes, Isabella is in our custody until you bring my Liubove safely back to me."

Stefan eyed the sword.

"That is not an option, Stefan. Even if you tried to kill me, what would happen to Isabella? What would happen to Aparator? What would happen to your precious Moldova?"

Clenching his jaw, Stefan pounded the table. The dishes rattled and several pieces of cutlery fell to the floor. He inhaled deeply and strode to the gear. Hefting it on to his back, he stomped out the door without uttering goodbye. It did not matter to Faur who was treated to a cacophony of curses in his head the likes of which he had not heard in centuries.

The young man was as angry as he had been since he saw Petru Aron holding his father's severed head by the hair, mocking, as if it were some kind of trophy. Suppressing the urge to retch, Stefan stormed over the path leading to the exit tunnel. Telly came after him, pleading with Stefan to slow down and listen. Stefan placed his hands over his ears in a futile effort to block out the octopus's palaver in his head. Since Telly had the map and was the only dependable source of light, Stefan gestured for Telly to go in front. By allowing the octopus to get far enough ahead to be out of telepathic range, Stefan spared himself having to listen to Telly's inanities.

It did not take Telly long to grasp that Stefan was shunning him. Rather than force the issue, he decided to use the time to work on the epic ballad of their adventures. This was a lot harder than he expected but as the hours passed, he was well along with a composition which would enthrall young and old alike. He was stymied at the stanza about how the brave human and his noble octopus friend slayed the dragon and saved the damsel in distress. Telly concluded that the writing of this stanza would have to wait until they actually did it.

By midday they reached the end of the tunnel. Telly manipulated some hidden mechanism, no doubt revealed to him by Faur, to open a passageway to the valley beyond. Although the trees were bereft of foliage, Stefan could tell that it was a verdant land. He surveyed the landscape and noticed a flurry of activity at an outcropping on the opposite wall of the valley. His jaw dropped when he saw figures flying in and out of a shielded area. *That must be the lair, but what were those flying figures?*

Chapter 22

"Those are the emuki of *Ismeju*," said Telly in a matter-of-fact tone as if it was common knowledge.

"Emuki? What the . . . ?"

"You think only humans have kids, Stefan? The emuki are *Ismeju's* children."

"They look pretty big and they can fly. How are we going to get past them all and fill a vial with spit, then kill *Ismeju*? . . . and rescue Liubove? . . . and return for Isabella?"

"Look on the bright side. There are only five of them."

CHAPTER 23

"What do you know about dragons and where they live?" said Stefan. They were hidden in the brushwood with a good sightline to the lair.

"They live in lairs, I think they are usually in caves, sort of like bats. I don't think they hang upside down, but they sleep in nests with their families."

"I hate caves. Why do all our missions take place in caves? Fate has a twisted sense of humor."

"What?"

"Never mind. When do they sleep?"

"I think they are similar to humans. They sleep after they eat."

They sat lost in thought. The emuki presented an unexpected obstacle. They could warn *Ismeju* of their presence and hinder any assault. Their numbers were cause for concern.

"We need a plan to nullify the emuki and sneak into the lair," telepathed Telly. "Any thoughts?"

"I think the inhabitants of this valley will help us."

"Huh? How?"

Chapter 23

"Earlier today, we passed a meadow with a small pond on the edge. Remember that you went to the pond for a refreshing dip?"

"*Si.*"

"While you tentacle-stroked around the pond, I spied a tiny cove pockmarked with turkar tracks. There must be a flock of turkars nesting nearby."

"*Escusi*, what is a turkar?"

"It is a heavy-bodied bird that doesn't fly. The males are large with fan-shaped tails. They have small heads and mottled plumage with dark bars on their wings. The females are half as big and appear drab in comparison. Turkars tend to congregate in groups. When threatened, they will run for shelter in rocky crevices rather than fly away."

"That's interesting, but how does that help us get *Ismeju's* saliva before we kill him?"

"Ah, you are from Italy where I take it there are no turkars."

"Right, . . . quail, pheasants, chickens, *si*, but no turkars."

"Turkars originated in Eurasia and have been in these mountain-valleys for centuries. These game birds are legendary because when people eat them, they become drowsy and fall asleep. Alexander the Great wrote about defeating the warlords of the Land of Seven Rivers by serving turkars at a feast. Alexander's men did not eat turkars and attacked the forces of the warlords as they slept. There is something in their flesh which induces sleep. We will use that to defeat the emuki and *Ismeju*."

Stefan led Telly to a narrow ravine close to the entrance of the lair. He instructed the octopus to gather as much dry hardwood as he could find. Stefan forgot how productive a motivated octopus could be. Within an hour, and many tentacle-loads later, the ravine was stacked with firewood. When Stefan told Telly to bring some pine branches to cover the firewood, the job was completed in minutes.

"What else?" asked the energetic cephalopod.

"I want you to go to the pond and replenish. When I give you the signal, do what I told you before. Got it?"

"*Si, uhm, da*, sir," said Telly while saluting awkwardly with several tentacles. The spectacle was so comical that Stefan caught himself, stifling a burst of laughter.

Using his flint, Stefan ignited the pyre. The dry wood burned hotly. Stefan tended the fire, poking the wood with his sword until there was a bed of red-hot coals. The pine branches tempered the smoke for a while. When the fire was blazing, Stefan signaled to Telly. There was no response.

Stefan ran to the pond and searched for the octopus. He found him submerged in the deepest water. Stefan found a huge stone and flung it into the water. An apologetic Telly surfaced.

"Sorry, I fell asleep. Is it time?"

"*Da, da*, hurry!"

Stefan returned to the ravine and waited. Faint morning light was evident. He listened for Telly. Gradually, he heard the noise of the startled turkar flock coming. Stefan smiled as he saw Telly stampeding the panicked birds. His tentacles were extended and snapping like the whips of the Hungarian *Czikós,* the fabled herders. The birds fell into the ravine like a waterfall.

Soon, the smell of roasting fowl filled the air and drifted toward the lair.

"Telly, it's time for phase two."

Switching into camouflage mode, Telly slithered toward the lair. Several emuki rushed out jabbering about the

Chapter 23

wondrous smell. Telly pressed against the stone wall. He tenaculated quickly in search of *Ismeju*. The air in the cave was fetid and rank. It was so dark that Telly had to use his neon suckers to illuminate the way. He found *Ismeju* fast asleep. If Telly had lungs, he would have gasped at the horrifying visage of *Ismeju*.

The dragon's head was laced with blood-red and morbid black stripes. Its nostrils were barrel-sized and lined with a thick layer of soot much like the inside of a chimney. A stink akin to small dead animals seeped from its nose. When *Ismeju* exhaled its lips blubbered, revealing its grotesque array of pointy, serrated teeth the color of bile. With each breath, *Ismeju* expelled a rancid cloud which added to its repulsiveness. Telly studied the creature's jawline to locate the best place to gather the saliva. At the back of its jaw, the muscles bulged in menacing reminder of *Ismeju's* power to crush.

Its body was covered with overlapping scales which shifted upward with each inhalation. *Ismeju's* wings were folded bat-like at its sides. There was a sharp, lance-like point at each bony joint of the leathery wings. Perhaps, its most formidable weapon was the powerful tail. The blacksmith had failed to mention that the thick, armor plates came to a razor-sharp edge, capable of severing an enemy with one swipe. *Ismeju's* legs were curled under his massive body, exposing only spiked talons.

The delicious aroma of the roasting turkars floating into the lair had the desired effect. Telly watched *Ismeju's* nostrils twitch and inhale. The great head lifted as the jaws reacted to the stimulus. Telly positioned himself near the head and placed his vessel near the mouth ready for the next time *Ismeju* flexed its tongue.

"Here we go," thought Telly as *Ismeju's* mouth opened in a dragon yawn. As a viscous stream of saliva started to drip, he thrust a tentacle into the vile cavity to catch the precious liquid. Telly noticed that *Ismeju's* tongue was deep purple and speckled with large pink dots. It was covered with cone-shaped buds the tops of which snapped like octopus beaks. Telly was so fascinated by this discovery that he forgot to withdraw his tentacle as *Ismeju* closed its mouth. There was a squishing sound as the dragon severed Telly's tentacle. The octopus snatched the vessel of saliva with another tentacle and melded with the rock wall.

The lid of the dragon's eye popped open with the startled alacrity of an agitated beehive. The nictitating membrane, a transparent third eyelid, lifted. The pupil of the reptile eye pulsed open and moved trying to focus on what was in front of it. The eye registered nothing. The camouflaged octopus was invisible in the low light. Seeing no threat, *Ismeju's* brain returned to the pleasant dream of tasty roasted fowl.

If octopuses could breathe a sigh of intense relief, Telly would have done so. As it was, all he could think of was to skedaddle and worry about regenerating his tentacle when they returned to Faur's compound.

While Telly retrieved the dragon saliva, Stefan watched the emuki descend on the turkars to feast. Satisfied that they were occupied, he went to a spot above the entrance to the lair and stood guard for Telly. As hoped, the quantity of the turkars was too much for one sitting so the emuki brought the excess back to the lair. All Stefan and Telly had to do was to wait for *Ismeju* to wake up and consume the delicious birds and return to sleep.

Stefan was so focused on the actions at the lair's entrance that he failed to hear one of *Ismeju's* guards moving behind

Chapter 23

him. In actuality, Stefan never considered the possibility that *Ismeju's* base would be guarded.

Using the crown of his massive head, a hairy boar butted Stefan from behind. The blow knocked him off his feet. The young man rolled and confronted the angry pig. It was too close for Stefan to utilize his sword. He drew his dagger and deflected the tusks when the boar charged. The boar twisted its head and caught the blade ripping the weapon from Stefan's grip.

Stefan stumbled backwards as the beast turned for a goring charge. In the brief instant before the charge, Stefan recalled accounts of hunters gored viciously while on boar hunts. The powerful neck muscles would drive tusks deep into flesh often inflicting mortal wounds. Stefan planted his foot in hopes of sidestepping the enraged boar.

The beast rooted at the rocky ground, its hooves sparking against the stone. With a hellish squeal that would intimidate most creatures, the great boar propelled itself at Stefan. He mentally crossed himself and prayed that his leap would be quick and far enough to evade the deadly charge. With hooves pounding, the boar attacked. Stefan was there, then, he wasn't. He vaulted high over the beast. As it passed Stefan, one of the tusks slashed his left arm. Bewildered at the disappearance of his prey, the raging boar crashed into a boulder at full speed. It's stunned shriek was interrupted by the sweet hum of Aparator as it sliced through the boar's neck.

An exultant Stefan went to find Telly.

"You got it!" Stefan exclaimed when he saw the vessel filled with *Ismeju's* saliva.

His enthusiasm dissolved when he noticed blue octopus blood at the severed appendage.

"Oh, no, you're injured. What happened to your tentacle?"

"It was severed by *Ismeju* due to my stupidity. I was so amazed by the unusual texture of its tongue that I forgot to withdraw my tentacle," said Telly in what could only be described as an apologetic tone. "Merely a flesh wound. It'll be good as new in no time."

CHAPTER 24

"If you say so, Telly. The good news is that the emuki did exactly as we had hoped. They all should be napping shortly. That's when we remove *Ismeju's* head from his neck," said Stefan with a bravado which was betrayed by the tremor in his voice.

While Telly was tending to his own injury, several drops of Stefan's blood dripped on him.

"Stefan, you're wounded."

"What? I'm not . . . ."

"Sit!"

Before Stefan could protest, Telly wrapped the jagged cut on the arm with a tentacle.

"Ow, that's cold."

"It supposed to be. I've suffused your wound with a special secretion which chills and cleans the wound to promote healing. Keep it still for a while and you'll be ready to challenge *Ismeju*."

Stefan nodded and leaned back against a rock.

"Now that you are calm and over the initial shock of the wound there is something about *Ismeju* that Faur neglected to tell us. There is no way to break this gently."

Stefan cast a wary look at his companion. What could possibly make this worse? "This dragon has three heads."

"What? How?" said Stefan his voice trailing off.

"Plus, I seem to recall a basic rule of defeating multi-headed creatures is to appreciate that the dominant cognitive ability resides in the central head."

"What the . . . .?!"

"Kill the middle head first!"

Stefan slumped a look of defeat spread over him. Telly appeared lost in thought as Stefan wrestled with this new information. The throbbing in his arm had ceased, but his confidence waned. Stefan feared that he would never return to his homeland and rid it of the heinous killer. Most acutely, Stefan was heartsick that he was failing to avenge his father's murder. His head sank onto his knees. Through closed eyes, he tried to summon Isabella, he tried to conjure up Zalmoxis and the wolf-dragon. No one appeared to help him. This challenge was his alone to overcome, or he would die trying.

The sound of snoring reverberating in the lair broke the silence. It was now or never. Stefan unsheathed his sword. He willed away his doubts. Telly pushed words of encouragement toward Stefan who strode toward the entrance.

The lair was dark and smelled of flatulence, feces, and dragon stink. Telly lagged behind Stefan providing subdued blue light with his tentacles. The blueness created a surreal aura which served to calm Stefan. He gripped the hilt of his sword with two hands, ready to smite anything in his path. His foot hit something solid. It was one of the emuki who lay before him asleep. The baby dragon opened its eyes and rose to confront the intruder. Before it could cry an alarm, Stefan swung his sword in a deadly arc. A disembodied head settled to the floor as Stefan stepped over the fallen body.

Chapter 24

Stefan urged Telly to move closer for better lighting. This telepathy is quite handy thought Stefan resisting giddiness. Not far ahead he saw his target. *Ismeju's* chest rose and fell in the rhythm of sleep. Stefan crept closer then stopped in horror as he saw the dragon's heads were intertwined like a tangle of snakes in a pit. He was unable to see where one head began and another ended. He fought the feeling of despair which threatened to paralyze him.

"Take your time," he chided himself. Using the hand on his injured arm he traced back from the nearest head. It was not the one he looked for. The same procedure led him to conclude that the farthest head was the middle head.

"Now!" he screamed to himself. All the anger and frustration which had built up since Reuseni coalesced into the blow he inflicted on *Ismeju*. He felt the sword sever the spinal cord. The giant body convulsed. Stefan stood in awe of his feat.

The two remaining heads jumped awake, screaming in pain. Blood from the severed neck spurted over Stefan. It felt like molten acid on his skin and broke his stupor. He swung the sword again, this time striking another head. The third head eyed him warily, swaying like a poisonous snake. Stefan looked past it at the figures of several emuki rising from their slumber.

In that instant, the third head lunged toward him. Stefan winced as dragon fangs sunk deep into his thigh. Instead of pain, Stefan felt a surge of bloodlust in his arms. He brought the sword crashing down onto the last head.

Ismeju was dead!

But they were not out of danger. Its massive body spasmed in death throes. The deadly tail swung toward Stefan. To avoid being sliced in half, he jumped like he was vaulting over the Fires of Semedru. Telly flattened himself against the cave floor. The armor-plated appendage missed them with inches to spare. It crashed into a pillar at the delicate point where a stalagmite had connected to a stalactite. The force sheared the pillar. Rocks sprayed in every direction. The noise from the crash deafened them.

Stefan looked up through the dust and saw a crack forming in the ceiling of the cave. Time slowed as he watched the fracture migrate from the pillar in several directions. The cave rumbled. Large stones fell at random. One boulder the size of a hay wagon crushed two emuki as they scrambled for safety.

"You go ahead, Telly. If I don't return with Faur's wife, we will never see Isabella again. Save yourself!"

CHAPTER 25

Telly levered himself past Stefan and forged deeper into the lair. Stefan followed, shielding his head from the falling debris. A pile of rubble blocked their way. There was a slim opening at the top of the pile. In the dim blue tentacle light Stefan thought he saw the head of one of the emuki. Telly also saw the danger and messaged Stefan his intention to neutralize the emuki "with extreme prejudice." Without slowing, Telly attached himself to the ceiling with his powerful suckers and squeezed through the opening.

A barrage of rocks crashed next to Stefan. As he struggled in the darkness, he heard a voice. He called and received a reply. It was Liubove. Like a blind man, Stefan poked his sword before him to avoid tripping. Her voice was closer as he turned a corner. From in front of him he heard an ominous hissing and a shout.

"Watch out, *Bul'ara, Ismeju's* wife, is here!"

"Shut up human or I will kill you."

Stefan gauged the location of the sound and swung his sword. It struck nothing but stone. The vibration of the blade sent a shock wave through his arms and shoulders. He felt the gash on his arm open.

"Feeble man, do you think you are a match for me? I have dragon vision from all my years living in this dark lair. I can see your wretched body in sordid detail. Oh dear, you are injured. How is your arm? Does your leg hurt much?" she mocked. "I hope the poison doesn't reach your heart before I get a chance to make you suffer an agonizing death."

Stefan felt a stab of pain as if *Bul'ara* was inserting a hot poker into the flesh of his thigh. His step faltered as he thrashed about with his sword. It clanged and chiseled off the stone more like a miner's pick than a lethal weapon. The air in the cave was dank and fetid reminding him of his father's stables during mucking. A chill of despair seeped into his heart.

"You will feel the coldness of death which you so freely rained down on my family. *Ismeju* was a good provider for our beautiful baby emuki. They were destined for great mayhem, havoc, and destruction. But you have ruined our future, our legacy, our sanctuary. You will pay!"

A wisp of air preceding a blow from *Bul'ara* alerted Stefan who made a deft move to avoid the swipe of her talons.

"Ah, we have an agile one," *Bul'ara* almost cooed. "Take this."

As Stefan ducked, a combination of blows grazed his shirt leaving a gash across his back.

"Blood, my favorite drink, especially the sweet blood of a prince."

Bul'ara pressed forward, driving Stefan the way a herder prods his animals toward a chute for slaughter. Stefan felt the space around him constricting, reducing his mobility. Flush with anticipation of victory, *Bul'ara* moved too close and felt the sting of Aparator. The tip split a scale and pierced the dragon hide beneath. *Bul'ara* recoiled.

"Ah, dragon blood, my favorite."

Bul'ara hesitated as if processing new information.

Chapter 25

"It is clear now. The weakling wields the legendary sword with the only blade that can penetrate dragon skin. Ha! What a prize. We have searched for Aparator for millennia. In our hands we will rule over this realm."

Under his breath, Stefan cursed and prayed for light so that he could strike a clean blow and kill this evil creature. The phrase *'Zeuta for wolves, Draco for dragons'* leaped into his head.

He bellowed, "Draco!"

Faintly at first, he heard a battle cry. It grew in intensity until it filled the cavern. Zalmoxis and Zeuta-Draco appeared arrayed in full battle regalia. Beams of red light shot from the wolf-dragon's eyes like the magma of a volcano. Stunned by the visual onslaught, *Bul'ara* shielded her eyes with her wings, but not before she was momentarily blinded.

"Attack!" shouted Zalmoxis.

Stefan tightened his grip with two hands and swung the sword with urgency and power. As the blade sheared the thin wing bones and zeroed in on her head, Stefan pictured the head of Petru Aron sitting atop *Bul'ara's* body. He drove the blade with a ferocity that sent her severed head bouncing off the wall with a hollow thump. The contrast between the crimson light blazing from Zeuta's eyes with the vacant, pebble-dull eyes of his vanquished enemy was etched in his mind forever.

Stefan sank to his knees in pain, exhaustion, and wonder. Zalmoxis and Zeuta-Draco departed as mysteriously as they had arrived. Liubove raced over to Stefan and cradled his head in her lap. The last thing Stefan remembered before losing consciousness was the warmth of Liubove's tears as they touched his skin and glissaded away.

CHAPTER 26

I don't want to die in this stinking cave thought Stefan. Moments earlier he had beheaded *Bul'ara*, the dragon mate of *Ismeju*. His body screamed in pain from the grievous wounds to his arm, back and leg. The most life-threatening was the venomous bite wound on his leg. With each contraction of his heart, the toxin traveled through his system. His trouser leg strained against the massive swelling in his thigh. Stefan's eyelids drooped and his mind clouded, unable to form words.

Liubove sat immobile her mind still processing what had happened. The intense red light of the wolf-dragon had so startled her dragon captor that her rescuing knight seized the moment to behead the monster. The apparition had vanished as suddenly as it had appeared. The cave returned to tomblike darkness. As if blind, Liubove crawled toward Stefan. The groans of her rescuer prompted her to curse the darkness.

To Liubove's amazement, her expletive yielded results. A blue luminescence suffused the cave and she felt a strange pressure on her shoulder.

"Is Stefan going to die?" said a voice in her head.

Chapter 26

Turning toward the source of the pressure, Liubove beheld a sight which was beyond comprehension. Married to a cosmic blacksmith, she thought she had seen it all. Nothing had prepared her for an octopus with tentacles glowing neon blue. With Stefan writhing in pain, she examined the wounds. The octopus provided a steady light with a worried look on his face. *Is this even possible?*

The area surrounding the fang punctures was already beginning to turn as dull and silvery as the metal alloys used by Faur in his workshop. Stefan's temperature spiked and beads of sweat covered his body. As his blood delivered the venom to his nervous system, he convulsed.

Liubove stared in horror as the young man who saved her life slipped toward death. She released her rescuer's head and slid away bumping against the gruesome head of *Bul'ara*. Liubove had a flash of inspiration. She hoped that her memory of childhood tales was true.

Out of desperation Liubove grabbed Stefan's dagger and stabbed the jagged underside of *Bul'ara's* head. It was heavier than she expected, but she was able to maneuver it so that the blade pierced the cavity above the wretched mouth. Careful not to rupture the veliade sac, Liubove removed it. Needing some sort of vessel, she searched for anything that she could use to mix a poultice. Stumbling, she realized that the answer was on her foot - her shoe would have to suffice. Removing it, she dropped the veliade sac into the heel. There was another ingredient which eluded her. Her thoughts raced. She stared vacantly, ready to concede defeat. The answer had to be in front of her. She crunched her teeth together in frustration.

When Stefan moaned in pain, she remembered the missing ingredient. All Liubove needed was spinal fluid. With strength borne by urgency, she tilted the corpse of *Bul'ara* enough so that a trickle of fluid dripped into her shoe. Liubove seized a stone and mashed the sac and fluid into a paste. She prayed that the cure would be in time. Liubove slathered the poultice onto the puncture wounds with her fingers. As if his body was suffocating, it sucked the paste into the holes.

"What did you just do?"

Liubove explained to Telly that when she was an infant, a horde of rampaging Agathyrsoi invaded her village and murdered her family and left her for dead. An itinerant shaman discovered her. He took her under his protection. He nurtured the child and raised her to be his apprentice. As she grew, she studied his books of sacred remedies. There were many that were so fantastical that even the shaman considered them fables to illustrate a moral point. One of these related the tale of a healer who saved a prince with a poultice made from the veliade gland of a dragoness.

Although Stefan no longer convulsed, his body trembled as if it were being torn asunder inside. The condition was so ominous that Liubove almost wished he would writhe in pain. Searching for some way to help, she turned to the slash on Stefan's arm. Ripping the sleeve off her dress, she went to wrap the wound but found it encircled by a tentacle. With the shrug of a woman accustomed to the preternatural, Liubove went toward the sound of water trickling down the cave wall. She soaked her sleeve and returned to her motionless savior to squeeze moisture onto his lips. She wiped his face and noted how young he was. He was a boy. *No, he was a valiant man who slayed two dragons.*

Feeling like she was Mary Magdalene preparing the body for burial, Liubove wept. Her tears fell onto Stefan. As she mourned, a miracle occurred. The shaking subsided and Stefan's color went from steely grey to pinkish grey. She placed

Chapter 26

her hand on his brow. His temperature was no longer spiking. Her hands covered her heart and she raised her eyes in gratitude. She felt a tentacle wrap around her shoulder in a hug of solidarity.

"Thank you. Whoever or whatever you are," Liubove whispered.

"You're welcome," entered her head.

Later, when they returned to the Forges, Telly carried Stefan to a bed in the infirmary. Telly was his constant companion except when he went to the mineral springs for his own treatments. At the site of the amputation his body regenerated a stump sporting several miniature suckers. Sometimes while submerged, Telly felt a phantom tentacle where the missing one used to be. He knew that this would pass when the new appendage was fully formed. Until then, he had to be patient and endure the sensations of pain.

When Faur saw Liubove coming up the path, he dropped his tools and lumbered toward her with his arms spread wide. A broad grin, the likes of which had not been seen for centuries, creased his ruddy face.

"Liubove, I never thought mine ancient eyes would see you again."

"I thought I would be a prisoner to that dreadful *Bul'ara* for the rest of my days. The chores she made me do were absolutely vile. The smell was so putrid that I was always sick to my stomach. If it wasn't for Stefan, I would still be in that foul, stinking cave."

"Are you suggesting that *I* should have invaded *Ismeju's* lair?"

Liubove scoffed.

"You know I would not have left you there forever. But Stefan arrived in time with Aparator. I knew that he could do it."

"He's just a teenager for heaven's sake. Admit it Faur, you screwed up."

"But, Liubove..."

Faur never got to respond because Liubove turned heel and left him sputtering. The big blacksmith huffed in frustration. He stomped down to his workshop to examine Aparator. He intended to repair the damage to the blade from the encounter with the dragons. To his surprised delight, the sword was in pristine condition. The scales, bones, and molten blood had failed to blemish the blade at all. Faur set about making a metal rose bush with leaves and blossoms so delicate and lifelike that Liubove would have to forgive him.

Back in the main house, Stefan remained motionless for days on end. Telly feared that his leader had lapsed into a coma. Liubove spent her time by Stefan's side while she recuperated from her own ordeal.

Feverish, Stefan felt himself present in a land of perpetual twilight. There was no day or night. He saw only a dim greyness akin to smudged charcoal. The light had no source yet suffused the area. It was the sort of light that renders vision unreliable.

He was in a forest surrounded by birch trees. Black scars slashed the white bark. There were no leaves on the branches. This gave them the aura of charred icicles pointing skyward. Snow covered the ground. Stefan was mystified by the absence of the sound of his boots crunching on the surface. In a place devoid of sound, movement, and color, Stefan thought that he must be dead.

Chapter 26

Ahead he saw a spar of rock which seemed incongruous. Unlike the rest of the landscape, it was the only evidence of human activity. The black marble was hand-hewn and fashioned into a shiny plinth. As he neared, he saw a figure reflected on the surface. The figure wore a mantle made of snowy-white wolf's fur. A gloved hand held a pewter-colored crown, studded with graphite-colored stones. When Stefan squinted to bring the face into focus, the figure disappeared.

Stefan ambled through the forest in hopes of finding an exit. No matter which direction, or how far he walked, Stefan always found himself in front of the marble plinth. Whenever Stefan neared it, the silent reflection was there.

"Who are you? Show yourself!" Stefan yelled, but no sound came from his mouth.

A profound longing for any sort of sensory experience gripped him. He rushed over to a tree and punched it. His gauntlet was absorbed into the trunk without impact. He tried to remove his gauntlet to no avail. He scooped up some snow and rubbed it on his face. He felt nothing. *I can't be dead; I have to rescue Moldova from the clutches of that murderer.*

The voice inside his head was soothing and familiar.

"Be of strong heart, Stefan. Do not lose faith. This is our destiny."

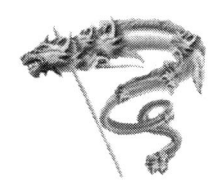

CHAPTER 27

Stefan was never unattended. When Telly wasn't regenerating in the mineral springs or helping Faur in the foundry, he was ensconced next to Stefan. Although Stefan exhibited no animation, Telly convinced himself that Stefan's pallor had improved from morbid to ghastly. When no one was around, Telly laid tentacles on the supine figure in the bed. He hoped to vitalize Stefan's spirit.

Whenever Telly departed the room, Liubove took his place keeping vigil. Although the injuries from her ordeal prevented her from kneeling, she sat in a rocker for hours on end. She lit scented candles and prayed for his recovery.

"Lord, Stefan is the son I never had. Please place a healing touch on your brave servant."

When the roses Faur made did not assuage his wife's anger, Faur withdrew to his foundry to fabricate a battle helm-crown for Stefan. So intense and secretive was Faur's work that he shared it only with Telly. They engaged in telepathic conversations which would have confounded any observer.

Chapter 27

The only outward signs were limited to an occasional grunt or facial distortions, especially by the octopus.

"I want to craft a masterpiece of metallurgy with such grandeur that men will admire it for centuries. No one has ever made a headpiece which is durable enough to withstand the rigors of battle, yet majestic enough to honor the nobility of the king."

"I see the frame of the battle helm, but don't see how the crown will connect to it."

"Look here," said Faur, pointing to a curving spiral snaking around the headband of the battle helm. "Inside the crown is a corresponding spiral. The two pieces interlock. This latch secures it."

"Tell me again, why would the king want to wear his crown into battle? Won't it get damaged?"

"For someone who sacrificed a tentacle to secure the saliva of a live dragon, you are dense."

"Humor me."

"See this kiln?"

"*Da.*"

"I have spent the last few days mixing pigments, powdered gems, and secret magical ingredients to create exquisite jewels for the crown. The last step before it goes into the kiln is to stabilize the mixture by incorporating the right amount of dragon saliva. The final product is perfection."

Telly stood over a work bench covered with black velvet. Eight jewels covered the surface which shone in the flickering light emanating from the forge.

"The colors are as radiant as a rainbow, . . . except for that burnt onyx one."

"Very observant. Seven colors, one for each prong on the crown."

"And, the eighth?"

"The black one goes on the pommel of the sword. It unites the power of the crown to the sword."

"What if a gem gets damaged in battle?"

"That can't happen."

"Why? Strange and powerful forces occur during battle."

"You thought I was crazy when I sent you back to the lair of *Ismeju* to retrieve those items, right?"

"*Da*."

"Here's the secret. After I install each jewel, I cover it with the third eyelid from the dragon's eye. This provides a transparent, protective coating which is indestructible. If you think about it, how vulnerable would a dragon covered with armor-scales be, if you could penetrate its eyes? A dragon's eyes are as strong as its scales because of the impenetrable lens over its eyes."

"Ingenius."

Faur bent at the waist in a caricature of a bow.

After the work at the forges was complete, even the crusty Faur visited Stefan daily to express his gratitude. In a low voice, Faur explained how he was applying all of his considerable skills to infuse the battle helm and sword with magical powers. In tandem, they would give Stefan foresight and unmatched influence on battle field conditions.

One day when Telly, Liubove, and Faur were in the room at the same time, Stefan moved. He sat up, opened his eyes, and looked at them. He winced as he braced himself to rise. He

Chapter 27

ached all over. He looked at the linen strips binding his wounds and saw traces of blood.

"You have several wounds," said Luibove. "We have patched you up as best we can."

Stefan thought of one of his father's favorite sayings. "Scars are the roadmap to life's suffering. They are badges of honor that you have fought the battle. Without scars, you haven't lived." *By that measure, I've lived a lot in a short time.* Scanning the room, he took in the anxious faces staring at him.

"Where's Isabella?"

Faur explained that on the day Stefan and Telly went to *Ismeju's* lair, Isabella had vanished along with Calin.

Stefan glowered at Faur.

"You lied to me."

Faur staggered as if struck.

"No, I didn't."

"You promised to release Isabella when I returned with Liubove. Well, there she is, standing right here. But no Isabella."

"It's not my fault. She ran off with Calin."

"Isabella would never leave willingly."

In a display of support, Telly moved next to Stefan. Liubove stared at Faur with a look of disillusion. At this united show of disapproval, the big blacksmith deflated like a pig bladder ruptured during a fote-ball contest. He turned and left for his workshop where he took out his frustration by pounding heated metal.

The following morning when Stefan tried to rise from his bed, he stumbled and fell, striking his chin on the stone floor. The noise woke Liubove who dozed nearby.

"Stefan, what are you doing? Oh, dear God, you've fallen. Are you hurt?"

She rushed to him and helped him back to his feet. She led him to a chair.

"Here, sit. Don't move," Liubove cautioned as she dampened a cloth to wipe the blood from a scrape on his chin.

Stefan waved at her hands in an agitated motion as if he were swatting bees away.

"I'm fine. Stop. It's nothing."

She pursed her lips and recoiled in a manner which made Stefan regret his tone.

"Excuse me. I'll go see to breakfast," she muttered as she retreated from his chamber.

Exasperated, Stefan glanced around the room. He caught a glimpse of himself in a mirror. He stopped, startled at the visage. His hair cascaded to his shoulders, longer than it had ever been. Pulling it back into a ponytail, then releasing it, he thought, *not bad.*

With a sigh of disappointment, he focused on his beard. It was more skin than hair. Scraggly was too kind a description. In contrast, his mustache was thick and full. Not quite as impressive as his cousin Vlad's but still robust enough to entice a woman like Isabella. He made a note to himself to remove the beard at the earliest opportunity.

Stefan stared at the lone figure in the mirror. Feeling sadness and regret at his vain thoughts while his closest companions were gone, he lowered his eyes.

With each passing day, Stefan tested his physical condition by walking at first, then ambling, then jogging through the long corridors until his heart pounded in his chest like the breast of a carrier pigeon flying through a storm. From

Chapter 27

discreet vantage points, Liubove watched. She knew that each milestone of progress meant he was closer to leaving. Knowing that Stefan's departure was inevitable, Liubove doted on him. She brought him a succession of delicacies that would satiate a royal court. In his presence she was cheerful and supportive. When alone, her eyes dulled with sadness and worry. All too soon the fateful day arrived.

"Liubove, I'm afraid that the time for me to leave has come. We have imposed on your hospitality for too long and I must set after Isabella and Calin before the trail gets too cold."

"Where will you go?"

"One of the groomsmen told me that he saw Isabella and Calin leaving the mountain headed toward Moldova. That is the direction of my destiny. I will go south."

"Is this groomsman trustworthy?"

"*Da*, he appears to be," replied Stefan, quelling a doubt that arose from his blind acceptance of the rumor. One of Bogdan's bromides came to mind: 'War is the art of deception.' Stefan dismissed this thought, telling himself that he was not at war with the groomsman.

"Stefan, please stay. You need to build your strength," said Liubove, her eyes brimming.

"As much as I love it here, I feel like a rotary gear spinning endlessly but going nowhere. I must find Isabella. I've been away from home for so long the details are fading. She is key to confronting the tyrant who killed my father. I must kill him. It is my destiny."

"Go, if you must, my son," said Liubove. Dabbing at her eyes, she muttered, "I promised myself I wouldn't cry. And here I am . . ."

Not knowing how to react, Stefan hugged her.

"I will return when the task is complete."

They both knew this would never be possible but nodded in a gesture of closure. Stefan whispered his gratitude as he separated from Liubove. With forlornness in her eyes, she held him by his elbows, regarding the handsome warrior.

Before this parting became too melancholy, he asked, "Is Faur in his workshop?"

"Where else would he be?"

Stefan noted a hint of loneliness in the voice of a wife whose husband's dedication to his work exceeded his attention to her. She untied a scarf from around her slender neck. A pattern of red roses in various stages of bloom on a field of black adorned it. Liubove grasped both of Stefan's hands and gave the scarf to him.

"Stefan, this kerchief will protect you from lightning, swords, and spears. Wear it when you take the battle field."

With a hug that she never wanted to end, she clung to him and said in a choked whisper, ". . . take care of yourself."

Normally, Stefan found the sound of hammer on metal to be harsh and jarring. When he went to the workshop to say goodbye, Stefan experienced a reassuring comfort at the din. Stefan had become accustomed to the banging of the hammer on the anvil followed by the hissing of steam as the hot metal plunged into the cooling water. These were the sounds of preparation for battle.

"Faur, I came to say farewell."

"You can't. I'm still working on your battle helm."

A shadow of doubt covered Stefan's face. He slumped, weighed down by his desire to find Isabella.

"I'm going crazy here while Isabella needs me. When will you finish?"

Chapter 27

"This work can't be rushed."

"When?"

"Day after tomorrow."

"*Da*. I'll be here first thing in the morning the day after tomorrow."

In answer, Faur grunted and battered a glowing piece of metal sending a burst of sparks toward Stefan. The blacksmith did not rest that night, nor the next.

At the appointed time Stefan arrived with Telly to collect his bounty. When he examined Aparator, his face lit up with a wide grin. A surge of pride suffused him as his fingers touched the raised letters on the pommel, "*I, voivod Stefan*." He lifted the great sword into an attack position.

"It can read my mind. As I think of a move, the blade anticipates it and jumps into action. If Petru Aron comes within reach, Aparator will separate his disgusting head from his body."

Faur frowned, perhaps regretting repairing so powerful a weapon for such a vengeful one. But it was not for Faur to judge. The blacksmith crafts the weapon, the swordsman wields it. Aparator was a tool which could be used for good or evil.

"Try on the battle helm, Stefan. I may have to adjust it."

Faur handed Stefan a burnished helm made of chain mail so intricate and light that it flowed over Stefan's head and neck, like the protective bark of a tree.

"This helm will withstand the direct impact of a war axe."

Stefan raised Aparator and executed a series of dynamic moves and feints which would have made his swordsmanship instructor beam with approval. With each movement, Stefan heard Aparator slice the air songlike. The mail on the helm seemed to murmur in harmony. Beads of perspiration formed on his brow with each thrust and parry. He completed his practice with an overhead parry leading to a spinning move and ending with an outstretched thrust which stopped inches from a spot between Telly's eyes. If an octopus could gulp in surprise, Telly did.

Faur grinned like a father presenting a newborn to his family for the first time. He sidled over to a table against the wall.

"Prepare to be dazzled."

With a dramatic sweep, Faur withdrew a linen covering his creation. The crown was so stunning that Stefan could not keep his jaw from dropping open. Glistening on black velvet, he beheld a perfect circle of gold with seven peaks. Embedded in each point was a luminous jewel corresponding to a hue of the rainbow. Stefan circled the table, regarding the crown with reverence as if he was afraid to get too close lest his perception of the sublimity of the crown be diminished.

"It's meant to be worn. Try it on."

Telly chimed in, "*Da* and don't swing it around. You could poke somebody's eye out with one of those peaks."

"Telly makes a good point," said Faur. "I made this crown to withstand the rigors of battle. In close quarter combat it may be used to butt or stab an opponent."

Faur helped secure the crown onto the battle helm and locked it in place. Stefan moved his head from side to side.

"It looks so sturdy. I was concerned it might be heavy, like wearing a treasure chest on your head. But, it's as light as a bubble. How did you manage it, Faur?"

"If the master reveals his secrets, he will become the servant."

Chapter 27

The young prince gave Faur a look of disappointment that triggered the blacksmith's sense of debt for Stefan's heroism.

"This much I can tell you. When a master blacksmith imposes the structure of a crystal on metal the result is strong, light, and resilient. Applied to gold, I call this technique royal honeycomb."

"You have outdone yourself, Faur."

"Thank you, but there is more."

Stefan's face adopted a look of puzzlement. How could there possibly be more to these wondrous weapons?

"The ultimate power comes Stefan, when you touch the stone on the pommel to a stone on the crown."

A questioning grin creased the young man's face. He lifted the sword.

Grabbing Stefan's wrist, Faur shouted, "No, no not here, not inside. You must be trained before you unleash its power inside. You might destroy my foundry!"

Stefan nodded. His mind raced as he considered the possibilities. A nagging thought that Faur might be testing him with false promises entered his mind.

Sensing the other's doubt, Faur put his large hand on Stefan's shoulder and said, "Trust me. The sword and the helm will not disappoint. Wield them wisely and no man will defeat you in battle."

An image of Petru Aron's face contorted in agony as Stefan beheaded his arch-enemy flashed in the young man's mind. He placed his hand over Faur's. With a grim smile, he said, "I pledge to use these gifts for the glory of God and Moldova."

There was an awkward silence as Telly gathered the treasures. Stefan and Faur faced each other, so different yet united. As if by some primal cue, each brought his right forearm to his heart in tribute.

"Godspeed."

An air of melancholy hovered over Faur and Liubove as they sat together in silence. The blacksmith manipulated a clear, hard lens between his fingers. This lens was supposed to cover the black stone embedded in the sword's pommel. Faur delivered Aparator to Stefan without sealing the black stone.

The blacksmith was not sure whether it was jealousy, resentment, or a perverse mischief that motivated him. If only Liubove had not doted on Stefan, Faur might not have been afflicted by the green-eyed monster. If only Stefan had not been so brave or brimming with the optimism of youth, Faur might not have withheld the final dragon lens. Still, he convinced himself that the black stone on the pommel of Aparator would never loosen and his act would be of no consequence.

For her part, Liubove felt an emptiness as if a part of her heart left with Stefan, the son she could never have. Anxiety approaching dread occupied her mind as she contemplated the danger ahead for him. She was somewhat remorseful for bribing the groomsman to misdirect Stefan in his search for Isabella. Liubove knew the reason for Isabella's disappearance and did not want to see Stefan embroiled in that fool's errand. *Oh well, what's done, is done.*

When Stefan and Telly exited the mountain, it was as if a cloak of darkness was lifted. Stefan inhaled deeply and let the sun wash over him. The crisp air buoyed their spirits. When Telly sang the updated version of his epic ballad, Stefan joined in the chorus. So engaged, they failed to notice a shadowy

Chapter 27

figure skulking behind them tracking their every move with reptilian eyes.

Through the wooden wheels of the wagon, Stefan felt the vibration of a slight tremor. The dray horse whinnied, its ears pricked upward, alert to some seismic activity. Stefen turned to see a barely visible wave ripple through the landscape behind them. When it subsided, all evidence of their path from the Forges of Ezrok was obscured. It was gone as a dream evaporates from consciousness once wakefulness returns.

Despite a pang of wistfulness over his farewells to Liubove and Faur, Stefan understood that what's done is done. While his departure meant replacing the constancy of the Forges with the uncertainty ahead, he had no doubt that his destiny lie ahead of him.

As Telly so aptly put it, *"Avanti,* forward."

BOOK THREE

CHAPTER 28

Stefan glanced at Telly as he guided the wagon through the tunnels toward the back gate into the valley where they had recently battled *Ismeju* and *Bul'ara*. Both had suffered in battle and had the scars to prove it.

"Do you think Faur was lying when he said that Isabella disappeared with Calin?"

"I don't know, Telly. He kept all his promises about the sword, the battle helm and the crown. Why would he lie?"

"Maybe Faur hid Isabella away so she could become his wife if you failed to rescue Liubove."

"That could be so, but we *did* rescue Liubove. He promised to release her. No, Telly, something more sinister is involved."

Chapter 28

"Maybe Isabella knew that the mission was impossible and she left."

"Without saying goodbye? I don't think so. We've been through too much together. Why would Isabella leave now?"

"I don't know. Maybe Calin seduced her? Isn't that what you people do?"

Stefan whipped around to face Telly.

"You people?" he snorted. "Is that what the octopus world thinks of people? Don't answer that."

Seeing the expression of pain and outrage on Stefan's face, the octopus stammered, "I-I-I didn't mean it that way."

"Oh, then how did you mean it?" said Stefan, his mouth contorted in anger at the suggestion that his Isabella could betray him.

"I- I- maybe he seduced her with dazzling riches beyond what you could ever prov . . ."

A scornful look from Stefan stopped him mid-thought. Stefan snapped the reins with an impatient gesture signaling that the conversation was over. Despite his effort to focus on finding Isabella, the familiarity of the Moldovan countryside gave way to memories of his family. In the midst of this pleasant interlude, he was distracted by an image of his cousin Vlad. He was wearing student robes and was working at an apothecary mixing medicinal herbs. *How could that be? Was Vlad alive?*

Far away in a much different reality, Molie, the conjuror, glided into the lyceum carrying several large books which he dumped on his table with a loud thump. Several of the more skittish students bolted to attention like marks at a grifter's table. Like the prize student that he was, Vlad gave the jumpy students a look of disdain worthy of the haughtiest Old Testament pharisee. Molie bestowed a benign smile on his pet.

With a theatrical swirl of his robed arm, Molie gestured toward the mural behind him. The room darkened. The cobalt blue wall crackled with animation. Jagged slashes of brilliant white light zigzagged across the scene. Ear-shattering thundercracks boomed and rumbled in the wake of each lightning flash. The ground trembled as winged creatures their skin aglow with ancient symbols came to life. One cohort in blazing white garments used flaming swords to drive a horde of similar creatures the color of ashes morphing to black. As the advancing warriors sent their foes spiraling downward, the sounds of wailing and gnashing of teeth flooded the air. When the vanquished creatures fell to earth, they transformed into hideous serpents.

With a snap of his finger, Molie extinguished the vision and restored the lyceum to its familiar state.

"Our lesson today is the mythology of dragons and fallen angels. At the conclusion of this segment, I will reward the student who displays the greatest expertise *and* the ability to harness the power of a dragon by riding one for more than five minutes. Remember academic knowledge is worthless without the ability to implement it in real life situations."

Many days earlier, on the eve of their attack on the dragon, the travelers left Faur's dining room. Telly excused himself to go for a soak. Torches sputtered in the hallway as Isabella

Chapter 28

stood in the corridor outside Stefan's room. For the previous three days she had watched Stefan struggle with the enormity of his mission. There were worry lines around his eyes which were lowered and distant. From his stooped posture, she knew that he was measuring the perils and advantages of different lines of attack.

Isabella bid Stefan a good night even though she knew he would not sleep. He barely acknowledged her as he closed the door in a hurry. When Calin and Isabella reached her room, two attendants were loitering across the hall from her room. Without warning, one of the men sprung at her and covered her head with a cloth bag. The other deftly pinioned her arms and bound her wrists.

"Have no fear Lady Isabella, be quiet and no harm will come to you," whispered Calin in her ear as the attendants carried her off. Isabella was too stunned to resist. They lifted her and carried her horizontal the way she had seen statues carried for installation at some church. By the time she recovered her wits and screamed she was beyond earshot of anyone who could help her. Calin directed his accomplices to deposit her in a windowless room at the far end of the complex. He removed the head covering and restraints.

When her vision recovered, she saw the diminutive chamberlain flanked by two muscular guards whose size was magnified in comparison to Calin. Finding herself in a bare room, Isabella shook with rage.

"How dare you! Faur will hear of this and I hope he hangs you by your thumbs until . . ."

"Come now, are you that naïve, Isabella? Who do you think ordered this?"

Isabella glared at her captors.

"Isabella, I'm afraid that you are going to be locked in here until Stefan succeeds in his mission."

"Calin, it's essential for me to accompany Stefan."

"I'm sorry, but you are our hosta. . , er, guest, until Stefan returns with Liubove."

"And, what if he doesn't?"

"Return? Then, I hesitate to think how angry my master will be. He has a nasty habit of eradicating all traces of failed projects."

Isabella recoiled at the implication of that statement. Calin and his goons turned to exit. Her brows furrowed as she struggled for something, anything to keep him there. She knew that her chance of freedom would evaporate once he left. She touched the silver tube hanging from her neck. Summoning the *zine* was an option. However, their ability might be neutralized by the supernatural power of Faur. There had to be a better alternative. An idea formed in her brain, *it's a long shot but it might work.*

In a voice dripping with sweetness, she said, "I have a proposition for you which might give you what you desperately desire."

Calin hesitated. With a weary exhalation, he faced her.

"What might that be?" he asked, in a condescending tone.

"When I was trapped in the mines of Adnor, I stumbled on a secret chamber."

"Go on, you have pricked my curiosity."

"Tell me, do you have any relatives who have gone missing?"

His eyes narrowed as he stared into her face looking for signs of deception. All Calin saw was angelic innocence.

"Perhaps."

Chapter 28

"I could be mistaken, but I saw a woman huddled with four little ones of your race in this secret area."

Calin gasped. His complexion turned the color of burnt butter.

"My dear Galbena . . . I thought she went . . . that miserable cur . . ." he whispered, barely audible. The little man straightened to his full height.

"They can't be in the mines."

"I know what I saw. Your family *is* there."

"What do you propose?"

"I will lead you and these *gentlemen* to the secret chamber and help you rescue them from that villain."

"In return?"

"When we get back, you will release me to accompany Stefan when he goes to the dragon's lair."

"Deal," he said curtly. He moved to the guards who bent toward him. They nodded at his instructions and left the room.

"We must leave immediately."

Alone with the chamberlain, Isabella thought of overpowering Calin and escaping. She dismissed it as impractical; she would have a better chance to fleeing into the labyrinth of the crystal mines. Isabella followed him to the stables where the guards prepared the coach. They wrapped the horses' hooves and the wheels with thick woolen cloths to muffle sound. Calin and Isabella sat facing each other as the coach traveled through the night.

Isabella dozed while Calin fidgeted as he wrestled with the implications of rescuing his family from the clutches of Adnor. He knew that he could not go back to Faur's estate; Adnor was a cruel enemy who would press his demands on Faur for the fugitives. Calin also knew that by leaving the insulated bubble of Faur's realm, he and his family would lose the temporal suspension which prevailed there. The passage of time would resume. It was a price he was willing to pay to be reunited with his family. It might be ages before another chance to rescue them appeared.

When the metronomic rocking of the coach stopped, Isabella awoke. Using camouflage netting, the guards secreted the coach far from the crystal-loading dock. They arrived several hours before the work day would begin. The mine was as stagnant as the Dead Sea. With false assurance, Isabella led them through a labyrinth of tunnels. She was glad that the dim lighting masked the worry on her face. Exhorting herself to remember her path through the maze, she wished she had paid greater attention at the time. But how could she recall something which meant nothing at the time?

"Lady Isabella, this is the third time we have passed this stalactite. I know because I marked it when we passed it before."

"I – I – I'm almost there."

"We are running out of time. Once the drones begin mining, we will never get away."

"Please, we are so close . . ."

"I'm afraid you are taking us on a wild goose chase, madam. Guards, bind her."

"No, don't."

The guards restrained Isabella and led her back through the tunnels toward the coach. Teary-eyed, Isabella shuffled forward. When she continued to urge Calin for more time, he berated her in a loud voice.

"Calin? Can it be you?" said a voice which sounded weak and fearful.

The little man halted and placed his finger to his lips. A look of agitation blended with hope covered his face. His skin

Chapter 28

tone morphed from dark mustard to the yellow of a ripe banana as recognition dawned. He cocked his head to hear better. The tunnel was silent.

"That was Galbena, wasn't it?"

"Shush, I'm trying to listen," said Calin, cupping a hand to his ear. "Galbena?"

"Oh my God, my darling. Calin, I'm over here," she said, her voice rising in excitement.

"Quiet, my love, we don't want to alert the guards."

Moments later, after a series of soft, guiding directions, Isabella saw Calin reunite with his wife. Their hugs and kisses produced a hue of golden bliss in the pair that made Isabella smile wistfully.

"Calin, I hate to be a killjoy, but we have to leave. The mine will be humming soon and we cannot be found here."

"You can leave," he replied, directing the guards to release her. They handed her the dagger which they had confiscated earlier.

"Galbena and I must rescue our children. She says they are in a cell down this tunnel. Goodbye, Isabella."

After a moment's hesitation, Isabella turned away and hustled back the way they had come. Isabella sensed a weak vibration coursing through the tunnels as she navigated toward the coach and the path to freedom. The sound of the drone miners chanting their doleful refrain signaled the beginning of mining. She crept toward the sound, a plan forming in her head. The egregore was the key.

When she got to the cavern, Isabella spied the egregore in the glass-enclosed booth. Marionette strings manipulated the arms of the wooden effigy which swayed like it was conducting an orchestra of drone miners. A subtle thrumming from a structure near the stream attracted her attention. This must be the power source for the mine. Isabella stayed in the shadows as she crept past several guards who wore the bored countenance which comes from mindless surveillance never resulting in activity.

She entered the structure and discovered an intricate waterwheel transferring energy to the mining operation. If she could disable it, there might be enough of a distraction to complete her plan. Fire would work. She searched for a flint without success. She could try to grab one of the torches lighting the tunnels but that would risk exposure. Isabella slapped her forehead for failing to think of the obvious.

Reaching for the chain around her neck, she withdrew the silver tube and blew a lengthy distress signal. While she waited by the entrance tunnel, she tried to count the number of guards on duty.

A smile creased her face when she saw a faint glow coming.

"Clopotica, it is wonderful to see you and the girls," Isabella said in the tongue-clicking language of the *Zinese*.

After exchanging pleasantries, Isabella explained the reason she summoned the fairies.

"You called all the way here with a distress signal to have us start a fire?"

Isabella nodded.

"You think that because we glow that we are pyromaniacs?"

Clopotica and her coterie pulsed with agitated flashing, mostly in vibrant red tones.

"Let me start over. I called you because we are going to liberate these drone slaves," said Isabella, gesturing toward the procession of chanting miners. "The only way to do this is to distract the guards while I disable the egregore."

"There's an egregore here? Why didn't you say so in the first place? Where is this building? Do you want a slow

Chapter 28

smoldering fire? Or, a rip-roaring flamer that will rival a Chinese New Year's celebration?"

"The latter," said Isabella, with a sigh of relief.

"We're on it. Come on, girls, battle-lighting, forward."

Isabella moved into position while a subdued cloud of *zine* snuck toward the target. As the building burst into flames, streaking flares of light erupted upward. An alarm bell clanged, summoning guards to the conflagration. Adnor raced to the fire, gesticulating and shouting orders to form a bucket brigade from the stream to the building, As the silvery water sizzled into the flames, it produced amber-colored steam.

Isabella raced to the egregore booth. What she encountered when she opened the door made her gasp. The egregore was a carved likeness of Petru Aron. Her shock that Stefan's enemy wielded dark power quickly evaporated. With a strong hand, she grasped the strings controlling the egregore and hacked at the cords with her dagger. The cords were made of piano wire and she struggled to sever them.

One of the guards saw her and ran to stop her. His pounding cracked the wood. He had broken enough boards that he was reaching in to turn the handle. As he opened the door, a buzzing, blast of brilliance attacked him. Clopotica and her coterie forced him backwards as he flailed at the *zine*. With one final surge, Isabella slashed the remaining cords. It was as if the drone miners were connected to the cords. They stopped chanting. They looked around as if awakened from a trance, eyes blinking and heads shaking to clear away cobwebs.

At the cessation of chanting Adnor's head snapped to the collapsed egregore.

"Get her!"

The guards dropped their buckets and ran toward Isabella. They surrounded the booth and stabbed with swords and pikes. Although the glass was reinforced, it cracked under the onslaught. Isabella's eyes widened as the booth shuddered. The noise attracted the attention of the drone miners who picked up whatever implements they could find and rushed to save their liberator. Hundreds of miners overwhelmed the guards and secured the egregore booth. They hoisted Isabella onto their shoulders and cheered wildly.

In the chaos, Adnor and several of his senior officers slinked away.

"But, sire, the slaves are escaping into the tunnels," said one of the overseers.

"Nothing to worry about. The tunnels are an impassable maze. Every miner who has tried to escape, has returned or we found their miserable bodies within a few days. This will not end well for them."

CHAPTER 29

After the brutal murders at Reuseni, Stefan fled in the dead of night like a scared boy. The Stefan who drove the wagon south from the Forges of Ezrok was different. Gone were the jutting chin and pretentious strut of his youth. Now, Stefan strode with purpose, posture erect with his gaze level. No longer did his eyes dart around as if he were worried about being exposed as a pretender. He had the eyes of an owl, exuding wisdom and strength.

As the sun set, a great weariness overcame Stefan. He passed the reins to Telly and crawled into the wagon bed where he fell asleep within seconds. His thoughts drifted to the last moments with Rico at the rope bridge when Petru Aron's squad of thugs chased them across the rope bridge. In his dream, Stefan shouted, "Noooo!" as Rico disappeared into the spume of the river.

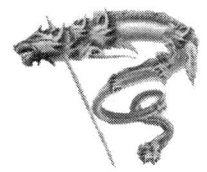

The bridge swayed and wobbled as Rico scrambled for safety. A bolt from Dryger's crossbow sped toward Rico. He looked into Stefan's eyes which were wide in alarm. An instant before impact, Rico thought he saw the silver tip of a projectile reflected in his friend's eyes.

Rico felt a powerful force strike him in the back like a sledge hammer. It was like the time an agitated stallion kicked him on the thigh. He was black and blue for a month. The impact of the projectile drove him off balance. Stretching his tall frame to its fullest, Rico reached for Stefan's hand but it was just out of reach. Rico grasped for the rope handrail as he staggered precariously over the gorge. It was limp. The bridge twisted and Rico tumbled downward, flailing.

The sound of the river sloshing through the crevasse grew louder as his fall accelerated. An agonized scream trailed him. His eyes meet Stefan's which were wide in helpless despair.

As he fell, Rico heard a strangely familiar buzzing. Braced for impact, he feared the worst. It did not happen. His fall was cushioned and it seemed like he floated gently into the water. The swift current swept him downstream while he struggled to keep his head above the roiling surface. After a sharp turn in the river, he lost sight of the fallen bridge and where he last saw his friends.

Chapter 29

An odd buoyancy supported him, as the river carried him away. Performing a mental inventory, he concluded that he had landed in one piece. Rico tried to comprehend how he survived his fall. He knew that it was more than luck.

His mind raced to his last seconds on the swaying bridge. An image of Isabella surfaced in his mind. She was doing something, what was it? Like a flash of lightning, he recognized that she was playing her flute. That was it. Isabella had summoned water fairies to save him.

At first, the chill water soothed the injury to his back. After a while his back stiffened. He could feel the no entry wound from the crossbow bolt. Rico guffawed at the fact that the arrow had struck his backpack right where he carried the iron pot which he had found in the cave of Zalmoxis. It had saved his life.

His float down river was a tonic compared to the recent danger and manic pace of their flight. Rico's state-of-mind was a mixture of survivor's glee and a desire to block out the trauma. He drifted for hours upon hours until he noticed that the water was turning warmer and warmer. The sun shone brightly and reddened his sun-deprived skin. A gnawing ache in his stomach convinced him to paddle to the shore to find some food. He landed in a strange and alien place.

The Land of Xeric

In ancient times the site of the fortress was a fertile, verdant paradise that was the crossroads of traders coming from the exotic lands. It was considered a free zone where peoples of all nations were welcome. That all changed when a horde of vagabonds led by the Bald One appeared from nowhere and pitched their tents. As was the custom, the caretakers accommodated their needs, liveried their mounts, and exchanged their hides for gold. The vagabonds found the environs so pleasant that they stayed. It wasn't long before they extorted money from the caretakers in return for protection from non-existent threats.

Within a year, they were charging tolls to caravans taking shelter there. Within three years, they had erected walls around the oasis, excluding travelers without the wherewithal to pay exorbitant prices for the previously free resources. Within five years after their arrival, they had built a foreboding fortress.

The leader of these thugs and criminals was the Bald One who was so bizarre and narcissistic that he invented special pronouns for himself – ze was substituted for he, zis was substituted for his, and zir was substituted for their.

No one knew that zis given name was Hekpac Vuk. Ze was known as the Bald One. Ze was the rare instance where genetic anomalies combined to form a creature of peculiar attributes. Few men had seen a creature afflicted with alopecia, a condition which renders the person hairless. Few men had seen an albino, a creature born without pigmentation. It appears white with pink eyes. Fewer had seen an androgyne, a creature born with a mixture of male and female sex traits. No one alive had ever seen a person with all three – that is, until they saw the Bald One.

Ze was tall, broad across the chest and hips, with multiple bulges that made both men and women blush. From beneath a pale, hairless brow, pink, bloodshot eyes appeared to glow like pastel embers used by magicians to startle an audience. Zis voice was alternately beguiling or stentorian depending on the Bald One's mood. The clothing ze preferred to wear was a mélange of leather and lace which was at the same time intimidating and bewitching.

Chapter 29

The Bald One was passionate about two things – horse-breeding and sadism.

Over time he bred horses that could withstand the thermal rigors of his adopted homeland. Eighty percent of the country was composed of desert so xeric and scorching, that the royal viziers called the expanse between the fortress and the borders, the Sulphur Hell-plains. There was no record of any wingless creature surviving crossing the hell-plains without a passport from the Bald One.

Early in life, the Bald One understood that his differences were too great for other mortals to ignore. As a youngster, ze was shunned, mocked, and abused. When he was a youngster, another anomalous creature was born. It was a cremello pony with rosy pink skin and pale blue eyes. One night the pony appeared on the Bald One's doorstep, a mocking gift to a fitting owner. On seeing the pony, he hugged its neck and kissed its muzzle with such passion that zis parents wept at the bond between the pair.

The Bald One and the pony were inseparable. Ze only found solace in the company of his pony. Unlike its master, the pony was incapable of judgment and accepted zis young master unconditionally. Zis fondest memories were of galloping through freshly-fallen snow or fragrant meadows of zis birthland. Many years later when the cremello died, the Bald One ran away in pain and embarked upon a life of a vagabond wreaking havoc on those less powerful.

When the Bald One and zis gang took over the oasis, ze had wealth beyond zis imaginings, enough wealth to indulge zis passion for horses. He constructed mews and a veterinary school that rivaled the Lipizzan stud farms of Slovenia. He interrogated travelers who came to the fortress about horse breeding practices across the world. The Bald One often purchased prime specimens which ze bred with choice mares. After many years and much selective breeding, the Bald One created a horse perfect for zis domain. A horse of massive haunches with a unique frog in a solar concavity of its hooves which minimized contact with the scorching surface of the desert. At full gallop, the horse appeared to fly across the landscape. The Bald One called him *Hayalet*, the Turkish word for wraith.

The true villainy of a despot revolves around the pain inflicted on victims. Every despot has a dungeon for incarcerating and punishing enemies. Usually the conditions are so dark, dank, and cold-deadened that prisoners die from infection or disease. The Bald One was a despot to be sure, but ze valued zis own hedonistic pleasure too much to locate zis headquarters in a northern clime where frigid conditions existed. Zis fortress was set in the middle of a vast desert. Zis dungeon was the antithesis of the stereotypical dungeon.

Rather than being in the bowels of the castle, the Bald One's dungeon was located at the highest tower, on the roof. It had no walls. It consisted of an anchor bolt embedded in granite to secure the prisoner's leg irons. There was more than one jailer and each had his particular form of brutality.

When the jailer used long chains on the leg irons, the prisoner was in danger of being blown off the tower by the jugo, the blistering hot winds of the endless desert. Only by lying prone and shielding the eyes from the biting sand could a prisoner survive. It was not uncommon for a guard to find a dead prisoner, hanging upside down by his leg irons on the side of the tower. Jailers who wanted to prolong the agony used shorter chains which anchored the prisoner to the center of the rooftop dungeon. The prisoner had to endure the relentless rays of the sun and heat radiating from the granite

Chapter 29

surface. No shade, no water, and no human contact quickly drove men to madness or death.

One of the prisoners was a battered traveler who wandered into the fortress in need of food, water, and medical attention. To his intimates he was known as Rico. The fact that he was handsome was enough to engender the hatred of the Bald One. Soon after Rico's arrival, the Bald One drugged his food and placed him in chains.

During his imprisonment on the rooftop dungeon, Rico planned his escape if he ever got the opportunity. He knew that he could not make it across the desert without help. His best chance would be to attach himself to a departing caravan by hiding amid the cargo. The season of caravans had passed, so he would have to bide his time until an opportunity presented itself.

From his perch on the dungeon tower, Rico watched the Bald One ride a magnificent stallion each morning. The young prisoner admired the deep chest and strong, well-muscled shoulders and legs of the horse. His ebony coat rivaled the morning sunrise in brilliance. When they returned from their ride, his hide shone dun with sweat. His tail was braided at the base and carried high and regal, a fitting complement to his proud, arching neck. Rico was too far away to see the large expressive eyes, flared ears, and wide nostrils capable of consuming massive quantities of oxygen to feed the powerful lungs and heart. No matter, Rico thought, as he nicknamed the magnificent creature Dravan, the word for marvelous in his tongue.

"I-i ie waui hwep ie."

"I-i ie waui hwep ie."

He opened one eye to see what was awakening him. His eyes were crusty from the nocturnal cleansing of dust and specks from his eyes. He barely consumed enough fluids for his eyes to function properly. With his hands manacled, it was difficult to rub the sleep out of his eyes. There it was, a pretty little yellow-green bird. He would later learn that his new friend was a yellow wagtail. But for the moment, he sat and enjoyed the prancing of the little bird. It seemed to stare intently into his eyes when it sang, "I-i ie waui hwep ie." It was as if it was trying to say something. The young man closed his eyes and concentrated.

"I-i ie waui hwep ie."

He shook his head. Could it be? No, the bird could not be singing, "I want to help you." Or, could he be losing his grip on reality?

"I-i ie waui hwep ie, I want to help you."

Rico scratched his head. Either this is really happening, or he was going mad. Either way, what harm would there be if he asked the bird "how?"

It had been so long since he had used his vocal cords, that his first few attempts sounded like dry croaks. He bit the inside of his cheeks slightly to stimulate some saliva.

"Hwew, hwew," he uttered.

The bird cocked her head and ruffled her feathers.

Rico nodded and repeated his question using his tongue to say it in more of a whistling manner. The creature wagged her tail, apparently a gesture of assent, and hopped over to the device connecting the chain to the anchor bolt. She pecked at it.

When Rico grasped that the bird wanted him to turn the lock over, his weather-beaten face erupted into a broad grin. The crinkling of skin around his mouth hurt. Not wanting to startle his new friend, Rico scooched slowly over toward the lock. He flipped it over, exposing the keyhole. The bird hopped

Chapter 29

onto it and defecated into the hole. Then she flew away. Rico shook his head and stared at the lock in disbelief, as if to ask himself, "What were you expecting?"

Several monotonous hours later, the bird returned. She landed on Rico's shoulder and dropped several purple berries into his shirt pocket. When Rico attempted to remove one, the bird squawked like her nest were being attacked by a weasel. Rico withdrew his hand.

"*Da, da*, I'll leave them alone," he muttered. They probably are sour anyway, he thought to himself.

The bird gave him a satisfied look and alighted on the lock. She aligned her rump over the keyhole and defecated. Rico leaned forward and sniffed. He caught a harsh, acrid odor that repulsed him. The small creature looked at him and shook her head. She kept him company that afternoon and when the sun set behind her it illuminated the bird.

"I think I'll call you Halo," said the man who tried whistling the name. The bird responded with a trilling noise that Rico could have sworn sounded like her name.

Over the next few days, they repeated this routine. A chalky, viscous sludge clogged the keyhole and Rico's pocket overflowed with purple berries. Rico could hardly contain his glee that the jailer was oblivious to the plot. When the man left him a cup of water and some dried camel bread, Rico had to keep from guffawing at the trick they were playing. Once, he thought that the jailer was wise to their game because he threw a stone at Halo. It clipped her wing and Rico worried when the bird failed to return after the thug left.

Rico stood and shimmied to the edge of the tower to see if he could find Halo. He was so weak that he tottered near the edge. Lightheaded, he braced himself with the only thing available. As the heavy chain came taut, Rico heard a faint click. He teetered near the edge about to fall. Out of nowhere a yellow figure flashed to him and gripped his shirt with her beak. The backward thrust of her wings was enough for him to regain his balance.

The young man stumbled and landed in a heap next to the lock. To his amazement, the hasp was open. Halo chirped a celebratory note. Rico gave her a double-take before comprehending that the acids in the bird poop had dissolved the mechanism. He separated the links from the hasp and was free. Halo flew into his face and alighted on the edge of his pocket. She jumped from there to the cup of water and back. She did this several times before it dawned on Rico what Halo was trying to tell him.

"You want me to put the berries in the water? Is that it, Halo?"

His friend fluttered up and down in front of him, chirping, "Ywew, ywew."

Rico turned his pocket inside out and plopped the berries into the tepid water. The concoction fizzed, bubbled, and sputtered. Rico watched as the berries expanded and rose from the cup. A strand formed on each berry. As they rose, the berries twisted and knitted into a cord that thickened into a rope which coiled at his feet.

The only evidence of dawn was a dim light vanquishing the darkness in the cloudless, eastern sky. It was a harbinger of another dreadfully hot day. Rico tied the berry rope to the anchor bolt and peered over the edge. He noticed that the fortress was still, there were only slight stirrings around the mews as the stablemen prepared for the day's activity. Soon the fortress would be teeming with activity. It was now or never.

Chapter 29

He tugged the rope to make sure it would hold his weight. Satisfied, Rico coiled his chains in one arm and leaped into space. Rico felt a surge of adrenaline as he rappelled down the side of the tower with the surefootedness of the lizards he had seen skittering on the fortress walls.

On the ground, he snapped the rope and it released. After spending so much time on top of the tower overviewing the entire fortress, he was disoriented at ground-level. He started walking and was about to stumble into the mess area where the Bald One's soldiers were entering for their morning meal. An urgent caw from Halo and tugging on his collar averted disaster.

Admonishing himself to be more careful, Rico reversed course and headed toward the stables. It wasn't long before his nose told him he was heading in the right direction. When he arrived, his heart jumped in his chest. The groom was adjusting the bridle on the magnificent stallion he had dubbed **Dravan**. The splendid creature snorted and jittered in anticipation of his morning exercise. Rico pounced on the unsuspecting groom, tying and gagging him with the rope.

In one fluid motion, **Rico** mounted **Dravan** with the mastery of the Mongol raiders he had seen invade from the steppes. The horse hesitated for a split second, gauging the lighter weight of his rider and the assurance of his directions. As if deciding that **Rico** was worthy, **Dravan** bolted into action. In a few strides, the giant beast was galloping toward the gate.

The guards who were accustomed to their master's often erratic moods hastened to open the main gate at the sight of **Dravan** racing through the fortress square. One of the guards on the wall saw that the Bald One was not the rider. He shouted an alarm. Tumult reigned as the guards below tried to reverse the gate opening. It was too late as **Rico** was speeding to the opening. Several soldiers moved to block his path, drawing their weapons. Rico felt the muscles of **Dravan** flexing and releasing in powerful thrusts as his hooves skimmed over the cobblestones. With a giddy sense of power surging up from **Dravan**, **Rico** uncoiled the chain and swung it over his head. It hit the guards with such force that it nearly cleaved them in two.

Almost free, he thought. Then he saw some guards pushing a wagon to block the gate. **Rico** could either pull up the horse or try to jump the wagon. He wasn't sure of **Dravan's** jumping ability and he was wary that the gate opening might not be high enough for them both to clear the lintel. **Dravan** must have sensed a relaxation in **Rico** as he made these calculations. The horse decided for him. As if propelled by a desire to liberty that surpassed **Rico's**, **Dravan** resolved to vault the obstacle to freedom. Feeling the horse accelerate, Rico leaned forward and whispered sweet encouragement.

In unison, the horse and rider soared over the wagon. Rico's long hair mingled with **Dravan's** mane as they soared through the narrow space under the crosspiece of the gate. After a perfect landing and evading arrows from the parapets, they were free.

At least, until an irate Bald One organized a hunting party.

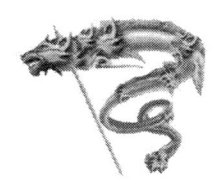

CHAPTER 30

After almost freezing to death in the mountains and almost roasting to death on the rooftop dungeon, Rico was ecstatic to be galloping toward freedom. Even though he was unsure of his destination, it was enough that he was on horseback, streaking away as fast as his steed could race. He tightened his knees and raised both his arms in triumph. A silly grin split his sunburned face.

It was difficult to discern which creature was more euphoric at their break for freedom. Dravan felt a sensitivity in this rider which contrasted to the oppressive style of his former rider. It was much more than the difference in weight, his new rider possessed skill and intuition. Most important, he did not rely on the whip and spurs to direct the horse. By the time they were out of range of the archers, Rico and Dravan were like a synchronized machine. As horse and rider merged, the distance covered by each stride increased until to a stationary observer Dravan would have seemed like a mythical Pegasus flying over the desert.

With the slightest lean Rico steered the stallion toward a dried riverbed whose surface appeared like a checkerboard made of squares with curled edges. He hoped it would lead to the river which had brought him to this God-forsaken place. If he never saw the Land of Xeric again, it would be too soon. Dravan skimmed gracefully over the desiccated bed. So swift and light was Dravan's touch that he left no imprints on the cracked, baked surface. Nor was there any telltale dust to mark their location. Rico fixed his eyes on the verdant mountains in the distance and prayed that they would find shelter there before the desert turned them into cinders.

Back at the fortress, the Bald One was in a rage which surpassed the most turbulent sandstorm. He bellowed orders at the captain of the guard with such speed and complexity that the poor man stood, nodding and quaking. He moved only when the Bald One slashed him across the face with his riding crop. As blood flowed down his cheeks and mouth, the captain shouted contradictory orders to the guard contingent which dashed about like a fire brigade during a volcanic eruption.

Amused by the spectacle playing out in front of them, the experienced soldiers among them took matters into their own hands and formed four squads, one for each compass point. They gathered provisions necessary for an extended foray into the desert. They knew that if the mission to recapture the stallion and the prisoner was unsuccessful, no one would be

Chapter 30

safe. Better to bring enough provisions to bolt beyond the wrath of the Bald One than return to hell.

The Bald One found the stable master and beat him senseless. Naturally, this delayed the saddling of horses. By the time the posse mounted for instructions, several hours had passed. In the interim, ze released four raptors from their cages in the mews, removed their hoods, and launched them to search for zis prey. These birds were magnificent flyers, bred for endurance and superior vision. The Bald One won the birds and their falconer in a game of chance with a sultan who was too enamored with the Bald One's courtesans to notice the Bald One switching the dice. In the end, the Bald One mollified the sultan by gifting him his pick of the harem.

By the time the posse was ready, the Bald One was frothing at the mouth. When ze finally raced out of the fortress into the midday sun, ze headed north and the other squads departed in their directions. The leader of the southbound group sighed in relief at the good fortune of heading in the opposite direction from his insane master. While his second-in-command was getting weapons at the armory, the leader stopped at the treasury and filled his saddlebags with pilfered jewelry. He figured that it was fair compensation for all his years of service.

Immediately after clearing the gate, the Bald One realized the inferior quality of zis mount. Ze missed the magical strides of zis beloved *Hayalet*. To make up for lost time, ze whipped the horse savagely and spurred its flanks viciously. Before they reached the dried riverbed, zis horse was lathered with a thick, white foam from the exertion of carrying the bulky rider, running in deep sand, and anxiety from harsh treatment. The members of the Bald One's posse exchanged glances. Their eyes expressed sympathy for the poor beast. When the Bald

One finally signaled for them to halt, exhaustion etched the faces of the men and animals.

"Where did they go? It's like that wraith disappeared into thin air," thundered the Bald One. "An extra 1,000 gold pieces to the man who captures them alive!"

"Do you want the man alive also, sire?" asked one of the soldiers, who was known for his savagery. The Bald One pounded zis chest with zis meaty fist clutching the bloody riding crop, making it clear that ze wanted the pleasure of inflicting an excruciating death on the man.

"We will split into three groups. Burak and Voyk, you come with me. Rico will follow the riverbed. The rest of you, head northeast and northwest. We will meet back at the fortress at the next full moon," said the Bald One whose baleful look made it clear that no one should return empty-handed.

The Bald One's anger was tempered by zis knowledge of the terrain. Ze knew that in order to escape from Xeric the fugitives must pass through Miasma, a quagmire inhabited by mysterious and murderous beings. Ze scanned the sky for signs of zis hunting birds. Ze mumbled zis displeasure at the empty skies and made a mental note to torture the falconer upon return to the fortress.

Rico and Dravan were far ahead of their pursuers and their lead increased with every stride. While he knew that his mount could outrun the posse, his odds would improve exponentially if they could find cover. He sensed that Dravan felt the same because whenever Rico sought to conserve energy, the big horse snorted, shook his head in defiance, and forged forward over the withered ground.

Feeling a stirring against his chest, Rico thought for an instance that he might be suffering from heat exhaustion.

Chapter 30

Looking down he saw the friendly face of Halo poking out of his shirt.

"Look who is awake."

"I-i ie waui ti whing."

"Where do you want to fly?"

"*Ti ie monstie.*"

"To the monster? You mean the Bald One?"

The bird jumped from his pocket and hopped onto his finger where she roused, ruffling her feathers with a ripple which pulsed along her body, ending with a flourish at the tip of her tail.

"*Da*, Halo, but return before we enter those woods up there," said Rico, pointing his chin toward the dark green shape on the horizon. The wagtail seemed to nod, then leapt into the air. Halo rode a rising gust and was last seen flapping toward the wilderness they had traversed. It wasn't long before she spied another bird flying in her direction. As the distance between them narrowed, Halo recognized the larger bird as one of the hunting falcons from the fortress. No doubt it was on a search mission for the Bald One. Halo knew that she was at a grave disadvantage in any direct confrontation with the trained killer with its large, powerful wingspan and sharp talons. There was one tactic that might work to divert this spying enemy.

A swift flurry of strokes thrust Halo high into the air. She turned and positioned herself so that she would be coming out of the sun. Summoning all her nerve, the little bird tucked her wings and dove toward the falcon. An instant prior to impact, Halo pulled up and landed on the falcon's back. She dug her claws into her enemy's feathers as if perching on a tree limb, and hunkered down.

The unexpected attack startled the falcon. Disorientation entered its bird brain. Nothing in its instincts or training had prepared it for an assault of this nature. Its first reaction was to peck at the intruder. When that failed, it tried to dive and ascend rapidly in hopes of dislodging its unwanted passenger.

With his focus on the green land beyond the desert, Rico did not see the antics of the irritated falcon as it swooped, dove, and soared across the sky. It seemed like the falcon was drunk. Its obsession with removing Halo off its back distracted it from its mission. For her part, Halo hung on for dear life and the little creature's heart pounded with pride and excitement. If ever a wagtail received a thrill ride on a falcon, it was Halo.

Through wind-driven feathers, Halo peeked around the falcon's head. She saw that Rico was almost at the trees and would soon be shielded by the forest canopy. She had to hold on for a little while longer. The falcon squawked and cawed in frustration. In a move that reeked of desperation, the falcon tried another tactic. It turned upside down.

Falcons are not anatomically designed for inverted flight. In seconds, the falcon was in free fall, accelerating toward the earth. The creature was so distraught by the presence of Halo on its back that it seemed to prefer a suicide dive to carrying a passenger. It was as if its normally precise flight judgment was addled. Halo had no intention of joining the falcon in its self-destruction.

As Rico entered the forest, he turned to see the falcon speeding toward the ground. He had never seen a falcon behave in this manner. As he watched, Rico urged the creature to pull up, to alter its course and swoop out of its dive. When it reached the point where even powerful wings could not avert a crash landing, Rico saw brown, grey, green and yellow, and black talons on the spiraling falcon. The bird hit the ground at full speed and disintegrated in a plume of feathers. Rico felt a surge of discomfort in the pit of his stomach over the demise of such a magnificent creature. *How bizarre.*

The Land of Miasma

As Rico and Dravan entered the forest, a feeling of apprehension permeated him like a toxic potion. He could not identify the source of his anxiety. The young man dismounted and led the horse along the riverbed which was no longer hard-packed and dry. The surface was brittle like an egg shell, but soft underneath almost as if a winter rain soaked it and drained quickly beneath the porous surface. Though still mostly sand, it held the promise of moisture. This made walking on it somewhat refreshing. Rico breathed in air which had a hint of humidity. It was a pleasant change from the air of Xeric which was as hot and scorching as the furnace endured by Daniel in the Bible.

A nervous sense of relief settled over Rico and Dravan. The forest canopy shielded them from the powerful mid-afternoon sun. Although they did not know the name of this place, it seemed an improvement over the desert. At its edge, the Land of Miasma exuded a welcoming humidity, the promise of refreshing moisture which seduced them into complacency.

"Have you seen Halo?" said Rico absentmindedly to the mighty stallion.

Dravan bared his teeth and whinnied. Rico chuckled, convinced that the horse's head shake was a coincidence.

"I told that silly bird to return when we entered this forest. I hope she's safe."

As he uttered these words, Rico recalled the spiraling falcon and the yellow mass he saw in the swirl. Could Halo have been caught in the crash? No, how could that be? Halo was too smart to get tangled with such a fearsome predator. Rico was about to chalk his fear off to the tension of recent events when he inhaled sharply. He had no choice; they had to go look for the crash. Halo could be injured and need their help.

Back in the blazing sun, they wandered in the direction which Rico thought was the falcon crash site. Rico replayed the scene in his head. Something about the swirling bird nagged at him. It was the patch of yellow that he saw as the predator plummeted. Maybe it was the yellow legs of the falcon, maybe not. He rushed over a small hillock and saw a bloody pile of mangled feathers and a carcass in the sand.

It was the falcon. Rico saw what appeared to be stark white sticks poking out of the feathers. He understood that he was looking at shattered bones of the creature. Rico knelt next to it. He felt a surge of bile rising in the back of his throat as he examined the remains of the once magnificent bird. A tug on the reins he held loosely in his hand drew his attention to an inert lump of yellow a few yards away from the falcon. Dravan was standing over something. He was nuzzling it.

Before he could rise, Rico felt a vibration in the sand, followed by the distinctive sound of men on horseback. A shiver of dread shot through him as he recognized the voice of the Bald One exhorting his band. Rico leaped toward Dravan and was about to mount when he spied what had attracted the horse's attention. Rico scooped up the motionless figure of Halo and placed it in his pocket. He would sort out the bird's condition later. At that moment, he had greater concerns.

CHAPTER 31

The Bald One and his men whooped a war cry when they cleared the low ridge and saw Rico. Their weariness with the search converted into wild energy. The Bald One spurred his mount mercilessly. The desperate horse surged forward. It was no match for Dravan who bounded into full stride with Rico clinging to his back low in the saddle to avoid the arrows that Burak and Voyk shot at him.

Dravan pulled away from their pursuers. Their lead lessened as they entered the unfamiliar territory of the forest. Following the dry riverbed, Dravan found what appeared to be a path deeper into the woods. The Bald One was in hot pursuit screaming curses and threats. Dravan's strides were so swift that he skimmed above the ground. The terrain was changing. As they got deeper into the forest, the surface became spongy and mossy. They followed the path to a bog. It contained various peats, cranberry plants, and stunted tamarack trees. Dravan increased his speed to avoid getting entangled in the vegetation below them.

Rico glanced at the plants and saw pairs of oval shaped leaves with spiky edges. The leaves were opening and closing as if they were the jaws of thousands of hungry green mouths. He blinked in disbelief as he saw the bodies of toads and other water creatures inside some of these things. Rico recalled hearing tales from his tribesmen about carnivorous plants but he always thought that they were stories meant to frighten the young ones. Apparently not.

While Dravan flew over the surface, the Bald One's horse struggled in the mire. Though valiant, the Bald One's horse was spent. When it hit a depression below the watery surface it stumbled, pitching its rider into the bog. Rico heard the screams of the Bald One calling to his companions to rescue him from the snapping plants. Rico turned to see the horse sinking into quicksand while Burak and Voyk threw lassoes toward the Bald One.

Dravan continued his dash from the enemy and resisted Rico's assurances that the danger was over. The mighty steed crossed the marshland and found higher ground which led to a riverbed. The sounds of rushing water filled the woods. Dravan slowed his pace until he found an eddy of water at a slight bend in the river which was flowing and glittering in the late afternoon sun. Rico dismounted and watched Dravan drink his fill of the crystal water.

Chapter 31

    Finding a stump to sit on, he gently removed Halo from his pocket. His friend's breathing was ragged and shallow. Although Halo showed no outward signs of injury, the bird twitched and cawed as if she were experiencing some kind of awful pain. Rico surmised that it had something to do with the ordeal suffered by the falcon. A veil of dread covered Rico's face. Halo's breath halted, then resumed when Rico gently massaged her chest. A sense of panic crept into his mind; he could not bear the thought of losing his deliverer. *Think, think of something.*

    A slight breeze ruffled the leaves. A whiff of fragrance captured Rico's attention. Honeysuckle. He went to a vine laden with delicate reddish flowers accented with bright yellow centers. Recalling his childhood, he pulled on the center stalk. A shining droplet of amber nectar clung to the edge of the pistil. Rico brought it to Halo and touched the golden liquid to her beak. Rico repeated this several times. Halo calmed and lapsed into a restful sleep.

    As the sun set, Rico shivered in a chill breeze. He gathered some kindling and lit a small fire. The effect was soothing and soon his head nodded. As he drifted, his eyes fluttered. He thought that Dravan moved toward the embers. Between blinks he saw the horse lower his head and bite into the fire. Dravan raised his head and nickered in satisfaction. It was as if Rico's mind was so exhausted that it declined to register the scene before him. Rico fell into an uneasy slumber.

    Well into the night, the moon was at its zenith and the forest was alive with nocturnal sounds. Owls, reptiles and night feeders roamed looking for prey. Gaps in the ground opened and released foul excretions as if the land itself was putrefying. Tree frogs croaked and insects trilled in a primal plea for a mating partner. The air was gauzy making visibility limited. The three refugees lay unsuspecting on a patch of grass.

From the adjacent foliage, a hand reached for Dravan and stroked his muzzle. The horse sighed. He remained asleep as the being petted the area around his eyes. His breathing deepened as a spell entered his brain. Dravan would be immobilized until the sun rose.

Apparition-like, figures arose from the forest. Their forms were unmistakably feminine and naked except for flowing diaphanous gowns which glowed with an erotic iridescence. Their faces were the essence of desire, the perfect blend of angelic innocence and barely disguised lust. Long tresses rippled around their faces and shoulders in sybaritic splendor. Entering the clearing with the grace of a ballerina troop, they encircled the camp. As they assembled, the delicate bells around their ankles tinkled ever so faintly. Halo stirred. They were in grave danger. Posed in a circle as if awaiting the conductor's baton were the *Ielele*.

According to legend, the *Ielele* were the spirits of Dacian High Priestesses. Although the group of *Ielele* appeared similar due to their garb, nothing could be further from the truth. Each embodied the wondrous variety of feminine beauty in shape, complexion, and features. Renowned for their beauty, these beings danced the *hora* with sensuous abandon capable of driving a man mad with lust. The *Ielele* were the aggregation of every masculine dream, vision, and fantasy. It was well known that the *Ielele* were extremely protective of the secrets of their ritual dances. The folk tales were rife with stories of squadrons of men being torn to pieces by *Ielele* who transformed into raging banshees on those who saw them dancing.

Chapter 31

The sound of the *Ielele* moving into position awakened Halo who watched in stunned silence as the *Ielele* finalized their circle. Each dancer held a candle whose flickering glow added a magical aura to the idyllic scene. By some unknown signal, the *Ielele* began by moving their arms in a series of sensuous motions evocative of branches swaying in a sultry breeze. A vague percussive beat arose from their ankle-bells as they stepped into the *hora*, moving around the circle.

Rico shifted in his sleep. His forearm was draped over his forehead, shielding his eyes from the moonlight. The sound grew as the pace of the dance quickened. As wakefulness returned to Rico his arm dropped. The *Ielele* clapped rhythmically and individual *iele* released cries of ecstasy. As Rico's eyelids twitched on the verge of lifting, Halo flew to him and smothered his eyes with her wings. She admonished Rico to remain still or forfeit his life.

They remained like this as the fervor of the *Ielele* dance rose to a fever pitch. The enticing figures of the *Ielele* glistened under the moonbeams. The sounds of their dancing coalesced into a music reminiscent of the song which tempted Odysseus. Whenever Rico attempted to peek through the feathers, Halo pressed down harder. With dawn nearing, the *Ielele* peeled off one-by-one back into the forest as mysteriously as they appeared. Halo waited quite a while before she relinquished her hold. Both were astonished when they saw that the *Ielele* had burned a perfectly-formed circle into the grass.

Over the following days, Rico and his friends traveled through Miasma. They followed the river leading away from the Bald One. Dravan raced ahead at a breakneck pace. It was as if he were an equine machine fueled by the large quantities of embers – which was exactly the case. Once he got past the improbability of it, Rico was aware that the stallion was a supernatural marvel. They traversed the Land of Miasma in record time and entered the lowlands of the Carpathian Mountains and Moldova.

They found the land devastated as if it had been the victim of biblical retribution. Traveling mainly at night to avoid detection, the little band slept during the day. Sometimes when they were near a village, Rico would go there for food, or to talk to people. In the short time since Bogdan's murder, goons sent by the new *voivode* confiscated food and supplies that the people had prepared for the winter. The constant refrain by the robbers was, "Petru Aron needs this more than you do."

On more than one occasion a farmer protesting this confiscation of his property was met with a cold, steel blade and left to bleed out in front of his wife and children. Rico heard stories of brigands abducting young maidens to become part of Petru Aron's harem.

"You know, Halo, tales of these atrocities enrage me. I only hope that Stefan will return with the repaired blade of Aparator to restore peace and justice. I will be at his side along with sweet Isabella."

"*Hie Isabella?*"

"What is an Isabella? That's right, you don't know her, yet. She is a beautiful, strong, wonderful angel. Isabella is the woman in white who saved us after the slaughter," he said, half to himself. As if recalling a pleasant memory, "Get this, Isabella calls me by my proper name."

The bird cocked her head with a quizzical look.

"Alright, I'll tell you but you must promise not to call me by it. Only Isabella gets to call me Viorico."

Halo chittered, trying to replicate the name.

Chapter 31

"You promised," said Rico in mock annoyance.

The man, bird, and horse searched for the place where Stefan, Isabella, and he had agreed to rendezvous if they ever got separated. Near the crossroads, he encountered a monk living in the trunk of an ancient cypress.

"Hail," said Seraphim whose sightless eyes stared vacantly toward the stranger.

"We come in peace and wish only to rest here for a while."

"Over there is fresh water for your mount. But I beg of you do not steal my meager provisions."

When Rico dismounted and walked toward the man, he cowered and twisted away in fear.

"You have nothing to fear from me, old man," said Rico who gazed at a welt on the man's face which resembled tenderized meat.

"Who did this to you?"

"No one. I fell on the gravel path."

The monk could not see the expression of disbelief on Rico's face.

"At least, let me apply a salve."

The Blind Monk acceded to Rico's ministrations and invited him into his abode. The monk pulled a jug from a hole in the dirt floor and offered Rico a swig. There was a strange purple-green ooze around the opening.

"It's mead I prepared last summer."

"I don't think so."

"What's the matter, young man? Are you afraid of disease?"

"It's not that. I have been traveling for a long time and my stomach is unsettled."

The monk took a healthy gulp from the jug.

"*Da*. Rest a while and I will tell you about another traveler like you who refused my drink. He went down a sorry road. His name is Vlad Tepes."

Like his head was on a swivel, Rico jerked toward the monk who had settled into a semi-reclining position perfect for spinning a tale.

"In the not-too-distant past, ___"

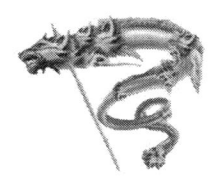

CHAPTER 32

As the horse-drawn wagon jounced along the rugged road, Stefan inhaled deeply. He woke refreshed at the new dawn. His nostrils tingled, welcoming the influx of fresh air. Since the tragic murders in Reuseni, he had spent more time in caves than he had ever thought possible. If he never saw another cave that would be too soon. As he steered the wagon away from the Forges of Ezrok, the simple delight of sunshine on his face produced a broad smile. He was not so sure whether his travelling companion shared his elation.

"Telly, how does it feel to be out in the great wide open?"

"It would feel a lot better if I wasn't stuck to this bouncy wagon. In case you haven't noticed, octopuses do not have asses to sit on."

As the wheels traversed a boulder, the wagon pitched to the side, sending Telly sliding into the seat rail. Stefan chuckled.

"It's not funny, Stefan," telepathed his companion.

"Don't fret. From the looks of your injured tentacle, you'll be back tentaculating through the forest in no time."

"*Si*, I hope that blasted *Ismeju* choked on my tentacle before you decapitated him."

"The sunshine on the budding leaves reminds me of the trips I took with my father to wine country. He would cut a bunch of grapes from a vine and squeeze it until the red juice flowed down his wrist and arm.

"This is the lifeblood of Moldova. It flows from mother earth to the vines into our bodies and becomes one with us. This liquid nourishes us and courses through our veins. In turn, we protect Moldova and its people. We will give our last drop of blood for our country. I miss him."

An anguished cry sliced through the air like a straight razor.

"What was that, Telly?"

"Probably just a crow."

"I don't know. I'm getting a bad feeling. Spring is coming. We should be seeing farmers working in the fields and orchards by now. The land appears barren. Look, up ahead, see that smoke? We must be coming up to a village. Time to go into stealth mode."

"*Si*," replied Telly as he slid into the wagon bed and covered their treasures with his camouflaged body.

The path to the village was familiar. It lay nestled next to a broad stream. Stefan recalled fishing there with his father

Chapter 32

when he was a youngster. It was the first time Bogdan had taken him fishing with some boyars. The memory of the trout he had hooked wiggled into his mind the same way the fish had wiggled out of his hands on that day. He visualized the slippery trout escaping from his grasp as he rushed to display his catch to his father. Stefan stumbled over a stone and fell headfirst into the rapid stream. He recalled the laughter of his father while he flailed helplessly after the fish.

"Bogdan, your boy just let our dinner swim away," joked one of the men.

"*Da*, he has a tendency to be all-thumbs. Another night of stale beer and moldy cheese for supper."

Bogdan's comment drew raucous laughter from the fishing party. Stefan's tears of humiliation were concealed by the water droplets from the stream. Wiping his nose on his sleeve, the young Stefan went back to the camp and spent the night in his tent nursing his wounds.

Telly was about to communicate that Stefan should dwell on the good memories when the sound of crying coming from a thicket interrupted him. Stefan reined in the horse and listened.

"Stay here. I'm going to check that sound."

The constant jouncing of the wagon produced a disorientation in Telly. He was exhausted and decided to use this opportunity to nap. Stefan received a groggy *da* in response. Neither heard the sound of steps nearby.

Stefan followed the sound of crying to the edge of the stream where he saw a young girl sitting on a boulder her head buried in her thin arms. From the looks of her ripped dress, he figured that she must have been living in the woods for a while. Hearing footsteps, she turned her face upwards. Dirt covered her face except tracks left by her tears. Her hair was matted and thick with twigs. She recoiled as he neared.

"No, no, don't hurt me."

She rose to flee but Stefan was quicker and grabbed her arm.

"Don't worry. I won't hurt you," he said in his gentlest voice.

When he knelt to be on her level, she sprang. In one swift move, she pushed his shoulder and scratched at his face with her other hand. The shove knocked him off balance, giving her the chance to race away. By the time Stefan scrambled to his feet, she had disappeared into the thick undergrowth. Grumbling about the thorns and brambles, Stefan let her go.

Back at the wagon, Telly was sound asleep in the wagon bed. It's odd, thought Stefan to hear another snoring in your head. Re-entering the sunlit road, Stefan sensed a note of discord. As his eyes adjusted to the light, he glimpsed a shadow near the wagon. Dagger drawn he circled the wagon. The undergrowth rustled as a figure fled. It must be the girl surmised Stefan. If he had paid attention to the size of the disturbance, he might have understood that it wasn't a young girl.

He mounted the wagon and clicked the horse forward. Rounding a curve, a village came into view. What he saw shocked him. A once bucolic village was now a mess of smoldering ruins. Fire had destroyed everything in sight. From his perch he could see burnt bodies lying amid the rubble. His sadness at the horror was interrupted by violent retching.

As they travelled through the province, they encountered similar scenes of death. The destruction left scarce cover for the stealthy shadow which kept its distance. Stefan's grip on

Chapter 32

the reins tightened and his jaw ached from constant clenching. There was no doubt in his mind that this devastation was the work of Petru Aron. This province had been strongly supportive of Bogdan and the inhabitants must have balked at the usurper's rule. Stefan imagined the terror of these peasants when the mercenaries attacked. Stefan closed his eyes as he envisioned the horror as the hellions raped and pillaged. His anger and dread increased as he approached his home village of Borzesti.

Stefan tried not to think of his mother and his siblings trying to defend themselves against these animals.

"Hai, dii! Giddy-up!"

The mare gave Stefan a backwards glance as if to say, we'll get there at my pace, son.

The sun was low as he entered the last stretch of forest before reaching Borzesti. Before Stefan could react, a man jumped from an overhanging branch and covered his head with a sack. Two riders came from nowhere and grabbed the bridle of his mare. In seconds, Stefan was a prisoner on his way to certain death. Muffled by the bag over his head, Stefan's protests were not loud enough to rouse Telly. The powerful octopus might have been formidable enough to thwart the abduction, but he was too busy dreaming about debuting his epic ballad at Stefan's coronation celebration.

Strong hands held Stefan in place as the wagon veered off the road onto a path that was more an animal trail than a road. The going was difficult and Stefan heard the mare straining. Through the scant light coming into the rough burlap of the sack, Stefan could tell that they were in the shadow of the forest canopy. He tried to communicate with Telly but received no reply. Once or twice, he heard his captors speak. Stefan assumed that they were passing through guarded checkpoints. They spoke in a dialect he recognized but could not place. He wracked his brain trying to recall where he had heard it before. Most likely, it was the speech of mercenaries who he had heard at the *petrecere*.

After an initial sense of heightened awareness, the tedium of the trip dulled his perceptions. He was brought back to awareness by the smell of cooking which got stronger after they splashed through a stream. When the wagon stopped, he steeled himself for his encounter with Petru Aron. Even though his hands were bound, Stefan would figure out a way to get one clear shot at the monster before his thugs killed him.

Yanked off the wagon and dragged into what sounded like a large camp, Stefan tried to maintain his balance as one of his captors pulled by the rope around his hands. He cursed under his breath. Then he heard Telly.

"Stefan, where are we?"

"Petru Aron's mercenaries have taken us prisoner. From the noise of horses and blacksmithing, it sounds like a camp of horsemen. They don't know about you, so stay hidden until I call for you. We have to protect Aparator at all costs."

"Will do."

Telly stayed in the wagon while it was driven toward the outskirts of the camp. He sensed being under the hate-filled gaze of someone or something.

The ruffians threw Stefan into a heap on the ground before a powerfully-built man. He was seated on a rough-hewn bench in a temporary wood structure that was built for quick exits. His unruly black hair resisted the colorful scarf which attempted to bind it.

"What do we have here?" asked an authoritarian voice.

"We caught him travelling alone outside of Borzesti. His wagon was empty except for some crystal residue."

Chapter 32

"One of Adnor's," the leader said to no one in a dismissive tone. "Take him to the pit for execution."

CHAPTER 33

As the guards frog-marched Stefan away, his mind filled with a thousand thoughts, none of them pleasant. The best alternative he could think of was to summon Telly. But to what end? Would the octopus be able to defeat what sounded like dozens of men? Even if Telly wielded Aparator, he would be grossly outnumbered. If only they had tested the combination of the sword with the battle helm and crown, maybe he would know his chances. They had been too driven to reach his family that they put it off until they had arrived. Hooded and bound, Stefan was in no position to do much of anything.

Chapter 33

"Wait! I am a citizen of Moldova and I demand my right to confront my adjudicator eye-to-eye. Not like this, like some low-born slave!"

A look of incredulity crossed the leader's face at this effrontery. His immediate reaction was to run his sword through this insolent whelp. Yet, there was something about that voice. He looked toward a woman standing at the edge of the gathering. Her dark eyes signaled reinforcement of his gut feeling.

"*Chavaía!* Stop!"

He gestured for the guards to remove the prisoner's hood.

When the coarse fabric rasped across Stefan's eyes, his vision was momentarily impaired. Though unfocussed, Stefan saw a large figure bounding toward him and he braced himself. An instant before impact, there was a shriek of recognition from the woman in the gathering.

"Stop! Bako, don't hurt him," shouted Ruxandra.

Bako grabbed Stefan with such force that the pair almost tumbled to the ground.

"O *Del!* Oh, God! You're alive!"

"It's a miracle!"

As Bako clapped Stefan on the arms, Ruxandra rushed between them.

"Bako, leave the boy alone, can't you see that he is stunned?"

"Stefan, you are with friends. It's me Ruxandra. You got my note! Praise God."

The young prince stood motionless, blinking, his brain working furiously to process the scene before him. One second earlier he was resigning himself to a bloody execution at the hands of his enemies. Now, his friends were hugging him, weeping tears of joy. With renewed clarity, Stefan recognized many smiling faces of people who had worked with his father.

"Here, sit, my son," said Bako Fotino, the leader of the *Calusari,* the secret society which supported Bogdan with the fiercest gypsy loyalty imaginable. He guided Stefan toward his chair.

"Get Stefan some wine and *sarma.* He needs some cabbage stuffed with meat and rice to put some flesh back on his bones," said Ruxandra as she pinched his gaunt cheeks.

"Look at you," she said. "This moustache makes you look so grown up."

With a self-conscious shrug, Stefan touched the growth. "I'm sorry..." he said without appreciating that Ruxandra was serious. Over the past few months, the changes in Stefan were more than the obvious physical ones. His eyes in particular, radiated a confidence and wisdom that comes only from trial by fire. Ruxandra saw the strength of a leader in Stefan.

With the guise of getting more food, Ruxandra slipped away. She returned with a surprise.

"Look who wants to see you."

As the creature strained against his leash, he whined with such insistence that it seemed his heart would break if he didn't reach his master. Stefan turned to see Panda pulling Ruxandra for all he was worth. At the risk of being dragged across the mess tent, the poor woman did the only sensible thing. She let the leash slip from her hands. Unfettered, the Molossian let out a joyful yelp and bounded toward Stefan. The big dog was like a puppy who bounced from side to side in a primal dance of joy. Stefan hugged him as the Molossian licked and slobbered over his face. Panda rolled onto his back his eyes imploring Stefan to scratch his belly. Sporting a wide smile, Stefan complied. The reunion brought smiles to

Chapter 33

everyone present. One person observed that Panda was so happy that he nearly wagged his rear end off. The exuberance of the dog released a wellspring of happiness in Stefan which he had forgotten existed.

The revelation that the prisoner was Stefan Musatin, the son of Bogdan, caused a commotion. His hosts barraged him with an onslaught of hospitality that rivaled the return of the prodigal son. Servers rushed helter-skelter trying to keep up with Ruxandra's orders for food and delicacies. Bako's aides dispersed through the camp alerting senior leaders of his arrival. Faster than a wildfire during a drought, the news spread. It passed from stable boy to farrier, from cook to scullery maid to milk maid.

In the midst of this hubbub, Stefan asked about his family. Gesturing for him to eat, Bako told him that Petru Aron's mercenaries descended on Borzesti the morning after Bogdan's murder. They overcame the resistance from the small contingent of guards his father had left to protect his wife and family. His home in Borzesti was burned to the ground and his family likely taken as prisoners to Suceava.

A solemn look covered Stefan's face as he clenched and unclenched his hands. His jaw muscles bulged with resolve.

"But all is not lost, we heard rumors that your mother and the children fled through a secret tunnel," said Ruxandra, with tears in her eyes.

Stefan nodded. He knew that his father had prepared an escape route and secretly kept boats at the river Casin because one of Stefan's chores was to maintain them.

"I know this is small consolation. By the time we got to Borzesti, there was nothing we could do except bury the dead," said Bako, shaking his head.

"This coup was well-planned. He probably had the support of *szlachta,* the Polish nobility. Within days, Petru Aron had soldiers in almost every village. They were ruthless. They arrested leaders and clergy who were loyal to your father. They confiscated anything of value that wasn't nailed down and brought it to that bastard's headquarters in Suceava. The worst of it is that the soldiers took food which the people stored for the winter. There is famine in the land."

"I'm sorry to interrupt, sir," said a young rider who hurried into the tent.

"Excuse me, Stefan. This is one of our scouts and it looks like he has important information."

Turning to the rider, he said, "Go ahead."

"Sir, we have seen movement of large numbers of men near the crossroads north of Reuseni. They are coming from the north and the west. We think that Petru Aron might be massing his forces for an attack."

A shadow of worry crossed Bako's face. In an instant, it was replaced by a look of resignation. His jaw clenched and the muscles along his thick neck bulged. The inevitable battle for survival was here. Stefan stiffened at the news. He thought that he would have more time to rally his own forces against the tyrant. His father always spent months preparing for his campaigns.

Bako signaled a trumpeter to blast an order of assembly. Men and women throughout the camp gathered to hear the news. Even the guards on the perimeter turned their attention to Bako. A buzz of excited anticipation charged the crowd as their leader went to a slight rise in the center of the camp and declared in a stentorian voice:

"*Calusari,* although we have suffered through a period of darkness, the time has come to rejoice. Stefan, the son of

Chapter 33

Bogdan, and future *voivode* has returned. We have received word that the enemy is amassing nearby. Fear not, Stefan is here. He will lead all Moldova to victory over the evil forces that murdered our beloved Bogdan, have terrorized our country, stolen the fruits of our labor and raped and slaughtered our fellow citizens. This night we will celebrate the return of our son. I give you Stefan Musatin!"

A raucous cheer erupted as Ruxandra led Stefan to Bako's side. Stefan blushed. Flying knots invaded his stomach as his eyes scanned the crowd. He had never addressed such a large group. His knees buckled as he resisted her pull. Stefan wished he had Telly's ability to disappear. He would never replace Bogdan. A tic appeared under his left eye and his extremities quaked. A calm voice urged him to breathe and embrace his destiny. Images of Isabella, Liubove and his mother floated into his mind. They were displaced by the anguished visage of his father's head held by Petru Aron. Stefan pressed his lips at the conclusion that only he could make it right.

The gathering began chanting "Ste-fan, Ste-fan." At the edge of the camp, he saw a friend encouraging him to seize this opportunity. From a tree near the barn, Telly revealed himself to Stefan. The young prince knew that this was the reason he had survived all the dangers. He straightened his shoulders and stood next to Bako. They raised their arms skyward in solidarity. After several minutes of applause, Bako and Stefan lowered their arms. Hundreds of rapt faces turned toward Stefan.

"My fellow Moldovans and *Calusari*, . . ."

The crowded erupted with a loud roar.

"Since the assassination of my father, Petru Aron has hunted me like an auroch."

Shouts of "Kill the bastard!" rang out.

"By the grace of God Almighty, I escaped Reuseni with the help of several loyal comrades. I have had many adventures. We lived in the cave of Zalmoxis where we discovered the broken celestial sword and a map to the Forges of Ezrok."

The silence was punctuated by awe and gasps as Stefan recounted the journey across the Alpine Sea, the betrayal of the forest *zine*, the escape on the wooden bridge from the thugs of the Bloody Scourge . . .

Stefan's thoughts were interrupted.

"Hey, Stefan, you left out the part where the heroic octopus saved the group by destroying the bridge."

"Be quiet, Telly. I'm trying to provide a summary."

If one could grunt in dissatisfaction then that's what entered Stefan's mind.

"Where was I?" said Stefan, returning his attention to the assemblage.

"Ah, yes, our journey took us to the dreadful mines of Adnor."

Stefan's voice strengthened with each cheer from the multitude. He glanced at Bako and Ruxandra whose faces were lit with pride. As Stefan retold of the mission presented by Faur, Telly nudged his leg.

"And so, we entered the lair of *Ismeju*. It was foul, fetid and frightful. We tricked the dragons into sleep by roasting a flock of turkars for them."

A knowing chuckle from many in the crowd indicated their familiarity with the sleep-inducing effects of eating those birds.

"When we attacked, my companion dispatched the vile offspring of the dragon. After we gathered the live saliva, I stood before the three-headed monster with just my sword."

Chapter 33

"Stefan, you skipped over the part where *Ismeju* chopped off my tentacle while *I* got the saliva," telepathed the octopus. Stefan ignored him.

"In spite of trembling, I knew that the time had come to destroy this foul creature. I unsheathed the great sword, Aparator."

At the moment, as if by magic, Telly placed the hilt of the sword in Stefan's hand. He withdrew the sword from the camouflaged scabbard and brandished it above his head. The crowd gasped. The magnificent legendary sword flashed in the sunlight.

"With powerful strokes, I killed the dragon. Smiting the central head, then the next, and finally the third. *Ismeju* lay dead at my feet."

He paused allowing the crowd to release its delirium.

"But this victory over *Ismeju* did not come without a cost. I was bitten on the leg by the fangs of the venomous third head. As I battled the effects of the venom, *Ismeju's* wife, *Bul'ara* attacked me. As I struggled in the dark against this wicked creature, a miracle occurred. Zeuta, the wolf-dragon of Zalmoxis appeared with a burst of red light. It startled *Bul'ara*. In her temporary blindness, I chopped her head off."

Stefan was interrupted by a loud shriek which filled the air as an enraged emuki swooped toward him with one thought.

"I will have vengeance!"

CHAPTER 34

Alerted by the malevolent thought of the emuki, Telly yanked Stefan's feet from under him. Stefan hit the ground an instant before the talons of the emuki snapped viciously over his head. Panda barked his head off and missed biting the dragon's tail by inches. When the emuki turned for a second pass at Stefan, it was thwarted by a barrage of arrows from the guards with the presence of mind to fire at the menace.

From ground level, Stefan saw the crowd cowering as they looked skyward at the retreating emuki. He leapt to his feet and adopted a defiant stance. Stefan held his head high, chin

Chapter 34

up like he was posing for a statue. Raising Aparator, he declared,

"Fellow citizens! That must be one of the emuki of *Ismeju* that escaped our slaughter by hiding in fear. Don't let that puny dragon intimidate you. Aparator will detach the dragon's head from its body and then chop its body into filling for a new dish – we'll call it dragon *sarma*."

With that dramatic declaration, the cloud of doubt evaporated. A buoyant enthusiasm replaced it. Stefan's energy spread through the crowd.

"My countrymen and women, God has ordained us to defeat this evil. We are destined to live free. We are destined for victory over the tyrant. Who will join me in crushing this affront to Moldova?"

In a frenzy, the crowd surged forward. Men closest to Stefan lifted him on to their shoulders and paraded around the camp. Stefan's chest filled with conviction – this was *his* time.

While emotion gripped his people, Bako gathered his senior officers and planned their next move. By morning, the camp was packed and the *Calusari* was on the march ready for war. Stefan, Bako, and Ruxandra led the column.

In a wagon next to the rear of the baggage train, Telly hid with the other treasures. He passed the time adding the previous day's events to his epic ballad. Telly concluded with the inspirational oratory of Stefan and looked forward to glorious victory in battle.

The Blind Monk lay on his cot. Although Seraphim was glad for the company of the polite young man with the slightly foreign accent, the monk felt an uneasiness akin to the onset of some physical malady. Throughout this restless night, Seraphim tussled with his threadbare blanket. Images of warriors clashing disrupted his sleep. It was as if the reverberations of metal clanging against metal vibrated in his bones. His repose was haunted by the gruesome death throes of men and horses as they succumbed to bloody wounds. As dawn broke on the battlefield, the smell of rotting gore wafted into his dream. He heard the caws of scavenging birds pierce the early morning quiet as they selected the choicest parts of the fallen.

Outside, a brilliant flash of lightning zigzagged through the darkness followed by a loud crash of thunder as storm clouds traversed the night sky. The violence of the storm joggled the tree abode as if the ground quaked. Startled, the monk opened his eyes. Momentarily awake, he listened to the storm recede across the valley.

When sleep returned, he dreamt that he walked past a bell tower into a classroom. The walls were decorated with a tableau of warriors engaged in battle against a background of cobalt blue slashed with firebolts. On the far side, a group of young people clustered around a long work bench. They were dressed in disparate garments from around the world - dashikis, kimonos, embroidered robes, and peasant garb. He noticed turbans, scarves, berets, and even a fez or two.

One young man caught his attention. Whether it was the menacing, elongated moustaches, or the aura of dread which he seemed to radiate, the Blind Monk recognized Vlad. He stood over a concoction of herbs, roots, and, viscous parts of

Chapter 34

small creatures. Concentrating intently, the young man raised his hands like a seasoned conjuror and exhorted, "*Pulvoce!*"

A stone pestle rose over the ingredients in a mortar and pulverized them into a poultice the color of an over-ripe blood orange. The monk identified it as a treatment for the skin disease known as St. Anthony's fire, or ergotism. A rising disturbance of wind and shaking marred the dream. The Blind Monk reached for Vlad's hand and they were enveloped in a swirling column of blue smoke. From the depths of his repose, he heard himself say, "The time has come. There is a convergence at the crossroads and you are summoned."

The Blind Monk awakened to the sounds of a fire crackling nearby. As dreams often do, his dreams evaporated into the foggy recesses of his mind. Rico groomed Dravan who nickered in anticipation of his morning meal. The young man shoveled embers into pile for the horse.

As Rico watched Dravan finish eating, a greenish-yellow figure flitted toward him.

"Good morning, Halo."

"Iew sul rie nor."

"I should ride north? Why? Is there something we should check?"

The little wagtail nodded her head several times.

"Let's go, then."

Earlier in the week, a young woman slept with her companions in a make-shift camp about a day's march away from the tree abode. The sheer effort of navigating through the tunnels from Adnor's mine until they finally reached the surface exhausted them. Although Clopotica and her *zine* tried their best, the column of escapees was too long to provide sufficient light. Each time one of the miners stumbled, Clopotica cursed the darkness.

At long last, they reached an opening to the surface. A feeble cheer erupted as the miners climbed to freedom. Isabella instructed them to congregate in a copse of trees until the entire party was safely out of the cave.

"Clopotica, we are in your debt . . . again. We could not have managed this without you."

"You know that we are only a whistle away when you are in need in the mountains."

"Tell the girls thank you."

In a flash Clopotica and the *zine* vanished.

Isabella led the ragged group south through a series of valleys. Most had been imprisoned for so long that they were unaccustomed to daylight and fresh air. Many shielded their eyes from the sun. They walked stiff-legged like sightless robots. As the sun traversed the sky, they stopped frequently to wait for faltering comrades. With many near the point of collapse, Isabella found a suitable place to rest for the night.

After making sure that all the miners were as comfortable as the circumstances would allow, Isabella nestled under a tree overlooking the path they had traveled. If Adnor had intended to follow them he would have shown himself by now. Still, they needed to remain vigilant. She tried to stay awake but weariness overcame her.

"Lady Isabella," said a timid voice. A hand nudged her shoulder. Startled, Isabella jumped up and was behind him with her knife at his throat faster than a bee sting. Her mind registered that he was short.

"Wait," he gurgled. "It's me, Calin."

Chapter 34

Seeing his red coat in the dim moonlight, Isabella relaxed her grip.

"What in blazes are *you* doing here?"

Calin's skin was the color of an overripe banana skin. Blotches of brown mottled his face.

"Where is your family?"

He pointed to some bushes. Isabella heard Galbena with the children. She hummed a lullaby while she knitted. The rhythm of the soft click-clacking of the needles produced the desired effect on the children. The scene of domestic bliss touched Isabella's heart.

"What happened?"

"When we returned to the coach, the guards saw Adnor's men attack you in the egregore booth and the rebellion by the miners. The guards got scared. One of the guards has a cousin who works for Adnor. He convinced the other guard to join Adnor. Good for us, they forgot us and ran toward the fire. We've been following you since. It was hard going with the children, they're exhausted. Thank God, we finally caught up with you."

"I've got my hands full here. You can stay tonight, but once we get moving, you are on your own. You bring nothing to our efforts to escape."

"What if I did?"

"Did what, Calin?"

"Give you something that you desperately need, Isabella."

She cocked her head and regarded him. There was something about the little man's air of confidence that stopped her from dismissing him. Isabella gave him an expectant stare, her posture seeking an answer.

"I–I–I know where Adnor keeps a storehouse," stammered Calin.

"What's there?"

"Food, clothing, and . . ."

"And what?"

"Will you help us?" Calin said with a confidence of a card player about to reveal the winning card.

Intrigued, Isabella repeated, "And, what?"

"Weapons."

"Is it guarded?"

"One or two men at most," said Calin, lowering his eyes.

Isabella glared at him.

"A-A-Alright. I don't know. Especially after the escape, I don't know."

"That's more like it," she nodded. "There's nothing we can do about it now. Try to get some sleep. We'll tackle this problem in the morning."

Her favorite time of day was before sunrise when she could listen to the dawn chorus of the songbirds. She loved to start each day absorbing the optimism of their joyous serenade. She lay on the ground propped up on her elbows with her eyes closed. Isabella pretended that she was alone on this glorious morning. The birds were chirping and small creatures were stirring in the forest.

The warble of one bird was particularly compelling. Her eyes were drawn to a greenish-yellow bird perched on a branch in front of her. The small bird wore an expression of unusual intelligence. Isabella chided herself for imagining that the bird was trying to communicate with her. As she dismissed the thought, a voice in her mind told her that it was no more preposterous than a telepathic land octopus.

Sounds of movement in the camp interrupted her peace. Isabella rose and sought out Calin. On seeing her coming, he moved away from his wife and sleeping children.

Chapter 34

"I'm gathering five of the most able-bodied men for this excursion. You are going to lead us to the storehouse. You better be right."

"Wait until Galbena wakes up, so I can tell her where I am going, Lady Isabella," he said in a hushed voice.

"No. There is no time to lose," she commanded. "We must use surprise to overcome the guards who will be armed."

Calin frowned. His pallor darkened with resentment at the harsh tone of the woman. He knew that he had to swallow his pride if he wanted to save his family. He pulled himself to his full height, pasted a phony smile on his face, and marched past Isabella.

"Of course, follow me," he hissed.

It was midday by the time they reached an outcropping above several buildings. No one noticed the small wagtail following them until they reached the storehouse. A rutted road ran from the clearing into woods on the far side of the compound. From their vantage point, Calin pointed to the storehouse in the center.

"The smaller building to the left is the barracks. The stables are off to the right."

Smoke rose from a lean-to adjacent to the barracks.

Isabella motioned for her team to assemble around her.

"There are four horses in the corral next to the stables. Calin, do you think that means four guards?"

"My guess would be two guards. Two of the horses are probably for the supply wagon over there," he said, pointing to an open wagon alongside the barracks.

"Makes sense. Here's the plan. Marko, you and two of the men go over to the trees next to the rear of the barracks. I'll take Timkus and Swolky to the area in front of the storehouse. Calin, on my signal you will scream and run toward the storehouse like you are being chased by the hounds of hell. Anything to get their attention. When they come out, we will attack."

To her band of miners, she said with fierce determination, "Remember, these men work for Adnor, the fiend who enslaved you. No mercy."

Isabella smiled inwardly at the resolve on the faces of the men. The team moved into position while Calin waited. As she crept low like a bird dog hunting quail, Isabella revisited her strategy over and over until all she could see were the flaws. She cursed herself for putting the diminutive chamberlain in charge of creating a diversion. The delay and her second-guessing filled her with doubt. She was on the verge of calling off the attack. Her knees were sore from crouching. Her men shifted and re-shifted. Timkus complained that his right leg had fallen asleep; the pins-and-needles feeling was driving him crazy.

After an interminable wait, Isabella waved to Calin. He rushed on to the trail leading to the compound. Between his red coat and yellow skin, the little man created quite a spectacle. The volume and depth of his voice surprised Isabella.

"ROBBERS! HELP!"

Isabella heard the guards inside the building.

"What's that?"

"What?"

"HELP! MURDER! RAPE!"

"That!" shouted one of the guards who swept aside the curtain on a nearby window.

"*Sfanta molie*. Holy moley. It's that yellow freak who works for Faur."

Chapter 34

"HELP! MURDER! FIRE!" screamed Calin who, on seeing the curtain part, fell to the ground writhing as if in death throes.

"We better check on the little guy."

"Yeah, Adnor will flay us if he dies on our watch."

As Isabella watched, Timkus and Swolky neutralized the unsuspecting guards. She heard a ruckus coming from the barracks. Probably Marko and his men securing the barracks. While her crew trussed the guards, Isabella entered the storehouse. Her eyes were adjusting to the dim light when she heard a noise behind her.

"Who are you? What do you think you are doing here?" said a burly man wearing an apron. He dropped a bag of corn meal and withdrew a large meat cleaver from his waistband.

"I might ask you the same question."

Isabella's reply befuddled the cook. His eyebrows furrowed. He scratched the side of his head with the cleaver as if contemplating a complex recipe conversion. Her dagger struck with lightning accuracy and sliced the man's jugular before he could react. She stepped back to avoid the blood spurting from his neck.

"Feel the taste of Damascus steel," whispered Isabella. He fell with a thud which was so loud that Isabella failed to hear his partner walk up behind her.

At the sight of his comrade bleeding to death, the second cook stood mouth agape. Isabella watched the dying man's eyes focus on the man behind her. She turned too late. He grabbed her. They wrestled, but Isabella was no match for his superior bulk. She scratched at his eyes. Shrieking in pain, he lifted her and threw her against the stone wall of the storehouse. Isabella smashed hard; her breath left her. As she lay motionless, an evil grin spread across his face. He had been stationed at this isolated post for too long.

"I'll show you the taste of real Polish steel," said the brute, as he unbuckled his belt.

CHAPTER 35

As Isabella lay prostrate on the ground, the cook unbuckled his belt. A green blur flitted into the storehouse and flew out faster than a ray of light.

The man was so intent on his evil designs on Isabella that he did not hear a black stallion thunder into the building. His rider leapt onto the man who was slow to react. Viorico was on the villain, throttling him with both fists.

Dravan nuzzled Isabella who lay unconscious, her clothes torn. A shock of surprise crossed Viorico's face as he recognized his friend. He lifted Isabella and carried her to the well. He folded his cloak under her head and wiped her face with a wet cloth. She lay motionless.

"*Hie de?*"

"No, Halo, she can't be dead," said Viorico, his voice choked. He stared down at her inert form, clenching and unclenching his fists as if grasping for a missing tool.

With an urgent flutter of wings, Halo flew away. When she returned, she held a spring onion in her beak.

"Halo, this is serious. Now's not the time to think about food."

The bird squawked in protest. She flew to Isabella's dagger and pushed it with her beak toward the onion. Viorico's eyebrows knit together as he tried to decipher Halo's actions. A hint of understanding lit his face.

"Of course, genius."

With the knife, Viorico sliced the bulb in half. His eyes watered from the pungent vapors. He held the plant under Isabella's nose. She stirred, blinking.

As if peering through fog, she focused on the face above her. Recognition crept into her consciousness. *I must be home*, she thought.

"Viorico?" she asked in a halting manner.

"Isabella! Praise God, you're alive."

She tried to rise, but instead reached for her painful head wound.

"What happened?"

"This animal attacked you from behind and threw you into the wall. He was about to have his way with you when my friend Halo, here," said Viorico gesturing toward the green wagtail. Her head bobbed in agreement.

". . . alerted me. I pummeled the bully into submission before he could complete his dastardly deed."

Chapter 35

Viorico tilted his head toward the ruffian who was bound and gagged in the corner. Isabella's eyes welled up.

"I suppose you are wondering how I ended up here after falling from the bridge."

Isabella whispered, "Out of desperation when I saw you fall, I sent a distress signal to the water *zine* in the vicinity."

"Ah, that explains it. My landing was miraculously cushioned and I survived only to be swept downstream to Xeric where I was imprisoned by the Bald One."

"I'm sorry to interrupt, Lady Isabella," said Calin. "Marko and his men have secured the barracks. We have loaded what we can onto the wagon. Men from the camp are on the way to transport the rest."

Isabella noticed Viorico's astonished look at the diminutive yellow man with the military bearing.

"This is Calin, the chamberlain to the blacksmith Faur."

The men exchanged nods. Calin pursed his lips and fidgeted.

"What is it? What aren't you telling me?"

After a reluctant pause, the chamberlain said, "During the altercation, one of the guards escaped on a horse and headed toward the mountain. If he escapes to Adnor . . ."

"Send two men after him and let's empty this storehouse as quickly as possible."

Calin snapped a salute, pivoted, and hustled toward the warehouse.

"You heard the Lady," he bellowed. "Get moving. We must clear these provisions with the utmost speed!"

Isabella and Viorico watched as men dressed in rags poured into the compound. With the skill of a person used to managing logistics, Calin directed groups to different tasks, making sure that the storehouse was emptied efficiently. At

Isabella's direction, he prioritized food and clothing before securing weapons.

"Who are all these people?" asked Viorico.

Isabella explained about the escape of the drone miners from the clutches of the evil Adnor.

"I will call them Isabella's Army," said Viorico with a chuckle. The young woman rolled her eyes.

"And Stefan and Telly . . . where are they?"

"When last I saw them, they were preparing to attack the dragon's lair. That was when that creature kidnapped me," she said, glaring at Calin.

"To save myself, I agreed to help Calin rescue his family from Adnor. I'm heartsick over my separation from Stefan. It is my sacred duty and I must find him."

"I know where we can find help."

The Blind Monk had trouble identifying the cacophony of sounds emanating from the forest. It was well past sundown when he heard men chanting a jubilant refrain. Among the snatches of words, he heard "full bellies and freedom" were a major part of the chorus. He was so used to the wind bringing sounds of pain and distress that he smiled at the convivial sounds of joy.

As the troop neared, the Monk smelled a mixture of sweat and corn meal. It was after midnight when Dravan led Isabella's Army into a meadow near the tree abode of the Blind Monk. Viorico and Isabella were astride the stallion. Calin sat next to Marko on a wagon loaded with sacks of grain. The rest of their party followed in wagons containing weapons and tools.

There was no need to carry the clothing from the storehouse, because the drone miners appropriated it the

Chapter 35

moment they saw it. In addition to new garments, there were articles of used clothing which Adnor had confiscated when he enslaved the miners. Apart from an occasional scuffle when a miner saw another man wearing a jacket previously owned by the first man, the group was fairly content as they headed back to camp.

Not far from the Blind Monk's meadow, a man on a lathered horse rode up to Bako who was leading the long column of *Calusari*, wagons and walkers. Stefan could not understand the conversation, but Bako's face brightened at the news. So far, they had traveled through narrow valleys and ravines which made them vulnerable to ambush. The *Calusari* showed the strain of the constant vigilance required. The lines on their faces were taut and, in the dwindling light, appeared as deep as the wrinkled hides of Hannibal's war elephants.

"*Calusari*, our scouts report good news. A short distance from here, they have discovered the ruins of an ancient Dacian outpost. It rests on high ground and there is ample shelter for the wagons and livestock. Let's push on so that we will arrive in time to set up a proper camp. We will have warm food tonight."

A loud "*Jolta!*" followed. Stefan smiled at the rallying cry. The column pushed forward until they reached a hillock rimmed with crumbling stone walls.

Spurring his horse to the summit of this rise, Stefan imagined the panoramic view this vantage point would provide on a clear day. Unfortunately, the waning light of dusk and a low ceiling of clouds obscured his view. These conditions did not prevent the sound of running water from reaching him. He dismounted, tethered his horse to a bush and headed downhill toward the sound.

Due to the steep face of the hill Stefan sidestepped down. As he descended, several rocks skittered and disappeared into a tangle of vines. The sound of water increased. Securing his sword, Stefan pushed aside the vines to reveal a crevice large enough for a man to enter. He peered into the opening.

He expected darkness but was nearly blinded by the reflection of the setting sun on the surface of a pond nestled in a secluded grotto. A slight haze hovered over the azure water which glowed as the last rays of the sun bounced off the crystalline floor of the pool. He entered the opening and walked down some rough-hewn steps toward the pond with the intent of availing himself of the opportunity before him. Hearing a sound behind him, he raised his sword.

"Whoa, Stefan, it's me, Telly."

Squinting toward the direction of the voice in his head, Stefan saw the octopus switch from camouflage mode to his normal coloration.

"Where did you come from? How did you get here, Telly?"

"I was in the outpost with Ruxandra when I decided to explore the perimeter. I went through the ruins of a small building when I found an opening in the back wall. I sensed that it might lead to water so I entered and found a cave which had been carved through the rock. That led me here. Oh, boy . . ."

The cephalopod brushed past Stefan and plunged into the pond.

"Ah, divine replenishment. Hurry, Stefan, this pool is thermal. Good for aching muscles."

Chapter 35

Needing no encouragement, Stefan slipped off his garments and dove in. A feeling that he had been there before consumed him. He broke the surface and backstroked around the perimeter. The reflection of the water on the rock ceiling triggered memories of Lake Zalmoxis. He recalled the surge of emotion he had felt for Isabella when they swam in Lake Zalmoxis and how crushing her rebuff had been. What did she mean when she said, 'I can't'? His heart filled with a desire to embrace his enigmatic guardian. He wondered where the mysterious beauty was.

Refreshed from his swim in the grotto, Stefan returned to the frenzied activity at the camp. Despite his efforts to slip back unobserved, Bako met him.

"Ah, Stefan, I was worried that you got lost as you reconnoitered the perimeter. I was about to send a search party for you," chided Bako.

In truth, the leader was so busy directing the reinforcement of the camp that he barely missed Stefan. The *Calusari* leader was agitated by the slow progress in making the area defensible against the threat of a mass movement of armed men reportedly heading in their direction. Dozens of men worked furiously with pickaxes and shovels to restore the outer walls of the Dacian fort. Stefan joined them until he was overtaken by exhaustion.

Stefan and Telly slept in their wagon. They awakened to the sounds of men working. Stefan sought out Bako for his work assignment. Flexing the fingers on his blistered hands, Stefan hoped for a job more suitable for his tender skin. With cephalopodic guile, Telly stayed camouflaged lest he be called to work.

"Go see Ruxandra, near the field kitchen," commanded Bako in a tone so brusque that it brought to mind the way

Bogdan had addressed him when he had bungled a task. With his shoulders slumped, Stefan walked past busy men. When he smelled the aroma of food cooking, his stomach grumbled, reminding him that it had been a while since his last meal.

"Stefan, Stefan, over here."

It was Ruxandra. She was standing next to a large wagon that the gypsies used to transport the gigantic black bear which was a dramatic finale to their traveling show. The wagon was constructed of sturdy oak planks and iron bars. Rusty gashes from the powerful claws of the beast marred the iron. The caged bear left a noxious animal smell which permeated the air near the wagon. Due to their emergency evacuation from Reuseni, Bako had released the bear so the wagon could be used for other purposes. At first the bear did not want to leave. A few well-placed pokes in the butt with a spear sent it scurrying into the forest.

"Our scouts have captured someone who claims to lead the armed force that is threatening us from the north. We have reports of other forces coming from the south and east. With the right persuasion, this one might help to assess these threats. Bako is too busy right now, so he wants you to persuade this prisoner to talk by whatever means necessary."

Stefan gulped. He knew from his battle tactics training, that interrogations were an essential part of intelligence gathering, but he had zero experience. Nor did he feel prepared to "use whatever means necessary." Was he even capable of torturing another human being?

"Come, Stefan, Bako needs results now!" said Ruxandra, coldly as she peeled back the tarp and unlocked the door to the cage. The heavy door opened with a harsh metallic screech.

He braced himself against the rank odor rising from the scat-strewn straw. He peered into the dark interior of the wagon. Huddled in the corner was a figure covered by a cloak besmirched with muck.

"Stand," he said in the most authoritative voice he could muster. He hoped the volume disguised the croak at the end of this command. Receiving no response, Stefan contemplated how to get the prisoner's attention. Unsheathing Aparator, he repeated his command, moving closer. As his eyes adjusted to the darkness, he experienced a sense of familiarity. *No, it cannot be.*

CHAPTER 36

Miles away, adjacent to the tree abode of Seraphim, the smell of porridge bubbling filled the meadow with a comforting aroma. A breathless Marko burst into the camp where Dravan was eating his early morning embers.

"Where's Rico?"

"Over by the stream with the Blind Monk," replied one of the miners tossing his head in that direction. Marko rushed to them.

"Sorry to interrupt, sirs, but a patrol of horsemen has captured Lady Isabella . . . ."

Chapter 36

"Marko, slow down, catch your breath," said Rico who grabbed the man by the elbows. He mimicked breathing slowly.

"Now, tell me what happened."

"Minutes ago, Isabella and I were at the edge of the woods searching for medicinal herbs when we heard several horsemen. They stopped and gazed at the encampment in the meadow. Then, they saw us. Before we could find cover, they were on us. One grabbed the Lady and tossed her across his saddle. I fought off the other with my knife. They fled into the forest."

"What? How could you let them take her? You were supposed to protect her!"

"I - I – we . . ."

"I don't want to hear it. Round up a couple of your most trusted men for a rescue party. . . and Marko, do it quietly. We don't want to start a panic."

The man nodded and turned to go. He paused.

"I don't know if this will help, but I heard one of the brigands say that they had to report to the outpost."

"Did you say outpost?" asked the Blind Monk.

"*Da.*"

"Rico, there is an ancient outpost not far from here. The Dacians built this forgotten fortress to defend against the invaders from the east – Tatars, Mongols, and marauding nomads. That is where they must be taking Isabella."

"Excellent, give me directions and we will storm it."

"That would not be wise. It is on a strategic hill. They will see you before you get within a half-mile of the entrance," said the Monk. He rubbed his beard. Sensing Rico's impatience, the Monk reached for his arm.

"Wait, there's another way. There is a secret passage into the far side of the outpost. Yes, if you travel along the north-bound trail, you will find a rock formation in the shape of a giant anvil. To the left, you will find a stream. Follow it to its source in the rock. There you will find an opening which leads to a tunnel. In Dacian times, the tunnel led to a chapel. Over the centuries, the outpost and its structures have crumbled into unrecognizable ruins. I don't know what you will find, but the tunnel will lead you into the outpost."

Without delay the rescue party raced north. Rico repeated the Monk's words in his head, "Look for the giant anvil." The soft forest trail soon turned rocky and steep. When they rose above the tree line, their pace slowed as the horses picked their way through the rubble. Rico fidgeted in his saddle. He patted Dravan on the neck. The great stallion whinnied.

At the top of the ridgeline, Rico shielded his eyes and scanned the panorama. In every direction, mountains rose like ocean waves as far as he could see. *We must be off track. Perhaps, the Monk was mistaken.*

"I say we turn back and pick up the trail where the brigands fled," said Marko.

Glancing toward the others, Rico saw nods of assent. He was about to agree and order them to turn around when Dravan snorted and shook his head. His mane whipped like a battle flag.

"No, Dravan is right. We've come too far. We must trust Seraphim. We will descend into this area between these two summits."

Marko stole a look with his companions, shrugged.

"Now, we are taking orders from a horse," muttered Timkus under his breath.

Chapter 36

It wasn't long before they reached the tree line where shadows enveloped them. With reduced sightlines, their sense of their surroundings heightened.

"What's that?" asked Marko, cupping his hand to his ear.

"It's just the wind, ya fool," replied Timkus.

"Shh," said Rico with his finger to his lips. He held the reins loosely. Dravan's nostrils twitched and his ears perked up. When there was a lull in the breeze, they heard water gurgling. As they headed toward the sound, the ebb and flow of the wind masked the direction to the stream. Their wandering led them to a wide flat surface.

"It's almost like the wind is toying with us. Rising and falling, giving us snatches of noises of the stream, then withdrawing them like a flirty maiden's kiss."

"*Da*, I had a girl like that once. When I finally got to kiss her, I was trapped. Now, she's my wife," joked Timkus, slapping his knee.

"At least she let you catch her, my maiden is back in Suceava still on the prowl," said Swolky in a tone of mock misery.

"You men stay here. Take a break. I'll check the surrounding area."

The men tied the horses to some scrub brush, allowing them to graze. Marko walked to the edge and sat, Timkus joined him, dangling his feet over the edge. Swolky walked past them onto a curved promontory. He peered into the distance for any sign of the outpost. His eyes were drawn to one peak, then another. Finally, he sat and started flipping stones into the trees.

"Ouch, you idiots, I'm down here."

Below them Rico looked up toward them and could not believe his eyes. He scrambled back up the path.

"My friends, I found the anvil."

"Where?" they asked in unison.

Rico pointed down.

"Where?" asked Swolky.

Marko slapped him upside the head. "We're standing on it, ya dolt!"

"Right, we have to follow the direction the horn is pointing and we will find the stream."

"Swolky, you stay with the horses while we search for the tunnel. If we are not back by sundown, take Dravan and ride back to camp. Tell Calin that we've been captured and he must break camp and travel west at day break."

"But . . ."

"Do as I say," said Rico in a voice which left the poor man quaking.

"*Da.*"

From a vantage point about halfway down the slope Rico, Marko, and Timkus looked back at the formation. In front of the flat top, there was a curved projection shaped remarkably like the horn of an anvil.

"Will you look at that," said Marko.

"*Da*, I wonder how the old Monk knew about it," said Timkus.

"It doesn't matter," interrupted Rico. "We must find the stream."

They followed the ever-growing sound of rushing water to a rockface where it vanished. Rico's heart pounded as he tugged at some vines to find a crevice in the rock.

Rico signaled to Marko and Timkus to stay outside while he entered.

"And, for heaven's sake, be quiet. We are in enemy territory."

Chapter 36

Both men nodded.

Rico unsheathed his sword and stepped forward. To his surprise, a blinding light overwhelmed his vision. He felt his way along the wall, thinking that this is how the Blind Monk must feel. As his eyes adjusted, he entered a magnificent grotto. Although he could not discern the source of light, he was relieved to be able to stand. He moved ahead, looking for the tunnel which would lead them into the fortress and Isabella.

With alarming power, something gripped his legs and yanked him into the water. He kicked with all his might but the grip was too strong. He recognized it; no, how could this be?

"Telly, is that you? Let go of me! It's me, Viorico, let go," his brain and mouth screamed simultaneously.

"Rico? Is it really you?"

Minutes earlier, Stefan stood in the bear cage with Aparator drawn facing a possible enemy leader. He felt a sense of familiarity. Was it due to the cloak? Through the dirt he recognized a color, a once-pristine whiteness . . . *No, he thought, it cannot be.*

"Isabella!?"

The garment slid from her face to reveal the subject of so many of his dreams.

"Stefan?" she said with a mixture of surprise and exaltation. "You're alive!"

Isabella rushed toward him, unmindful of her shackles. They jerked her to a stop.

"Ruxandra, unlock these irons. This is no prisoner; this is Isabella."

"Who?"

"My . . . friend . . . my guardian . . ."

Ruxandra bowed sheepishly.

"I didn't know. Go to the mess tent while I get the lady cleaned up," the gypsy said, ushering Isabella toward the women's tent.

Normally, the enticing smell of rabbit stew was all the invitation Stefan needed. On this occasion, although he was famished, Stefan could not eat. He waved off the ladies bringing food to him. He was too anxious to speak with Isabella. His brows were furrowed and lips were pressed tightly together as he struggled with his emotions.

At the sight of Isabella entering the mess tent, Stefan was dazed. She wore a peasant blouse with puffy sleeves, a floor-length skirt patterned with brightly-colored flowers, and a green scarf trimmed in blue which covered her dark hair from her forehead to where it was tied at the nape of her neck. The contrast of the colors with her usual basic white made Isabella look as fresh and dramatic as a bouquet of springtime flowers. The radiance of her new clothes rekindled the ardor he had experienced at Lake Zalmoxis.

"This is the first time in months that I have changed clothes."

"The gypsy clothes suit you well. The colors . . . ," he stopped, embarrassed by his staring.

"Isabella, you abandoned me when I needed you most. I awoke thinking it could well be my last day on earth. Then, I assured myself that with you at my side I might be able to slay the evil *Ismeju*. Imagine my despair when you were nowhere to be found. I have never felt so alone."

Tears welled in Isabella's eyes.

"When Faur told me that you ran away, I started shaking. I couldn't stop. It was only after Telly embraced me that the

Chapter 36

tremors stopped," said Stefan with a bitterness that pierced her.

"Stefan, I am truly sorry for your ordeal, but it is not what you think."

A raised eyebrow was Stefan's reply.

"That dragon almost killed me. I was in a coma for I don't know how long."

"But you are well now."

"No thanks to you."

Stefan turned away. Isabella's hands went to her face. With tears streaming down her cheeks, she said, "I am so sorry, Stefan."

She placed a hand on his shoulder. Her fingers felt something, as if a crust fell away from his heart.

After an awkward pause, "So, tell me what happened to you at Faur's."

Isabella related her abduction by Calin and the search for the chamberlain's family in the mines of Adnor. She told him about how she found the family and then released the slaves by destroying the egregore. Isabella related how she summoned the *zine* to guide their escape and their attack on the storehouse. She omitted the part where the brute almost raped her.

"How did you end up a prisoner here?"

"I was so grateful for our good fortune that I awoke before dawn. I headed toward the nearest hill to gather herbs for medicine. I never heard the *Calusari* patrol. Before I knew it, a sack was thrust over my head and I was brought to that foul cage."

"I know the feeling. They captured me the same way."

The blood red flag bore the image of silver vipers in a circle facing outward. The two men entered a makeshift command tent along a river not far from the crossroads.

"Well, well, well, what do we have here?" said a bent-nosed man through mirthless lips.

"Petru Aron, you know very well who I am," spat out the burly man.

"*Da*, if it isn't the Crystal Lord, himself."

"Do I detect a tone of derision?" replied Adnor.

"Derision? Why would there be derision for someone who spends all his days underground mining chunks of glass? I much prefer to be up here in the light."

"I have been accumulating wealth beyond your wildest imagination by mining those 'chunks of glass.' The last I heard you were a wretched mercenary who was barely surviving as a sword for hire," said Adnor, his narrow pig eyes burning with disdain.

"Pah," scoffed Petru Aron. "You call those chunks of glass wealth? You don't look wealthy to me. As a matter of fact, you are beginning to look like the mole that you are."

When Petru Aron screwed up his face like a rodent, Adnor lunged at him.

"How dare you!"

Before Adnor reached the other man, several guards restrained him and Dryger had a blade to his throat. The one-eyed man stared at his master looking for an excuse to slash the outsider's throat. Adnor's jugular vein bulged under the elaborate dragon tattoo on his neck. As the vein pulsed, the

Chapter 36

dragon undulated in a manner reminiscent of the torso of a belly dancer. Petru Aron fixated on the throbbing dragon for several seconds.

"Look at that!" chortled Petru Aron. "The dragon comes alive when the master is threatened."

With his nose almost touching Adnor's, Petru Aron said, "In case you haven't noticed, my friend, things have changed around here. I am the *voivode* and you will show respect."

"*Voivode*? Since when?"

"Since I severed Bogdan's head from his body," said Petru Aron.

Nodding to his guards to release Adnor, the *voivode* said, "Now, if you wish to keep your head attached, you will state your business."

Adnor twisted out of their grip and glared at Dryger as if to signal that this is not over.

"I am here to recover my slaves and seek vengeance against the damnable woman who incited them to rebel. Have you seen this woman in white?"

"I think I know who you mean, Adnor. When I was hunting the wretched spawn of Bogdan, I heard rumors that he was in league with a woman in white. If we find where she is, we will find Stefan. I say we combine our forces to destroy this pestilence."

Adnor and Petru Aron clasped forearms to seal their alliance.

"To murder and mayhem!"

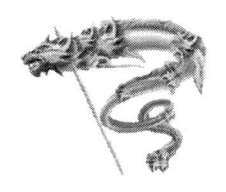

CHAPTER 37

The concussive blast jolted the class to attention. With his ears ringing shrilly, Vlad watched Molie the magic instructor appear on a cloud of smoke. During his time at Solomanta, Stefan's cousin had excelled in his studies into the occult. His desire to avenge his father's murder provided strong motivation to master the lessons taught by the legendary Molie.

"Gather around my darlings, today you will discover the joys and dangers of the conjuror's weapons. We generally accomplish our goals using spells, potions, and manifestations. There are occasions when direct, forceful

Chapter 37

intervention is warranted. Weapons, like enchanted spears, fire-throwing staffs, and explosive devices can be quite effective in the proper circumstances."

Muttering an archaic incantation, the master wizard turned the lyceum into an open field spotted with weapons stations.

"You will pair up and rotate through these stations. When you have mastered a particular weapon, you will proceed to the next one until you have completed all. Oh, yes, these weapons are fully active. Mishandling or ineptitude will get you or someone else killed. If you kill a classmate, you will be transported to the realm of eternal servitude. Go have some fun."

After several days of intense learning, Molie reconvened his students.

"I am pleased with your efforts. We achieved a course safety record with only two fatalities and one banishment. One student distinguished himself by completing mastery of the weapons in the fastest time in two centuries. That student is none other than Vlad Tepes. Come forward."

"Vlad, for your outstanding performance your reward is this quiver of firebolts," said Molie who placed the strap over Vlad's lowered head. The arrows sparked and crackled in a unique, translucent container.

"Congratulations. These projectiles are rechargeable and the quiver will modulate its luminescence depending on the stealth you desire."

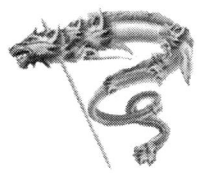

Back at the fortress, Stefan and Isabella sat in the mess tent when the sounds of men trying to restrain an animal shattered the calm like a grenade exploding.

"Watch out. He is going to stomp you," yelled one man.

"Hold the reins tight. I'm going to lasso his neck."

Stefan recognized Bako's voice. If anyone could control an enraged stallion, it was the master horseman. When Stefan exited the tent, he saw a magnificent, black horse whip his head with such ferocity that the sturdy Bako flew as if launched from a cannon. He landed with a thud and rolled to a stop at Stefan's feet.

The jet-black stallion reared on his back legs and tore the reins from the other *Calusari*. He was free, his eyes blazed as if they were charged with glowing embers. The horse was about to trample Bako when Isabella stepped from behind Stefan.

"Dravan, settle down. No one will harm you."

The horse pricked his ears and his eyes alighted on Isabella. Terrified onlookers gasped in surprise as the big horse calmed and walked docilely to Isabella. The crowd buzzed at the sight of the young woman petting the animal.

"How did you get here, Dravan? Where is your master?"

As if on cue, Viorico and Telly appeared from the rear perimeter. Wearing perplexed expressions, Marko and Timkus trailed the odd duo. Dravan shook off Isabella's hand and cantered to his master.

Open-mouthed, Stefan struggled to process the calm with which Isabella confronted the wild stallion. That was nothing compared to the startling appearance of Rico. The shift of emotions from fear and dread to shock and surprise occurred with the speed of a thought.

Chapter 37

Telly interrupted the shock by asking Bako if they could use his tent. The *Calusari* leader was brushing himself off, still upset at the animal which would not yield to his will. Unsettled by a request that he only heard in his mind, Bako muttered, "Of course, of course."

Telly led Isabella, Viorico, and Stefan toward the leader's tent. Years later when the tale of the entrance of Dravan and Rico was recalled in song, it was Telly who subdued Dravan and rescued Rico. That's what happens when the octopus chronicles the events.

"Before we share our stories, I have an important offer for you," Isabella said to Bako, "My men are skilled miners who can help rebuild these fortifications. Shall I summon them?"

"Yes, yes, as quickly as possible, my men are exhausted doing this work."

Addressing Marko and Timkus, Isabella said, "Go to the meadow encampment and tell Calin to send the miners here immediately. Stay with him and the women and help them break camp. But send the miners ahead. We need them here as soon as possible."

Viorico slapped his forehead.

"In all the ruckus, I forgot about Swolky. He was with Dravan. Does anyone know where he is?"

"Your friend, you call him Swolky?" said Bako.

"Yes."

"We jailed him when we captured the horse."

"Please release him Bako, he's one of ours."

"I will see to it right away."

The reunion of the comrades was filled with grand emotion as each related their adventures since they were parted. When it was Stefan's turn, Telly interjected with graphic embellishments. As Viorico and Isabella laughed at Stefan's embarrassment over the octopus' frequent self-aggrandizing, a small bird alighted on Rico's shoulder.

"Pardon me. Halo has returned from a scouting mission."

They engaged in a few moments of excited conversation in a series of squawks, whistles, and chirps.

"Rico, what's wrong?" said Stefan.

"Terrible news. The Bald One is advancing on this position. He means to kill everyone who interferes with his recovery of his beloved *Hayalet*."

"*Hayalet*?"

"That's Turkish for wraith. It was Dravan's name before I changed it."

After Calin deployed the miners, he entered Bako's tent.

"Excuse me, milady. There is a matter of importance which I need to discuss with you."

"We are busy here. Can't it wait?"

"No, it can't. Unlike some cheeses, bad news never gets better with time."

"Calin, what is it? What is so urgent?" said Isabella with more than a touch of annoyance.

"Adnor is amassing his forces to the north of here. The men are afraid that they will be recaptured and returned to the mines. What should I tell them?"

"Tell them to prepare for the battle of their lives."

Outside, Bako watched the miners as they assessed the challenges of making the outpost defensible. The design consisted of two parallel stone block walls which were separated by compacted gravel. The Dacians built these walls to absorb the shock of massive projectiles hurled by Roman catapults. The miners worked with gusto borne from self-interest. Inspired by their surroundings, they chanted old

Chapter 37

Dacian work songs as they labored. The spirit of the ancients revived morale in the camp.

Satisfied that the reconstruction of the perimeter walls was in good hands, Bako directed the *Calusari* to set up makeshift forges for sharpening their weapons and readying their horses for combat. Soon, the sounds of smithies hammering metal joined the robust noise of picks on stone.

Ruxandra interrupted the reunion, announcing that Bako had called a council of war. Stefan watched Bako confer with the scouts who had returned from the surrounding area. Their faces were grimy from long hours in the saddle and taut with concern. As Stefan neared, he heard snatches of conversation. The chief scout was advocating for retreat by the *Calusari* before it was too late. Bako raised his hand to silence him, nodding at Stefan. Bako dismissed the scouts who exited through a side tent flap.

"Let's get started," said Bako as he gestured for the group to gather around a crude map stretched across the table, its edges held by horseshoes.

"Calin, what's the status of the wall?"

"The men are working hard to rebuild the walls in accordance with the original design. They have figured out a way to hoist the fallen blocks against the gravel buffer without excavating the foundations. Ingenious actually."

"Good," said Bako. "Our scouts have reconnoitered the terrain and have drawn this map. It is rough, but will serve our purposes. We are here," he said, pointing to the map's center.

With everyone focused on the map, Stefan looked at Isabella. Her lips were pressed tight and she leaned forward with her thumbs and forefingers splayed at the edge of the table. She reminded him of a cat ready to pounce. Calin was beside her, his eyes darting back and forth. With a slight tilt, he leaned toward Isabella as if trying to absorb strength from her. His pallor was more gray than yellow.

Viorico tapped his fingers on the table and his clenched jaw was moving slightly as if he were trying to grind a kernel of wheat into flour. Stefan had seen this look during training when his friend was ready for action and losing patience with the instructor. His mien screamed, 'Enough talk, let's attack.'

Bako continued, "By all reports we are surrounded. Adnor from the north, the Bald One from the south, and Petru Aron from the west. Fortunately, we have a mountain wall at our backs. We have ample water to withstand a siege."

"It's quite refreshing," interjected Telly.

Those unfamiliar with the telepathy of the octopus, blenched at the intrusion into their minds. Only Ruxandra seemed unfazed, tilting her head at Telly with the inner twinkle of a kindred spirit. Stefan exhaled an embarrassed chuckle.

"Sorry about that. I should have alerted you to the way Telly communicates."

The young man nudged his friend, raising his eyebrows and pursing his lips in the universal sign of don't speak unless you are addressed.

"Since they outnumber us, we will deploy our forces to counter three different threats. We will use messengers for essential communications – and I have a miser's definition of essential," said Bako. "Isabella, you and Calin will lead the defense of the north perimeter with your miners. At the end of the day, Adnor cares only about lucre. If we can withstand the first wave of his attack, we may get him to leave by paying him off."

"Rico, what can you tell us about the Bald One?"

Chapter 37

Rico closed his eyes recalling the screams of pain and terror which echoed through the Bald One's fortress.

"He is an evil sadist who revels in the pain of others. This monster is vengeful and relentless."

"My men have heard that he is obsessed with this horse. How do you call him . . . ?"

"Dravan," said Rico, coldly.

"Yes, Dravan. Do you think the Bald One would accept Dravan in return for peace?"

Rico scoffed, giving Bako a hard look, which said it was out of the question. Bako exhaled, his shoulders slumping.

"*Da*. Rico, we can spare you a squadron of the *Calusari* to defend the south perimeter."

"The *Calusari* will defend the center against Petru Aron and his savages. Stefan, you will deploy wherever you are most needed," said Bako, with an edge that caught Stefan by surprise. Then, he remembered that Bako was part of the triumvirate with Tramo and Bogdan who ran their country. Bako had lost as much as anyone when Petru Aron brutally murdered his two dearest friends.

Almost as if Stefan's recognition of Bako's suffering and motivation spread to the others, a strange silence blanketed the group like the shroud of a penitent. They were lost in thought over the loss which brought each to this juncture.

Stefan knelt and the others formed a circle with him. He thrust his hand into the center. Isabella covered his hand with hers. The small chamberlain placed his dainty hand on top, his grayish, lemon-hued skin contrasting to Isabella's lily-white skin. Calin's hand disappeared when Rico placed his meaty paw over it. Bako and Ruxandra followed suit.

Stefan paused to absorb the collective energy before speaking. The solemnity of the moment was broken when

Telly joined the stack of hands by wrapping it with a tentacle. The sensation of suckers on skin was unexpected. A ripple of amusement followed the initial reaction and served to dispel the tension.

"Lord, we submit ourselves to Your protection. We wrap ourselves in the armor of God and pray for Your favor in the upcoming battle. We humbly petition You for courage, strength, and victory. As the battle rages back and forth, let us not lose faith. This is our destiny. Amen."

Entering his quarters, Stefan recalled the humiliation which Petru Aron had inflicted on him at the *petrecere* when he smacked him across the face like Stefan was an annoying house pet. His most painful memory was the sight of Petru Aron swinging Bogdan's head as if it were a demonic version of a priest's incense thurible. His hand went to the hilt of Aparator as he pictured how it would be when the sword sliced through Petru Aron's neck. His fingers twitched, reliving the sensation of Aparator as the sword severed the heads of *Ismeju*.

Stefan unlocked the velvet-lined case which held his crown and battle helm. He fingered the inner rim of the crown where it fastened to the battle helm. There was a slight oily film on its precision grooves. He screwed the crown onto the track ringing the battle helm until it locked. According to Faur, the gold alloy used in its fabrication was stronger than the hardened heart of Satan. With a whisper of resolve, Stefan tied Liubove's scarf around his neck. He inhaled deeply as he lifted the battle helm. The burnished helm draped over his head and neck like a monk's cowl.

The first attack came at night. Adnor led a contingent of men against the north wall of the outpost. The miners were

Chapter 37

barely able to repel the initial attack. The sight of Isabella and Calin standing on the ramparts fighting fiercely rallied the men. Due to his training at a youth fencing academy, the chamberlain was quite adept with an epee. He dispatched more than a few of Adnor's brutes. After one particularly skillful display of swordsmanship, Calin caught Isabella looking at him with admiration. He brought his weapon to his face and bowed gallantly in her direction.

On several occasions, Adnor sent three-man teams to undermine the walls while his main force engaged Isabella's Army. With night-vision honed by slavery underground, the miners were able to thwart these attacks.

Adnor regrouped and tried a different tactic. He ordered that his carpenters retrofit the tongues of several wagons so that a team of horses could push the wagon rather than pull it. He ordered the men to load straw and wood into the wagons. In the dead of night, Isabella saw horses pushing blazing wagons toward the ancient walls so recently fortified. As the wagons gained speed, Isabella saw that the horses were blindfolded and that men were on the horses' backs whipping them. She commanded the miners to withdraw, hoping that the walls would withstand the impact.

The combination of sounds which followed was unlike anything heard in the natural world. The crashing of wagons travelling at high speed into immovable stone blocks was bad enough. The mournful sounds of the horses as their momentum carried them into the flames or, in some cases, flipped them onto the walls with a mortal thud was sickening. The screams of the men and neighs of the horses as the fires consumed their broken bodies made a blood-curdling sound which covered the fortress like a curse.

Designed with the flexibility to withstand forceful impacts, the walls held. The engineering genius of the Dacians had saved them. Isabella paced along the wall exhorting the miners to stand strong. She chanted the miners' mantra, "Full bellies and freedom, Victory must be won." She repeated this refrain until it was picked up by Marko, Swolky, and others. Soon, the song of Isabella's Army filled the outpost as the other contingents joined in.

As the flaming wagons rolled toward the fortress, Isabella saw Stefan racing to her wielding Aparator above his head like a guiding star. At the moment of impact her attention was diverted and she lost sight of him. She did not see a squad of infiltrators sneaking toward her. Stefan did, and with the power of Aparator coursing through his body, he attacked the would-be kidnappers with savage determination. The celestial sword crackled as it hacked, stabbed, and sliced through the enemy.

Knowing that Isabella was safe, Stefan wheeled and raced back to his post. In his hurry to return to defend the center, Stefan did not see Galbena run to Isabella waving her arms wildly. Her dark yellow skin was illuminated by the fires as she threw herself at Isabella's feet, her hands clasped in petition. Stefan was back at the center when the reason for Galbena's agitation was revealed.

With a flourish of trumpets, Adnor strode to front lines surrounded by men holding torches. Behind him a team of men was pushing something through the throng. Drummers joined the trumpeters increasing the suspense. The men wheeled a small, wooden enclosure into a clearing beside Adnor. Inside a glass-windowed booth was Calin.

While Isabella's Army was focused on the flaming wagons, a party of Adnor's men had kidnapped the diminutive chamberlain. Isabella shivered as if an ice bolt had been shoved into her spine. Her dismay grew as she saw that his complexion had turned the color of dried mustard. His eyes were blank, entranced. In the flickering torchlight, Isabella could see the reflection of wires which were attached to his limbs.

Adnor held up his hands signaling for silence. With the skill of a seasoned conjurer, he proclaimed Calin as the egregore with power over the miners. In a low voice, he chanted in an ancient language. With a stronger voice, he repeated the chant. Calin's arms jerked like a marionette leading a grand chorus. Adnor's army repeated the chant to the rising beat of the drums.

The chant rose with such volume and intensity that it overwhelmed the singing of Isabella's Army. Isabella knew that if she did not stop Adnor's chanting the miners would fall under his spell and all would be lost.

But, how could she stop it?

CHAPTER 38

Meanwhile at the center, Petru Aron, unlike his allies, employed a more deliberative tactic against the seasoned *Calusari*. The *voivode* was in his home territory and had ample provisions for a lengthy engagement. He was in no rush to expend his resources. He preferred to let Adnor and the Bald One absorb losses while they weakened their common enemy. Of course, when the three leaders parlayed, they had all agreed to attack simultaneously; but the others had failed to heed the warning inherent in the treacherous viper banner of the usurper.

Chapter 38

Neither Adnor nor the Bald One would have cared much anyway. They had little respect for their opponents. After all, how much resistance could a band of emaciated slave miners present? Or, a single squadron of *Calusari*?

After a sumptuous meal in his tent, Petru Aron retired.

"Dryger, we don't need to waste a lot of effort on this rabble. We will let our friends from the north and south bear the brunt of the attack."

"*Da*, my Lord. How shall I proceed?"

"How's our supply of arrows?"

"We are well-supplied."

"Good, let's keep shooting flaming arrows into the fortress until the gypsies surrender."

"My Lord, the entrance consists of an opening which is wide enough to allow two columns of horsemen to enter. The gateway is unprotected except for a hastily-constructed barricade of upturned wagons and barrels. We can easily breach it. I recommend using our superior numbers to overwhelm them with a full-frontal assault."

"Dryger, Dryger, why should we risk our fighters when we can achieve victory without losing our men?"

"My Lord, the best victory is achieved quickly."

"My dear Dryger, I know that the savage within you craves blood. I promise you this way is better. Once we force them to surrender or burn alive, you will be bathing in gypsy blood."

"Instruct the archers to aim with a high trajectory so that those heathens will think the arrows are the wrath of God coming down from heaven."

Dryger's expression of scorn was hidden from Petru Aron as he marched out of the tent. The Butcher of Greben preferred to attack. He was aware of too many instances where the fortunes of war shifted and sure victory turned to bitter defeat.

Although a barrage of flaming arrows was a sound strategy under normal circumstances, these were not normal circumstances. The typical town under such a barrage would have incurred severe fire damage. Inside this recently-occupied Dacian fortress, there was not much to burn. The *Calusari* had travelled with only their horses and wagons which had been parked safely out of the range of the fire arrows. The incendiary barrage continued for hours, but produced minimal damage. The fire arrows landed in the dirt and died, or hit the stones scattered around the interior, and extinguished. Between the volleys of arrows, gypsy children retrieved the projectiles.

Knowing that Petru Aron expected to awaken to a conquered fortress, Dryger grew frustrated by the ineffectual tactic. He ordered a frontal assault on the barricade protecting the gate. The thumping sounds of charging horses replaced the swish of arrows.

Bako ordered his horsemen to mount up. He looked in vain for Stefan. Where was he? Since his inspirational speech, the *Calusari* believed that they were invincible with Stefan leading the charge. Bako saw disappointment in the faces of his men.

As the sounds of the galloping invaders grew louder, the horsemen steadied their nervous mounts. From behind the formation, Bako heard the pounding of hooves and jangle of a bridle. With a spray of dust, Stefan reined his horse into formation. While Bako's steely eyes admonished him, the commander released an ancient gypsy war cry.

Wrapping the reins around his fist, Stefan unsheathed Aparator and waited in formation with the other horsemen inside the gateway. Bako signaled to the archers manning the walls. Sweat poured down Bako's face as he withheld the signal to fire. When the calvary was yards away, Bako dropped his

Chapter 38

sword. The archers aimed at the first row and rained down a storm of arrows on the charging calvary. Horses tumbled, riders flew over their wounded mounts and the riders behind them, having no clear path, also fell. The archers made the most of the kill-zone and routed the attackers. The horrid noise of men and horses dying filled the air.

The sounds of engagement reached Petru Aron in mid-snore. Confusion fogged his mind as he awoke. Sensing something amiss, he scrambled into his battle gear. His armor was burnished black; even the metal of his sword and dagger was tinctured black. In his right hand he held his demi-gaunts, gloves made of reinforced leather combined with armor to protect the back of the hand and wrist. These provided protection without compromising flexibility.

He strode to Dryger and demanded a report.

"The flaming arrow attack failed, Sire."

"What did you do?"

"My Lord, I ordered a frontal assault by our horsemen. I wanted to present you with a victory when you woke."

"And?"

"It was a slaughter."

"It doesn't sound like we won. Were our men the ones slaughtered?"

"*Da,*" replied Dryger.

With all his might, Petru Aron struck the big man in the face. The spikes on the gauntlet tore a bloody gash in Dryger's cheek.

"Dryger, it's time, unleash *Samael*. Have you incited it enough to use its fire?"

"*Da*, we have drilled this baby on the best use of its deadly fire power."

"*Bun*, I was worried that it was too young to harness its full destructive force."

"Sire, we have trained it with the harshest techniques we use to train war dogs. It is vicious and now deploys its flame with murderous effect. Once it learned to use it, it seemed to enjoy incinerating things."

Excellent, that mongrel band of *Calusari* will not be able to stop the rebel archangel of flame and death."

The man with the eye-patch turned and walked to a large, boxy wagon. It quaked and jerked wildly on its springs as something large and heavy smashed into the walls.

On the other side of the outpost at the southern perimeter, Rico chafed at Bako's order to wait for the Bald One to make the first move. With the patience of a true sadist, the Bald One waited.

When the veteran *Calusari* were told they had been assigned to defend the south wall under the command of Rico, many scoffed. How could this youngster from the steppes command them in battle? Now with the enemy amassed across from them, they saw Rico in a different light. Mounted on the mighty Dravan, Rico cut an impressive figure. Erect in the saddle, his broad shoulders and strong neck were the perfect platform for his majestic head. His eyes blazed with the fire and passion of a true warrior. They saw him as the personification of the mythical warrior *Goyahkla*, the hero-model for all *Calusari*.

After hours of nervous waiting, dim eastern light began to chase the darkness. Halo suggested it was time for her to scout the Bald One's position, Rico nodded. As the little wagtail alighted, he thought that she must be spending too much time with Telly because she was becoming adept at reading his

Chapter 38

mind. A slight smile creased his lips as he watched her disappear.

Rico scowled raising himself on his stirrups to view the enemy camp. His eyes were drawn to a pink-and-magenta-striped structure which was the freak's command tent. A burgundy flag bearing the image of a rose-colored horse rearing flapped above the camp. He imagined how he would thrust his sword into his foe's pale, hairless, chest.

With that action emblazoned in his mind, Rico watched the Bald One ooze from the tent draped in a prismatic robe. An epithet which Rico had not heard since his childhood on the steppes burst from his lips. The vehemence of this curse startled even him. Rico vowed that the sun would never again rise on this vile creature.

Ze thrust zis arm skyward and a plumed projectile flew into the air. The Bald One repeated this action several times. Rico's neck and shoulders tensed. These sharp-eyed birds were vicious hunters whose talons the Bald One usually enhanced with razor-sharp blades. On this occasion, the Bald One had not fastened the blades because he instructed the falcons to capture their prey.

Rico's head swiveled as he trained his eyes on the birds while trying to locate Halo in the hope that he could somehow warn her. He whistled vainly into the high ceiling of clouds. He caught sight of Halo the instant two larger figures dove toward the small bird. They surrounded her, forcing her downward. Rico could almost hear the evil creature cackling at the prize before him.

"Excellent, my pets. Let's see if we can extract some information from zer. Tie zer down and put zer head in this vise."

The Bald One gesticulated theatrically, making it clear that ze was going to torture zis prisoner. Ze withdrew a white cloth and shook it with a flourish as ze placed it over the inert figure on the table. The Bald One motioned for a water pitcher. In the midst of this charade, ze glanced sideways toward the outpost to gauge whether zis plan was having the desired effect. Ze knew that Rico was familiar with this particular form of coercion where water is poured over the prisoner's mouth to create the sensation of drowning. It was quite effective at loosening tongues.

At the garrison, Rico watched in horror. He knew that Halo's tiny lungs could not withstand such an ordeal. Rico spurred Dravan into action.

Defying gravity, the big stallion bounded over the battlements and flew toward the garish tent. In barely the time it took for the guards to register the threat, Rico was upon them. As he was about to slash his way through the perimeter something strange happened. The Bald One adopted the stance of a conjurer with zis hands extended. Ze spewed an incantation. Rico felt the reins yank back and Dravan screeched to a dead stop. It was all Rico could do to stay mounted.

Rico urged Dravan forward, but he did not budge. The horse's ears flicked back and forth and his eyes darted as if searching for an escape. His hooves juddered on the earth as he ran in place against his will. A force tugged the reins from Rico's grip. His eyebrows spiked and his mouth opened as he tensed his legs in the stirrups like an acrobat ready to spring. The reins hung, suspended in front of the stallion's face. The Bald One continued to mutter in an ancient tongue, all the while moving closer.

Chapter 38

With Dravan on the verge of submission to the Bald One, Rico looked around. The Bald One's gang of blood-thirsty thugs closed in around him. They menaced him with swords, pikes, and maces. Without Dravan to power his way of this predicament, Rico lowered his eyes and prayed for an honorable death. He knew that he could expect no mercy from the Bald One. The monster was already planning to inflict a slow and painful death on zis enemy who had escaped zis clutches once by stealing zis favorite horse. The Bald One would not allow Rico to escape again.

When the center held, the men of the *Calusari* cheered and replenished their quivers. Bako barely breathed a sigh of relief when a courier from the southern perimeter arrived. He told Bako that the Bald One had captured Rico, Halo, and Dravan. Before Bako could react, Stefan spurred his horse and raced toward the south wall. Bako's eyebrows and mouth registered shock at the young man's abandonment of his post.

"Bako, let him go. We have bigger problems," Ruxandra said pointing skyward.

A dark object grew larger until they all recognized the ominous figure of the emuki. With powerful strokes of its wings, the dragon swooped toward the outpost. The archers sprayed arrows at it but the arrows bounced off its armored skin. *Samael* strafed the walls with flames driving the archers away. With one mighty blast of flame, it ignited the barricade. The fire roared and consumed the last barrier between them and the invaders.

Samael's flaming aerial attacks wreaked havoc on their already vulnerable position. Several of his officers had suggested that he order a full-scale retreat. Bako refused, concluding that this would have to be their last stand against the tyrant. The *Calusari* leader knew that his people could not outrun the bastards and that Petru Aron would hunt them down and kill every last one of them.

Bako withdrew, looking to marshal his forces for a last-ditch defense. At that moment, a courier from the northern perimeter arrived.

"Sir, our forces repelled the first three waves of attack by Adnor."

"Good. Dismissed," said Bako, exhaling in relief at some good news at last. He focused on the map before him.

The courier lingered. He wrinkled his brow and bit his lip.

Shaking his head with impatience, Bako lifted his gaze to the boy.

"Don't just stand there. Out with it!" shouted Bako, who immediately regretted his harsh tone.

Tears dribbled down the boy's cheeks.

"It's alright, son, what else do you want to report?"

With his face tilted toward the floor, the boy blurted, "Adnor kidnapped Calin and has declared an egre-something . . ."

"Egregore?"

"*Da*, egregore over the miners. Calin is egregore over the miners."

Bako exchanged a knowing glance with Ruxandra. She gave a sigh of resignation at her fear that the miners would be entranced by the egregore and stop resisting Adnor.

"Son, go back to Isabella with this message," said Bako, handing the boy a quickly-scribbled note containing two words.

CHAPTER 39

Back at the northern perimeter, the sound of Adnor's egregore chant pulsed for hours and hours over the earthen walls of the outpost. Isabella scrunched her brows in concentration. *Was the chant of the egregore increasing?* She shifted her feet and rubbed her neck wondering how that could be. It dawned on her that the increased volume was coming from behind her as some of her men picked up the refrain. Unless she acted, the miners would come under Adnor's spell and all would be lost.

Scanning the no-man's land between the outpost and Adnor's forces, Isabella detected movement. Despite the smoky air, her trained eye watched Telly in camouflage mode. With his mantle flattened, he tippy-tentacled across the divide. The webs between his arms were stretched to their widest so that they were like an umbrella almost touching the ground. She wondered what he might be concealing. Whatever it was, she must create a distraction to prevent the enemy from discovering him.

"Sire, I'm sorry to disturb you," said the captain of the guard as he nudged Adnor's shoulder.

"Can't you see that I'm resting?" shouted Adnor. He glared at the man who continued to speak but Adnor could not hear him. All he could sense was the man's lips moving with no sound emerging. The master thought he might be losing his mind until he remembered that he had inserted wax earplugs into his ears to earscape the chanting. With a grimace, he removed the plugs.

"This better be important," Adnor grumbled.

"We found her."

"Who?"

"The White Lady. Stefan must be nearby."

"Show me."

The captain preceded Adnor from the tent. A brilliant light assaulted his eyes. His first thought was that he must have napped longer than he thought because the light was as bright as the midday sun. As the cobwebs of sleep faded, Adnor comprehended that he was not looking at sunlight. Attempting to discern the source of the light, he shielded his eyes with his hands and tilted his head. To his astonishment, he was seeing pure, white light emanating from a being. A woman in white vestments stood on the ramparts of the Dacian fort radiating dazzling light. Adnor squeezed his eyelids shut. The image persisted in the back of his eyes.

Chapter 39

Inside enemy lines, Telly opened the egregore booth and cut the wires which held Calin. The octopus moved swiftly and the chanting abated with each snip. When the chanting ceased, Adnor shook his head as if awakening from a spell.

Before he could react, a diminutive woman confronted him. She was the color of an egg yolk. He vaguely recognized her as related to the chamberlain of Faur. What was she doing here, he wondered?

Emitting a primal curse, Galbena moved with the speed of a viper. She stabbed Adnor below his ribcage with two brass knitting needles. Galbena grunted as she drove the pointed rods up, piercing his internal organs.

Adnor's eyes stared in disbelief. His hands reflexively reached for his midsection. He clasped Galbena's hands as he staggered backwards. The big man fell gasping in pain, holding Calin's wife on his chest. Although she wriggled with all her might, she could not escape his clutches. Their eyes met; his questioning, hers defiant.

The guards were shocked into immobility such that they might as well have been statues. Even if they had been propelled into action what happened next was even more spellbinding. Telly swept into action. He was already carrying Calin with one tentacle. He brushed past the stunned captain of the guards and enveloped Galbena in his grasp and yanked her free. With both his compatriots in his grip, Telly tenaculated across the divide untouched.

After releasing Calin and Galbena, Telly went to Isabella and performed his most gracious four-tentacle bow.

"*Proptea*, Angel, for you . . .." he telepathed before collapsing at her feet like a deflated balloon.

At the southern perimeter Rico and Halo were strapped down on adjoining torture tables in front of the garish command tent of the Bald One. Dravan was tied to a nearby post. The monster prolonged the ordeal in the hopes of luring Stefan into the fray. Rumors of the discovery of Aparator and the celestial crown created by the cosmic blacksmith had reached the Bald One's covetous heart. With such treasures and the mighty *Hayalet*, the Bald One could easily expand zis puny desert kingdom into an empire.

Heedless of his own safety, Stefan vaulted over the southern ramparts and galloped across the divide between the outpost and the Bald One's camp. He was driven to save his friend. Horse and rider dipped into a swale and emerged to see lines of bow men aiming at him. The first row was kneeling and pointed crossbows at him. Standing behind them were longbow archers at the ready.

Determined to breach the line, Stefan spurred his horse forward. He raised Aparator to his forehead. When the hilt of the sword touched the battle helm, Stefan felt a strange sensation as if lightning had struck the sword. It sizzled and glowed with an ethereal light. Neon blue sparks arced up the blade.

At that moment the archers unleashed their bolts at Stefan. He uncorked a barbaric yawp:

Traiasca Molda, Long live Moldova!

Stefan swung his sword in a vicious upward arc. To the shock and awe of all present, the arrows and bolts swept skyward and headed back toward the Bald One's camp. The arrows hit their marks.

In the ensuing pandemonium, Stefan stormed up to the torture tables, dismounted, and slashed the bindings holding

Chapter 39

Rico and Halo. The Bald One sprang toward Stefan with his scimitar slashing wildly.

Stefan parried the blows and sidestepped the charging man. As the Bald One streaked past him, Stefan head-butted him. One of the peaks opened a gash at the Bald One's forehead. Blood gushed from the wound into his eyes.

The last thing the Bald One saw before Aparator pierced his chest and cleaved his malignant heart was a smile of Stefan's face. With a triumphant scream, Stefan plunged the blade into the Bald One and twisted it for good measure before yanking it free of the evil corpse.

Wiping Aparator clean on the burgundy flag with the cremello horse emblazoned on it, Stefan shouted,

"Let's go, we have to get Petru Aron!"

Back at the center, with *Samael* spewing his incendiary blazes on his *Calusari* with impunity, the end was near. When Isabella entered the bailey, she found Bako and the remaining *Calusari* hunkered down under any stone slab they could find. She gagged at the smell of burnt bodies. A palpable sense of fear permeated the air. All that remained of the wooden barricade blocking the entrance were charred boards and metal wheel hoops poking out of a smoldering heap of embers. With resigned bravery the *Calusari* waited for Petru Aron's horsemen to come barreling through the breach and finish the slaughter.

"Where's Stefan?" asked Isabella

"He went to rescue Rico from the Bald One," said Bako, nodding his head toward the southern perimeter. Wedged under the ledge behind him, Ruxandra muttered an incantation and bit her knuckle in a menacing gesture. An instant before *Samael* gushed fire on Isabella, Bako grabbed her wrist and yanked her under the stone.

"Child, you must be more careful. That dragon would delight in turning you into a cinder," admonished Ruxandra.

With a distracted look, Isabella nodded. She berated herself for failing her obligation to stay at Stefan's side . . . again. She hoped she would have a chance to redeem herself. In her pocket, she clutched the note from Bako. Its message, "Save Stefan" reverberated in her mind. She acknowledged to herself that she was driven by more than her duty to guard Stefan. Was it possible that she had fallen in love?

"I've got to go find Stefan."

"Not while *Samael* is patrolling the skies," said Ruxandra, pointing at the dragon who was gliding in for another fiery barrage. The noise made by his leathery wings was as deafening as a blizzard howling through the Bicaz Gorges.

"Isabella, squeeze in," said Bako, drawing her closer.

In the distance she saw a lone figure heading toward them. Appearing like an apparition floating in the smoky air, his cowl obscured his identity.

"He's going to get incinerated walking like it's a Sunday afternoon jaunt."

"Hey, you there, come here before the dragon burns you to death," yelled Bako, waving wildly.

The stranger turned to Bako and gestured with an open palm that all was fine.

The arrival of new prey did not escape the attention of *Samael*. After inflicting mayhem unopposed, the dragon was bored and hungry. So, when it noticed the stranger, the dragon saw the opportunity for sport and a snack.

Chapter 39

Almost as if he were tempting the dragon to inspect him, the stranger halted in the center of the outpost. He unfurled a large brightly-colored silk scarf and laid it on the ground.

"He's going to get himself killed," said Bako with sadness in his voice.

"No Bako, I recall a legend about magic silk from a mythical spider which was said to be potent enough to harness a dragon," said Ruxandra.

"I detest spiders," said Bako.

"God made all creatures," said Isabella.

"So, what. Spiders never did anything worthwhile."

"Not so. Don't you recall the story of David and King Saul?" Bako shook his head.

"After David killed Goliath, King Saul was so jealous of his fame that he sent soldiers to kill him. When David hid in a cave, God sent *Akkabish*, the spider, to weave a web across the cave's opening. The king's men passed by the cave because a spider's web sealed the entrance," said Isabella.

"There is something magical about spider's silk," added Ruxandra.

"What does that have to do with *Samael*?" countered Bako.

"Watch and learn."

The stranger cupped his hands and directed a slow, mournful incantation in an ancient dialect skyward. *Samael* tilted his head and adjusted his flight to a spiral descending toward the stranger. The stranger twirled the scarf in complex movements akin to flag-signaling by military units. As *Samael* got closer, the singer increased his cadence, repeating the incantation. *Samael* spread its wings and glided toward the stranger. It landed about twenty feet away from the man who stood rigid, continuing to chant.

From their hiding place, the trio had the rare opportunity to observe the dragon up close. Although by dragon standards *Samael* was still a fledgling, he was as large as an elephant. Thick, charcoal-gray scales covered his body. On reaching maturity, he would molt and his outer coat would turn iridescent black like the plumage of a raven. After a century, the dragon would molt and grow an additional head. This occurred again after another century and stopped at three heads.

The dragon's chest was broad as might be expected given the power needed to fly. The bony structure of the wings reminded Isabella of the bats she encountered in the crystal mines. At that instant, *Samael* released a nasty digestive gas from its rectum. They gagged and covered their faces.

Isabella studied his grand head. The most striking feature was a pair of bulbous glands adjacent to the holes of his nostrils. These glands smoldered, emitting an acrid smoke resembling a cannon that had been fired. No doubt these organs were the source of the deadly fire which *Samael* used to cause so much devastation. She followed thick cords from the glands down the side of its neck where they probably connected to an organ which produced fluid for the fiery emissions.

The stranger raised his hand in a friendly gesture the way one would greet a pet dog. Bako braced himself when the mighty beast moved his rear legs. Instead of coiling them to pounce, the dragon settled down onto his stomach with its legs splayed out.

Continuing to chant but almost like whispering a lullaby, the stranger went to the dragon and, to the amazement of all, petted the dragon's head. *Samael* closed itseyes. A low rumble,

Chapter 39

not quite a growl rose from the beast's core. Isabella shook her head in disbelief; was the creature purring?

The stranger gathered the scarf in his hands and tossed it so that it fluttered over the dragon's neck where it settled like a cape. He tied it around *Samael's* neck.

Meanwhile across the divide between the opponents, an agitated soldier scanned the horizon. He rubbed the black leather patch over his empty eye socket as if that might help him find *Samael*. He ground his teeth in frustration.

"Where is that blasted dragon? Something that big cannot just disappear."

"The last I saw him, sire, was when he sunk below the ramparts of the outpost."

"I know, I know . . . but it makes no sense. The *Calusari* have no weapons to hurt him. Why would he land there? He must have flown off behind a cloud of smoke when you weren't looking," said Dryger.

"Maybe the White Lady cast a spell on him," said the other.

"I'll bet that one of the dark wizards from Solomanta entranced your dragon. They are the only ones capable of such powerful magic," said another soldier.

"Rubbish," snarled the Bloody Scourge who bulled his way forward.

"Mount up and prepare to assault the fortress. We need to finish this business now. Kill everyone you find."

"*Da*," said Dryger, his eyes filling with blood lust.

Alone with Petru Aron, Dryger said, "I have heard that Stefan attacked the southern perimeter and killed the Bald One."

Petru Aron glared at him.

Stefan and Rico rode fast, hoping that they would be in time to prevent a slaughter. Rico restrained Dravan so as to maintain pace with Stefan's steed which was flicking foam from its mouth. Stefan held Aparator aloft, ready to engage with any enemy forces. As the bailey came into view, both men reined their horses hard in shock.

In the center, a man was petting the dragon.

"Hello, Stefan, Rico," said a familiar voice from beneath the cowl.

"Vlad?"

In the second it took to recognize the voice, Stefan dismounted and raced toward his cousin. *Samael* opened an eye, and drew its legs up under it.

"Relax, my pet, these are my friends. They will not harm you," said Vlad in a treacly voice. He scratched the beast behind one of its horned ears. As Vlad hummed the tune of the incantation, the dragon released the tension in its limbs.

"My friends, sheathe your swords and don't make any sudden moves," hissed Vlad. Both nodded nervously. Their hands remained on the hilts.

"I know you must have a million questions. We have little time," said Vlad. "After you left me at the crossroads, I ambushed Dryger but only succeeded in taking out his eye. The lucky bastard. Anyway, I escaped and took refuge from the snow in a cave. While there, supernatural forces took me into the school of Solomanta where the great wizard Molie taught me many magical spells. I have bewitched this dragon . . ."

"They're coming," yelled half a dozen panicky voices.

"Time to go. Good luck, cuz. I will see you on the other side," said Vlad.

He shouted a command to *Samael* and vaulted himself onto the dragon's back. Kicking his heels into the creature's

Chapter 39

ribs, Vlad yanked on the scarf. The dragon shook head to tail, like a dog emerging from a lake. His rider wobbled slightly, then shouted, "*Zbura*! Fly!"

Petru Aron and Dryger entered the gate leading a column of horsemen, with swords, axes, and maces drawn. There was blood lust in their eyes. As *Samael* elevated, its wings sent a giant cloud of dust and debris toward them. Through shielded eyes, they watched the magnificent creature rise into the sky.

During the distraction, Stefan and Rico remounted and drew their swords. Along with the few *Calusari* remaining, they charged the invaders. Rico reached them first swinging his sword violently at Dryger. The sound of metal hitting metal echoed through the bailey. Stefan aimed directly for Petru Aron.

With the speed of acid through paper, virulent storm clouds surged over the fortress. This unexpected phenomenon petrified the combatants who stared at the dark clouds with apprehension. A loud whooshing sound pierced the air. The shrieks of man and beast commingled as *Samael* and Vlad reappeared and dive-bombed like a winged predator homing in on its prey.

With the silk scarf of *Akkabish* in his teeth, Vlad held his bow, nocked with a firebolt. It glittered in the darkness. The combatants paused in shock at the spectacle. The man/dragon accelerated. The rear legs of the dragon levered forward exposing its sharp talons. Vlad fired. The firebolt exploded in front of Dryger's mount. The horse reared.

By the time Dryger comprehended the target of the attack, it was too late. The dragon plucked him from his saddle like an eagle snaring a salmon. Dryger wriggled like a slippery fish as Vlad screamed a primal howl. With a few dynamic wing-thrusts, they disappeared.

CHAPTER 40

"Where is everybody? Did I miss anything?" wondered Telly who surfaced a bit groggy from his emergency plunge in the grotto. After his extraordinary rescue of Calin and Galbena, Telly suffered from hyper-dessication. He was totally depleted and barely made it back to the outpost. Now, although his hydro-replenishment was incomplete, he forced himself to the surface to join his friends in battle.

His message reached Ruxandra first. She told him to join her and the others at the tollhouse near the front gate.

"Telly, the battle is over, well, almost over," she told him.

Chapter 40

"It's over for us," said Bako.

"You men," he said, pointing to a few of his officers, "collect all our weapons and bring the horses to the area where all the wagons are. The rest of you men, divide into three teams. Gather our fallen countrymen and prepare them for burial. Be careful to avoid *marimé*, contamination from the bodies."

"Telly, Isabella told us about how your heroism saved the northern perimeter. You should be quite proud of yourself."

"Thanks, but I don't have time for that Ruxandra, where are Stefan, Isabella, and Rico?"

"They are pursuing Petru Aron."

Looking around at the burned-out fortress, Telly asked, "The dragon?"

"That's a different story. We're still trying to understand what happened," said Ruxandra as she hefted some quivers onto her shoulders.

"After the dragon burned everything possible, we had almost given up hope. Out of nowhere, this stranger walks through the haze and chants some sort of spell in an ancient language. He spreads out a silk scarf, signaling the dragon to land there."

"*Samael* the dragon who had destroyed our fortress and killed so many, landed. It was as docile as a puppy under the hands of the stranger. At that moment, Stefan and Rico arrived. It turns out that the stranger was Vlad, Stefan's cousin. After he failed to kill Dryger at the crossroads, he learned the dark arts of charming dragons."

"And then?"

"Well, Petru Aron and his men galloped into the bailey intent on killing us. Vlad and the dragon flew off. Before the battle started, they returned to snatch Dryger and carry him into the clouds. Petru Aron was so shaken by the sight of Vlad flying on the dragon that he turned and fled with his coterie of men. Stefan and Rico pursued him into the mountains. When Isabella learned the others had gone after Petru Aron, she followed," said Ruxandra.

"Do you know where they went?"

"Telly, I cannot be sure, but most likely they followed Petru Aron into the region known as the Bicaz Gorges and . . ."

"Tell me how to get there," thought Telly, exuding agitation.

"Follow this road until you get to the Bicaz River which will take you into the mountains. The river will narrow into a stream which runs along a single path through sheer cliffs which rise several hundred feet on both sides. The cliffs are studded with caves. For centuries this area has been the refuge of outlaws and fugitives."

"I must go join them."

The last light of the day faded with the sunset. Isabella picked her way through the mountain trails. Given their head start, she knew that Stefan and Rico were far ahead of her. Stefan was obsessed with avenging his father's murder. Neither ice, storms, nor darkness would deter him from this mission – even if he died trying. His companion was so dedicated to Stefan that he would ride Dravan against an army of Goliaths to serve Stefan. Isabella sighed. Not only was she obligated to defend Stefan from all manner of external menace, she had to protect him from himself. She had to find him and convince him that Petru Aron's death was not as important as saving his country.

In pitch blackness, Isabella forged ahead. Her horse stumbled. Stones bounced off the path and careened down a rocky wall. She dismounted and left her horse. At risk of falling

Chapter 40

off a precipice, Isabella thought about calling the *zine*. When she put the tube to her lips, she saw a flickering light up ahead. She creeped closer, listening.

Through the darkness, she heard whispering.

"I know it's risky to start a fire, Stefan. I need embers to feed Dravan. He is starving. We need him at full strength."

"No, I forbid it. You'll betray our position."

"I'm sorry. It must be done."

Stefan grunted.

Isabella's heart raced. They were right there in front of her. She started to rise when a gust of wind whistled through the ravine. The smell of sweat, smoke, and bad breath caught her attention. Others were nearby. She heard the barely-perceptible sound of leather creaking as large men shifted their weight.

When a silhouette extinguished the flames, darkness returned. The only sound she heard was the crunching of the embers by Dravan. By the time Isabella heard the noise of figures retreating into the night they were almost on her. Too concerned with their own stealth, they did not detect her. She followed them.

After a while, she saw their destination. They headed toward a dim orange glow coming from the mouth of a cave. A fire crackled from inside and she heard faint voices. Isabella drew closer, smelling smoke and meat cooking.

Moving to the entrance in hopes of overhearing them, she pressed against a rock wall. She felt an indentation and followed it with her fingers inching along as if she were blind. It felt like a ledge. Quietly, Isabella placed a foot on it and hoisted herself up. She stepped side-by-side along a ledge which rose above the cave. It led to an opening which was large enough for her to enter. She crawled toward the light until she was almost above Petru Aron and his band of thugs.

"Now that we know where they are, I have the perfect plan to lure them into *Gatul Iadului,* the neck of hell," said Petru Aron who patted the sack next to him. This was followed by a cackling laugh which echoed throughout the enclosure.

Isabella stifled a gasp. She had to warn them. As quiet as a shadow, she slid backwards out of the narrow cave. When she was near the entrance her foot dislodged a stone. It tumbled out and landed in front of the cave entrance with a slight clatter. Isabella held her breath. Petru Aron raised his hand, gesturing for silence. His eyebrows drew together in concentration. He cocked his head, listening. The only sound he heard was the fire crackling.

The *voivode* mouthed an order to one of the men to station himself at the entrance. Isabella heard the man assume his position – directly in the way of her escape route. Resigned to the fact that she was trapped, she curled up her legs and closed her eyes. A tear rolled down her cheek as she contemplated her next move.

Hours later, Isabella heard Petru Aron and his men breaking camp. When the last man vacated, Isabella slid from her hiding spot. She wasn't sure if she should find Stefan and warn him, or follow Petru Aron and locate the trap. Figuring that her friends would proceed cautiously, she followed the villains.

Isabella watched as they went through a narrow ravine which was barely wide enough for a single rider to pass. A surge of worry flooded her mind as she envisioned how this pass would trigger Stefan's fear of confined spaces. At the far end, it opened into a wide circular area with a floor of granite. The surface was concave, shaped like a giant bowl. This would

Chapter 40

make it difficult for horses to cross. Rock formations along the perimeter were perfect to conceal archers. Opposite the entryway was a broad flat surface shaped like an altar. The only exit from this area was an opening into the ravine behind the flat rock.

Isabella was careful as she climbed above the ledges where Petru Aron was stationing his bowmen. A stab of fear pierced her heart as she assessed the danger. It was ideal for an ambush. There was limited room to retreat or exit and the shape of the ground was slippery for horses. Movement at the altar caught her eye. Petru Aron hefted a sack onto the surface. What he did next horrified her. She knew she had to stop Stefan and Rico from entering this slaughter pit.

CHAPTER 41

It was too late for Isabella to stop Stefan and Viorico. The Bloody Scrouge had lured them into a killing field. The monster had orchestrated a trap which negated any strength his enemies had and accentuated his own position to the point where a swift death would be a merciful outcome.

One of the guards signaled to Petru Aron that horsemen were coming. Isabella heard the clip-clop of hooves as her friends followed the trail into the neck of hell. The confined space made them vulnerable. There was no room to turn around; once a rider entered, he could only go forward. She heard Stefan breathing loudly as if fighting to control his

Chapter 41

impulse to bolt out of the narrow pass. A suffocating dimness permeated the passage. At this time of day, the only visible light illuminated the far side of the opening. There, Petru Aron stood at the altar in bright sunlight. His black armor seemed to absorb the light like an abyss.

"Welcome, wretched spawn of Bogdan," said Petru Aron in a tone dripping with disdain. "I am the Bloody Scourge and I have something for you which used to belong to your father."

Stefan clenched his jaw, trying to suppress the impulse to charge the bastard.

"And, your mother sends her regards. I'm amazed how much she enjoys humping with a real man," said Petru Aron in a voice dripping with malice.

"Ignore the lying bastard. Archers, left and right," whispered Rico. "I'll take the right."

Stefan nodded, figuring he would neutralize the threat on the left before charging the bastard. All he needed was for Petru Aron to cooperate by standing still. A taint of doubt said 'good luck with that.'

Stefan and Rico tapped their hearts in solidarity and coiled for their assault.

"Don't worry about the archers on your left. They are mine," telepathed Telly.

"Nice of you to join us. Was your night in the river enjoyable?"

A slight smile creased Stefan's mouth. The secret presence of the octopus leveled the field of battle, even though the floor was still treacherous.

"Behold what I have for you, worm," shouted Petru Aron, lifting the head of Bogdan from the sack. Decomposed flesh hung from what once was a face. Attached by stringy fibers, one eye swayed back and forth like the pendulum of a metronome. The killer cackled maliciously and taunted Stefan, "Come and get it, if you can!"

The grisly spectacle incensed Stefan. He raised Aparator, touching the hilt to his battle helm. The great sword crackled and glowed supernaturally. At that moment, the sun hit the jewels in his crown, sending shafts of light toward his nemesis. The bastard was briefly blinded and flailed with his free hand to shield his eyes.

Screaming, *"Prepare to die, Petru Aron!"* Stefan spurred his mount forward. Before he could raise Aparator to create enough force to disrupt the enemy, one of the crossbowmen fired. The horse skittered on the smooth granite and reared. The bolt struck Stefan in the flesh above his ankle and passed through into his horse's ribcage. The impact knocked Stefan off his mount. When he hit the ground, the pommel of his sword smashed into the granite floor with such force that the single stone there dislodged. The white-hot light coursing up the blade fizzled and died.

Stefan stared uncomprehendingly at Aparator. How could its magic disappear at this crucial juncture? As his wits returned, Stefan saw the gap in the pommel and scrambled to find the jewel. He saw it just beyond his reach, as if fate was mocking him. Before he could reach the stone and restore it, Petru Aron attacked.

While a stealthy Telly dispatched the archers on the left, Rico attacked the ones on the right. Dravan had no trouble gaining purchase on the granite, he glided above it. The big stallion leapt over a boulder trampling an archer hidden there.

Seeing Stefan lying on the ground, Petru Aron sprang from the altar and struck at his prey with murderous blows. Rico saw Stefan's precarious position, he wheeled Dravan and sped to Stefan's aid. The twang of a bowstring releasing an arrow

Chapter 41

reverberated through the cramped space. With a level trajectory the arrow would have bounced off his armor. This bowman was cowering from Dravan's hooves so the trajectory was upward. The arrow struck Rico under his armor above the elbow and drove up into his shoulder. He fell from Dravan, banging his head on the granite. There he lay bleeding and unconscious.

Barely able to fend off the blows of the enemy, Stefan crab-walked away from Petru Aron. He figured if he could reach the wall, he might be able to get upright and fight his nemesis. As the blows rained down, he parried them as best as he could.

One murderous blow caught Stefan under the chin. Expecting a river of blood and a decapitated enemy, an astonished Petru Aron cursed. For the moment, Faur's chain mail had saved Stefan from his father's fate.

Isabella leapt from her hiding spot and performed a series of handsprings. Accelerating rapidly, she tucked into a ball. By the time she reached Petru Aron she was a white blur of kinetic force. As Petru Aron was about to deliver a mortal blow to Stefan's stomach, Isabella smashed into him. The collision whipped his head back and knocked the wind out of his lungs. He smashed into the stone wall and crumpled in a heap, entangled with Stefan and Isabella.

As they shook the cobwebs out of the heads, trying to recover, Telly strangled the remaining archer. From the fringes of the bowl, several men rushed to Petru Aron. He groaned as they lifted him. His left leg dangled at a freakish angle and both his arms were strangely bowed as a result of trying to brace himself when he hit the wall. His reinforced gloves saved his wrists but the force was so great that his elbow joints popped out. When his men put him on his horse, the bastard unleashed a scream of pain as if he were already suffering the agonies of hell. They raced off through the far exit.

Through groggy eyes, Stefan watched Petru Aron flee. When he stood, his wounded leg collapsed under him.

The bowl was awash with blood. Stefan knelt next to Isabella who was still unconscious. Blood streamed from a gash where her scalp had smashed into Petru Aron's armor. Stefan's horse thrashed in death throes, ragged rasping breath escaping from the blood-soaked foam around its mouth.

Telly led Dravan by his reins to where Stefan sat, his head still ringing.

"Where's Rico?"

"Gone. During the melee, he was wounded and knocked from Dravan. Several of the villains bound him and threw him on the back of a horse. Muttering something about a ransom, they fled into the ravine"

"What? Nooooo! We must give chase," yelled Stefan. He bolted to his feet and limped toward Dravan. He never made it; he collapsed from the loss of blood.

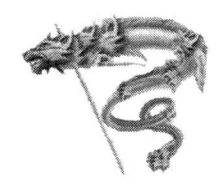

CHAPTER 42

The sharp pain in his leg reminded Stefan of his helplessness as he watched enemy soldiers load his father's murderer onto a horse and ride away. His heart ached at the thought of Rico being held prisoner. A trace of his gloom lifted as he thought of Isabella turning herself into a dynamic projectile and smiting Petru Aron. Her bravery saved his life. His stomach tightened at the sight of Isabella lying unconscious, blood flowing from a scalp wound, in the aftermath of the violent collision. Using the healing power of his tentacles, Telly stopped the bleeding from their wounds.

When Stefan and Isabella were stable, Telly helped them onto Dravan.

Both riders slumped forward as Telly led the great horse out of the neck of hell. In their semi-conscious state, Stefan and Isabella took comfort in the closeness of the other. Telly delighted in eavesdropping on the private thoughts of affection forming in their unguarded minds. Telly wondered how he might incorporate details of this ride into his epic ballad.

When they arrived at the outpost, Bako was supervising the evacuation of the *Calusari* for their return home. A sentinel shouted.

"Bako, a column of mounted soldiers is approaching."

"To the walls. Sound the alarm for all the able-bodied to take positions on the walls."

Turning to Ruxandra, Bako's eyes told her that this was the end. They could not repel Petru Aron's army again. Her demeanor sagged in resignation. She blew a kiss to him with tear-soaked fingers.

"I'll bring Stefan and Isabella to safety in the chapel," she said to his retreating form.

Groans and panicked shouts resounded through the camp. Over the last few days, they had been stretched to their limits. And now this. A mood of despair permeated the air as men dashed to their posts. Across the divide, a column of soldiers came toward them at a slow pace. Bako screwed his eyebrows, a puzzled expression plastered on his face. Why were their weapons sheathed? Why weren't they charging?

"Bako, I see a white banner. It's a raven with a gold ring in its beak."

As his brain comprehended the identity of the heraldry, Bako's face transformed into a palette of joy.

Chapter 42

"It's the White Knight! Put down your weapons!"

When Janos Hunyadi and his soldiers entered the outpost, they were greeted by cheers of relief. The happy tumult was so loud that it roused Stefan and Isabella from their beds. With help from Ruxandra and Telly, they hobbled to the entrance where Bako welcomed Commander Hunyadi.

"Stefan, Bako informs me that you have vanquished Petru Aron and the monster has abdicated to parts unknown. I look forward to presiding over your coronation as *voivode*."

"I thank you for your kind words, but there is unfinished business with that bastard."

"Yes, Bako also told me that your friend is being held hostage. My men and I will rescue him as soon as we refresh our horses."

"Sire, I will join you. I cannot rest until that villain's head is severed from his odious body."

Looking at the young man quivering from the effort to remain upright on his one good leg, the knight shook his head. With a gentleness which seemed incongruous given his size, he took Stefan's face into his hands and stared deeply.

"Your courage is commendable but you are in no condition to pursue him. No, I will go. I pledge to you, as one warrior to another, to bring him back in one piece so that you can impose whatever sentence you deem appropriate."

Buoyed by the respect he saw in the knight's eyes, Stefan nodded.

The journey to Rueseni was bittersweet. The anxiety over Viorico's fate dampened their feelings of achievement. As word of the defeat of Petru Aron spread, people came to celebrate. Soon the town was teeming with boyars, farmers and tradesmen. Much like the awakening of the earth in spring after a long, dark winter, a festive atmosphere prevailed.

Stefan was resting when he heard an uproar at the edge of the town. When he heard a crowd chanting, "Hail, mighty commander," Stefan rushed to see Hunyadi.

"Where is he? Did you capture the bastard?"

The Commander brushed some dust off his cloak and expelled a weary sigh.

"No, son, we chased Petru Aron and his mercenaries all the way to Poland. We were close to catching the scum, but our efforts were thwarted by King Cazimir. The foolish young king believed the lies of Petru Aron and granted him sanctuary. With our limited numbers, we were in no position to challenge the king's decision. Your day of justice is deferred for now."

Coronation day broke sunny and clear. Every person in the town lined the main street which led to the modest church. When Stefan entered the street, there was a collective gasp. Mounted on the majestic Dravan, Stefan cut a powerful figure. He wore the robe of crimson velvet, embroidered with gold celestial symbols which his father had worn at his coronation.

On his hand, Stefan wore a golden signet, embossed with the head of Urias, the auroch and the numerals 317. The ring was far more than jewelry. It was made of a special alloy to withstand the rigors of its primary function. The crown atop Stefan's head shone brilliantly. The dragon stones at the seven peaks reflected a rainbow of light rays which enthralled the crowd. If ever God had ordained the ascension of a person to be a ruler, it was Stefan wearing the crown worthy of an emissary from heaven.

"Commander Hunyadi, clergy, boyars, farmers, tradesman and all citizens who have come from far and wide, I present to

Chapter 42

you Stefan of the House of Musatin, the son of *Voivode* Bogdan II, and grandson of Alexandru cel Bun. By virtue of his exalted lineage and heroism in defeating the usurper, Petru Aron, we are here today to coronate Prince Stefan," proclaimed the Blind Monk.

"In accordance with our tradition. I have examined Stefan for the mark which is burned with a hot signet onto every royal heir at birth. I am proud to confirm that Stefan is the rightful heir to the position as *voivode* of Moldova."

The crowd erupted with a jubilant cheer. Stefan blushed at the memory of the cleric examining his ass with his fingers like it was embossed leather. Situated next to the Blind Monk, the White Knight stoked the passions of the multitude by pumping his palms skyward. The chant of "Stefan, Stefan, Stefan," echoed through the front courtyard of the church.

"Kneel before the people," instructed Seraphim who turned to the crowd.

"Stefan Musatin is truly a man chosen by God, he is the good ruler, the brave, the one full of love and divine gifts. Do all agree that he be your ruler?" thundered the Blind Monk.

To a man (and woman), the crowd called out in one voice: "May you rule for many years."

"You kneel as Stefan Musatin," said Seraphim as he hefted Aparator toward the young man. "And you will rise as *Voivode!*"

There were nervous looks and gasps as the Blind Monk touched him with the blade on both shoulders. When a ray of light glinted off the steel with the brilliance of sunlight reflecting off ice, those present took it as a sign of divine favor. A jubilant Stefan rose and accepted the sword.

"I understand fully that Aparator means Defender or Guardian. I will honor my ancestors by using Aparator to bring peace and prosperity to Moldova."

"Now, let us celebrate," said the monk, directing the assemblage to the rear of the church where he smelled the presence of dozens of tables filled with food and drink. The sweet music of a string quartet accompanied the coronation banquet. Stefan received all manner of well-wishers, friends, and sycophants on a reception line which stretched as far as the eye could see.

When the last celebrant had passed, Stefan looked at Isabella with so much emotion that he thought his heart might burst from his chest. As he went toward the banquet hall, he pulled her into an alcove. They stood face to face, holding each other by the elbows.

"This is why I came," whispered Isabella.

"After all that we have been through, I . . ."

Isabella put her finger to his lips, quieting him. With her other hand she touched the signet.

"You have puzzled over the numerals hidden in the face of the signet."

Stefan nodded.

"What do they mean?"

"They refer to the Book of Ecclesiastes where it is written that for everything there is a season. Chapter 3, verse 17 says:

> God will bring into judgment
> both the righteous and the wicked,
> for there will be a time for every activity,
> a time to judge every deed.

Your people need you, Stefan. Petru Aron is not worth your attention. You must focus on your destiny."

Chapter 42

The voivode nodded and was about to ask an important question when he heard a voice in his head.

"Well done, my Lord."

Stefan scanned the party for Telly until he came upon an astounding sight on a slight knoll in the rear garden. Telly was the string quartet! Two tentacles played the viola, two the cello, and the last four played dual violins with perfect pomp and pageantry.

Raising his hand in salute, Stefan thought, "Bravo, you show-off."

The octopus gave him a Telly-version of a grin and telepathed, "And now for Your Royalness, the magnum opus - 'A Tribute to Stefan.'"

With Telly playing superb music, Isabella joined Bako, and Ruxandra to sing the epic ballad in perfect three-part harmony.

THE END

ACKNOWLEDGEMENTS

The genesis of this book is a story itself. Moldova was a satellite state of the Soviet Union when it collapsed. To assist former Soviet-controlled countries the United States assigned American states to several dozen eastern European countries. My current home, North Carolina, was assigned Moldova, a sliver of a country between Romania and Ukraine. North Carolina's Secretary of State, the Honorable Elaine Marshall, has spearheaded the Moldova-North Carolina Partnership since its inception in 1995. With the support of many public and private institutions, she has helped enrich the lives of countless Moldovans. Secretary Marshall and her staff, including Rodney Maddux and Lora Sinigur, deserve the highest commendation for their efforts.

This work would never have occurred with the constant encouragement and friendship of Donna and Jerry Flake. During a visit to Moldova several years ago, I had the good fortune to met numerous Moldovans who have been helpful and supportive throughout this process. I apologize for any I omit, but I extend special thanks to George Teodorescu and Silvia Ciubrei, Dr. Evelina Gherghelegiu who has been especially dedicated to the success of my work. She introduced me to Dr. Andrei Prohin whose insightful review and comments improved *Stefan and the Celestial Sword* considerably.

No writer can thrive without beta readers and encouragement from colleagues. Gigi Warner, my daughter Jenna, and Richard Dobberstein gave generously of their time to improve the manuscript, as did my writer friends and buddies Shaun Cherewich, Dr. Lee Mendez, Lee Ewing, and Tom Olsinski. I would be remiss if I failed to thank Gilda Adler who not only helped as a beta reader but gave us permission to use the image of her son Eric as Stefan on the cover. Thanks.

Christy Meares has been a patient godsend during the evolution of this project. Her incredible imagination, dedication, patience, and talent as a designer have made the production of this book a collaborative masterwork.

Most of all, I want to express my love for my wonderful wife Rhonda who is the only reason I accomplish anything.

Made in the USA
Columbia, SC
11 January 2022